WE, THE SURVIVORS

By the same author

TASH AW

We, the Survivors

4TH ESTATE • *London*

First published in Great Britain in 2019 by
Fourth Estate
An imprint of HarperCollins*Publishers*
1 London Bridge Street
London SE1 9GF
www.4thestate.co.uk

Copyright © Tash Aw 2019

1

The right of Tash Aw to be identified as the author
of this work has been asserted by him in accordance
with the Copyright, Design and Patents Act 1988

A catalogue record for this book is available from the British Library

HB ISBN: 978 0 00 831854 3
TPB ISBN: 978 0 00 831855 0

Typeset in Meridien by Palimpsest Book Production Ltd,
Falkirk, Stirlingshire

Printed and bound in Great Britain by
CPI Group (UK) Ltd, Croydon CR0 4YY

MIX
Paper from
responsible sources
FSC
www.fsc.org **FSC™ C007454**

This book is produced from independently certified FSC™ paper
to ensure responsible forest management.

For more information visit: www.harpercollins.co.uk/green

For Francis

'Here we received the first blows: and it was so new and senseless that we felt no pain, neither in body nor in spirit. Only a profound amazement: how can one hit a man without anger?'

Primo Levi, *If This is a Man*

I

OCTOBER

You want me to talk about life, but all I've talked about is failure, as if they're the same thing, or at least so closely entwined that I can't separate the two – like the trees you see growing in the half-ruined buildings in the Old Town. Roots clinging to the outside of the walls, holding the bricks and stone and whatever remains of the paint together, branches pushing through holes in the roof. Sometimes there's almost nothing left of the roof, if you can even call it that – just fragments of clay tiles or rusty tin propped up by the canopy of leaves. A few miles out of town, on the other side of Kapar headed towards the coast, you'll find a shophouse with the roots of a jungle fig creeping down the front pillars of the building, the entire structure swallowed up by the tree – the doorway is now just a shadowy space that leads into the heart of a huge tangle of foliage. Where does one end and the other begin? Which one is alive, which is dead? Still, on the ground floor of these houses, there'll be a business or a shop, some kind of small operation, an old guy who'll patch up your tyres for twenty bucks. Or a printing press that makes those cheap leaflets advertising closing-down sales at the local mall. Or a cake shop with nothing in the chiller cabinets except for two pieces of *kuih lapis* that have been there for three weeks. The packets of biscuits on the shelves are covered in the dust that drifts across from the construction sites nearby, where they're building the new railway or shopping mall or God knows

3

what. These people haven't made a decent living for twenty years. They're seventy-five, eighty years old. Still alive, but their business is being taken over by a tree. Imagine that.

That night, after the killing – or the *culpable homicide not amounting to murder*, as you politely call it – I walked for many hours in the dark. I can't tell you how long. I tried to hang on to a sense of time, kept looking at the sky for signs of dawn, I even quickened my stride to make each step feel like one full second, like the ticking of that clock on the wall over there, that right now sounds so quick. Tick, tick, tick. But that night each second stretched into a whole minute, each minute felt like a lifetime, and there was nothing I could do to speed things up.

My shirt was wet – not just damp, but properly wet – and it clung to my back like a second skin; only that skin did not belong to me, but to a separate living organism, cold and heavy, weighing me down. As I walked further and further away from what I now come to think of as *the scene of the crime* (but didn't then – it was just a darkened spot on the riverbank, indistinguishable from any other), I listened out for the sirens of police cars, expecting to hear them at any moment. I kept thinking, They're coming for me, this is the end, the mata are going to catch me and throw me in jail forever. I said out loud, *You're finished. This really is the end for you.* Hearing my own voice calmed me. Nothing had ever felt so absolute and certain. The police would arrive, they would lock me up, and from then on, all my days would be the same. The thought of being in a small empty cell with nothing to think about for the rest of my life – the idea of this existence comforted me. When I woke up each morning I would see the same four walls that had been there when I fell asleep the night before. Nothing would ever change. What I wore, how long I slept each night, how many times a day I could eat, wash, shit – every decision would be made for me, I would be just the same as everyone else. Someone would take control of my life, and that would be the end of my story. Part of me still wishes things had turned out that way.

I walked through the long grass – it was stringy and sharp and slashed my legs right up to my knees. It was hot, I was wearing shorts, my skin started to sting. Twice, maybe three times, I crossed a bridge and continued to wander along the opposite bank. At first I was looking for my car, but soon I realised I was trying to get as far away from the scene of the crime as possible. The only problem was that I couldn't remember exactly where it had happened. At some point I started to feel mud between my toes and I realised I'd lost one sandal, which must have got stuck in the swampy ground, so I kicked off the other and walked barefoot. It was late, but not so late that there wasn't any traffic on the highways beyond, and on the bridges overhead. Their headlamps would sometimes illuminate the tops of the trees above me, and suddenly little details would leap out at me, things I wouldn't have noticed if I'd been walking there in the daytime – kites with smiley bird faces snagged in the branches, or plastic bags, lots of them, hanging like swollen ghostlike fruit.

Sometimes I'd see strange shapes drifting in the middle of the river. Fallen tree trunks and bushes uprooted by the storms upstream, tangled together in huge rafts that looked like some sort of mythical beast from *Journey to the West*, the kind of nonsense that adults tell children to scare them into behaving themselves, but that no one actually takes seriously, not even children – what kid actually believes in a nine-headed bug? – until one night they're walking alone on a riverbank, and then those demons seem real and terrifying. Other times, snagged in the reeds right by where I was walking, I'd see a dead creature, a body so bloated that I couldn't even tell what it was – a could-be cat or a could-be monkey. When a body's been in the water for that long, its shape starts to blur, softening around the edges until it becomes impossible to distinguish one kind of animal from another.

My arm ached, I was moving in a funny way, one side of my body less mobile than the other. I realised that I was still holding the piece of wood, the length of tree branch that had felt so light in my hand just a short while ago but now seemed to weigh a hundred pounds. During the trial, when people in court referred to *the murder weapon that was never retrieved*, I remembered the damp two-foot piece of wood that I held that night. It was just a fragment of a tree. A few hours earlier, when I'd struck the man for the first time, the broken length of wood had seemed so insignificant that I thought it incapable of causing pain. I expected it to shatter, I expected the man to laugh at my ridiculous choice of weapon. Now it felt as if I was lifting an entire tree, the weight of the world clinging to its roots. I raised my arm, wanting to throw it far out into the middle of the river, but suddenly I found that I had no strength left in my body. It slipped from my grasp and fell just a few feet away.

I realised after a while that the police were not going to arrive. No one was going to come for me. Not that night, not the following day, and maybe not for weeks. In the end it took them more than two months to arrest me – but you already know that. You also know why it took so long. When the victim is that sort of person, the police don't really care. Yes, that kind of person. A foreigner. An illegal. Someone with dark skin.

Bangla, Myanma, Nepal. When the police come it's all the same to them. Even Africa. It's as if they all come from one big nameless continent. Back when I was living in Puchong, I saw a group of Africans by the side of the road, a dozen men. Some were sitting on the pavement, others were standing up, laughing, joking, drinking beer and liquor. One or two were dancing – they had a big portable set that played their tunes so loudly I almost couldn't hear my own music. I was listening to Jacky Cheung on my phone – back then we only had those small Sony Ericssons that made every song sound crackly, as if you were listening to it on the radio in a faraway country. Maybe you're too young to remember those phones. I was on the other side of the road, outside the 7-Eleven, eating a Ramly burger with Keong. This was seventeen, eighteen, maybe even twenty years ago. Back then you didn't see so many Africans around. People didn't know anything about them – which countries they were from, why they'd come here. Ask anyone what they knew about Africa and they'd say, *Lions*.

Keong was looking at his phone, pretending he wasn't interested, as if he'd grown up with black people. But he couldn't help making comments. *Wahlau, Muhammad Ali brought all his friends!* I remember laughing, even though I didn't really find it funny. Most probably I made some comments too. It was so long ago, I don't recall. There was a light breeze that night, I remember that. Next to us an old Indian stallkeeper was clearing up his stand for the night. Business was slow, there weren't many people out on the street. 'Every Friday night,' he said. 'Every week they come here and raise trouble. Friday supposed to be holy day – these *guys*, they don't respect anything.' In fact he didn't say *these guys*, he said *these Mat Hitam*. Better not translate that.

I said, 'They're Nigerian.' I'd seen an article in the *Nanyang Siang Pau* about Nigerian students coming to Malaysia, falling into debt after they graduated and being

7

unable to buy a ticket home. I remember thinking, Must be really desperate to come to college here.

'Shut your mouth,' Keong said. 'Nigerian your ass. You don't know anything.'

As I looked at them, I got the feeling that they were floating through the city, unattached to anything around them. Their music was the only thing that seemed real – a link to their home. That was why they were listening to it so loudly, I thought. But they were thousands of miles away, and something in the way they talked to each other, shouting over the music and laughing in the half-dark street, made me realise that they would probably never return to where they came from. And suddenly I thought, *I am just like them, I am floating through life.*

'What the fuck,' Keong said. There was a note of excitement in his voice. Two guys in the group had started fighting, that kind of messy scuffling that happens when people are drunk, not really a proper fight, just grappling with each other, tumbling into the road. A car passed by and had to swerve to avoid them. The driver leaned on the horn for a long time – it was a Kancil, the noise of the honking as it drove off was high-pitched, like a cheap child's toy that you buy in the night market. It made us laugh. A few minutes later the men were joking and talking again as though nothing had happened. We stopped looking at them – they were nothing special, they were just like us, just hanging out with friends. Keong was texting his new girlfriend, reading out her messages to me. Of course he was exaggerating. I knew she didn't think he was the handsomest guy in the world. In fact I'm sure she didn't even exist. But I went along with it – that's what you do with old friends. You take an interest in their lives, even when they're lying.

Then suddenly we heard a commotion – more shouting. We looked up from our phones and saw three police cars and another three unmarked ones surrounding the Nigerian guys. Everyone was yelling. There were a lot of cops, I couldn't count them. They pushed one guy against a car. I could hear him shouting in English, *No drugs no drugs I don't have anything!* But they handcuffed him anyway and made him sit on the kerb just like his dozen or so friends. At first the Nigerians were arguing, shouting at the police. They were big guys, much taller than us, and maybe they thought they could get out of trouble by being loud, but they didn't know what the police were like. I couldn't see what happened, there were too many bodies in the way, but all at once everything became quiet, and one of the men was lying on the ground, one arm around his head, the other one stretched out as if he was reaching for something. He wasn't moving. After a while, some of them started to plead – we could hear them from across the street. Their voices were soft and rich and deepened each time they said the word *Please. Please.* The sound of the word made me feel as if I was stepping off solid earth and falling into an abyss. I wanted it to stop.

'Just pay them,' Keong said. 'Get all the damn cash out of your pockets. *Just pay.*' But we knew they had no money to bribe the cops. I'm sure they understood the system just as well as we did, they just didn't have the money. Keong shook his head. '*Aiyo cham lor*, lock-up for you tonight my friends.' When you've grown up in the kinds of places that we have, you know what's in store for you.

A big police truck arrived and picked up all the Nigerians. While it was still parked, one of the cops came over to buy some cigarettes. We asked him what was going on. He said, 'Local people – we don't like seeing *Mat Hitam* around.' He lit a cigarette with a silver Zippo lighter. 'We're like the town council, just cleaning the trash off the streets.'

We laughed loudly – as if we were best buddies with

him. *Yeah, clean it all up.* I can't remember what else we said, can't recall exactly what kind of jokes we made, but we wanted the police to think we were on their side. We knew they wouldn't be hassling us that night, that there was someone else they were more interested in. Even though I was young, I thought I already understood the way things worked. But that night made it clear to me, like the words to a song by a foreign singer. You know the melody by heart, but you can't quite make out the words, you can only understand fragments of English here and there, you sing a line or two from the chorus and sort of understand the message, but then one day someone explains the words to you, and suddenly everything clicks into focus, the whole song makes sense. It's no longer just a pretty tune, it's got meaning – and that night, the message became clear: no one wanted to know about you if you were dark-skinned and foreign. Who would come looking for you if you were thrown in Sungai Buloh jail? Or if you sank slowly to the bottom of a river? No one would ask questions. Not until it was way too late.

I don't know why I'm telling you all this. I guess I want to empty out the contents of my head after all these years. That's what you asked me to do right from the start. Don't hold back, be as honest and open as possible. Just talk, you said. No judgement. So that's what I'm doing. Just talking.

I have nothing to complain about these days. Every day is the same, and this is a blessing. Nowadays people think variety is the only thing that gives meaning to life, but they forget that routine is a privilege too. No disruptions, no crazy ups and downs, no heartbreak or distress – there is something divine in sameness, isn't there? A gift sent from the gods. I'm lucky. I live on my savings – the small amount of money I made when I sold my house in Taman Bestari that I'd lived in with my wife. To my surprise it was still worth something when I came out of jail, so I sold it and moved into this place, a smaller house with just two small bedrooms, a bit further out of town. Twice a week, someone from the church visits me with a food hamper – basic groceries with a few treats thrown in – and if ever I'm in need, I can always go to church to talk to someone, and they'll usually give me some biscuits or leftover fried rice – whatever they have in the kitchen. It's called Harvest Assembly. I've been going there for nearly six years, ever since I got out of prison.

Apart from that, small sums of money come through to me from time to time from a Chinese charity. You know, the L-Foundation. That happened through the lawyer who tried to get damages from the prison service for the injury I suffered during my time inside, but of course it didn't succeed. I could have told them that before they even started. Who in the world ever gets any damages from the police or the prison service? But because of the lawyer's efforts, someone heard of my case, even though it was never famous, never in the newspapers for long. Somebody took pity on me, even though God knows I wasn't worthy of sympathy then. Next thing I know, I get a cheque for six hundred ringgit. To you it probably seems like nothing, but for me it's a lot. I thought it was a one-time deal, I was happy with it, but the cheques continue to arrive – not regularly, just now and then, with no warning or reason. Sometimes 250 ringgit, sometimes four hundred. On those days I'll walk to the bus stop and ride into town, get there just before the old *bak kut teh* places shut, and have a big breakfast before strolling around Little India. Sometimes I like to spend a few hours just wandering around a mall in the new town, usually Klang Parade. I treat myself to a meal at Texas Chicken, and always order the same thing: Mexicana Burger and Honey-Butter Biscuits. Sometimes I think I should be more adventurous and try something else – I really like the look of Jalapeno Bombers. *Bombers*! They sound great. But then I think, what if I don't like them? The thought of getting something new makes me nervous. I want my day to be happy, I don't want to be stressed, I want everything to be calm, to remain the same.

I sit and watch the teenagers in school uniforms sharing their fried chicken and showing each other photos on their phones. The boys pretend to be tough, they use the same language I did when I was their age – you know, Cantonese cursing, which sounds really crude and aggressive. If you'd heard me and my friends at that age you'd probably have moved away to the next table. But these kids, they're not like me – they come from the new suburbs close by, they've got decent families. Fourteen, fifteen years old, but they're just babies, relaxing in the mall together after school and

12

playing games on their phones. Even after a whole day at school their uniforms look freshly laundered, not crumpled and grey with sweat – you'd almost say there was starch on their white shirts. Nothing troubles their lives, and in a strange way, their happiness makes me feel innocent again, and hopeful. Those days out in town are special. I have money in my pocket, I feel independent and free, even if it's just for a day or two. That's what those cheques mean to me – a day of freedom. I never pray or even make little idle wishes for them, they just appear. That's how God works, I guess. Always surprising, always giving.

With the injury I suffered in prison I can't work. As you can see, I still have a slight limp, though it's not so notice-able when I'm walking slowly. You only notice it when I have to move quickly, like when I'm running for the bus and just can't shift my leg the way I want to. My brain says, *Faster, faster*, and for a few seconds I think I can do it, I really think I can get up and sprint for the bus – but my leg just drags. That's when I notice that I'm limping badly, my body sloping from side to side. I also can't pick up heavy loads as I could before. I used to be famous for that. The guys at the factory I worked at when I was a teenager would set me a challenge, see how many crates of fish I could lift at a time, and I'd always surprise them, even though I'm pretty short. It's my stumpy legs that give me balance. People say it's a Hokkien trait, that our ances-tors needed short thighs and calves to plant rice or harvest tea and whatever else people did in southern China two hundred years ago, but who cares? All I know is that my legs always served me well, until I got to prison. [*Pauses.*] It's because of a nerve in my back, something to do with my spine that I don't really understand. The doctors showed me x-rays, but all I could see was the grey-white shapes of my bones. They couldn't correct it without surgery in a private hospital in KL, but who can afford that these days? At the hospital I laughed and said, 'I'm not a cripple, so let's just live with it, OK?' Someone from church suggested I could get a different kind of job, something that didn't involve manual labour, but any kind of job that allows you to sit down in a comfortable office also requires you to have diplomas and certificates and God knows what else these days – and I don't have any. I was never very successful at school.

One time, just a year after I got out of prison, some fellow churchgoers found me a job in their family business, a trading company that imported goods from China and distributed them throughout the country. I had a nice desk, there was air-con in the office, and I didn't have to answer the phone or talk to anyone I didn't know. All I had to do was add up numbers – such an easy job; nothing can be more certain and solid than numbers. I made sure invoices tallied, checked receipts, that sort of thing. Even though I'd never done that kind of work before, I knew about how to manage money. But at that time, I got a bit anxious whenever I encountered anyone new, in a situation that wasn't familiar to me – I guess it must have been my time in prison that did that to me. Nothing serious, you understand, just some hesitations in replying whenever someone spoke to me, lapses between their questions and my answers that made them think I had mental problems. Five, ten seconds – who knows? I watched people's expressions change from confusion, to concern, then irritation. Sometimes frustration, sometimes anger. Some people thought I was doing it on purpose. Once a guy in the office said, *Lunseehai, such an arrogant bastard!* He shouted it out loud right in front of me without expecting a reply, as if everyone thought the same of me, and that I was deaf and mute and couldn't hear what he was saying. 'Whatever the case,' my boss said after a few months – she was very nice, she understood – 'we think it's better you stop work. Just go home and rest.' Up to that point, I hadn't understood how much I had changed in the previous three years, but losing that job made me appreciate that I had become a different person. Exactly how, I couldn't tell you, but I was no longer the same. I had a couple of interviews for office jobs after that, but nothing worked out.

That's why I say I'm lucky. I don't work, yet I'm alive. My days are calm. I'd even say I was blessed.

[*Long silence.*]

Sometimes . . . [*Hesitates; reaches for and picks up cup of tea but does not drink.*] Sometimes, yes, of course I think of that night. How can I not? I think of the two men who were present, Keong and the Bangladeshi guy. I know what you're expecting me to say: that I see their faces, and that I'm tortured by the sight of them – but that's not the way it is. I don't feel anything about either of them – not hate, not pity. Maybe I should have felt anger towards Keong; maybe things would have turned out differently if he hadn't come back to see me. He had choices. He didn't have to ask me to do all those things.

Now when I think about him, I don't see the Keong of that night. I see the version of him that appeared in court three years later, when my case was being appealed. His white long-sleeved shirt, his neat hair, even the way he spoke to the judge, softly and respectfully – anyone would have thought he was a salesman for an IT company in Petaling Jaya. I didn't recognise him at first, I thought it was someone else, that the prosecutors had brought the wrong guy to the courtroom. The lawyers asked him questions about himself, and he supplied the bare facts – he owned a business importing frozen dumplings from China, his income stream was steady, he owned a Toyota Camry and had a home loan from Hong Leong bank. He'd recently been on holiday to Australia and was saving up to send his daughter to boarding school there in seven or eight years' time, when she was old enough to travel on her own. Right now she had just started at a private school in Cheras, close to where he lived, so he could spend a lot of time with her at home. The moment he finished work, he'd rush home to his wife and daughter and they'd spend the evening having dinner, doing the daughter's homework together and watching a bit of TV. She was a studious girl – she really loved science!

He answered quietly, as if he didn't want me to hear what he was saying. On the other side of the courtroom I had difficulty making out some of his words. *Mortgage. Laptop. Playground.* The man speaking seemed to be embarrassed by the way he lived. Why would someone feel shy about having a life like that? That was when I realised it was Keong – the same one I had known since my teenage years, and I knew why he appeared so awkward. He was ashamed because of my shame – or to be more precise, he was ashamed of being happy while my shame was on display to the world. We'd shared so much as children. People used to say, 'No use giving Ah Hock any ice cream, he'll just give half to that little bastard Keong.' But *time* – that was something we couldn't share. It could only favour one of us.

And I thought, Of course he's changed. All those years in prison, when I went through phases of either sleeping all day and all night, or lying awake all day and all night – phases that lasted weeks and broke down my sense of time, my resistance to the idea that every day should be different – during that time, Keong was changing himself. Anyone could have become a new person in that period, anyone could have acquired a brand-new life. He'd been

so proud of his hair, the long fringe that he'd dyed a shade
of coppery orange when he was fifteen, and that he'd kept
right up until that evening when we last saw each other.
I used to joke with him. 'Hey, big brother, going to become
father, still keep that gangster hairstyle meh?' He called it
'blond', thought it made him look like a Hong Kong pop
star. He always used to do this [*sweeps hand theatrically over
forehead, throws back his head in slightly camp fashion*]. Made
me laugh. You're a nobody, just like the rest of us – that's
what I used to say to him every time he tried to show off.

That hair was gone now, trimmed short and allowed to
go back to its natural colour. I hadn't seen him with black
hair since we were teenagers. He'd put on weight, which
made him look younger, not older, like an adolescent who'd
once been chubby but was starting to shed all his puppy
fat and turn into a handsome man. I could tell that he'd
given up smoking, that he was eating better – his
complexion was smoother, the deep crease between his
eyebrows which he'd had since he was a child had disappeared. Ironed out by those three years.

At one point the lawyers started asking him questions
about my character. Did he ever know me to be impulsive?
Had he ever seen violent tendencies in me? Was I someone
who felt sorry and regretted bad deeds? At first he answered
clearly and simply, without hesitation, just like the serious
businessman he'd become. It wasn't a role he was
performing, it was who he really was now. Both his English
and his Malay had improved, and he used them carefully,
considering every word before saying it. But as the questions continued, he began to feel at ease and started
speaking more freely, sometimes using expressions you
might consider rude. He even told a little story from our
teenage years. *One time hor, I steal biscuit from the store, I
share with him but I steal so much we cannot finish, he say must*

return, must return, I say no way, poke your lung, but he lagi force me so next day we go give back biscuit. Your mother. Make me lose face! But he say how can steal, she also no money.

'OK, OK, Mr Tan. I think that will do.' When the lawyer said that I laughed. Even in his new life, Keong couldn't resist talking too much. For a few seconds, when he was recounting that incident – which I couldn't recall – I saw the years and the extra weight he'd acquired fall away. I saw the skinny kid with a sharp face and earrings again, the one I'd grown up with and had always thought would end up in jail. We even joked about it when he left KL to find work elsewhere. 'Don't worry about an address,' I'd told him, 'I'll just come looking for you in prison.'

After the lawyer's admonishment he fell silent once more – a husband, a proper father, someone you could trust to hold a family together. That's the image of him that comes to me from time to time these days. A respectable man, beyond hatred.

It was only much later that I realised I'd only spent three years in jail. Three years – that's nothing! Why did it feel so long when I was in my cell? And how did Keong change so quickly? That's when I felt bitter. I'd never held a grudge against him, not even for coming back to Klang and bringing Evil into my life. When I talked about it to members of the church some years later they said, You must forgive him the way God forgives you. And I thought, There's nothing for me to forgive; I don't feel anything towards him. But when I saw him in the court-room and thought of how quickly he'd changed, I felt angry. He had taken hold of time and mastered it, I had let myself be crushed by it. It was only three years, I told myself, *only three years* – you can make up that time and turn things round for yourself. But I knew I was no longer capable of changing my life. Evolution is a funny thing.

For the longest time, you believe in the power of change – in your ability to mould your life through even the smallest acts. Even buying a four-digit lottery ticket feels loaded with optimism, as if those five bucks might turn into a twenty-thousand bonanza and transform your life. Then one day it disappears, that blind devotion to hope, and you know that even if you pray all day, nothing will happen to you. My anger was directed at myself, I didn't blame Keong. Seeing him reminded me of the person I could no longer be.

As for the other man, his face remains a blank, even though it should be the one thing I remember from that night. In my defence, it was very dark when I first saw him. What's more, he turned away from me before I picked up the piece of wood. I couldn't see his face when I struck him.

Towards the end of the trial my lawyer tried to explain to the jury the kind of childhood I had experienced. She was young and clever, she worked for free, she wanted to help me. I understood that my life was being used as an excuse for many things. I listened to her speak about me, and though the facts were true, I felt as if she was describing someone else, someone who had grown up close to me, maybe in a village a couple of miles up the coast. Another guy who shared my name, which she kept repeating. Lee Hock Lye. Lee Hock Lye. Always my full name. Sometimes she said, Lee Hock Lye, *also known as* Jayden Lee, which made the name sound fake, as if I'd made it up – which I had. But still, it was my name – had become my name. I had chosen it when I'd found proper work and things were going well, just before I got married. It sounded good, people liked it – they hadn't heard anything like it before. It was a cool name that looked professional on the calling cards that I had printed when business started going well. Jayden – that was me, but each time she pronounced the name in front of the entire courtroom it felt as though she was referring to someone else, because she said it as two separate words. *Jay, Den.* As if she found it unnatural. Every time I heard it, I felt as though the name was being prised away from me, and that I never truly owned it. *Also known as.* I should never have taken that name, I was foolish to have chosen it.

20

The person she talked about was miserable, badly-educated, hopeless. Someone who had no choices in life. Anyone listening would have pitied him. A woman in the jury was nodding her head slowly, her face twisted in a frown. Even I nearly felt sorry for the person being described. But then I thought: Wait, this is wrong. I also thought: I was happy. I was normal. I knew my lawyer was trying to help me, but I wanted her to stop talking. I started humming a tune to block out the noise of her words. I closed my eyes and tried to imagine being back in the village as a child. I tried to remember what it was like to be myself again, but it was ridiculous. That life was gone. What a stupid thing to do, trying to recapture your childhood while you're being tried for killing someone. Recalling my life wouldn't make it any more real – the truth of it existed in the version being described by my lawyer. I laughed at my own stupidity. I laughed quite loudly, and couldn't stop, so I had to put my face in my hands. The lawyer turned around to look at me. She stopped speaking in the middle of a sentence and stared at me – the kind of look you give someone when you think he might be having a heart attack but you're not yet sure what's happening. The judge said, 'I don't think the defendant's life story is relevant. Please continue with your legal arguments.' My lawyer tried to dispute this, but my laughing and the judge's scolding made her lose her concentration; all the intelligence and conviction and vigour I had admired up to that point dissolved in that stuffy courtroom. It was very hot that day, the air-con wasn't working, I had trouble breathing. She stumbled over her words a couple of times, and couldn't hold her thoughts together. I was glad it was all going to end soon.

She got the details wrong. Everyone got the details wrong. Maybe you can set things straight once and for all. Is your phone recording all this? I was born in Bagan Sungai Yu, not in Kuala Selangor town as all the court documents said. The two places are separated by a sharp curve in the Selangor river, and that small distance – forty, fifty feet in places – sometimes felt like an ocean between two continents. These days, with the bridges and good tarmac roads, people think of them as just one place: Kuala Selangor. I get the papers and read articles about new seafood restaurants built on jetties over the water, I see pictures of day-trippers from KL enjoying Sunday lunch, and I think: *That's not Kuala Selangor, that's my village*. But that's the way things go: the big swallow up the small, everything becomes part of something else. It's just funny to think that when I was a child, even at primary school, we had to take the ferry over to town, or cycle miles to get around the bend in the river, and when we got to the other side, it felt so busy and important that I thought I was in Tokyo or New York. That map that you're looking at on your phone, it can't show you the real distance between our side of the river and town on the other.

My father was a fisherman, just like my grandfather before him. In fact, every man in the village was a fisherman. The country left us no choice – the river coiled around the village, blocking our route south towards the towns, forever nudging us towards the sea. On the other side were the jungle and the plantations, which offered prospects even worse than the sea. Back then it was Indians who harvested the palm oil, now it's Bangladeshis and Indonesians – whoever was doing it, we only had to look at their lives to know that their fate was worse than the storms and tides and tangle of nets that we lived with every day.

All of us worked at the mercy of the elements – the storms, floods, snakes, worms that burrow into your feet. Nature is beautiful when you look at it from afar, or from a car that passes through it with the windows rolled up.

When you have to work outdoors it doesn't seem so beautiful. Yesterday I read an article on Facebook that said: *We should all spend more time outside!* I looked at the photos of people walking in parks, hugging, drinking water from small bottles, eating slices of watermelon. Lying down on the grass without a mat, without shielding their faces from the sun. Everyone was having fun, no one was sweating or getting heat exhaustion. There were all kinds of people in the photos. Asian, African, every colour under the sun – but they were all behaving like white people. I mean, who else actually enjoys going out into the wilderness apart from these crazy *angmoh*? You get a day off work, you want to go out into the jungle? Those happy Westerners, they don't know what 'outdoors' is like around here.

I remember once, when I was thirteen, fourteen – old enough to have started feeling that if I didn't escape the village I would go mad – I spent a whole day cycling as far as I could, in every direction I could think of. I went inland into the plantations in the shade of the palm-oil trees until the mud tracks got too soft for me to cycle. I looked ahead of me, thinking, How long would I have to cycle before I came out on the other side of the estate? I could only see the perfect rows of trees disappearing into the darkness, so I headed back to the coast, cycling along the dirt path that ran along the rocky shoreline, the red earth staining my toes. All the way to Sekinchan and beyond, that was all I could see: red earth, rocks and mud, the sea stretching back towards Indonesia, so flat and shallow, like a sheet of silver without end. No wind. No shade. The sun so hot on my head and arms that my skin felt stripped away with sandpaper. The light too sharp for my eyes – the same light that I'd known ever since I was a baby. I knew that all my days as an adult – every single one, to the end of my time on this earth – would be spent under that burning sun. In that moment, I suddenly got the feeling that all the things I'd ever known – my family, my home, the trees, grass, water, food, the bare earth, the huge, huge sea: everything – were strange and foreign, as if I'd never known them at all. They were mine, handed down to me at birth, the only heritage I'd ever know, and yet at that moment they didn't seem to belong to me. This land that was supposed to be part of me, and I part of it – in that instant we felt like strangers. I didn't want it. One day, it would kill me.

[*Pause; long sigh.*]

I like my life indoors now. If I had children I would make sure they never had to go outside, ever.

What made us different from the Indians who laboured in the plantations was that we worked for ourselves. If it rained we wouldn't eat. If the catch was plentiful we could save some money and replace our worn-out shoes, buy a tarpaulin to stretch over the front yard to keep the rain out of the house – small things like that. The equation was simple for us. But they worked for the big corporations, the ones the government took over from the British. New owners, same rules. Times change but the workers' lives never improve. They had bad pay, bad housing, no schools, had to work with poisonous chemicals all day, had no entertainment in the evenings other than to drink their home-made *samsu* that made them go blind and mad. But what else could they do? Run away to the city and live on the streets? At least back then they had papers. Now it's all Bangla and Myanmar workers – I don't think a single one of them has an ID card.

We seldom spoke about the Indians on the plantations, except to say how miserable their fate was. *Poor black devils, dead but not dead* – repeating these kinds of expressions made us feel that by comparison we were comfortable and easy. We never mixed with them – our lives were totally separate. We didn't want anything to do with them, in case their misfortune rubbed off on us. All the time I was growing up, I shared the villagers' sense of being scared of the plantation Indians because they might infect us with their poverty, and we really didn't need any more of that in our lives. Maybe it was just another superstition that we Chinese specialise in – you know, like: Don't look at a funeral procession or you might die too. Looking back now, I guess it was because they made us realise that we were not so different from them. So they just *existed*, a constant presence on the plantations *over there*, which is to say right next to us – a reminder of how bad things could get.

I guess you could say it was Geography's fault that I was born into a family of fishermen – that we became who we were. But history played its part too. Like most of the people in the village, three of my grandparents arrived from Indonesia in the first years of the Second World War, when it wasn't safe to be Chinese over there. They'd heard about the internment camps, the summary executions, young girls being raped – all the stuff I'm sure you've studied at college. Even I heard about that in school. They knew it might be the same story here, but they took their chances. What makes a person leave a country for another country where they could be persecuted for exactly the same thing? You get on a boat in Sumatra, cross the Melaka Straits, knowing that you could get rounded up and put in a prison camp just like you were before. Why did they do it? I'll never know. *Aiya, they made it through the war, we're all OK now, why do you care?* That was what my mother said when I asked her about my grandparents. Stuff that went on in the war – forget it. Old Chinese folk never talk about that, so don't go asking.

For many years, my grandmother refused to register to vote. The address on her ID card was her aunt's in Teluk

Intan. She'd spent a few years there when she first got to the country, and thought of it as a sort of home. She was the youngest, barely fifteen when she arrived. I'm not sure how long exactly she spent there, but the moment she got to our village she didn't move for the rest of her life. It's not like the rest of us actually bothered to vote – we didn't, or only occasionally. It would never make much difference to us – politicians change, our lives stay the same. But with my grandmother, it was more than just not caring. She actively wanted to be hidden from view. *If they come for us, they won't know where I live! I'll have one, two, three more days to escape.* That's what she used to say. *Not like the rest of you! They'll know your address and when the time comes they'll know where to find you.* Crazy old woman. People used to laugh at her. Who's going to come for us? No one cares about us or what we do! But she was convinced that one day there would be a government decree, a law that would be passed overnight, and everyone with a Chinese name would be rounded up and put in camps, just as they were during the war. Hey Po-po, just chill out! We have internet now! Facebook Twitter Insta Snapchat, can Skype with someone in Russia while listening to Super Junior on live stream, team-play video games with people that you never met in Harbin and Copenhagen. You actually believe that in this kind of world, we can just round up millions of people and put them in a prison camp, or kick them out of the country? You think you'll wake up one day and hundreds of thousands of people are going to be walking across the border into Thailand with nothing but the shirts on their backs, and all the homes and villages and entire cities we've built, with skyscrapers and malls, are going to be abandoned, just like that? Keep up with the times, Po-po!

She wouldn't listen. For the rest of her life, she was obsessed by keeping her address secret, thinking it would protect her when Chinese doomsday arrived. When she was very old – I'd long since moved out of the village but was back living in the area – she fell down one day while reaching up to pick a pomegranate from the small tree she'd planted outside her house. A scrawny plant that never grew well, no matter how much she looked after it. That was another one of her obsessions, that stupid plant; in the end, it nearly killed her. The small plastic stool she'd climbed up on to reach its branches was brittle and cracking, and couldn't take her weight when she stepped on it. She fell, broke her hip and ended up in hospital. When I arrived I found there were many forms to fill in. Each time I did so, she insisted I wrote her false address. 'What the hell is the use of doing that?' I said. 'If they need to do any follow-up tests they'll go searching for you fifty miles from where you live.'

'Good,' she said. Maybe it was because she was so young when the war broke out, only fifteen, and only sixteen or seventeen when she had to get in a boat and cross the seas to Malaysia. She knew what could happen to girls of that age in times of war. I guess that's why she wanted to remain in the shadows. To be invisible is to be safe. Kids nowadays, their whole lives are on the internet – every minute of their day broadcast to the universe. Thank God my Po-po never knew Facebook – she'd have been anxious and stressed all the time. *Die lor, police see computer know where you are!* She was the opposite – wanted her history, her entire self, to be scrubbed out from the world.

That was when I understood that for her, our village was a place of comfort. We were trapped in obscurity, hard to get in, hard to get out. If anything happened, she could just slip away into the sea. Again. It suited her just fine.

My grandparents were all originally from Fujian province. According to my calculations, the ones who came from

Sumatra – they'd only been in Indonesia for ten years max before they had to move again. Imagine that – you come all the way from China, you leave behind war, famine, getting in and out of small boats drifting on the ocean for months, eventually land in some tiny town in Indonesia, find some way of earning a living, working the land or the sea. You think you own that tiny bit of scrubby jungle or marsh or wherever it is you've landed, you think you can start a family, start a new life. Then, just when your days and weeks start to feel normal, when your notion of time begins to stretch out into a year, two years, a future – when you look at the place you're in and it no longer feels as if every tree, every blade of grass is out to hurt you, you have to move again. More war, more boats, more swamps.

Guess that's why they never wanted to leave the village once they got there. For them, that was it. End of the road. Stop. Don't look back. Don't look ahead. Even if this new place turned out to be as bad as the one they'd left, they'd take their chances there. No going anywhere, ever again, not even to Klang for a movie. Their children were the same – all the people of my parents' age seemed to be attached to that coastline of rocks and mangroves and driftwood, sheltered by inlets and swamps. They started to fish, firstly to feed themselves, then, after the war, to sell in the small markets down the coast. One generation handing on its work to the next – the only heirloom we had. The men out in the boats at sea, the women sewing the nets in the village, the children gutting the fish in rickety shacks perched on stilts over the muddy banks – a way of life that didn't change for nearly half a century, until the first bridge was built across the rivermouth in the early 1980s.

The other day at church I was sorting through the pile of books and magazines that people had donated – old paperbacks and textbooks dumped on a table in the hall where we have tea and cakes after mass. One of my little jobs at church is to arrange the books and empty the donations box. There's rarely much money in it. Sometimes people might take a copy of *Twilight*, but they don't put any money in. That day someone had left a whole stack of old *Time* magazines from 1979, 1980 – just a few years after I was born – and out of curiosity I took them home with me. I stayed up all night looking at the photos. The president of the United States was shot. *Shot!* Can you believe that? John Lennon got shot too. Hundreds of thousands of people on the streets in Cuba. Russians fighting in Afghanistan. The whole world was changing. Our own country must have been changing. And all I could think was: How did we stay the same? The people of the village – my grandparents, my parents, even the children – we must have been trying to protect ourselves against all of the things going on around us. That's what our village meant to us: it existed to prevent us from knowing what was happening in the world. There can't have been any other explanation.

But once the bridge was built, things were different. Not long after, the businessmen from down south started building small factories around Kuala Selangor to clean and process the fish and distribute it around the country. We caught mainly white pomfret and prawns – delicate produce that required careful attention. The factories worked faster than we could, and more hygienically too, they said. That was what all the big supermarkets in the cities wanted, those giant air-conditioned spaces that were just starting to be built, so we sold them our catches cheap and let the flimsy gutting shacks fall slowly into the sea.

It was better that way, the villagers said – now at least we can save time and catch more fish, and our kids can go to school instead of cleaning fish and repairing nets with the women. But still we didn't go to school. We were

supposed to, but no one really did. We turned up sometimes if we felt like it, we messed around, we cut classes,
went out instead into the fields and plantations, smoked
cigarettes, planned our escape from the village. Hong Kong,
San Francisco – we imagined those places were just across
the water, and that with a bit of cash in our pockets we
could hop on a ship and start afresh there, just like our
grandparents had when they'd come from Indonesia, or
our ancestors who'd made it across from China a century
before we were born. It seemed so easy.

But when I think back to that time, I realise that of
course we didn't seriously believe we were going to end
up living in America. It was just a vague idea – a longing
to be some place better than where we found ourselves.
Those kinds of ambitions belonged to people like you, not
people like us. You know what I mean – people who lived
in the cities, who went to decent schools. We were just
village kids, messing around. One or two of the kids, the
serious ones at school who worked hard and passed all
their exams, they would only end up in a college nearby
in Klang, or train to be a teacher. Keong and I and the
rest of the children from the village, we didn't want that
life. We wanted to be tycoons. But the funny thing was,
we also *knew* we weren't going to become tycoons. How
to explain this? The more we longed for something, the
more impossible it became. You only dream about things
you can never obtain.

We heard about people from nearby villages moving to
KL or Singapore, or going abroad to Australia or the US,
and when they came back they were *rich*. We were eight,
ten, twelve years old – we didn't even know what that
meant, didn't know how they got rich or what they did
for it, or even how much money you needed to be considered *rich*. All we knew was that they had left their homes,

and now they had more than us. Sometimes they'd come back for Chinese New Year or Cheng Beng and I wouldn't even recognise them, these men and women who'd been part of my childhood. They had big new Japanese cars, Honda Accords, that sort of thing, and all the smaller kids would climb into them. I remember crawling over the seats, rubbing my face on the upholstery and sniffing the newness of it, while another kid pretended to drive the car even though he couldn't even see over the steering wheel. The very presence of such a vehicle in the village made everything else look shabby and poor. The smooth curves of the silvery body were beautiful and effortless and powerful – like a shark cutting through the water. All around it, our houses looked tired. Fragile. Concrete blocks and timber, patched up with zinc sheeting and planks of wood, every element a different colour and texture. If a storm blew through the village at that precise moment, everything else would have been swept away and only the car would have been left standing.

As I grew older and started to learn about the world, I could have asked them what they did in life, what kind of jobs they worked at, how they managed to leave the village and all that, but I never approached them. From a distance I watched them unload presents from the boot, carrying the boxes slowly into their family homes so that the rest of the village could see what they were – a colour TV, a Japanese rice cooker, a hair dryer. It wasn't just their clothes that had changed, but their voices too – not much, just a bit louder and clearer than before, with more English and Mandarin thrown into our dialect. Enough to make me feel that I couldn't communicate with them any more. Or maybe I wasn't that interested. I didn't have to go away and do what they did. I had a belief that life would improve for me, even if I didn't know how.

I wasn't the only one who was optimistic. Around this time, when the new roads and factories were starting to be built, as well as the first of the new suburbs further down south with their shopping malls and car parks, everyone in the village was happy that we didn't have to gut and clean all that fish any more. We were delighted that someone else took our catch from us and cleaned it in a *processing plant*. Simply hearing that expression made us feel that we were becoming more sophisticated. We knew that we were selling the fish more cheaply than we had before, but it didn't matter. Now we could spend more time at sea. Now we could start farming cockles in the mudflats that stretched out for hundreds of yards right from our front doors. Auntie Hong found a new recipe for prawn crackers that became so famous that day-trippers came up from the city at week-ends to buy them, and one day an article appeared in the national newspapers under the title 'Forgotten Seaside Charms'. I can still remember the photo of her, dressed up nicely in a red blouse, with matching lipstick and blue eyeshadow that made her look like a completely different person – who even knew that she had make-up? But there she was, proudly holding a bag of crackers in one hand, and a raw prawn in the palm of the other.

For about ten years, right up until I left the village, we got used to the excitement of the harvests of cockles – the distant sound of the shells as they were emptied from the boats into huge blue plastic tubs for cleaning. A bright sharp drumming noise that you could hear from hundreds of yards away. It was easier than going out to sea for long stretches, men and women could work together, they didn't have to be separated from their families for so long, could see the storms coming and take refuge. The children helped sort through the harvest. We picked out all the empty shells or those already half-open and dead. By the time I left the village, I knew that I would be one of the last of the children to be doing that job. Each year the harvests grew smaller, and we started to find more plastic bags in the mud that got dredged up with the catch, wrapping around the shells and suffocating them. One year I found dozens of condoms too. Maybe a factory had dumped them there, or they were carried downstream in the river – who knows. The younger kids had no idea what they were – they blew them up as though they were balloons, wore them on their fingers and clawed the air pretending to be a Pontianak or some other evil ghost. We laughed a lot that year.

Then some of the kids started getting a rash on their hands – red and tender, like the raw flaking patches that follow a burn, except more itchy than painful. I was the only one who guessed that it was from the mud – some of the villagers had the same problem on their feet, from wading in the shallows during the harvest. People started visiting the Monkey God temple to make offerings and prayers. We burnt paper-money – we thought it was our fault, that we hadn't done enough to appease the heavens. Everyone said, If we were richer, we could make more donations to the temple, we'd have better catches. They didn't realise that there was nothing they could do about all the pollution flushing down the river that went right through the cities and emptied into the sea in front of our houses. Or from the offshore prawn farms that had started further up the coast where the water was deeper – you could smell the chemicals sometimes, late in the afternoon when the wind was blowing in the right direction. A sour stink, like old catpiss. Even though I wasn't good at school, I understood that all those big industries further inland which were making cars and air-conditioners and washing machines and American sneakers – they lay close to the same river that washed over our cockle beds, forty, fifty miles away, and they would just carry on emptying their waste into the river, more and more as the years went by. I didn't even feel sad, or angry – why get mad over something you can't change? That was just the way things were.

The only thing that infuriated me was that no one wanted to listen to me when I told them what I thought was happening. *Pollution*? My grandmother repeated the word as if it was some bizarre other-worldly phenomenon, like an interplanetary collision in another solar system. She turned her back on me and went to the temple. 'Don't know what they teach you in school these days.'

Whenever anyone came back from the temple, they'd talk about destiny. *To live like this is our destiny*. I never thought about the meaning of fate and chance until I was in prison, and ideas just came to me during those long hours when I was lying on my bed doing nothing. What would have happened if my grandparents had landed further up the coast, or drifted south? If the winds or tides had been stronger or weaker and had carried them to Perak or Johor, or to Port Klang itself? Would I have been a dock worker or a sailor, or maybe a ship's captain? That would have been fun. If they'd landed somewhere else on the coast, where they weren't trapped between river and sea, maybe they'd have travelled inland and gone straight to a city. Maybe then, I would have become you.

I'm just kidding. Of course I couldn't have become you. I know it's not that simple. And I don't mean that I want to *become* you, or someone like you. It's just that sometimes I can't help thinking about whether I was really destined to be me.

October 10th

The dispute was about money, as it always is. That's why the man died. It wasn't because of a woman, as some of the papers suggested. People like us don't fight over love, we fight over houses, land, sometimes cars, mostly money – things that make a difference to the way we live.

About five, six weeks before the night in question, I got a call at work. Hendro, one of the Indonesians who'd been working for us for some time, came running up to the edge of the water, shouting, *Boss, boss, telephone.* His head was wrapped in his usual blue-and-white bandana, his hands blackened with grease as he signalled for me to go to the office. From a distance, he looked like a superhero cartoon toy, stout and smiling, even though he'd been working since daybreak, tarring the dirt yard in front of the small office building with a few of the other guys, transforming it into a proper car park with a tarmac surface so the cars and scooters wouldn't churn up the mud in the rainy season. We were getting more and more visitors then, people coming up from KL and as far as Alor Setar to inspect the farm and witness for themselves the quality of our produce, our new filtration systems, the freshness of the water, the hygiene levels. They needed to be sure of these things before they signed supply contracts with us, so we had to impress them. We couldn't have their cars sinking into the red mud or arriving back in town looking as if they'd driven to the Sahara and back. My boss had money then, business was good.

I started to make my way across the walkways, back towards the shore. I'd been supervising the release of the newest batch of hatchlings. Sea bass, that's what we were concentrating on that year, we knew the price of it would be high. There'd always been demand from Chinese restaurants, but then the upscale Western places started serving it too. A couple of our customers, who ran a neighbourhood restaurant somewhere in Petaling Jaya, showed us their menu – our fish might be selling at the same price as fancy imported produce like salmon and cod. 'You kidding me?' I said. 'Local people really paying these kinds of prices for sea bass – you sure it's not Westerners?' They assured my boss it was easy. Their clients preferred fresh local produce, they didn't want stuff that was frozen and flown all the way from Australia or Alaska. Their restaurant was just a café, it didn't look anything special, but it was selling sea bass fillets at fifty, sixty ringgit a serving. I thought of that money as I watched the tiny fish swim slowly out of the plastic bags, shimmering against the dark water like a bright silver cloud. A hundred bucks each on someone's plate in the city.

I couldn't stop thinking about the value of those fragile little fish as I walked along the wooden planks lashed to the floating oil drums. The farm had grown in recent times, and each year we added another few pens to the existing ones – floating cages framed by timber squares on the surface that served as walkways, the nets suspended in the water below. That year, the twelfth of the farm's existence, we had grown to twenty enclosures, five of them added in the last few months alone. I liked the neatness of the grid, knew my way around it, was quick on my feet, never losing my balance even if I had to run along the narrow decks in bad weather, when the water was choppy and the wind was up. I'd stand and look down at the fish thrashing at the surface of the water as the men threw in the feed, feeling the platform bob gently under my feet as the fish disturbed the water. And I'd be happy that I no longer had to jump in to repair the netting or retrieve plastic bags and bottles and other debris that got blown in by the storms. I'd grown up by the sea, but it remained unpredictable to me, always capable of change and destruction.

It took me a while to get back to the jetty, and I thought that the caller would have hung up by then. People get fed up of waiting, especially young people – everyone is in a hurry all the time. Hendro walked to the office with me, complaining about all the work they had to do. It was just him and two other Indonesians resurfacing the car park – Budi and Joyo, who were newer, who didn't know how to operate the machinery. They were slow, he had to show them how to do everything. Hendro had to deal with one of the generators too, which had blown up the previous night and needed to be fixed by the end of the day. A cage had been ripped and needed to be mended. One of the jetties had to be repaired. Then there was the maintenance of the pens, checking the water filters, doing the feeding rounds – he was having to do it all. *They stupid, boss, they stupid.* I laughed. When I started out here at the farm, I did all that work myself. And I never complained, I just did what needed to be done. '*Aiya*, people these days,' I told him, 'they just like to complain about everything. *Damn migrant worker also complain, how can?*' We laughed. 'Get the tarmac done first, the other jobs can wait until later.'

He knew that if he did everything well and didn't cause any trouble, with all the new work we were getting, I'd make sure Mr Lai gave him some extra cash at the end of the month to send back to his wife and daughter in Java – nothing much, fifty, a hundred ringgit maybe, two hundred at Hari Raya. Sometimes, if I felt that he'd done a lot of work that month, or if we'd had a particularly difficult time with the weather or supplies, and the boss only gave him a small tip, I'd give him some extra cash from my own pocket. He'd been with us for four years, and I thought he deserved something good – it was unusual for a worker to stay that long.

The boss didn't notice all that – the physical work we did on the farm, or the men who did it. He'd started spending more and more time on the road, searching for bigger clients farther afield – his latest obsession back then was the big supermarket chains in the Klang Valley, Tesco and Carrefour and suchlike. Some weeks he didn't even show up at the farm one single day. Most days it was just me keeping an eye on the place, supervising twelve workers. It was always difficult to find good Indonesians, men who'd stick at the job and didn't steal or cheat or gamble their earnings away – that was what the boss always said, and I think that's why he could never remember their names. He didn't want to know about their lives, didn't want to think of them as real people – it was easier that way when one of them suddenly didn't turn up for work. You lose a man like that, of course you wonder what's happened to him. Maybe he'd been hit by a bus in the night while coming back from one of the brothels down near the port, or he'd died in a fight or got picked up by the police, or just decided enough was enough and headed back to Kalimantan without bothering to collect his wages.

Stay in the business long enough, you hear all kinds of stories about what happens to these foreign workers. Just that week, three workers from the sheet metal factory down the road went missing and were found two days later, in a shack on the edge of a plantation, their eyes bulging and bloody, their mouths gone – no more lips or tongue, just a mess of bone and blood, dissolved by acid. That's what happens with paraquat poisoning, it burns a hole in your throat – this bit here [*touches throat, makes gurgling noise*] – and all the blood and whatnot comes bubbling up. One of them was a woman, a girl really, not even twenty-five years old. Who knows why they decided to commit suicide together. Workers kill themselves all the time here, and I can't say I'm surprised. I know it's wrong, it's a sin. Everyone knows that. When I started going to church that was one of the first things people told me – I guess they were concerned about my mental state, afraid I might try something stupid once I started to repent and realised what I had done, as if I hadn't realised before. *God will punish you if you commit suicide!* Churchgoers told me that all the time. But sometimes, when you see the way these Indons and Bangladeshis live, it makes sense. [*Pause.*] What I mean is, if there's no ceremony or leisure in your life, why would there be in death? If I worked eighteen hours a day and only had two rest days a month, and hadn't seen my family for seven years, I wouldn't be thinking of a luxury funeral with all my friends and huge bouquets of flowers and black cars the way you sometimes see in town, when some big boss dies. I wouldn't be thinking about whether my family will take out a full-page ad in the papers to announce my passing, like those Chinese tycoons do. I wouldn't be thinking about a portrait of myself dressed in a suit and tie. I'd think: it's time to go. And I'd go. No messing about.

The boss wasn't interested in all that. As long as the farm kept running well, and no one stole any money or machinery, he didn't care who worked there, how long they stayed, whether they were happy. *Ah Hock, that's why I have you!* He used to joke that I was half-foreign – that maybe my dad had been with a prostitute, and that's why I got along with the workers so well, because I had Indon blood in me. 'Don't know how, but you actually *understand* these guys,' he used to say. Sometimes, when clients came to visit and remarked on how smoothly things ran, the boss would tell them that it was down to me. 'My foreman does everything, makes sure the boys work well – *village boy, easier for him to communicate with them, hor.*'

I was proud that he boasted about me like that. Although I grumbled from time to time about his absences, it secretly felt good to be trusted like that. I'd been working on the farm for nearly ten years, and I'd got to that point in time when one year began to resemble the next, changing in ways I could anticipate, in ways that I wished for. My salary was going up only slightly, but it was increasing all the same. I'd got used to small surprises – a nice *angpow* at Chinese New Year from clients or machinery suppliers, sometimes a present when the boss came back from holiday, like that box of special Hokkaido wafers when he went to Japan one time.

When life evolves like that, one small gift coming on top of another, you start to feel strong. Your salary, which surprises you at the beginning – because its regularity is astonishing, because it keeps coming to you even when you think it might stop abruptly at any moment – starts to feel as if it has always been there. An unshakeable part of the universe, like atoms or the cells in your body. You receive it month after month, one year, two years, four, eight – it can never end. You start to feel complacent, though it doesn't strike you as complacency, but a sensation of solidity that surrounds you, so thick that sometimes you wake up in the night and believe that you can reach out and touch it.

Put it another way: I was thankful. I'd left home a few years before that – moved away from the village and drifted through a number of jobs in KL before returning to the area. I worked in a hardware store in Klang for a couple of months, then a shop that sold small agricultural tools and equipment just opposite the train station. I was loading some bags of fertiliser onto a customer's truck one day when I saw he had a big watch, a Rolex. This was the kind of thing that my time in KL had taught me to notice – shiny, expensive objects worn by their owners as a sort of challenge. Look at me, resist me. Covet me, reject me. I kept loading the bags, flipping each one up onto my shoulder and carrying it from the shop to the truck, fifty pounds a time, and all I could see out of the corner of my eye was the watch on the man's wrist as he stood there, hands on his hips. He checked the time. It was noon. It was hot.

When I finished he reached into his pocket and I thought he was going to give me a tip, maybe two–three ringgit, something like that, but instead he gave me his business card. 'Ever need a job, just ring me,' he said. He was called Mr Lai, and he owned a few vegetable farms near Sekinchan, some orchards, a goat farm. Plus, he was the middleman, the one who employed the groups of migrant workers to harvest the rice for the Malays who owned the biggest ricefields in the area. He arranged everything for them, got the groups of Bangladeshis and Indonesians in for the season, paid them their wages in cash, then sold the rice for the land-owners. Of course he took a cut from everything – not much, a bit here, a bit there, enough to end up a wealthy man. People make job offers all the time, but when you call them, the work isn't there any more. I'd got used to that way of living. A promise isn't a promise. Still, I kept the card.

A few months later, when I had a problem with my employers – they accused me of stealing, which wasn't true, not at that job, anyway – I just turned around and walked out. The boss-lady was sitting at the desk, the cash register open, scolding me, her voice as harsh as a drill into concrete.

You want the money for what, buy drugs is it? Owe money to a loan shark? What? Her husband stood behind her, his arms folded across the top of his paunch. Above them the clock showed nine o'clock. I could feel the sentences forming in my head, explaining that it was a mistake, that if they looked at the books again, the numbers would add up, that I wasn't the only one in charge of receiving the money. Or maybe I'd made a mistake, hadn't counted the notes properly when a big payment came in – who knows? But she was shouting too loudly, one question layered on top of another, and I couldn't keep up, the sentences in my brain never stitched together to form a clear line of defence. I wanted to scream all kinds of swear words, smash the glass cabinet in front of me with my bare fists, kick down the shelves of paint and screws and weighing scales, see all that cheap shit fall to the ground. But instead I grinned. I didn't even know I was pulling a silly cheerful face until the boss-lady said, '*Smile what?* Crazy boy. Where you going? Come back! Why you smiling?'

'Hei.' I shook my head. *Pok kai.* I turned and walked out of the shop. I'd never liked her. She was always prying, always asking me questions about my family, where I came from – things I didn't want to talk about. *Sei pat por.* In my memory I actually called her these things to her face, told her exactly what I thought of her, but maybe I didn't. The way I'm talking now, you won't believe me, but I've never been one for saying much, especially in situations like that. She was still shouting as I left and walked out. I crossed the street and had some *bak kut teh* at Seng Huat, just under the iron bridge by the river. Even in the shade of the huge rusty columns and the trees that stood next to them I could feel the heat of the morning sun gathering in strength, making my shirt stick to my back. All around me, office workers and old retired couples were having a quick snack before heading off to more important matters – they ate quickly, slurping their soup, not looking up at the people around them. I shared a table with a young family, a mother and two children, a boy playing his Nintendo and a small girl who looked at me and smiled as her mother read a novel. I smiled back and made a face, a big happy clown face with bulging eyes and a wide smile. Her laugh was so clear, so weightless and free, and in those few seconds I believed that I could live life exactly as I wanted, that no harm would ever come to me, not on that morning or ever after. Her mother looked up and scowled at me. She put her arm around her daughter and said, 'Don't stare at the man. Finish your food, we have to go see *ah-ma* and *ah-gong*.'

When they were gone, I thought, Here I am again, no job, *kaput*, *habis*, finished. It wasn't the first time, and it wouldn't be the last. I knew I'd find another job soon enough. If you're willing to do anything, you'll get something. But there's always that moment when you feel stuck, one door closes and all the others disappear. You can't even see them, never mind think about how to open them.

I hadn't forgotten Mr Lai's card. It was still in my pocket, floppy and dog-eared from the sweat that seeped through my clothes. I found a phone booth and rang him. On the plastic dome over the telephone someone had scratched some graffiti, like some rare and delicate artwork carved in glass – the prime minister's name, followed by the word 'PANTAT'. The words had been written on the outside, and it took me some time to make out the letters in reverse. I started to laugh. Who takes the time to stand outside a phone booth and call the prime minister a cunt? That was exactly when Mr Lai answered. I tried to explain who I was, and why I was calling, but it was difficult because I was still chuckling. 'You're in a good mood,' he said. 'I like cheerful people.' A week later I was working at his fish farm near Tanjung Karang.

At first I worked as a farm hand – a labourer – repairing, lifting, transporting. There were only two cages to start with, but more were already being built, and I was soon joined by two Indonesians, Halim and Adi, then Rio, Indra, Yudianto, Satria, Bayu, Adit, Rendy, Adra, Eka. [*Pauses.*] Rama, Hanif, Abdi, Firman, Leo, Dimas, Denny, Fariz, Endang – they came later. After all this time I can remember all their names. Very few of them stayed for long. Six months, one year – that wasn't uncommon; a year was good, two years was unusual. Even after all the agencies started making big bucks by bringing in workers and tying them to three-year contracts, and deducting a whole year's salary from their pay packages before they even started their jobs, they'd still go missing. When you saw how hard they worked, you'd understand why. It wasn't that their spirits could not accept the wages – four, five hundred bucks a month – it was that their bodies could not tolerate the work.

Not long ago I read something on Facebook that talked about minimum wages for migrant workers. I don't know how it came up on my Facebook – usually it's a lot of links to Joel Osteen videos or other devotional stuff, or badminton or soccer – but this time it was an article about how some people in KL, a human rights group or something, were trying to establish basic rights for the millions of foreigners working here. Of course they were going to fail! Even I could have told them that. They kept complaining about the lack of political will – government this, government that. What struck me and made me shake my head was all the nonsense they said about money. *Migrant wages are degrading, they humiliate the soul.* They didn't understand that it wasn't the pay that destroyed the spirits of these men and women, it was the work – the way it broke their bodies before they could even contemplate the question of salaries. The way it turned them from children to withered old creatures in the space of a few years. Anyone can work with their body like that for a year, two years, maybe even more. But when those years stretch out before you like the sea on a calm hot day, waveless, with no change or variety – when that kind of life becomes your only future, that's when you flee. Even if someone pays you ten thousand a month, your body won't accept it. Your mind tells you to stay, to earn money for your kids back home, your old parents who need help. But your body says: *Run*.

The first few months, I worked with the foreigners, some-times even getting into the water to fix the cages with them, or carrying ten tons of sand from one end of the land to the other in wheelbarrows when we were constructing the office and other farm buildings. We wore loose-fitting shirts to protect us from the sun, but later, when the sun had gone down and we were bathing, I could see how our bodies were marked by the sun – the skin on our faces, necks and hands was three shades darker than the rest of ourselves, as if it belonged to someone else, a person less fortunate than us. I took to tying a small towel around my neck to keep the sun from burning me. I knotted it at the front, so that I could untie it easily to wipe the sweat from my face, and the men started to make fun of me. *Hey Mr Cowboy*, they joked. *John Wayne just came to work!*

One day Mr Lai arrived and found me mixing concrete with the Indonesian labourers. I heard him shouting even before he stopped the car. He rolled down the window. 'Why you waste your time doing this kind of work? Go check the generators, check the inventory – something useful.' I stared at him, blinking. Sweat was dripping into my eyes and suddenly I felt very hot. '*Stare what?* Foreman also do this dirty work? Give them instructions already can, no need to join in.' The word *foreman* stayed in my head as I washed myself in the makeshift shower we'd built in the shade of some trees. The newness of the word spun gently in my head, as clear as the sunlight that was filtering through the thin canopy of leaves above, falling around me like shards of splintered glass. Maybe there was something wrong with my eyes that day, maybe I'd been working too long in the sun.

I understood that I would hold power over other human beings – that it was possible for me to impose my will on the actions of men who were just like me, whose bodies worked like mine, whose desperation and joy I not only recognised but shared. Were we friends? Of course not. I never went to their lodgings, they never came to mine. In the evenings they disappeared into the night, and I withdrew to my own space. We understood that we would never be buddies, but somehow that drew us together. Friendship is not a requirement for closeness. During the day, those long, long days under the sun and rain, we experienced pain in the same way, and satisfaction and laughter too, but mostly hardship, and that is what bound us.

Now, someone had given me the right to tell these men what to do. In the space of a few seconds, we were no longer the same – perhaps we never had been, and I had been a fool to think otherwise. It sounds stupid, but all at once I did feel different from them. As I walked back to the grey concrete box that housed the office, I looked at the men shovelling sand and cement, wheeling barrowloads of hardcore, carrying sacks of grit on their shoulders. Not one of them looked up at me – they just continued in exactly the same way. It was as if they knew that something had changed, that I had detached from their world, and no longer belonged to it. I didn't know what to do. I felt like calling out to them, making a joke about Adi's

46

permanent limp or how Bayu couldn't stop talking while he worked – the usual bad jokes that we made all the time. But it didn't feel right. A space had opened up between us, and they recognised it as much as I did. Mr Lai was nearby, walking down to the jetty, and if I'd called out to the men and joked with them, he'd have heard and said something nasty. I had no choice but to walk on.

I tucked my shirt into my trousers and went into the office. All around me there were piles of papers and files containing bills, invoices. I opened a folder and stared at the words and numbers that meant nothing to me. Soon, in just a few months' time, I'd learn how to decipher what was going on, but I never completely forgot the panic that I experienced that first day. You won't understand that feeling – being powerless in front of a sheet of paper. I told myself, *It's just a stupid piece of paper*. The last time I saw so many pages of numbers or words I was at school, and that had been years ago. Even then, I'd been defeated by them – more or less flunked my SPM, even got a D in Chinese and mathematics. Only got one good grade, in history – C4 – which was a joke, because the past means nothing to me. Nothing. All across the country, probably no one failed as badly as I did. Seventeen years old, couldn't wait to leave school. Already, back then, I'd thought: damn waste of time, thank God I won't have to bother with reading and writing ever again. How would I know that I'd have to learn it all over again?

I looked out at the men working in the yard, listened to the sound of the shovels against grit, the soft rumble of the cement mixer – all of it was like the rhythm of a strange music, lulling me to sleep as I sat in front of the files. The table fan was blowing in my face and making me drowsy. Wake up. Wake up. I knew that if I truly wanted to become the person I was supposed to be, I would have to make sense of those papers in front of me.

I heard Mr Lai approaching, and pretended to be examining the files as he walked in. 'We have to get some parts for the generator,' I said. 'Nothing major, just one small fitting that will help us save money in the long run.' I don't know how I knew that, but I did – must have picked it up in a previous job. Mr Lai hesitated, then nodded. 'I'll give you some cash.' He was almost out of the room when he turned back and said, 'Tell you what, I'll buy a safe for the office. I'll bring over a few thousand bucks to keep in it – you can look after it for the time being.'

After he left I sat at the desk and watched the men work. Their arms rising and falling, their legs planted deep in mounds of earth and sand, trousers rolled up to their knees. Rio was wearing a pair of fake Real Madrid shorts that were too big for him, tightened with a belt and hanging past his knees. He and Halim were hauling some bags of cement towards the mixer, walking swiftly with small steps, their bare feet making tracks in the earth. Their knees buckled slightly now and then, and I remembered that same sensation in my own legs just a couple of hours before – that feeling of forcing your body to do what it didn't want to do, until it became so familiar that you no longer knew how *not* to force your body, and simple acts like lifting a cup of tea or a bowl of rice to your lips felt strange and lifeless. Overhead the sky was turning dark. Soon, when the afternoon rain showers arrived and turned the yard to mud, it would be more difficult to walk, and the men knew this, which is why they were pushing themselves now. Run, lift, throw. Anticipating the rain, Bayu had taken off his shirt, and I could see the dark scar on his back from his last job on a construction site in Seremban – a long curved line, the width of a finger, that looked barely healed. As he emptied a wheelbarrow full of rocks, he slipped and fell to the ground. His head hit the handle of the barrow with a dull thud, and he fell awkwardly on an outstretched hand – the kind of fall that shocks the wrist and collarbone. *Aiiiiie*. His cry was like a small child's, high-pitched and weak – it didn't match the width of his shoulders, the stockiness of his legs. The others laughed. If I'd been out there I'd have done the same – laughed and teased him for being clumsy. He rubbed his head, dusted his arm and started running with the empty wheelbarrow, ready to collect a new load. Of course he would cry out like a child. He was not even twenty years old.

I sat in my chair and looked at my hands, turning them over a few times. The backs were much lighter in colour than the palms. I closed my eyes. All of a sudden, I was tired. I lay down and went to sleep, cooled by the table fan.

With each year I distanced myself a little more from the physical work on the farm. On a few occasions early on, when I was supervising a group of workers in the construction of a brick storehouse or a new net-cage, I'd get frustrated if I thought they were too slow, or weren't carrying out the task correctly – I felt the urge to jump into the boat and drag the nets up from the water to untangle them, as I'd done throughout my childhood, or to spread the mortar evenly and align the bricks myself. As I stood watching the men at work, my body felt as though it was trying to escape my control. Now, as before, I had to force it, but in a different way – this time to remain still, because it was not used to being so. The more my inaction frustrated me, the louder I shouted at the workers.

Still, the body can unlearn the lessons of a lifetime, and soon the idea of taking off my shirt and working in the sun felt so foreign to me that it became distasteful. Why would I do it? I spent my time doing the rounds, making sure the fish were healthy, that the pumps and filters and generators were functioning. I also supervised all the building and repair work. The farm expanded, and after a few years we had a sales manager and a secretary.

I started saving money and having a life outside of work – the kind of evenings and weekends that I'd always imagined normal people had. I got married and bought a house. We started going out of town – an overnight drive to Penang, a five-day tour of Bangkok. Even when I took time off, I drew my salary – I got used to the idea of receiving money even though I wasn't working. In August that year, I remember going to the bank and checking my account, and not even feeling any great pleasure in seeing that my pay had been safely deposited – 1,900 ringgit. I had no way of knowing that it would be the last time.

When I think back to that day when Hendro came running to tell me there was a phone call for me, I some-times wonder how things might have been if the line had gone dead, which sometimes happened, because our connection wasn't very reliable. I know it's God's will, and that things turned out the way they did because He intended it. But still. I sometimes imagine Hendro saying, 'Someone called but said, "Forget it, don't worry if Ah Hock is busy right now." ' Instead, I remember his breath-lessness as he walked briskly beside me, peeling off to rejoin the other men in our soon-to-be car park. In the office, the phone's receiver was lying face-down on the table, away from its cradle – I didn't know if the caller had hung up since Hendro answered it.

'Hello?'

'*Wai*, little brother! It's me.'

'Who are you?'

'Heyyy . . . it's Keong.'

She sits and stares at me without blinking.

I noticed right at the start, from the very first interview. She never blinks. Not even when I run out of things to say. In moments of silence she holds my gaze and smiles. It's always me who looks away first.

I didn't like her at the beginning, and part of me still doesn't trust her. You can never really believe anything they say, these educated types from the big city – they're too ready with their smile, too interested in you. She looks me in the eye when I talk, as if what I'm saying is the most important thing in the world. Every so often she nods, like she truly understands what I'm saying. Sometimes she makes a noise, like *Um . . . umm,* as if to say, *Yes, I'm with you.* She frowns and looks at me as if she's absorbing every single word I say, even when I'm just talking about unimportant things – the kind of underwear I once bought in Sungai Wang Plaza, what kind of noodles I ate one evening in 2003, that kind of thing. Sometimes I do it on purpose. I want to see if she gets bored and hurries me along to talk about other stuff.

But she never loses her composure, always pretends to be fascinated. Never yawns, never checks her watch. Her Samsung Galaxy is on the table in front of me, recording everything I say, but she rarely looks at it. She just scribbles notes in her notepad from time to time. I feel like I'm a politician giving a press conference on live TV.

I'm the one who keeps glancing at the phone, just to make sure it's still recording.

When I got her first email about two months ago, I thought it was junk, like the rest of the stuff in my inbox. Beautiful China Bride, USA Diploma Online, Viagra Direct. That day I noticed a message headed *Request for interview*. I ignored it – it was as meaningless to me as all the others. About a week later, I noticed another email from the same person, headed: *Fw: Please indicate your response*. Who actually clicks on this kind of email? Every day I read about people being scammed. You click on a link and your whole computer is infected, a hacker in Russia gets all your bank info. Someone takes your hard-earned cash. They even take your identity.

However, I am the kind of person who clicks on these links. I have no online banking, no credit card, no spouse to discover the stuff I look at on the computer – I have nothing to lose. I waited for a week, then two, reading the email a couple of times each day. Finally I thought, She's confused me with someone else.

But there was no mistake. She had been doing research for her studies in America, and had heard about my case. Now she was returning to Malaysia to spend some time conducting *field work*. She wanted to interview me, *to try to understand the circumstances and events surrounding the case*. A fraudster, I thought immediately. Someone pretending to be someone else. I'd say yes, and 'she' would come into my house with ten armed men and rob me of what little cash I had left.

I would like to talk to you on an informal basis, to build a portrait of you as a human being. I am interested in your personal history. We could have an initial chat and see how things progress.

I wrote back because I was bored. She replied, with a reference letter from her university as proof. I Googled her and saw her college photo. Tan Su-Min. I asked the pastor at church to ring the number on the letter, just to be sure.

New York, ah? he said. He read the letter slowly and said, doctorate in sociology – *wah*, no joke. It's OK, it's genuine, no need to call.

The first day, she rang the bell once and opened the metal gates without waiting for me to come to the door. She had crossed the small concrete porch before I could even make it out of the kitchen. I thought, She isn't scared at all. The dog next door started barking – lots of people round here have dogs because of the break-ins. You wouldn't think there's anything to steal in a neighbourhood like this, but these days robbers do anything for a TV or a stereo set. The slightest thing that happens – a motorbike pulls up in front of a house at night – all the dogs start barking. But she wasn't at all bothered by them.

She should have been apprehensive, but instead I was the one who hesitated. I stood watching her through the grille of the front door. Hair cut short, like a boy's. Or like Faye Wong's in about 1995. (I told her this a few weeks later, when I felt comfortable enough to make jokes with her.) The same height as me, about five foot seven, wearing shorts so long they looked like army trousers, with big pockets down the side. More cheerful than in her college photo. She took off her sunglasses and put them on the top of her head.

You're OK with chatting in the house? she said. We could always go out and have our first conversation somewhere else if you're more comfortable that way. Whatever you prefer. Her question felt more like a command to me.

It's OK, we can stay here, I said.

As soon as she stepped in, she started to look around. She turned to me and tried to be polite by making small talk – *Thank you for agreeing to meet, I hope it isn't too inconvenient, isn't it hot, there's been no rain recently* – but her eyes didn't focus on me, she kept gazing at things around the room, so often that I turned to see what she was checking out. But there was nothing there, just the same room I'd known all these years, the old rattan furniture that people from church donated. A Korean drama was playing on the TV. I'd forgotten to turn it off when she arrived, and the actors' voices filled the room. *Oppa, myo haeyo*. On the table across the room, a pile of newspapers. *Nanyang Siang Pau* and *Sin Chew Jit Poh*. A bible. A small cookie tin that I use to put my Magnum 4D and Big Sweep tickets in. I couldn't figure out what she was looking at.

I offered her a drink, as I do when people from church call round – a carton of Yeo's chrysanthemum tea. Good for hot weather, I said.

She laughed and took the carton in her hand. She looked at it as if she'd never seen one before. She took a photo of it with her phone and studied it for a while before peeling away the little straw glued to the pack. Very high sugar content, she said.

Her first few questions were simple and dull. How long had I lived here, what was I planning to have for dinner that evening, was she interrupting my daily schedule – that sort of thing. I'd been nervous beforehand, wondering if she was going to ask me uncomfortable questions that I wouldn't be able to answer. Maybe I wouldn't even understand them. But all at once I felt I had nothing to fear.

Yes, you're interrupting *Legend of the Blue*, I said, pointing at the TV set. She turned to look at the screen. A man and a woman sat astride horses, looking at the sky. She laughed, as if what I had said was really funny.

So you like Korean shows? she asked. I do too.

I wasn't expecting that from someone like her – foreign-educated, clever. A rich girl with fancy leather sandals. I wouldn't have thought she'd watch Korean TV. I started talking about the things I watch to fill my days, about *Scarlet Heart* and *Descendants of the Sun*, and also my favourite series from previous years, like *Secret Garden* and *Moon Embracing the Sun*. I told her about the time a couple of years back when I had spent a whole evening drinking beer and eating fried chicken wings while watching *My Love From the Star* just to feel in tune with Jun Ji-Hyun's character in the show, and that I'd loved my *chimek*-and-TV night so much that I had another the next day, with more beer and wings and Korean romance, right up until the street lamps went off and the skies began to lighten. When the church group called round that morning they were shocked to find me surrounded by beer bottles and looking a bit sick. They thought I was slipping back into bad ways, so they made me go to church with them to see the pastor, who talked to me about how the devil can get inside me without my even knowing it. If I wasn't vigilant at all times, and didn't pray for God's protection, I would be vulnerable, and though I felt sorry and knew what he said was true, I also knew that I wouldn't stop watching Korean shows. I would just stop the beer – it was too expensive anyway.

All that time she was nodding in agreement, occasionally laughing – a soft giggle that encouraged me to talk even more. She scribbled some words on a notepad now and then, and set her phone down on the table, recording.

But I'm just talking rubbish, I said.

No, no – it's *really* interesting. Please, go on.

As I spoke I couldn't stop wondering why she was so interested in me. But I couldn't stop talking. What's more, to a total stranger. The way she nodded and silently wrote her notes made me feel both important and uneasy. Sometimes she would say something simple like *Those situations must have been difficult for you*, and those few words were like a match to a trail of gasoline, lighting up a path ahead, making me talk even more. I tried to resist the impulse to speak, but failed. What revelations would I make, and regret later? I liked her for letting me talk. I hated her for making me talk.

She spoke Mandarin in a way that made it obvious that it was a second language to her – sometimes clear as a textbook, other times halting, mixed in with a bunch of English words. Everything about her seemed alien to me that first time, even though she came from only thirty miles away. Her foreignness made it easier for me to speak as freely as I did. I could tell her anything I wanted, and she would have to believe me. That first day, even though I tried to be formal in the way I spoke, I felt myself lapsing into dialects, my country Hokkien surging out of me from time to time, or else the odd Cantonese swear word popping up before I even realised I'd said it.

Suddenly I would be aware of my speech, the difference between the crudeness of my voice and the polish of hers, always under control, never too loud or too soft. Sometimes I would say something inappropriate and I'd think, Now she is going to realise she has made a huge mistake. Now she will start making excuses to leave. But her expression never changed – always balanced between interest and amusement. She stayed for four hours.

We've seen each other once or twice a week, sometimes three times, for the last two months. Every time, without fail, she comes to my house and sits patiently while I talk. We drink Chinese tea or chrysanthemum tea from a carton, and I might snack on some biscuits. She never eats anything, not even a dried melon seed. If a stranger walked into the room they would see a couple of acquaintances, or perhaps relatives – a young woman dutifully listening to her older cousin. But they are not as intimate as it appears. They are separated not just by ten or fifteen years, but by something else that neither can properly identify.

For example, how do you explain this incident? One day, not long after we first meet, maybe four or five sessions in, I'm talking about random, unconnected incidents from my childhood – from the time we were living with my uncle, after my father had left us and we had nowhere to call our own. I was only ten, but I hated that house. I spent all day outdoors, walking along the streams and inlets that ran into the river and eventually fed into the sea. I knew all the ricefields and the forests, I knew how to set traps for fish and shoot birds with my catapult. Sometimes the birds I shot wouldn't be killed, they would just fall to the ground and flap around weakly with broken wings. Sometimes I felt pity for them, and regretted hurting them, but even as I felt that sorrow I knew I would do it again. The only way I could stop their suffering was to kill them, usually by dropping a big rock on them, or by twisting their necks – just like *this*, I show her with my hands.

She nods and continues to take notes, but I notice something – a tiny change in her expression, something like a grimace that breaks through her half-smile, just for a moment, before she composes herself. So I continue. I describe how I would hear a soft crunch under the rock as I dropped it on the bird. How their bones were weaker than twigs in my hands. She nods, as if she understands, but I know she has no idea what it means to put an end to a life.

She has no idea what I felt, at that moment or any other.

I begin to tell her about the cat, the small black-and-white kitten, that I found by the side of the road one day. It had been injured, its hind legs broken and bloody. It was squealing loudly, and for a second I thought maybe I should take it home as a pet. I would heal it, give it some medicine and fix its legs. But I knew that it was hopeless, it was too weak to survive. It would not even last the journey home. As I picked up the rock I thought, I'm sorry,

57

but this is the way life is. In this world, some of us are strong, others are weak. Some will live, others will flourish, all will die. I wanted to feel pity, but I didn't. I brought the rock down hard on its head. Then I lifted it again, trying not to look at the black-red mess staining the hard earth. I hit it with the rock another time, harder, to make sure the cat was no longer suffering.

She continues to look down at her notebook, but she has stopped scribbling – her pen is poised over the page, waiting. Her jaw hardens, twitching slightly on the right side. For once, she does not look at me, but focuses on her notes. At last she smiles again, but her brow is still tight – the corners of her eyes a little creased. She says, Umm, but then she has to clear her throat. As if she's going to cough, only she doesn't.

Today is a normal day, meaning we're relaxed, and conversation is easy. I don't have much to say of interest, but that's OK. She doesn't mind if I ramble. We have a couple of moments' silence, but nothing that lasts too long. We don't have any of those awkward pauses we used to have in the early sessions, when I sometimes felt like fleeing the room. I'm talking about all the things I intend to do if I strike it big on the lottery one day. Maybe go travelling. Maybe get some training on computers. She's smiling while she writes in her notebook. She raises her eyebrows as if to say, *That's a great idea.*

But as I'm talking, something comes to mind, as it sometimes does when I'm with her. I remember the look on her face after I told her about the cat – her lips pulled into a smile, but her eyes narrowed, accusing me of something. But what? I don't know what to call the look on her face. I don't know if I can call it anger, or contempt, or sadness.

And I can't stop the thought from forming in my head: she cares more about the cat than she does about me.

The first time I ever saw Keong, he was beating up another kid. The boy's lip was puffy and split, and there was a trail of rich red blood down his T-shirt, matched in colour by two angry marks on his leg, parallel straight lines that ran from knee to ankle. He was half-sitting, half-crouching on the floor – Keong was gripping him by his wrist with one hand, and in the other he was holding a stick, about three feet long. They both looked up when they saw me in the doorway. A pause. Then Keong delivered another blow, and another, as if I hadn't appeared at all – as if the sight of me had been an illusion, a trick of the light. I didn't know what offence the other kid had committed to deserve the beating – what form the insult had taken. Later, I learned that it didn't take much for Keong to feel insulted.

The fight, which I guess you would probably say was an *assault*, was taking place in a disused shack on the edge of an inlet where the smaller boats were moored, sheltered from the storms that blew in from the open waters. The tide had gone out, and I was picking my way through the mangroves, hoping to dig out a crab from the mud – just killing time, as usual. I was twelve, I spent all day outdoors. I heard a quick suffocated groan, someone who wanted to cry out but didn't – the scream squeezed in the throat so that when it emerged it was only a weak impression of the noise it should have been. I recognised pain in that fleeting sound, which most people wouldn't even have noticed – I'd heard it many times in my own family – and instantly I knew where it had come from. The shack had once been used for storing nets and jerry cans, but it had been cleared out when our smaller boats started to become superfluous with the arrival of the large vessels capable of fishing over a much further range. Parts of it had rotted and fallen into the mud below, joining the skeletons of wooden boats that we'd simply abandoned over the years.

I stood in the doorway for a few minutes, watching until Keong had finished with the boy. I didn't try to help the victim or intervene. That was how things worked in the world, in our world at least – we didn't get mixed up in other people's troubles. Keong brushed past me as he walked out into the bright sunlight. I still had the feeling that he hadn't noticed me, but a few moments later he turned back and said, 'Come with me.' Now I realise that it wasn't a command but a question, but at that time it didn't seem as if I had a choice. As I walked with him back towards the village, I thought about the boy lying on the broken floor of the broken hut – his body broken too, defeated. I wondered if I should go back, try and help him. I didn't want him to be alone. I could have gathered the other boys in the village and reported what I'd witnessed. But instead I continued walking with Keong.

Nowadays I realise that it was only natural that our relationship would end up being what it was. What is born out of violence ends in violence.

His family had recently moved into a place on the edge of the village, where the houses began to thin out, overwhelmed by the mangrove forests and patchy orchards struggling to thrive in the salt-soaked earth. He was only four or five years older than me, but already belonged to a different world, one I had heard and dreamed about but didn't yet recognise, didn't yet know was even real – it was only just starting to draw into focus in my imagination, and it was Keong who made it real. I'm talking about the city – I don't mean Klang, which was thirty, thirty-five miles away, but Kuala Lumpur, only another ten, fifteen miles further. I'm not sure exactly, I just know that it's the biggest fifty-mile gap you could think of.

Keong had just moved down from there, and couldn't wait to return. His mother was from these parts – Kuala Selangor, I think – but had moved up to KL to find work. She'd got married, given birth to Keong, but then things started to get tough. Eventually she got divorced, and soon she was struggling. A young woman with a fourteen-year-old kid on her hands – you don't need a PhD to figure out it's a bad situation that's only going to get worse. A Chinese boy in the city with no money and no parents to keep him in check – they only do one thing. Join a gang.

It wasn't long after his parents got divorced that Keong started cutting class – a couple of lessons here, a half-day there, then whole days and even entire weeks. He might as well have quit school completely. He told me how he'd once strolled into class late, in the middle of the lesson, while the teacher was explaining how the earth's land masses are built on continental plates that are constantly shifting and pushing against each other – he remembered the neat picture she was drawing on the board, remembered thinking, *Maybe I should just pick up a piece of chalk and mess it up right now.* She was so shocked by how cool and brazen he was, sauntering in halfway through class, that she just stopped talking, her mouth hanging open. Didn't dare challenge him, didn't say a word. After a few seconds she went back to her diagram, and pretended not to notice when he put his feet up on his desk and rubbed his cock through his trousers as if to say, *Fuck this, I'm bored.* By then, she knew he was a gangster – a small-time gangster but a real one nonetheless, not just a bully who acted tough. His dyed coppery hair, the rings he wore – those were signs of someone you wanted to avoid. There were stories of what these boys did, even at fifteen, sixteen – stories of teachers being beaten up at the school gates, of a mean sonofabitch headmaster taking on a young tough guy and giving him a public caning at morning assembly, and the next day finding his car on fire. A giant ball of flames and black smoke that you could see five miles away. Bang. Three years' salary, gone.

One day he walks in and blows a kiss at the teacher. She knows all about him, knows his reputation, so she ignores him. She knows that he does this all the time: strolls in late, puts his feet on the desk, rubs his crotch, makes loud comments that distract the other boys. She says nothing. *The only volcanic pressure I know is right here*, he says loudly, pointing between his legs. The other boys laugh, throw scrunched-up paper balls at each other. Still the teacher says nothing; she carries on talking, through the laughter and disruption. When the boys have calmed down, Keong takes out a pack of Salems, carefully puts one between his lips and closes his eyes, as if he's taking a nap. Waits for a reprimand, but the teacher says nothing. Maybe she doesn't care – why would she care about him? Then he takes out a lighter – its flame is blue and dances like a demon as he lights his cigarette and takes a deep, deep drag. He sees the teacher staring at him through the cloud of silver smoke. *Oooooooohhhh*. The other boys' low moan is both a sign of respect and a challenge – respect for him, challenge for the teacher. Still she says nothing. She stands staring at the class, piece of chalk in hand, then walks out the door. (Crying – she was crying! Keong laughed as he told me this story.) A couple of weeks later, Keong is expelled from school. No big deal, he thinks. I was going to drop out soon anyway.

Facing his mum is another matter. Every morning, even after he is expelled, he puts on his uniform and pretends he's going to school. He has his rucksack with him, slung over one shoulder, trying to look serious. His mother asks him how things are going at school, and he says, OK, not so bad. Maths is fine, I like maths. Geography is fun too. He means it, too, because – here's the thing – he thinks more about class and about his lessons now that he has been expelled than he ever did when he was at school. When his mother smiles and says, 'Good boy. Education is your future. Study hard so that you don't end up like me,' he feels a sudden quickening of his pulse, the guilt cutting at his insides like the knife he has started to carry around for the gang fights that he will very soon get involved in.

(At this precise point in time his mother is between jobs. Every morning she goes out in search of work, every day she comes back with nothing to show but a promise of work that never comes true. This lasts about a month, until she becomes a shampoo girl at a salon in Cheras called Angelique D'Style.)

He decides to get some cash. It's the only way to relieve his guilt. (This is my analysis of his situation, not his – he never talked much about things like *guilt* or *obligation*.) By this time he's hanging around with boys who are nineteen, twenty, even a bit older. They've been running businesses for a few years, selling fake DVDs, small electronics – you know the type. Their friends and associates own stalls all over the city, Chow Kit Road, Low Yat Plaza, the top floor of Sungai Wang, you name it. But mainly their money comes from drugs – the boys are low-level dealers. *Syabu*, *fengtau, ice, G, K* – whatever name it goes by, they sell it.

You're looking at me like you don't know what all that is. Amphetamines, in all their forms, streaming over the border from Laos and Thailand. There would have been harder, more expensive stuff floating around too, heroin and coke I guess, but Keong and his friends wouldn't have got their hands on that kind of junk so often, if ever at all. He's still a kid, remember, barely sixteen. The cash he makes is small change for a serious dealer. Most of the time he just sits at the front of a cramped stall in Bukit Bintang selling portable electronics, Discmans, VCR players, Nintendo – the sort of thing every other stall in the area seems to sell. Every so often someone asks him for some pills, and he casually walks over to another stall fifty yards away, and after a few minutes one of his friends will come over with a small packet. Sometimes he's the runner, carrying a plastic sachet from one place to another. He's young enough for the police to ignore.

Still, the money he makes allows him to buy new clothes, the kind all the young gangsters favour – 'carrot-cut' trousers, baggy around the ass and clinging tightly to the ankles, shirts with sharp shoulders, a small diamond stud in his left ear. He wants to look like Alan Tam Wing-Lun or one of the other Hong Kong singing superstars. He does look like Alan Tam! That's what he thinks. But really – even I could see it when he proudly showed me photos of him and his *heng tai*, who were not really his brothers in any sense of the word, because they wouldn't come to his aid when he needed them – he ends up with the look that his teachers at school would identify as *samseng* or *Ah Beng*. Boys who will soon quit school and become stallholders or *dim sum* waiters on the outside, petty gangsters on the inside.

One evening Keong is delivering some bundles of cash to a building in Jalan Pudu – he doesn't know who or what the money's for. He's just been given the address, which he's committed to memory so he doesn't have to write it on his palm like he did the last time. *Sor hai, no brain, meh?*

64

his friends had teased him (how innocent and stupid he'd been!). He's only delivering a thousand ringgit, hardly enough to buy a decent second-hand scooter, but still, not worth taking the risk. Not that Keong recognises much risk – he feels invincible these days, with his band of brothers and cash in his pocket. It comes as a surprise when two police motorbikes pull up ahead of him – big powerful white bikes, surprisingly quiet, unlike the noisy scooters that his friends ride. He assumes they've stopped for someone else, or are just taking a break for an early-evening drink, but instead they walk swiftly towards him, backing him up against the wall. He doesn't care, he acts tough. Why you stopping me? he says, somewhat aggressively, which only inflames them further. You got warrant? No warrant cannot arrest. Why? Because I'm Chinese is it? They push him against the wall, take off his backpack and find the money, neatly bound by rubber bands in tight little stacks. When they take them out, they look like small bricks.

Chinese kid with a load of cash in his bag – no further explanation needed. *Samseng*. They slap him round the head.

Still, he is proud, unrepentant. At the police station he sits in a cell waiting for his brothers to turn up, maybe even the legendary ultimate big boss, who he knows by reputation but has never met, the one people say is best friends with the inspector general of police. After he's been there a day, then two, he realises that he's been forgotten. Even the police who patrol the cells seem barely to notice his presence. They give him water and rice with sambal – no egg or chicken or anything – that he eats quickly because he's so hungry, but it makes him sick, gives him terrible diarrhoea that lasts for a whole day, so when they finally let him out it's obvious that it's only because he was stinking up his cell too much. Even the two Indonesians in the lock-up were complaining about how disgusting it smelled.

In the end it wasn't his brush with the police that ended his brief career as a gangster, it was his mother. He'd thought she'd be happy with the money he gave her from time to time, that even if she suspected what he was doing to earn it, she'd turn a blind eye because they needed it so much. Now she could pay the electricity bill. Now she could buy some herbs to make chicken soup to give herself strength for work. Twice he'd bought her a blouse from Petaling Street because he wanted her to have new clothes to wear to work, but she made a point of never putting them on – and it hurt him to see how these gifts disgusted her. He'd thought she would be happy, but she just accepted whatever money he gave her without expressing gratitude. She looked away each time he handed it to her, the notes folded up so she couldn't see exactly how much it was. 'Being a part-time waiter pays well these days,' was all she said. And then, one Sunday when they were both at home watching TV, she said, 'I had a craving for noodles yesterday after work, so I went to Wanchai Noodle House. Asked if you were working there that day.'

Keong waited for her to say, 'They told me they didn't know anyone by that name.' Waited for the embarrassment and guilt and anger, wondered for a second how he should react, whether to be confrontational, scream at her, smash the furniture, set something on fire – anything to deal with the pain. But she said nothing more, just continued watching TV silently.

Two weeks later they were down here, living in our village.

What a shithole.

His mother had found a job in a factory processing fish – gutting and scaling them and packaging them for delivery to supermarkets. My mother had once worked in that factory too. It was new, it wasn't so bad. Her hours were long but regular, her salary small but regular. She'd been born in the area, spent her whole life until the age of twenty-two in Tanjung Karang, just up the coast. A relative had told her about a house that had become vacant in Bagan Sungai Yu, two bedrooms, a big front room, a kitchen – just right for a woman, not young, not old, and her son, no longer a child but years away from becoming a man. It was a bit out of the way, but she didn't mind, she had a scooter and Keong could cycle into town if he needed to. There were bridges across the river now, it wasn't so hard to get around. She didn't know what they'd do, she didn't have a plan – she just knew she had to move back to these parts and stay for as long as she could.

She still had family up the road, an aunt and an uncle, two cousins, and that seemed plenty. She could call them and get together for dinner once in a while – it wasn't a fancy life, but it felt as if it would never change much, in fact hadn't changed much since she'd left two decades before. What she'd hated back then, she now loved: the sense of continuity, of surrendering to something stronger than her – the pulling in of her horizons, the comfort to be found in the death of ambition. She had forgotten what it was that she'd wanted to accomplish when she'd left home for the city, but whatever that dream was, it had caused too much anxiety and pushed her towards bad decisions. Now it was gone, she could start to live again. Years later, I would recognise the same feeling, and I would think of her, this round-faced woman who said little but smiled a lot, her cheeks pulled into small dimples. Auntie Chai. She always asked me to come round for some biscuits and a cold drink whenever our paths crossed, but somehow it rarely happened, even in a village as small as ours.

Only problem for her was Keong. Almost seventeen, bored out of his mind, he despised every minute of his life here, resented being dragged away from KL, where he had felt strong and grown-up. He hated the way his mother had tricked him into moving here – she'd told him that they were visiting relatives for Cheng Beng, that they'd only be gone a week, long enough to tidy the graves and say hello to a couple of distant cousins. They had to pack everything because she was giving up the lease of their apartment in KL, but would be getting a new one when they came back. How could he have been so dumb? He should have just insisted on staying put when he found out – he could easily have made his own way in life. But what else, really, could he do? A mother is a mother. If he'd stayed in KL, chances are he'd never have seen his mother again.

The eighteen months he lived in the village were the longest of his life. 'If I'm still here when I'm twenty, I'll kill myself. Swear to Buddha, Goddess of Mercy, every damn deity you can think of. I'll do it.'

The other kids in the village stayed away from him. When he passed them in the road he just looked straight ahead, didn't stop to say hello. They didn't like outsiders, and he could tell that they weren't going to accept him as one of them – which was just fine, because he didn't have anything to say to them either. 'Me and you – you guys, I mean, all of you – we got nothing in common. I don't know anything about digging prawns from the mud,' he told me.

'But prawns don't live in the mud.'

'Then why are you sea gypsies always picking through the mud as if it's the most interesting thing in your life?'

Up to then, I'd never questioned our relationship with the mudflats – our whole life by the sea – but all of a sudden this image of us crouching anxiously in the sticky grey muck seemed ridiculous. Why would anyone want to spend their days sifting through the mud for shellfish that sell for a few bucks per kilo?

'I don't even like the sight of you,' he once said, laughing. 'Don't you guys have anything to wear other than rags?' He continued to wear his city clothes, real shirts with long sleeves buttoned at the wrist, but his copper highlights had faded, and his hair was now just as black as everyone else's, distinguished only by the long locks that fell over his forehead – a style that the other boys secretly made fun of. He sneered at us, we laughed at him. Sometimes, when I remember how he looked and spoke in court when testifying at my trial – how different he had become from me – I think back to his early days in the village, and realise that I should have known there would always be an unbridgeable distance between us. We both should have known that. But at that age, how could we?

It was only at games – on the small dirt patch that passed for a soccer pitch, and the basketball court that the temple had donated to the village – that the other kids had any real contact with him. Keong watched from the sidelines for a couple of weeks, smoking and pretending not to be interested. Then one day, during one of our daily late-afternoon games, just casually shooting hoops without really meaning to play – we were tired from school and from working with the nets and the cockles – the ball rolled out of play, directly into Keong's hands. He took a shot, a long graceful arc of the arms, surprising for a kid as skinny as him. He missed, but then, as if to atone for his mistake, stubbed out his cigarette and jogged towards us, waving his hands to receive the ball.

During that first match, and every subsequent one, Keong's entry was a sign that things were about to turn rough. He hustled for every ball, elbows jabbing, bumping into you just to let you know he was there. It wasn't the way we usually played, and when he wasn't there we were as lethargic and half-hearted as ever. Keong made us forget the heat and the fatigue – he made us want to fight. He put his hands in our faces, scratching our arms, inviting a punch-up, which he duly got. Once, a boy older and taller than him squared up to him, and when Keong spat at him, the boy threw a punch that floored Keong, to the laughter of the others. The next day at soccer, the same boy slid into a tackle, bringing Keong down face-first into the dirt. This time Keong was prepared. He had a rock in his pocket, which he held tightly in his fist as he swung at the boy's head. It was the dry season, and the blood marked the earth for many days afterwards.

On other occasions, the smallest insult would ensure that Keong stopped dead in his tracks. He'd stand still and walk towards whoever had offended him, fists clenched. It could be anything, whispered words that didn't mean a thing – *lia ma*, *cheebye*, really, just meaningless expressions – but Keong would always react in the same way, throwing the first punch, launching himself with the full force of his scrawny body at whoever had muttered the passing vulgarity. I'm not sure why they continued to insult him. He lived in a house at the farthest end of the village, and didn't go to school, so they had little contact with him. Maybe it was simply that he wasn't one of us. Or maybe that without knowing it, we were bored by the regularity of our lives – scared by the way our fate was determined by the weather and the tides, the way the slightest change in the moon's position could mean that we would have little to eat for the next month. With Keong, the equation was so much simpler. Call him a bad name and he'd react in exactly the same way every time. I never understood why he kept turning up at our games, when he knew it would always end in a fight. I guess he needed to do that to remind himself that he would never belong in our village – that he was hated there, and had a good reason to get the hell out of the place.

That I became his only friend in the village was not a surprise. He never expressed any gratitude for my silence over his beating up of the boy, but I knew he was thankful that I hadn't caused any further trouble for him. I wanted to explain that it wasn't because I cared about his welfare that I didn't snitch on him, it was just because I didn't want to get involved in anything messy. I was always like that, even as a kid. But somehow, at that age, explanations don't come easily, and don't seem necessary either, so the episode became anchored in the depths of our shared history, never talked about, but never forgotten either. It was the same in the days and weeks following the killing, when I was waiting for the police, for someone, anyone, to discover what I'd done. I didn't know when or how it would happen. I was scared of life's sudden uncertainty, but I was sure of one thing: that Keong would not tell anyone about the incident. If no one else found out, that terrible act would be silently swallowed up by our past.

He and his mother were my closest neighbours – the first people we saw when I cycled into the village. At that point we were living in our own house about a mile away from the village proper, and at night I could just about make out the lights of their house from across the fields. Physically separated from the rest of the village, it was easier for us to strike up a friendship that went unnoticed by the others, who found Keong's urban manners unnatural and ridiculous – his cowboy swagger, arms and shoulders swaying, his constant chatter, always comparing things in the village unfavourably to what he had experienced before. I knew he was an idiot too, but I couldn't resist his stories of life in the city, even though I suspected that they were exaggerated, and maybe plain untrue. Being with Keong and listening to his tales of fights in alleyways behind shopping malls, or making so much money you couldn't fit it all into your pockets, was like watching a movie that enveloped me completely, that made me feel I could be part of the action if I wanted to, even when I knew it was made up. Just reach out and I could touch that world. Just hop on a bus and I could be living in it. The more I lapped up his accounts of his life, the more he talked, spinning ever more outrageous tales. *Your mother, of course it's all true!* He needed me to be his audience even more than I needed to be entertained by him – without me, his memories of the city would have shrivelled and dried in the salt and sun of our coastal village. We all have our own way of surviving, and telling stories was his.

He got work up the coast as a waiter in a seafood restaurant in Sekinchan, one of those big noisy places perched on stilts that rise up over the mudflats, popular with day-trippers from the city. He didn't like taking orders from everyone, being shouted at by the boss and the customers, but he put up with it for a time because he liked seeing the people from KL, who reminded him of his life back there – his real life, not the temporary hell that he was enduring. He chatted to them as he cleared away the dishes, found that he carried himself differently; and he realised, shockingly, that in just a few months he'd started to shuffle lazily like a village boy, instead of swaggering like he used to. How could he have changed so much in such a short time? 'Hey, what's up?' he'd say as he approached a table of tourists from KL to take their order. He could see in the way their eyes widened slightly before they broke into a smile that they were surprised to find someone like him at a restaurant like that, way out in the country. In the briskness of his voice and the sharpness of his speech they saw him as one of them, and in their recognition of him, he finally understood himself.

Best of all were the girls. That's really why he stayed in the job – the discreet eye contact, the smiles, the fact that he knew – he knew! – that they found him cool, these sophisticated women from the suburbs of the capital. One time an entire table of young women arrived for lunch on a Sunday, eight of them, without a single guy in sight, can you imagine that? What a chance for Keong. He was all over them, buzzing round the table like a wasp, never settling for long – taking their orders, bringing them a glass of warm boiled water even when they didn't ask for it, offering them extra dishes of groundnuts behind the boss's back, slipping in a casual compliment here and there, like, '*Wah*, nice handbag,' and even encouraging them when they ordered Tiger beer and started to get a bit noisy. '*No need to be so traditional hor*. Women should have an independent life, not just with their husbands all the time!' He knew what city folk liked to hear – the kind of expressions I would never really be able to use convincingly, no matter how I tried – and loved communicating with them. At last he could speak to people who understood him, instead of these country idiots with their lazy tongues and plodding minds. Sometimes, as with that group of women, he would strike up such a bond with the customers that they'd start calling him by his name whenever they wanted anything, and for those few hours he'd feel as though he had friends.

He wrote his name on a restaurant card and gave it to one of the women who had smiled at him in a way that suggested she had appreciated more than just his hard work that day. He was sure of it! 'Anytime you come back, just ask for me and I'll get you a nice table, right on the water's edge.' She gave him her business card, said she was always looking for new employees, though she never said what her business was. He kept the card for months, waiting for the right moment to call, but when he finally did, the number was dead. I was with him when he rang from the phone booth outside the post office in Kuala Selangor town. Three, four times at least, before he gave up. 'Ah Hock, you try,' he said, handing me the receiver. I put a coin in the phone and carefully dialled the number. The funny thing was that I didn't hear any message saying that the number was out of use, or even a flat continuous tone, like the one in movies when someone dies in hospital – when you know for sure that there is no more hope. There was just a silence, an emptiness so vast it could have stretched forever.

As I stood there with the receiver pressed tightly to my ear, I watched Keong sitting on the stone kerb, absently plucking the long grass that was growing next to him, throwing it into the air. He seemed to have shrunk in the eighteen months he'd spent in the village – or maybe it was just that I'd got bigger. There were rain clouds out at sea that were threatening to blow inland, and a sudden breeze troubled the tops of the trees. I got tired of waiting and hung up, but as we cycled home the silence on the phone seemed to be replaced by an even greater void. Neither of us spoke. Maybe it was the approaching storm, which made the air feel sticky, too heavy to breathe – and this in turn made time stretch out before us, endless and frightening.

Not long afterwards, Keong left the village and headed back to KL. I thought I'd never see him again, but a few years later I felt the same urge to leave that others before me had experienced – the restlessness that affects boys and girls alike when they reach a certain age and can't stop thinking about being somewhere else. It was like an ailment, a virus that I always thought I would be immune to, but there I was, just like everyone else, desperate to escape. I went to Keong's mother's house and got his number. When I went to the phone booth to call him, he answered after just a few seconds.

This was in 1996 – the last months of my teenage years.

She stares at the plate as if she's trying to work out what's on it, even though it's obvious.

It's *chee cheong fun*, I say. Early lunch.

I know.

Have some. I bought enough for both of us.

No, it's fine, I'm not hungry.

Hei, don't be so polite. Have some. It's from Long Kei, you know, just down the road in Taman Eng Ann. The best in town. I went specially.

Really, that's kind of you, but I'm not hungry.

You need to eat! You're too skinny.

I start to dish out a portion for her, and she slowly sits down in front of it. She looks sad as she stares at the plate.

I promise you, it's delicious. They make their *tau pan jeong* fresh every day.

It's not that.

What's the problem then?

I don't eat carbohydrates. Well, not at the moment, anyway.

Carbohydrates?

Yeah. Noodles, bread, potatoes, rice, anything like that.

Not even rice?

No.

My God. Not a good idea! That's why you're so thin.

It's fine, it's not a big deal. I can eat some with you.

The way she says it makes me feel bad for insisting. Maybe it's a religious ritual that I don't know about, a

Buddhist tradition. She cuts off a piece the size of her fingernail and puts it in her mouth. I wait nervously.

Mmm. It's good.

I told you! *Ha*, eat – eat some more.

Wait, she says. Is there meat in the sauce?

Don't think so.

Shit, I think. She's a Buddhist.

You know what, I really appreciate this, but I had a really big breakfast before I came.

No rice or noodles or bread – how can you have had a big breakfast?

Why don't you take your time and finish your *chee cheong fun*? I'll sit and look over my notes, and when you're ready, you just let me know and we can begin the interview for today.

OK.

I try and take my time eating, enjoying every morsel of the noodles as I usually do. But even though I don't look at her, I can see her out of the corner of my eye, sitting in the rattan armchair, looking through pieces of paper in her folder. She isn't doing anything in particular. She doesn't look at me or try to talk to me, she just looks at her notes, turning the pages over, rearranging them. I try to ignore her and concentrate on my food, but it's impossible. I eat quickly, then take my usual seat opposite her.

She looks up and smiles. Shall we begin?

October 15th

Bottled-gas delivery man.

Waiter, several times.

Night security guard.

Strange. I'm trying to remember all the jobs I did in two and a half years, but it's hard – I can't answer your question fully. I know I'm forgetting one or two.

For the first ten days after I moved to KL, I slept on the floor of Keong's room in Puchong. In spite of his boasts on the phone, I knew that his life in the city wasn't going to be as glorious as he'd made it out to be – that the life of kids like us, who'd dropped out of school at sixteen, seventeen, would surely have its limitations. All I hoped for was that these limits would be higher than the ones in the village, or at the very least, different.

Life in the city didn't seem to have provided Keong with the fulfilment he'd craved during his brief years in the village. He rented a room in a small apartment owned by a thin old Cantonese woman who rented her two bedrooms to young people like us, new to the city and looking for work. She herself slept on the rattan sofa in the living room, in front of the TV that was never turned off in the ten days I stayed there. Two in the morning, it was on; 8.30 in the morning, it was on; four in the afternoon –

78

every time I walked through the door, it was on. Often, she'd be asleep, sitting half-upright in a chair, but the TV would be on. She had no family, no phone, no one to keep her company – all she looked forward to was collecting the two hundred ringgit from her tenants at the start of each month, which she kept in a biscuit tin under the sofa.

'Dangerous thing for a granny to do,' Keong joked with her. 'Someone could just walk in, beat you to death and take all your money.'

He had been there for ten months, the longest he'd stayed anywhere since he moved back to KL a few years before. It was because of the view, he said – from his window on the tenth floor he could see the city spreading out before him, obscured by two other blocks of flats but present nonetheless, twenty-four-seven, reminding him of all the glorious possibilities available to him. The blinking of the lights in the evening, the smog in the daytime, drifting across the seas from Indonesia and settling over the skyline. That year the gigantic Twin Towers had just been completed, and the glow it threw up at night meant that you could see the dust particles suspended in the air, shifting constantly. Even when nothing moved, the city was changing all the time. That's how he felt. Only problem was, he was stuck in that bedroom, often sleeping until lunchtime despite the light forcing its way through the thin curtains. Why get up early when you don't have a steady job?

A couple of months after he moved back, he'd tried to educate himself – saved a bit of money and enrolled in evening courses in computers and typing, and another one in *feng shui* and astrology. Everyone knew that the future was in technology. If you could use a computer you could become a millionaire in three months by investing in stocks and shares, which was just another form of gambling, after all – and God knows he was a demon when it came to gambling. All you needed to do was to reduce the variables of fortune – and that's where *feng shui* came in. You simply harnessed the powers of the universe, and once you were in harmony with the elements, there was no limit to what you could achieve. The internet had just arrived in the country, and shops started to appear all over town where you could go and find the news and other information on computers. That was only twenty years ago – just yesterday, it feels like. But it was a pain to go to the computer store every day, and when he did make it there, the internet connection often didn't work, and he would spend hours trying to perform the simplest tasks. He should have given up right from the start and realised that the sort of career he'd imagined for himself was reserved for people who worked in offices, who'd finished their diplomas at the age of twenty-one, twenty-two, who knew how to speak foreign languages – people like you.

During the brief period I lived with him, he rarely stirred before I'd come back from a morning's search for work. We'd sit and share some *kuih* that I'd bought from the street hawker outside our block, and Keong would smoke three cigarettes in a row on the narrow balcony. He asked a lot of questions about the village, wanted to hear the latest about various kids our age, whether they were still in Kuala Selangor; how my mother was; whether the fishing had been good; whether Uncle Kam's papayas were still as tasty as ever – the most mundane things you could think of. 'You're joking, meh?' I said. I never knew that he'd even noticed anyone else apart from me in the village. He'd always seemed so detached, deliberately distant, but now he was interested in the news of specific people. I have no idea why these individuals mattered more than the others, why they'd left an impression on him, but he seemed happy nonetheless to hear that Little Hong had started a small business making dumplings and *bao* down the road, or that Fei-fei was now married and living in Klang, with a young child and another on its way. Maybe Keong had had a crush on her, who knows. I can't remember him ever having met her. He didn't take his eyes off me when I told him about the village, drinking in everything I said and forgetting to smoke his cigarette. I watched it burn steadily down as I talked, big clumps of ash falling to the ground. Beats me why he found any of it interesting.

Sometimes I suspected that he went back to bed after I left to spend the afternoon looking for a job. When I got back in the evening – eight, nine o'clock – he would be preparing to go out, looking after the evening shift at his friend's CD stall in Chow Kit, which I understood was code for something else. Later, after I'd moved out and was struggling a bit in between jobs, he would make a few attempts at getting me involved in his line of work – a low-level dealing in pills and powder and cash – but I could never tell the difference between *fengtau* and Ice and G and K, and was always worried I'd make a mistake. He thought he was doing me a favour. 'Guys like us, it's the only way we can make a bit of money quickly.' But I could see that his heart wasn't in it, and he never tried very hard to convince me. He mentioned how much money he made from it, and I realised why it was dangerous – not because the drugs could kill you, or get you killed by rival gangsters or the police, or land you in jail for twenty years, but because the money was just enough to keep you going for a while without a proper job, but never – never, never, never – enough to make you feel comfortable and safe. One weekend he would earn a wad of cash big enough to last two months, other times he'd go weeks without making anything, or would have to pay his share of protection money, or subscriptions, or whatever he called it, to someone bigger and meaner, or pay a bribe to the police or the city enforcement officers who came snooping round his CD stall – always, always bribes. That one payment would dry you out for a month while you waited for your next windfall. And so on.

Once, towards the end of my time in KL, he talked about helping out a friend in a new line of business: girls. 'Helping out?' I said. 'I don't even want to know what that means.' He smiled and said, 'You're still as big a dickhead as ever.' When he laughed I could sense that what he was telling me was not a boast but a confession, a strange silent plea for help, though God only knows what I could have done. What was I supposed to do? I didn't want him messing with prostitutes. That kind of stuff was serious. I'd had over two years in the city by then; I knew when things were getting out of hand for him. I guess he wanted me to persuade him not to do it. He imagined us getting into an argument and insulting me for being a coward, and later, when he'd jacked it all in, he'd say he had only done it for me. I was the reason he'd turned down a perfectly lucrative job. But I just said nothing – what could I have said that would have made sense? *Go get yourself proper employment?* He was just doing what he had to do.

Those first ten days, sleeping on the floor of his tiny room, I didn't realise that he had already become stuck in a place he didn't want to be. I know now that he must have been taking drugs from time to time. That's why he had such strange sleeping patterns, why one time he didn't come home all night, and the next day was full of energy despite the circles under his eyes that were so dark I thought someone had punched him. Those were things that only dawned on me later, when I'd had time to figure out for myself the way the city shaped you without you even knowing what was happening to you. But right then, all I thought was, Why is Keong so miserable?

I felt the complete opposite – the entire city was at my feet, I couldn't wait to get going. I found a job as a waiter at a Chinese seafood restaurant in Old Klang Road. That was my first, and also the best, though maybe I felt that way because it was the first, and I hadn't had time to realise that it was actually pretty lousy. After just a week of ferrying the orders from the kitchen to the tables and waiting until someone more senior came and served the dishes, I was given a promotion of sorts and allowed to lift the dishes from the trays and place them with a flourish on the tables before the hungry diners, while *someone else* stood holding the tray. Such a fine distinction, invisible to the customers – I mean, do you ever notice who puts the food on the table, or who's standing like a dumb statue with the tray in their hands? – but to me it felt like a huge step up in the world.

Right away, I was better than that *someone else* – the sullen, silent person holding the tray – who was always foreign. Mostly Myanmar, Nepalese, sometimes Cambodian. They'd stand there looking at me, waiting for me to give them instructions. I'd only been there a week, ten days, but already I wielded power over them, mysteriously and without me even asking, by virtue of being the same colour and race as the forty-something-year-old couple who owned the place. I could feel it in the way these migrants looked at me, and in the way I returned their fragile smiling gazes. We both knew that one word from me accusing them of laziness or insolence and they'd be in trouble. Between their word and mine, there would be no argument. Luckily, there was no reason at that restaurant to invent a story about a foreign employee drinking on the job, or groping a Chinese waitress's ass, or being rude to a client, or some other exaggeration following an argument or a dispute over small amounts of money – mild fabrications just to get the guy sacked. Later, there would be – but not at that place.

Can you blame me for feeling happy? Suddenly, I had an income – I was making a living in the city! – and at work I felt that strange sense of authority over others. For years you think no one cares about you, then all at once, in your first job, you find that there are people out there who are terrified of you. It changes the way you feel about yourself, doesn't it? The shifts were long. Twelve, thirteen hours, with a brief lull in the afternoon when the last of the stragglers from lunch had gone and the tables had been cleared, the kitchen cleaned and re-stocked for the onslaught of dinner in just over an hour's time. Most of us took a quick nap, seated near the entrance, under the ceiling fan, resting our heads on the table in front of us with our folded arms as a pillow. Sometimes, when I didn't have time for a break I'd watch the others sleeping and think that they looked like birds at rest, curled into themselves and oblivious to the world for those few minutes.

I got paid eight hundred ringgit a month, which seemed a lot to me, and I could afford to rent a small room in a flat not far from Keong's.

I left the seafood restaurant after about six months because I was bored and wanted more – more money, yes, but also more of everything else. More variety, more fun, more work, even. I didn't know that all the jobs I'd get would end up giving me the same sensation I had towards the end of my time at that first seafood restaurant (there would be others) – a mixture of boredom and fatigue caused not so much by the constant movement of my body over twelve hours, but by the sense of a whole universe of ease and satisfaction existing just beyond the horizons of the world I was living in. All I had to do was push beyond a silky-thin membrane and I'd be there, part of a world where comfort produced greater comfort, day after day for years without end. The thought that all that was almost within my grasp made whatever job I was working at meaningless – all that mattered was what came next.

My next two jobs were also in restaurants. Neither lasted long. They were smarter establishments than the first, and I thought I was moving up in the world. Air-con and black-and-white uniforms, and carpets in the second place. Keong laughed when I told him I was quitting again. 'Restaurant jobs are for girls,' he said. 'Young guys like us, we don't mess about taking orders from people. Brother, you got to *give* the orders, not take them.'

I worked in a tyre-repair shop and got what you might call a bit of training, but I never got used to the constant hiss of air valves and pumps and the stench of hot rubber. The guys who worked at the garage said I was good with my hands, they could see I was strong, but how long can you stay in a job like that? The oldest guy who worked there was in his seventies, Hainanese uncle with bald head and long white eyebrows. Sometimes he'd just disappear without a word, and we'd find him slumped deep in the plastic-wire armchair, fast asleep with his mouth open and spit dribbling down his chin. The trembling of his brow was the only sign he was still alive. The other guys laughed. Old Boon, wake up! They'd shout his name and sing songs, knowing that he wouldn't even stir. He'd need to sleep for at least half an hour, sometimes more, before being able to start work again, but when he did he was swift and sharp with the tools. And then, suddenly, *bang* – KO'd again. When I looked at him I thought, I will light twenty million joss-sticks at the temple and pray to every god in the heavens, go to Chiengmai to worship magical monks, anything to avoid a fate like that.

On my nights off I realised I was starting to avoid Keong. At the beginning I'd seek him out whenever I had some spare time, and we'd go down to the stalls and eat Hokkien mee with the beer we'd bought from the 7-Eleven, or else we'd take a ride out somewhere on our scooters looking for a cheap *fengtau* club that Keong had heard of, where he might be able to do a bit of business. He was slowly giving up on regular work, and had a lot of free time on his hands. I knew that he was dealing more and more in pills. (He changed lodgings often, and one time I arrived at his place while he was searching for a lost fifty-ringgit note. All the drawers were open and I saw his stock of pills, one or two each in neat little plastic bags, every colour you could think of.)

We turned up at this nightclub once, called W- disco. Of course I can't tell you the real name – for all I know it might still be there and the police might go and raid it, and then the owners will send some gangsters to chop me up. I thought Keong had taken me there to introduce me to nightlife in the capital, but we just hung around outside, smoking and chatting. 'You waiting for someone to turn up?' I asked after a while. Keong laughed and replied, 'Maybe.' I didn't think anything more of it – Keong had never behaved in what you might call a conventional way, even when we were in the village. I didn't mind either, I felt comfortable there, sitting on a low cement barrier in the car park, smoking and watching the people go past – mostly young men and women who looked like us, spoke like us, but a few rich kids too, climbing out of their Toyotas, and a sprinkling of Malay guys in skinny jeans and death metal T-shirts. Even outside, the music from the club was loud enough that we had to raise our voices when we spoke, and I remember thinking, *I'm a hell of a long way from Bagan Sungai Yu*. I wondered what was going on in the village at that precise moment, 11.30 on a Tuesday night, the sea flattening out into the darkness, the last light in the village long since switched off, with only the street lamps to indicate the presence of human existence. Nothing, probably. I thought of my friends, the ones who hadn't left, asleep since 8 p.m., getting ready to wake up in the pre-dawn hours to supervise the boats, the incoming catch, the trip to the wholesalers. I smiled. Fuck, what those guys would say if they saw me now.

'Wait here.' Keong got up and strolled casually around the people gathered there, smoking and chatting just as we were doing. I watched him for a while, disappearing into the crowd, emerging now and then, exchanging a greeting here and there. He'd come back and start talking about random things, like the wars in the Gulf and the Balkans, or whether McDonald's ice cream was actually made of pork fat. And he'd ask questions like, 'In a war between America and Russia, who would you support?'

Just as I was laughing, this rich kid came up to us, nervous as hell, and said to Keong, 'Don't rip me off, OK?' You know the type – neat hair, bright blue Ralph Lauren polo shirt, genuine for sure, not a night-market counterfeit. Silver watch, pale skin. Probably same age as me but looked about sixteen.

'Heyyy, little brother, go back and relax with your friends for a while,' Keong said. 'I'll let you know when it's good. Don't believe me? Just ask your buddies.' He lit another cigarette once the kid had gone away. 'First timers – pain in the ass.' He passed me a pack of Salems, even though I was only halfway through the cigarette I was smoking. Then he gave me a fistful of cash and some instructions – told me to get into the club, leave the pack in the toilets, wait a while, and watch out for the Ralph Lauren kid. In moments like that you think, Why didn't I just say no? It would have been so easy to treat it as a joke, as just one more no-meaning thing that Keong had come up with. I could have just stood up and walked back to my scooter and said, '*Your mother. You've gone nuts. Seeya next week. Some of us have to work.*' And gone back home. But things don't work that way – sometimes your brain doesn't recognise danger or risk until much later – days, weeks, years – and it's only then that the event feels scary, because the passing of time has made it seem that you had a choice. But at that moment, sitting there with Keong, options did not exist for me. It felt like the most natural thing in the world – the only one, in fact – to provide him with the answer he wanted, and grant my approval. '*En.*' You might say that I could have bailed out at any time, but once I was inside the disco everything I did became melded together to form part of one continuous decision; every tiny action felt necessary and unavoidable – making my way to the toilets was the only way to escape the mass of people dancing with their heads shaking wildly; pretending to wash my hands was the sole means of making myself appear innocent; waiting for Ralph Lauren boy to appear was my way of assuring my friendship with Keong and being part of city life. I had placed the pack of Salems on a ledge in front of me, slightly to my right, in between two basins, so that if the police burst in I'd be able to claim ignorance, but if anyone else tried to take them I'd say they were mine. Don't ask me how I figured that out, I just did – throw someone in the sea and they'll find a way to swim. The more I tried not to look at the pack, the more it appeared in my field of vision, green and white, crushed along one edge. I pretended to wash my hands. Washing, washing, waiting. People came in, they went out. No one touched the cigarettes. Finally the kid walked in. I motioned with my chin towards the pack, and made to leave. He said, 'Wait.' We were alone. He opened the pack, took out the three cigarettes that were inside and dropped them to the damp floor, where they immediately started to soak up the dark yellow muck of piss and dirty water. He shook the pack and cupped a pink tablet in his palm. Quickly, he put it in his mouth and left without looking at me.

Outside, Keong was still sitting on the low concrete wall, and when I joined him he said, 'If the world was taken over by aliens, what would be your final meal?'

'*Fuck* you. *Chaohai.*'

'Relaaaax. Nothing bad happened to you, right? Calm down and grow up.'

He was right. It wasn't a big deal, it was just part of life. I'd helped out a friend from my village, nothing more. That's how I tried to square things in my head, and sure enough, after a few days I didn't think I'd done anything out of the ordinary that night. I'd just helped a buddy with something he had to do.

Still, I began to drift away from Keong, and though we'd occasionally meet for late-night supper down at the stalls, our lives were pulling apart and I felt less and less desire to search him out. He was drifting through life, experimenting with things that would lead nowhere – what else could he have done, to be fair? – but I wasn't ready for that in-between life, the fun always shadowed by fear. We're young, he once said, Life is long. But he knew that wasn't true, that people like us didn't have time on our side. We weren't like the cool Ralph Lauren boy who time favoured, we were already hustling for a living, already looked ten years older than him. For us, it was the opposite, in fact, and every day I told myself, *Hurry, you don't have much time.* I was in the city, I had to learn things, see things; I had to nail down some kind of life for myself.

One night, over noodles and beer at a *dai cau* place in Puchong, Keong told me he'd pack it all in one day, take off to Guangzhou, where big business was starting to happen – it would be easy for people like us because we could speak Cantonese. We start a business, marry a girl from Chaozhou and make a fortune. Doing what? I asked, but he just shrugged. 'Whatever,' he said. 'Whatever it takes.'

I don't know where he went, whether he actually made it to China as he said he would, but a couple of weeks later he was gone. I went to the DVD stalls in Low Yat, Chow Kit, all the places he'd worked at, but the answer everywhere was the same. Keong is gone, and no one knows where. I should have been worried about him – in his line of work, the people he hung around, he might have been hurt, or in jail, or chased out of town – but instead I was relieved. Happy. The kind of quiet joy that made me feel airy and weightless, like a shred of cloth swirling in the river when the tide pulls in. Because maybe he really had achieved his dreams and gone to China to find wealth and a pretty bride. But mostly because he had slipped out of my life and I wouldn't have to see him again. I hadn't realised it, but his presence was like the little thorny spine in the base of my foot – hardly a problem at all, barely noticeable most days, but present nonetheless, and always threatening to turn into something more painful, even if I never knew exactly what shape that pain would assume. It was that threat – that idea of something terrible that might or might not happen – that disappeared when Keong left town.

On the surface nothing much changed in my life. I kept working, and looking for work when I wasn't working. I never spent more than a few days without employment. No big change, some would say – still a loser's life. But without Keong, I felt free.

My last job in the city was at a neighbourhood restaurant called Fatty Crab, which was much more profitable than you'd think if you saw it – it was just a coffee shop on the corner of a typical block of shophouses in a housing estate, which wasn't so rich back then, but I guess not poor either. All around that estate, new ones were being built, bigger and smarter, providing an endless supply of customers.

A deep open drain ran by the side of the restaurant, and over the years the grease from woks and grills had turned the cement black, so it looked as if you were staring into a bottomless chasm. But that didn't put people off, and neither did the cramped tables and half-broken plastic chairs and ceiling fans that didn't work. Maybe it was precisely because it was a simple restaurant, modestly priced, that it was so popular. People drove across town and waited patiently for up to an hour to sample the crab and satay and chicken wings, and it was full all the time.

The boss-lady, Ah Leng Chee, drove a Mercedes SLK. Can you imagine that, old auntie driving a German sports car? Dressed like an auntie too, old nylon trousers and plain blouses, dyed black hair thinning so much that you could see her scalp, powdered face to keep the heat at bay – you'd never know she was rich until you saw her climb into that car. Arrived from Kuantan nearly thirty years previously, and now look at her – driving a Mercedes and raking it in. She was nineteen when she moved to KL – exactly my age when I did. Maybe that was why she loved me as she did, not because she didn't have a son, which you might have been tempted to believe was the reason, but because she saw a version of herself in me. That's why she paid me a thousand a month to supervise the seating of the customers and keep an eye out to make sure the orders were delivered on time. It wasn't a demanding job, so in the afternoons I helped the Nepalese workers with the heavy manual work, unloading the sacks of rice and vegetables, and late at night, stacking the dozens of tables and hundreds of chairs before sluicing down the floor. '*Gone crazy, meh*?' she'd bark when she saw me with my trouser legs rolled up to my knees, sweeping the grime from the floor while Bhim or one of the other Nepalese aimed the hosepipe. And though she never smiled when she said it, I knew her words were meant as praise. Sometimes I'd look at her while I was carrying out this final task, late at night, watch her patiently adding up the receipts, and I'd try to imagine her arriving in the city, a young woman my age, all those years ago. But I'd never really be able to visualise it – she was always just a kind old auntie to me.

She had a daughter who lived in San Francisco, a few years older than I was back then. She came to visit once, dressed in jeans and a T-shirt with the name of her college printed on it – I can't remember which one now. [*Pause.*] It was getting to the end of the lunch hour, but the restaurant was still full and noisy, with voices and laughter on top of the clatter of plates and the shouting from the kitchen beyond, with the din from the passing traffic in the street mixed into all of it. She stood behind the counter watching us rush from table to table, her mother helping us take orders and even serve the food. We were short-staffed that day, I seem to remember, though I can't recall why. I thought she was taking it all in, as if she was enjoying a movie, and I began to worry what she thought of us, that maybe she found us shabby and dumb. *Primitive.* That was the word that came to my mind; she found us primitive, unsophisticated. She'd have looked at the four Nepalese, two Burmese and me, and thought, *Poor things, they're so underdeveloped.* But as I walked past the counter

92

on the way to the kitchen I noticed that she wasn't looking at us at all – her eyes were just staring into space, even though her lips were pulled into a smile. She was sweating, wisps of hair stuck to her forehead and her temples, the ceiling fans doing nothing to relieve her discomfort. At one point I thought I'd caught her eye, so I smiled back, but she just kept gazing into the distance, her pleasant expression intended for no one. That's when I realised she didn't want to be there at all, that it must have been torture for her to be in that cheap restaurant. No air-con. Oily floors. Half the customers wearing soccer shorts or clothes that could have passed for pyjamas. When I saw things through her eyes I felt sorry for her, having to put up with the noise and heat and grease.

She was missing her fiancé, Ah Leng Chee explained later, and couldn't wait to get back to the US. 'Her boyfriend *angmoh* is it?' I asked – I don't know why it felt important. She lived in San Francisco, it wouldn't be surprising if she lived with a white guy. Ah Leng Chee nodded and fell silent for a long while. 'Yes. Getting married next year.'

'Not coming back to take over the business?'

Ah Leng Chee shrugged. 'You young people, you just do what you want.' It turned out her daughter already had a Green Card, and was planning to live in the States forever. 'When I moved to KL she was just a small child. Look at her now.' She visited two, three times in the space of a week, then I never saw her again.

One night, just as the dinner sitting was winding down and the last of the customers were at that point where they were thinking about leaving but couldn't, because they'd eaten too much and were feeling too lethargic, and the place was quieter, less rushed, and the staff starting to relax – a couple of scooters pulled up outside. I don't know why, but I noticed them immediately – scooters buzz up and down the road all day and night, but these were different. The deliberate drawing to a halt, one in the laneway next to the kitchens, the other right in front of the restaurant, engines killed almost at the same time. I've often heard it said that in such moments time expands, things happen in slow motion. People talk about being able to recall every detail, about watching dumbstruck and not being able to react because the actions they observe are out of step with time. But I can't believe that. When you're in the midst of violence, everything occurs swiftly. It swirls around you, envelops you, doesn't let you go, and you react, God knows you react. And so it was that even as I saw the three men enter the restaurant, the long curved blades of their machetes raised in the air, I rushed over to Ah Leng Chee, who had just started to count up the day's takings, the piles of cash arranged neatly on the counter.

That was her money. [*Pause*.] *Our* money.

And she did not remain silent as those slow-motion stories of terror would have you believe, but was already screaming as I reached her side and tried to shield her from the men. She was making a noise I didn't think she was capable of, a high-pitched cry that repeated and repeated as I grappled with one of the men, and suddenly a couple of the Nepalese workers were with me, throwing their slender frames at the robbers. In a few seconds it was over, and as the men escaped on their bikes Ah Leng Chee ran out, as if she was going to try to catch them, shouting, '*Damned black devils! Damned black devils!*' There was cash all over the floor. I started to gather it up – all our pay, what we needed to survive, scattered across the restaurant. As I started to collect it I noticed long streaks of blood across the chipped grey tiles and thought, *She's hurt*. But Ah Leng Chee was still standing at the threshold of the restaurant shouting out into the darkness. I looked up and saw Sujan, the Nepalese cook, sitting on the floor, propped up against the counter with his hand clutching his arm. The others were standing over him, talking to him, cajoling him the way a mother would when she tried to lull a baby to sleep, only they were trying to keep him from falling unconscious, their voices low and urgent, as if their own lives depended on him staying awake. His fingers gripped his arm so tightly that I had difficulty prising them open, and when I did, I caught sight of bright white bone amid the ribbons of purple-red flesh. One of the boys handed me a clean cloth for a tourniquet, and I lashed the wound as tightly as I could.

Ah Leng Chee was still shouting into the darkness, her voice starting to get hoarse. I noticed that my arms and clothes were covered in blood – a gash ran across my forearm. The diners were standing up, arranged in a neat semi-circle behind some tables that we'd started to stack up, like a row of spectators at a show, watching silently. 'Can someone please take this man to hospital,' I said. The money was still strewn across the floor. A man replied, 'We should call the police.' No, I said, *take him to the damn hospital*. Finally a young woman raised her hand and pointed to a BMW parked outside the restaurant. Five of us carried Sujan out to the car, with Bhim cradling his head and shoulders. The woman opened the door to her car and we placed him flat on the back seat. Even in the half-dark I could see the blood spreading over the pale leather upholstery and trickling into the seams, and I felt bad because the woman would have to spend a lot of money cleaning it all up. As I climbed into the passenger seat my arm began to sting, a sharp pain pushing through the numbness that had been there before, yet all I could think of was that the blood was going to drip onto the car seat, and I tried to think of ways to get rid of the stains, maybe rub salt and vinegar into them. I worried about that a lot on the way to the hospital.

Next day, Ah Leng Chee sacked the Bangladeshi guy who worked as a kitchen porter. Just like that. She was convinced that he'd tipped off his friends and told them about the cash she counted out every night. 'They weren't foreign, they were locals,' I said.

'You saw their identity cards, meh?' she asked. 'Anyway, *these guys* – they're all the same.'

[*Pause. Rolls up sleeve to display a scar.*]

I don't know how I didn't feel it when they slashed me, but the cut was clean and deep, and took a while to heal. [*Traces finger along the diagonal mark, about four inches long; other smaller scars also visible.*] I guess you could say that it left me with some memories of that evening. [*Laughs.*]

About six months after that, I arrived at work and saw that Ah Leng Chee was already there, which was unusual – I was normally the one who opened up the restaurant each morning, just before ten, and closed up around midnight. She trusted me with tasks like that, she knew I'd keep things safe. That day there was a lot of dust in the air – not the usual haze that floated over the city, but thicker clouds of it coming from the construction sites nearby, where those patches of sparse city jungle were being cleared to build a new housing estate. Ah Leng Chee was wearing a surgical mask that covered her mouth and nose, which in those days was a rare sight. Now even fashionable people wear them, but back then it was something that only people in Japan and Taiwan knew about, and I used to laugh at it. 'You think you're a Japanese scientist?' I used to joke, but that day I have to admit that I wished I had one too. She lowered her mask and said, 'Ah Hock, you can't work here any more.' Business hadn't been good, she hadn't been making much money for some time. She had taken out a loan, and now she was struggling to make the repayments. She had decided to get rid of me and three other workers, the ones who earned the most; the ones who remained would just have to manage a bigger workload. She wasn't going to lie: if business picked up again she'd employ another foreigner rather than rehire me – they were so much cheaper. 'So, you can't work here any more.' She pulled the mask back up over her nose and mouth and returned to her calculator and the pile of receipts.

I stood watching the clouds of red dust and the bulldozers in the distance, the grit in my mouth and throat starting to itch. She hadn't said, 'I'm sorry, I have to let you go.' Or, 'You're lazy, I'm going to sack you.' Or, 'Business is bad, I can't afford to employ you any more.' She'd just said, *You can't work here any more*. She'd said it as if it was inevitable, as if nothing on earth could prevent the termination of my employment at Restoran Fatty Crab – as if the end of my time there was as natural as the monsoon season that arrives and disappears without fail each year. But even that wasn't guaranteed. Some years we didn't get any rain, others we got too much. Why couldn't I continue working there, even for just a few months longer? Because the city was going to be destroyed by an earthquake? Because we were going to be invaded by extra-terrestrials? If so, I could accept it. No one would have a job, so why should I? I'm not an unreasonable man. Give me one good reason and I always walk away quietly.

'Ah Hock, why are you just standing there?' she said at last. 'Don't be like that, it's not my fault.'

I looked at her. Didn't do anything else, just looked at her – and that was enough to get her worked up, because she thought I was being insolent. Challenging her for a better reason, or financial compensation, or something else she couldn't provide. She started talking – shouting, really. About things that weren't important to me, explaining about her balance sheet and her daughter on the other side of the world, who still needed money, about the pressures of the job, of being a mother. About how I was so ignorant I didn't know how the world worked. Didn't I know about this thing called the Asian Financial Crisis? Why didn't I read the papers a bit more, and take an interest in the world? That was the kind of thing she was shouting at me. Every country in Asia had been suffering, and there I was behaving like a spoilt child. *Twenty-two years old, still acting like a kid!* All the bribes she had to pay, protection money, price hikes – did I even know about all that? I had no idea how tough running a business in this shithole country could be, she said; I had no idea what it was like to be a woman her age, all alone, trying to run a stupid restaurant. 'When you get to my age you'll know what it feels like.'

'What about the others?'

'Go back to Myanmar lor. Nepal, Bangla – like you care?' Then she cursed, just one rude word, not a big deal, but coming from a nice lady like her it sounded so funny that I started to laugh, and then I couldn't stop. I was standing in the middle of the restaurant, the tables and chairs in piles around me, laughing like a demon in an old kung-fu movie, and I could see the others who'd arrived for work staring at me as if I was dangerous. 'Crazy! What the hell are you laughing about?' Ah Leng Chee was shouting. 'What's so funny?' The more she yelled at me, the harder it was for me to stop. I closed my eyes, and all I could see was the image of her, sweet old auntie, saying that bad word, and I laughed so hard I was crying and feeling my

98

ribcage compress so much that I had trouble breathing; and the dust in my throat was getting worse, so I was laughing and coughing at the same time. Some of the other workers were giggling too, and Ah Leng Chee said, 'That's it, he's gone mad.' When I walked out of the place I was still laughing.

I thought that was the end of the matter. But at the trial, nearly ten years later, the prosecution brought up this episode. I was amazed that anyone remembered it, but they did – they spent a long time asking questions about that day. About my laughing – somehow it had become proof of my madness. My instability. *My inability to recognise the gravity of serious situations.* They'd found the girl from Yangon who washed the dishes, her plump boyfriend who worked on the satay grill. How did the police find them? I didn't think they'd last more than a few months in the country, I didn't think they even had papers – but here they were, just short of a decade later, answering questions in passable Malay. *Would you say that the defendant was disconnected from reality?* When I'd known them all those years before, I'd sometimes joke with them, call them rude names in Malay, but they just smiled – they didn't understand a word.

When it was Ah Leng Chee's turn to take the witness stand I knew she wanted to help me, to tell everyone that I wasn't crazy or dangerous. Several times she started to say, 'He's a good boy, hard-working . . .' but each time they cut her short. 'Just answer the question, Madam Wong. What was his reaction when you told him you were sacking him?'

How long did he laugh? Five–six–seven minutes without stopping?

So, would you say he was . . . hysterical? Out of control?

You said at the time he'd . . . gone *mad*?

She looked at me from across the courtroom, and I got the feeling she was asking for forgiveness, which was strange, because she had done nothing wrong. She was answering the questions truthfully, just as she was expected to do – there was nothing for her to be sorry about, nothing for me to forgive. I remembered her yelling at me that day, remembered the other people arriving at work, the restaurant starting to come to life – the two Indian guys delivering gas canisters, the booming metallic sound they made as they lowered them to the concrete floor in the kitchen, the Tamil song they were singing, *Nila, nila odivaa* . . . and the waiters, Bhim and the others, pulling back the shutters, the light falling on the sacks of vegetables. Sujan struggling to set up a table on his own, his right arm healed now but stiff, like a puppet's. Ah Leng Chee's single, sharp swear word. As I remembered the sensation of laughing at how beautiful and ridiculous it had all been, I put my hand over my mouth to hide my smile, but I couldn't stifle the laughter that was starting to force its way out. Ah Leng Chee looked at me from the witness stand and smiled back. I remembered, also, the folded notes of cash that she used to give me now and then – just ten, twenty ringgit – and the little gifts, like a bar of chocolate or a keychain, whenever she came back from a trip out of town. I started laughing. [*Pause.*] I covered my face with my hands.

The prosecutor had been speaking in long elegant sentences that rumbled gently like distant thunder, but he interrupted himself for a second to turn and look at me. Through the tiny gaps in my fingers I saw him glance at me before starting to talk again. The tone of his voice changed slightly, as if to say: You see? I was right – this guy is mad.

After I left Restoran Fatty Crab I drifted about for a few

days, and got turned down for a couple of jobs. There wasn't a lot of work available, but in truth I wasn't looking too hard. I know this sounds like one of the stories you're interested in, about a boy from the village who comes to the big capital city and gets crushed by how brutal it is, but that's not exactly right. I wasn't defeated by KL, I got bored of it – I wanted something better. A couple of weeks later I was back in Klang, and quite quickly found the job at the fish farm. If I hadn't left KL, I wouldn't have started making a decent living so soon. Someone like me, with no qualifications at all – I didn't think anyone would want to marry me, but they did.

The thought comes to me suddenly, in the middle of a sentence.

It's a normal session, nothing out of the ordinary. I'm talking, she's sitting back in her chair with her notebook in her lap. I can see her handwriting, tiny and perfectly neat. Now and then she stops to underline a word. I guess it's something I've said. All at once I think: I've talked too much. I talk all the time, while she remains silent. She knows everything about me, I know nothing about her.

Are you all right? she says.

I nod.

You were starting to tell me about your mother and the relationship she had with your uncle.

Can I ask you a question?

Sure.

What's your family like? I mean – you have sisters or brothers? How old are your parents? Do they still work?

That's a lot of questions. I have kind of a normal family. Parents still around, still at loggerheads like the proverbial black sheep and white sheep on a bridge. Three brothers, all doing different things.

Three brothers? Must have been tricky being the only girl.

Yeah. I had to learn to survive. Actually, they're quite sweet. When they're not being assholes.

Your parents work?

Dad still does, yes. Anyway, enough about me. I'm interested to know about your mother, the time she started living with another man.

But I'm interested in your background too. Your life.

She smiles and shrugs her shoulders.

We're here for your story. This is about you.

You said we'd have a conversation. That's a two-way thing, isn't it?

It's nice of you to ask. But yours is the story that counts. I'm here to listen to you.

I wait for a few moments, hoping she'll change her mind. In the pause, I can hear an ambulance somewhere in the distance.

All right, she says. You were talking about your mother?

Why? That's what you want to know, just like everyone else. But like the others, you're going to be disappointed. Many people asked me the same question. My lawyer did, numerous times – 'just to establish a motive', she explained. The other lawyer, the one prosecuting, asked all kinds of questions, some of which seemed to be unconnected to the actual crime, like, 'Where did you have dinner that evening?' and 'How would you describe your mood that night?' but I understood that they were aimed at the same thing: trying to figure out why I did it.

My wife – my ex-wife, I mean – didn't come to the trial. Why would she, after all? But I saw her photo in the newspapers. Some journalists found out where she lived and wanted to speak to her, perhaps just the way you're talking to me now, in the hope of understanding a little more about me. If you manage to locate the newspapers I'm talking about, you'll see a series of photos of her walking hurriedly, the journalists holding their microphones a couple of steps behind her. But she doesn't want to say anything, she pushes past them at the front gate, shielding her face from the cameras with her handbag. But once she's inside and tries to lock the gate, she has to use both hands. She's forced to lower the handbag, and that's why they were able to get those photos of her face, crumpled from the heat, from discomfort and frustration and many other things I can't put my finger on. In the main picture

she looks up, straight at the camera, and although –
according to the report – she never uttered a single word,
her expression screams out the same question: Why?

When I looked at the image, I knew that the question
was not directed at the journalists but at me. She didn't
need to know why they were harassing her – that was
obvious. Her *why* was meant for me. Why did I do it? *Why
why why why*.

I met Jenny by mistake. She was destined for someone
else, someone better, but ended up with me. I first saw
her name on invoices we'd been sent. Jenny Teoh, Accounts
Manager – she always made sure to include her title, even
on the smallest bill, and when we started to use email,
hers were still signed with her name and position. *Received
with thx, Jenny Teoh ACCOUNTS MANAGER*, so I always
knew she had an important position. This was a few years
after I joined the fish farm, when business was growing
fast and we were starting to sell our products to restaurants
and supermarkets all over the Klang Valley, even as far
south as Johor. I was working outdoors all the time, supervising the construction of the new cages and the growing
number of outbuildings, and back then we were even
considering building staff quarters within the compound
for the Indonesian workers. The closer they were to work,
the less likely they were to run away, the boss said. Mr
Lai had firm ideas about how to run the business. He didn't
like it when workers quit suddenly, when they disappeared
and none of the others could tell us what had happened
to them. One day they were working normally, next day
they were gone. It was because they had to travel a long
way to work, two to a scooter, sometimes even on foot
– a journey like that gives you time to think about what
you're doing, and when you reflect on your life, it isn't
pretty. That's when people bail out.

Not long before that I noticed a flimsy camp appear on the edge of the jungle, about twenty feet from the road, built around a small abandoned concrete block that must once have been a grocery store or coffee shop. A few bits of tarpaulin stretched from tree trunks to the derelict house. A fire was burning, small children sat around it idly throwing sticks into the flame. You could tell in an instant that it was a migrant camp, and Mr Lai was worried that one or two of our men might have been living there. 'The rains come, they're gone. Police come, they're gone.' He wanted them as close to work as possible, so they wouldn't have any excuses for not turning up.

That month alone we'd lost two men and were struggling with the workload. Mr Lai was pushing us all the time, and he'd just bought the piece of land that backed onto our existing plot – the men spent all day cutting down the trees, and Mr Lai himself was on site to plan the dormitory block as well as a new generator plant. I was doing everything – hours in the sun again, doing the work of the two men who'd just disappeared, then trying to help out with the paperwork. The sales manager, a city-boy type called Toh, was complaining that he was always on the road, always driving, always arriving home after dinner, that he never saw his young children because they had long since gone to bed by the time he got home. One day he'd be in Seremban, next day in Rawang, last week he even had to go to Tapah. What the hell. On top of all that he had to call in at the farm at least three times a week to collect samples, make sure the paperwork and money were in order, check his messages. 'Everyone's pulling me in different directions. Soon I'm going to snap,' he said. 'Break into a thousand small pieces.'

'Still complaining meh?' Mr Lai shouted. 'No work – cry. Too much work – also cry. Go die, eh.'

I couldn't stop myself from smiling. Toh earned a lot more than me – I don't know how much but it was substantial, at least twice as much, I'd guess. I didn't ever make a thing of it, not to him or to Mr Lai – it was only normal: he had an education, he was good with computers and numbers and papers, quicker and more at ease than me in the office. Those things count in life, I understood that. Still, it gave me a small feeling of satisfaction to hear Mr Lai slap him down like that. Two days later he called in sick – or rather, his wife did. He was too ill to get to the phone, she said, had barely been out of bed for thirty-six hours. 'What a feeble excuse,' I said to Jezmine, the secretary, who'd answered the phone. 'Such a coward, had to ask his wife to call.' He could have done it himself from bed – everyone knew he had a mobile phone by then.

Pok kai, ham ka chan, sei lun tao. Mr Lai couldn't stop cursing, the worst words you can imagine. Just as well you don't understand Cantonese – I'm too shy to translate that. There was a big contract that we needed to close, our main client was thinking about doubling the amount of stock they bought from us for distribution in Singapore, and that lazy wimp Toh had fallen ill just when he was due to conclude the deal. When Mr Lai had regained his breath he stood in the office with his hands on his hips and looked at us – me and Jezmine – as if he was noticing us for the very first time. The top button of his shirt was undone, and he was fanning himself with a folded copy of that day's *Nanyang Siang Pau*. 'You two will have to attend the meeting this afternoon. Don't screw up.'

Jezmine shrugged. She was twenty-three years old, only a couple of years younger than me then, but she wasn't ruffled. She looked at her watch and said, 'We leave in an hour.' Then she returned to her desk and started reading the *Nüyou* magazine that she'd been poring over earlier.

'Don't we have to do some . . . I don't know, preparations?' I asked.

'Sure. Do whatever you want.'

As we walked into the client's office – two floors of a modern air-conditioned row of shophouses in Taman Bukit Kuda – I silently repeated the key figures that I'd memorised earlier – our annual sales, turnover, and so on. I'd highlighted them in green fluorescent ink so I wouldn't forget them, and placed them in a folder of documents I'd prepared for the meeting. I'd put on the clean shirt I kept at the farm in case of unexpected visits from clients – in the past, there'd been occasions when I'd been helping the labourers dig the soil or prepare the foundations for new buildings, and had been surprised by the sudden arrival of buyers who wanted to inspect the farm. When fancy people turn up, it's better not to greet them with half-dried cement on your hands, walking around barefoot with your trousers rolled up to your knees like a peasant, so I learned to keep a spare set of clothes in case of emergencies. Now, as we walked up the stairs, I felt that I at least looked convincingly professional.

It didn't take me long to realise that the Jenny who greeted us was the same one who signed all the invoices. The fact that she didn't speak much, the directness of her tone when she did, the matter-of-fact manner of asking questions that sounded ironic, like 'So, is your business actually profitable these days?' – all that was exactly the way she wrote her messages to us. She didn't intend to be rude or sarcastic, that was just the way she was. She looked at me and said, 'If you're the foreman, I guess your job's just to look after all the manual stuff – so why are you here?'

I started to reel off the facts and figures I'd learned by heart, but even as I was speaking I knew I was getting it all wrong, all the numbers and terminology I'd rehearsed silently in the car, trying not to move my lips so Jezmine wouldn't catch on to what I was doing – I was messing it all up, stumbling over my words and flicking through the documents in my file to try to find the relevant information. But paperwork and me, we've never got along, and I knew that the answers I was looking for were not going to surrender themselves to me, no matter how hard I searched. I could see her watching me struggle – she was only a few years older than me, about thirty, I'd guess, but her neat blouse and dark businesswoman-type trousers, with sharp creases down the front, made her seem older and wiser. For a few minutes, no one spoke – only the shuffling of my papers broke the silence in that small glassed-off meeting room.

'Remember the floods last year?' Jezmine said, almost excitedly – exactly the way she might have done if she'd been sitting in McDonald's and chatting with her friends over a milkshake. 'We were the only farm in the entire state of Selangor not to be affected!' She started to provide information on our business the way the clever students recited poetry during competitions at school, without consulting any notes, pausing at the right moment, the rise and fall of her voice as steady as a stream of music – but instead of feeling stupid as I might have done at school, I felt relief, even gratitude. I sat smiling while she spoke, nodding when she employed terms like 'year-on-year profit', even though I didn't understand what they meant. I knew she was doing enough to secure the business that the farm needed. 'And all that is because Mr Lee here insisted we made our fish cages bigger and deeper than industry standards, and installed an expensive filtration system to ensure the highest-quality products.'

I blushed. It was true, though – I had done that.

Jenny looked at me and smiled for the first time in the

meeting. Turning to Jezmine, she said, 'I guess men have their uses after all.'

I can't remember how we ended up going on our first date – we never experienced a big turning point, no moment of rupture between our professional relationship and a personal one. That moment in Korean dramas where colleagues realise that, *Yes! They are actually in love*, or even just, *Hey, something is happening here* – we didn't experience that. Instead we simply progressed from one meeting to another, until it turned out that we were a couple. Much later, in the middle stages of our marriage, when we finally felt comfortable in our married skins, she would tease me for my lack of romance. 'You never courted me,' she'd say, and I'd reply, 'I wanted to let you court *me*.' In a sense, the gradual evolution of our beginning – so slow that neither of us recognised it as the start of something – would set the tone for our marriage. Things crept up on us, stealthily, and were almost over by the time we could even put a name to what we were experiencing – we could neither savour what was beautiful nor remedy what was bitter, we merely clutched at the final impressions of what-ever it was we'd experienced and thought, *It's finished*. Tenderness, anger, regret – we didn't recognise them until it was too late.

After that initial meeting, Mr Lai had been so pleased with the signing of the new contract that he put me in charge of managing affairs with Jenny's company. I told him that it shouldn't be me, that Jezmine was better with numbers and at talking to customers, but he insisted that I deal with them. 'That pretty accounts manager, she prefers to deal with a man.'

Jenny and I got used to seeing each other from time to time, and one day she texted me to say that her office was under renovation, and could I meet at the *bak kut teh* place across the road instead, but when I got there I found the noise from the traffic was as bad as any construction site, and we had to struggle to make ourselves heard over the scooters and buses passing by outside, the chatter of the breakfast crowd. I tried to tell her about developments on the farm – Jezmine had prepared a few sheets of figures to show how well we were doing – but Jenny kept shaking her head, asking me to repeat myself, and when our bowls of soup arrived we both felt grateful for the excuse not to talk. We ate with our heads bowed, concentrating on the food – I ate mine slowly, taking great care not to slurp it too noisily as I normally did. We went some time without speaking, and finally she said, 'It's like we're on a date. Ever notice how people on a first date seldom talk? They're too awkward to express any emotion.'

I blushed. And although I'd been trying hard to remember my table manners, I found myself lifting my bowl to my mouth and gulping down the remainder of the soup and savouring the thick sediment at the bottom, the best part. '*Wah*, you eat so quickly,' she said. I noticed that her meal was only half-finished. 'I guess it's habit, working on a farm like you do.'

I nodded. I didn't want to explain that in fact the habit came from childhood – I'd always eaten quickly, even as a kid.

After that we started meeting more regularly, always for dinner at the end of a day's work, when I'd ride into town on the new Yamaha I'd bought. We'd go to places she knew – simple spots tucked away in Pandamaran, Bukit Tinggi, even in areas you wouldn't expect to find decent eating places, like Taman Sentosa or Teluk Kapas. At first I was worried she'd mind being on a motorbike instead of in a car – a girl like her who worked in an air-conditioned office – but she never complained, and I was grateful for that, until the day I arrived at her office to collect her and she showed me a bag of shopping from Jusco mall. She'd bought some clothes for me – a fresh white shirt and light-coloured slacks that she'd washed and pressed, as well as some black leather shoes. 'You want me to treat you to somewhere fancy tonight, is that it?' I joked as I got changed in the men's restroom.

She just smiled and said, 'I should have bought you some new underpants too.'

She insisted on leaving the bike and taking a taxi, even though it was only a short distance to the restaurant, a Nyonya place in Taman Bayu Perdana that was a bit fancier than the coffee shops and street stalls and open-air *dai cau* joints we'd usually go to – but still not what you'd call a luxury restaurant, and I couldn't understand why she'd made such a big deal about taking me there. We were seated at a quiet table close to the counter, and after a few minutes the owner himself emerged from the kitchen – a well-preserved man in his late sixties, I'd guess, shirt tucked into his trousers, a small shiny gold buckle on his belt. His hair was thick and black, combed to one side and slick with Brylcreem. I remember thinking: *His hair is younger than his face.* He stopped and stared at us for a while before smiling.

'Pa,' Jenny said, 'this is Hock Lye. The one I've told you about.'

I stood up and shook his hand.

'Hock Lye. You're Hokkien too? That's good.'

As I exchanged pleasantries with Jenny's father, I realised that the previous three months had in fact been our period of courtship – that beautiful time when young men are supposed to romance their prospective partners and future wives – yet I had done nothing of the sort. Instead I'd just drifted through our meetings without making any effort to impress her at all. Now, in a matter of minutes, we had become boyfriend–girlfriend, and it was down to her.

Mr Teoh sat down with us and chatted while we waited for our food. He'd opened the restaurant about six or seven years before, one last big venture before he retired. He'd started out as a Hokkien *mee* seller in the Old Town, just a stand in a coffee shop – sweaty, hard work, but he was young and energetic and business was good, so after a few years he was able to open his own *kopitiam* on the other side of the river, not far from the bus terminal, where he continued his noodle business but rented out three other stands too. And here's the thing – he decided to buy the lot that the coffee shop occupied, including the two storeys above, a huge investment at the time. People told him, You're crazy, you're too young, you'll go bankrupt. But he thought, What the hell, even if I go bankrupt I'll just start again, I'm only twenty-eight years old. Who'd have thought that property even in boring old Klang would increase in value so much? Business continued to be good, and when he sold up, he started not one but two new restaurants, and so on.

He was only telling me all this to share the lessons he'd learned in life. He could see that I was the sensible type and wanted to achieve success. But no doubt I'd have my own ideas, he joked. 'In the end, every man must follow his own path, yes or not?'

Of course, in the meantime he had got married to Jenny's mother, who had been a primary school teacher. His poor wife had died of cancer a few years back – she was still young, it was so unfair. Oh, he was lucky to have met her – imagine, a teacher getting married to a noodle seller! But he was clever, he had waited until he was financially secure before looking for a wife, and he was able to offer her everything she wanted. Her entire life, she didn't have to worry about food on the table or paying the electricity bill. 'Will *you* be able to provide the same for *your* wife?' he asked, smiling.

The food arrived and Mr Teoh stood up to leave. I bade him goodbye and watched him climb into a Suzuki 4x4 parked outside. Why a restaurant owner needed an off-road car like that, I didn't know. It's not as if he needed to drive across the Sahara. Maybe that's just one of those things you do when you've got money – you buy yourself things you don't need.

Unusually, that evening I found I had no appetite. 'What's wrong? Don't like the food?' Jenny asked.

'No no, it's nice.' I helped myself to more even though I didn't feel like it, and forced myself to eat.

'Then what?'

I shrugged. I couldn't explain it. 'Nyonya food is a bit too rich for my liking.'

She laughed and ruffled my hair. 'You have such country-boy tastebuds!'

When we got married four months later, we moved into a small house in Taman Sentosa, just next to the Klang Bypass highway – a single-storey link-house with a cement yard out the front, almost identical to the one we're sitting in now. You know the type, you see them all over the country on the outskirts of towns – rows and rows of them, street after street, mile after mile. East coast, west coast, north, south, everywhere the same. You could kidnap me from this house right here, blindfold me, dump me in a house in Muar, and I'd wake up in the middle of the night to take a leak and still be able to find the toilet. The second bedroom wasn't big enough to fit anything more than a child's bed, so we used it as a store room. Jenny wasn't ready to have a baby, and neither was I. The way things turned out, thank goodness we didn't – that's what you're thinking, and I don't blame you.

Sometimes, when I was in prison, the image of that tiny room crammed full of boxes and piles of folded clothes came to mind. I imagined clearing out all the junk, bit by bit, until the room was empty. Then I'd paint the walls white and add colourful stencils. A rainbow. The sun and the moon. Some stars. I imagined carrying a baby's cot into the room with Jenny and placing it carefully away from the window. Once I'd gone through all these steps in my head, I'd think: It's just as well we never had a baby.

When I was about fourteen or fifteen, I accompanied my mother to Klang on one of her visits to the hospital, and I remember gazing out of the window of the bus as we travelled down that long stretch of road that led into town, flanked for miles by housing estates that had just been built, and I knew – with the kind of certainty that only a child can possess – that when I was an adult, that was where I wanted to live. I'd thought for years that it was just a fantasy, but as I arranged a loan from Mr Lai and another one from the bank, I told myself that there was no longer any need to doubt those childhood longings. As an adult, I knew it wasn't anything fancy, but I also knew it was a decent way to start my married life.

Almost as soon as we moved in, however, I realised just how much a person changes in fifteen years. Maybe it's just living in this country that does this to you – maybe in Canada or Japan or Texas or places like that, where life doesn't change so fast, people are different. My aspirations had changed – they had swelled without me even knowing, and were too big for that little house, which was already fifteen, twenty years old. All along the main road, from town to Meru, new housing estates were being built on every spare plot of land, and we could see them from our house, take in all the details of their construction as we drove past. I was embarrassed, almost ashamed, by our

115

house – a pain exacerbated by Jenny's pretence of hating the new houses we were forced to look at every day. 'Those gardens are too big,' she'd say. 'The people are going to have problems keeping them tidy.' Or, 'The second storey looks too small for a house that size – the shape is all funny.' Or, 'The fences are too low, I'd be worried about security if I was in their shoes.' Almost every time we drove past a construction site she would find something negative to say about those expensive new houses, as if she would hate to live in any of them – as if ours was the most wonderful dwelling place in the area.

Things were continuing to go well for me at the farm, and I knew that if I just kept my head down, we'd be OK. At the back of my mind I had Jenny's father's story of humble beginnings turning into a prosperous existence. Imagining simply waking up one day and owning a business – his progression seemed so natural that I thought it would just happen to me too. To *us*. I was twenty-eight years old, Jenny thirty-one; time was on our side. All we had to do was keep working, and in a few years' time we'd have more money and a bigger house, and then we could start thinking about having children.

I was working longer and longer hours, and sometimes at weekends, in the hope that Mr Lai would reward me with some extra cash at Chinese New Year – which he did: half a month's salary in fifty-ringgit notes. I wanted a pay rise too, and he kept promising he would do something. 'Ah Hock, if anyone deserves a pay rise it's you,' he'd say from time to time, and I would just shrug my shoulders and carry on with my work, trying to hide the fact that I was excited. But each month I'd check my pay and find that it was still the same. Once he arrived at the farm very late in the day, about 6 p.m., having just driven all the way from Johor, where he'd been trying to raise some business. From the generator block I watched him get out of his car and walk slowly to the office, and when I went in there a little later he was slumped over the table, half-asleep. Without looking up he said, 'I'm too old for this. You're young – I should give you half the business.'

I was so excited that my journey home that night seemed to take twice as long as usual – I couldn't wait to get back to tell Jenny what Mr Lai had said. She'd bought some Cantonese fried noodles on the way home from work and was tipping them out from a plastic bag onto a large dish – we were eating a lot of takeouts at the time, usually quite late, after we got back from work. I said, 'My boss is going to pass half his business to me.' By then she was shaking some chopped green chillies from a sachet into a plastic dish, and didn't seem bothered by what I'd said. She just breathed out – a kind of a laugh – and said, 'Let's wait and see.' I wanted to shout, *Can't you see? I'm going to own half of a huge fish farm one day! I'll be a genuine, real-life tycoon!* But I let it pass, allowing her caution and doubt to hang heavy in our little house until they became real.

Thundery without rain. Know what that means? One of the few elegant idioms I remember from school. Means 'empty promises'. That's exactly what they were. Who knows, maybe one day when he was seventy and I was fifty, Mr Lai might have given me half of the business as he had said, but that first mention of it turned out to be the last. After that, zero. Maybe he changed his mind, but he didn't even talk about a pay rise as a kind of compensation. I didn't have the guts to bring it up with him. How could I do it? It wasn't my place to ask – *paiseh*, isn't it? I've always been too shy to make a fuss. I was lucky to have a steady job with steady pay. No qualifications, no college diploma, nothing. I couldn't complain.

Jenny started working overtime three, four times a week.

'You don't have to,' I told her. 'I can manage.' We were OK, never late with bills, had enough food to eat. I thought we were doing fine.

'Those loans you took out – we're paying too much,' she said. She didn't feel comfortable with debt, she wanted to be saving money, to start thinking about having a child. I'd come home late and find her sitting at the dining table with her calculator and a mass of bills and bank statements spread out in front of her. In the harsh white light of the fluorescent tube overhead she looked like a ghost that might vanish at any moment. She'd lost weight recently, and her skin was drawn. Sometimes she'd be sitting in front of the computer, playing Tetris, or looking at news of celebrities from Hong Kong, and wouldn't acknowledge me when I walked in. I wanted to hug her, or stand behind her and massage her shoulders while I joked about Andy Lau's perfect face being the result of plastic surgery, and kiss the top of her head. But she wouldn't even turn to look at me, and in the moment of hesitation an invisible curtain fell between us, a small separation, and I'd suddenly be afraid to touch her in case she felt it was inappropriate, given how hard she'd worked all day. I know it sounds stupid – we were husband and wife, weren't we? But I became aware of a space that belonged only to *her* and not *us*, and I didn't want to intrude into it.

I thought: It's the house, this damn old house, starting to disintegrate in ways that other people would probably say were minor, of no importance – but add all those small things up and they start to weigh down on you until you're powerless. Yes, each little problem was fixable, but together they were overwhelming us. A broken pane in the window (*Never mind, you can still close it*). A section of the metal grille on the front door rusting away and crumbling, actually falling off before our eyes (*Don't worry, only a cat or a*

118

small dog could get in, not even a child robber could squeeze through that). The cracked cistern, the leaky toilet that dripped all night (*Can still flush, can't it?*).

One evening I arrived home and kissed Jenny lightly on the cheek. She was lying on the sofa leafing through *Her World* magazine, half asleep. The TV was on, an old martial arts movie playing, but the volume was turned nearly all the way down, so all I could hear was the short clashing noise of punches and crossed swords. I went to take a shower and noticed a bad smell, which increased to a stench when I opened the bathroom door. The toilet had broken some weeks ago, and wouldn't flush properly. We'd put a plastic pail in the bathroom, half-filled with water, to pour into the toilet after we'd used it, and sometimes it worked well, other times less so. I lifted the seat and saw that the toilet was filled with shit. Light brown, almost yellow, foamy. Flecks of it all over the bowl. I didn't know if the disgust I felt – the bitter nausea that swelled up inside me, rising into my throat – I didn't know if it was because of the smell or the sudden sadness I felt, a kind of helplessness standing in front of that pile of excrement. Jenny must have had diarrhoea. Maybe she'd had it all day, and hadn't told me. How could she? She'd been at work, and so had I; we didn't have time to speak to each other. I sluiced the mess away with the water from the bucket and filled it again. Four, five times, and still the water in the toilet was dirty. I tried to fix the flush but it was hopeless – something in the mechanism was broken beyond repair.

I went back to the living room and held Jenny tightly. She put her arms around me lightly, but it didn't feel like an embrace – her body was heavy, almost lifeless. She'd had stomach cramps towards the end of her day at work, she told me, and she'd rushed home just in time, before the worst of it started. She'd been vomiting, had thrown

119

up at least five, six times, and then the diarrhoea began. She was so thirsty, her throat burned and her mouth stank from the acid in her stomach that she could taste on her tongue, but she couldn't even hold down a glass of water. Every time she drank a few mouthfuls she would throw it all up again. After a few hours, she didn't even have enough strength to fill the bucket and wash away the worst of the filth.

The toilet was broken already, it's not your fault, I said. But she just pulled away from me and went to bed.

I sat in the dark watching the near-silent *wuxia* movie. A woman fighting two men and a woman, three against one. She used one weapon after another, battling away until it broke – the eighteen forms of Chinese combat. A thought formed in my head: Maybe it *was* Jenny's fault. If she hadn't got diarrhoea we wouldn't be sleeping next to a bathroom that smelled of shit. We wouldn't have to be reminded of a broken toilet, a broken house. *But it's not her fault, it's not her fault*, I kept repeating to myself. *Shit happens*. Isn't that what people say in America? Shit happens shit happens shit happens. I whispered the expression to myself, quietly. It was not her fault.

The next day I picked up a leaflet from the UOB Bank branch down the road, about low-interest home loans. I announced, 'Next year we're moving house.' Jenny was watching *Akademi Fantasia* on TV while eating pumpkin seeds, cracking them open carefully with her teeth with barely a sound as she stared at a cute Malay girl singing a romantic song.

'Shh. It's Whitney Houston,' she said.

'We should get a new place. Somewhere better.'

Still she didn't look at me. She laughed, but I didn't know if she was laughing at the singing or at me.

A few weeks later she quit her job to start a new line

of work: 'MLM'. She explained it to me three, four times, but in the end we both knew that I wouldn't be able to understand exactly how it worked. *Multi-Level Marketing.* That didn't sound like a proper job to me. 'Are you sure it's OK?' I asked.

She snorted. 'Huh. You men. What kind of question is that? You work on a farm where you don't even wear shoes, but still dare to look down on my work? Always putting me down.'

'I'm sorry, I didn't mean that. I just want to be sure. To be safe. Just in case.'

'In case what? In case I earn so much money I make you feel inadequate?'

I hugged her and told her I hoped her work would be a great success, that she would make a fortune and be able to keep me like a gigolo. She pushed me away gently. '*Gigolo*?' she laughed. 'You don't have the looks.'

I asked her to explain. Again. I wanted to understand. She sat me down in front of the papers and flow charts she'd laid out on the table and spoke slowly. 'It's a big American company,' she said, pointing to a photo of a sprawling complex of buildings with snow-topped mountains in the background. 'You think they're going to cheat me?' she laughed. 'This isn't some lousy local business that's going to rip you off at any time.' She read from the brochure: '*Skin-Glo. Founded in 1983 in Colorado. Annual turnover, US$1.1 billion.*' There was a diagram in the shape of a pyramid. 'Right now I'm down here, but all I have to do is recruit a few people and I'll move up one step, then another, then one day' – she traced her finger all the way to the apex of the pyramid – 'that will be me.'

'Soon, right?'

'Maybe. Probably. Ten years. Our children will grow up as rich people.'

She opened a box of creams and lotions of various sizes – beauty products that achieved amazing results. 'This one firms your neckline.' She dabbed a little marble of cream on her skin and began to rub it in. 'You see? You apply it like this, it's a special cream that requires a special technique.'

'If I were a customer I'd buy a whole box from you right now.' It was true. She was so convincing I felt that even I could improve my looks just by buying her Skin-Glo products.

The next few weeks it was as if we were newlyweds again, living a life that was full of promise. I even took a day off work to fix things around the house – the broken cistern, the loose tiles in the kitchen, the cracked window pane. I bought a new Panasonic water boiler so Jenny could have fresh-brewed tea all day while she worked from home. Often, if I came home early, she would be explaining how Skin-Glo products worked to other people – ex-colleagues of hers from the super-market distribution company, or neighbours I recognised but had never taken the time to say hello to. I realised that we'd all been living completely separate lives, each family tucked away in their little two-bedroomed single-storey house, linked to each other by walls less than a foot thick, yet also divided by that same thin layer of brick and cement. All of us just trying to get on with the day-to-day of our lives. And now we were together, in my house, with Jenny serving cups of tea, laughing, as though this was the life we had always been destined to have, filled with people who could become friends. Teenagers just about to start college, old retired uncles and aunties, professional-looking men and women of our age – they all sat at the table and dabbed creams onto their cheeks. Their eyelids would flutter lightly as they waited for Jenny to spray a fine mist onto their faces. 'Wait for it, relax,' she said – '*It'll feel as light as mountain dew!*' I loved that expression, even after I'd heard it twenty times. I loved the little sigh of pleasure or the giggle that followed the quick *shh* of the spray.

She recruited ten, fifteen, eventually twenty-eight people – all of them friends now as well as business partners of sorts. I looked at them when I came back from work on the farm – watched them sitting in the bright glow of the fluorescent light above the dining table, making jokes I didn't quite understand, constructing a glorious world of promise around them. They'd fill in forms, and I'd imagine those pieces of paper making their way across the Pacific Ocean, over mountains, all the way to Colorado. Sometimes I'd think: I don't even know twenty-eight people in the entire world. One day I found a smartly-dressed woman, barely older than me, sitting in our house, sipping coffee from a Starbucks cup. She sat with her back perfectly straight, perched lightly on the edge of the armchair as if reluctant to come into contact with it. She'd driven down from KL and was one of the company's star salespeople, who'd come to congratulate Jenny for all the people she'd recruited (thirty-three and counting).

'Why does she care how many you recruit?' I said when she'd gone.

'My recruits become her recruits. Of course she cares.'

'What? So *you* recruit for *her*? *She* gets the money?'

'That's how it works,' Jenny said as she turned on the TV. 'If my recruits hire more people, they become mine.'

'And then they all belong to that woman?'

Jenny laughed at something on the TV – a game show with people hitting each other with bouncy-foam sausages. 'She has *thirteen thousand* salespeople below her.' As if that explained everything.

I couldn't stand the idea of a woman in KL making so much money from all the time Jenny was spending with people she barely knew – all the nights that we could and should have been going out to the movies, driving to dinner at a seafood place on the coast. All the things we'd once shared, not so long ago. But I said nothing, I didn't understand the way these things worked. *Shit happens*. The words came to me, forming in my head like thunderclouds, and I tried to stifle them quickly. Everything would work out.

From time to time Jenny would show me a text message from the woman in KL, a line of encouragement. *The only person who can stop you is YOU. Go for it! Jia you!* Sometimes she'd show me a photo of the woman posing in various locations – Hong Kong airport, Vancouver airport, in front of Big Ben in London, the Eiffel Tower in Paris, and other places I'd never heard of. Jenny had bought a new phone, a Samsung, one of the first that could receive photos, a square blur of colour that didn't mean anything to me. At home she started following this woman – who she called her 'mentor' – on the internet, and spent long hours staring at the computer screen, scrolling through pages of photos of things that seemed unconnected, to me at least. Cars. Beauty salons. Fast trains in Japan. A hot-air balloon over African plains. A gym in Los Angeles. When I asked about them she replied, 'It's work.'

I'd come home in the evening and she'd be in front of the computer, so I'd eat dinner on my own, quickly, trying to avoid the feeling of being cut off from her even in our own house. We went to bed at separate hours, woke up at different times. I barely even noticed that she was receiving fewer and fewer new business contacts, or that the boxes of Skin-Glo products stacked up along the wall remained unopened. I asked her once how it was going, whether she'd made a lot of recruits recently, and she started shouting at me. Why was I always trying to criticise her? Why couldn't I understand anything? Why was I so ignorant and low-class? Why couldn't I get some education so that I could figure out complicated things in life?

It was true, I didn't understand complex arrangements for business, I couldn't figure out how Jenny's line of work was profitable. But there were more straightforward things I could work out. I asked Mr Lai for a loan, and added the money to my savings, which made me appear better-off than I actually was, so the bank lent me more money to buy a new house in Taman Bestari – three bedrooms, a garden at the front and a small concrete yard at the back, in an area that had only been developed a few months previously. No one had lived in it before, and it gave me a sense of freedom: in the space and light of this new house I was going to become someone different – someone better. The smell of glue and paint and cement, the powdery feel of concrete dust that covered every surface – all that seemed thrilling, but also reassuring, as though the place had always been destined to be mine. Someone had built this house just for us.

For a while I thought the house had saved us. Jenny used one of the bedrooms as an office, her computer set up on a desk on one side of the room, the screen always on, flickering and colourful even late at night as I walked past the door just before bedtime. She started inviting people over to the house for Skin-Glo meetings once more.

We carried on this way, each of us working at our jobs, our separate lives, until it all seemed normal, not even worthy of comment – by me or by her.

And then Keong rang me at the farm and came back into my life.

I recognise the tune she's humming, but I can't remember where it's from. Just a few notes, repeated on and off throughout the morning, whenever we take a break.

What's that song?

Huh? Oh. She laughs. It's nothing. An advert on TV, I think.

You had a good week?

I guess so. Actually, yes.

She looks at her papers and puts the phone down, ready to record our conversation, but she doesn't press the bright red button to start the way she usually does. Maybe I should ask her more questions, but I remember what she's always saying: We're here for *your* story.

What have you been up to? I ask after a long pause.

Oh, this and that. I mean, it's been very busy. Lots going on.

Like what?

I went on the Bersih march. You know, the anti-corruption demonstration. Felt I needed to be in the streets, physically protesting against the government and not just observing and writing.

Sure, I saw it on Facebook.

It was such an incredible atmosphere. So many people on the streets. Tens and tens of thousands. Maybe even a hundred thousand. I was standing on the overhead bridge outside Masjid Jamek and I couldn't see a single square foot of empty road. Every street was crammed full of protestors. I've never felt such excitement in my life. It was as though people were breathing each other's optimism. There was anger too, don't get me wrong. But it all mixed into a weird kind of energy, as if the air in KL was carrying an electrical charge, like it does during a lightning storm, when everything feels dangerous and unstable, but also, I don't know, alive with the possibility of change. It felt as if every political structure in the country, every outmoded social custom, can be torn down, and that was like, wow, scary, but also just so damn exhilarating. Every so often there'd be a small cheer, some people making a rallying cry, and then their voices would gather more voices around them, and more and more, and you'd hear this wave of voices swelling and growing, moving through the crowd, just like an angry sea. A tsunami. People would start chanting around me, and I'd join them without even thinking. Late in the afternoon, standing in the crowd in front of Public Bank, I've never had such an extraordinary feeling of belonging to something bigger than just myself or my family. Something that stood for change. For the betterment of society.

Were the police there?

Of course. Dozens and dozens, everywhere. Armed policemen, and drones overhead taking pictures. And some pro-government supporters too, trying to intimidate us.

You weren't scared? I mean, you're young.

You mean, was I scared because I'm a woman? Of course not! At least half the people there were women. There were entire women's groups out there, all kinds of people. Old, young, rich, poor. I was next to a group of old Chinese aunties from Kepong. They were all wearing baseball caps, and when the police drones flew overhead they said, Hey miss, hide your face! And they all pulled cloths over their mouths and noses. They knew the drones were taking photos. They were carrying backpacks with little bottles of water, in case of tear gas. They'd been there before. It was amazing.

You're very brave.

It's got nothing to do with bravery. It's about changing our country. Making the world a better place for everyone, regardless of race or religion.

You make it sound like a big party. I wish I could have been there. But my legs, my body . . . I don't know if I could have made it through the day.

It was a fight, not a party. We're all fighting, remember. For something better.

You really think things will change?

Of course. Why else would I have gone?

Sometimes we act because we have no choice. Especially nowadays.

Hmmm. She nods and tilts her head, as if she's about to disagree with what I said, only she doesn't. Well, she says. Let's see what happens. Politics is crazy right now, anything can happen. Even me and my friends, we argue about stuff all the time. I had some people over for a housewarming party the other night, we just sat among all the boxes and ate pizza, drank wine. And guess what? People started arguing! I guess we were all still pumped up about the demonstrations. Someone said something, someone else took offence. It was nuts. We're all supposed to be friends.

You moved house?

Yeah. Crazy time to move, huh? It was time, though.

Time for what?

She pauses, and her smile tightens. I get the feeling I've asked her too much, and now she feels that she's said too much, that she shouldn't be telling me things about herself. Maybe she's afraid of telling me where she lives, what her family does.

Time to make a commitment, she says at last. I thought, well, it's as good a time as any to move in with my, my partner. She hesitates, as if she's searching for the right word. *Airen*. My sweetheart. We've been seeing each other for a while now, and it gets to the point where you either commit or separate. So, we committed!

Congratulations, I'm happy for you.

Thank you. It's only been a few days, but I'm enjoying the experience so far.

When are you getting married?

You must be joking! It's too early for that. Anyway, I don't believe that two people need to marry in order to live together.

Don't talk nonsense, of course you do. Besides, if your *airen* doesn't marry you, another man will steal you away sooner or later.

Actually, she says. She holds my eye without blinking. Actually, my partner is a woman.

Oh. A woman.

Yes.

I'm sorry. I didn't know.

She laughs and opens her folder, leaning forward to check her phone. It's absolutely fine. But in the future, it might be better not to make assumptions about people's sexuality based on traditional gender lines.

I nod. I'm really sorry.

Oh, it's fine. Now, shall we begin?

I had never seen the other man before that night. He wasn't one of the migrants who drifted in from the plantations seeking work along the coast. You saw them often, skinny red-eyed Bangladeshis with patches of skin on their arms and faces rubbed raw from all the pesticides they sprayed. Always on the move. Always giving the impression they were in search of something, yet always slow in their movements, as if the air around them had turned to water and they were wading through the world. Swim-walking. The oxygen sucked out of their world so they were forever in motion, but never making progress.

That man, the one who waited for Keong and me on the riverbank that night, he didn't have the same restlessness as the others. He was Bangladeshi too. You already know that, you've read the court documents, done your research – but that's all you've got. Where he came from, maybe his name, age – nothing else. You might have seen a photo, the one he used on his identity card, the same one that supplied you his name. *Mohammad Ashadul*. I heard that name only once, in court. I'm surprised I remember it. The rest of the time he was referred to only as *the victim*, or *the deceased*, in public and in private. My lawyer, the prosecutors – they never used his name, so I'm not sure why I remember it.

Nowadays I'll often come across news reports on Facebook about men and women who die the way he did,

130

and always they're just called 'a 33-year-old Bangladeshi man', or 'a 28-year-old Myanmar national', or 'a 40-year-old Indonesian female'. Maybe that's why the man's name lodged in my head – because all the time I spent hearing him being discussed in front of me, I remembered the way he stood, his feet planted widely apart so that he seemed solid and unmoving, unlike the other foreign workers. Rooted to the earth, that's how he seemed. As much a part of the landscape as the trees around us. He wasn't going anywhere. The sharp smile on his face. His watch that glinted in the dark. The way he addressed me as *brother* – the single English word that popped up amid his broken Malay. The surprising warmth of his laughter.

These are details about the man that you cannot possibly know. You, the police, the lawyers, the judge, the jury – no one knew, and no one asked. But I knew. And that's why his name has stuck in my memory all these years, because I thought: My friend, you and I, we're pretty similar after all. Your name has been forgotten, just as mine will be very soon. I, at least, have existed for a brief moment, a few days when my name has been hauled from the shadows and repeated in public, but in less than a week I'll disappear too. I'll have a prison number, and the photo they'll take of me will make me look just like any other small-time Chinese gangster, a *dim sum* waiter who made a couple of bad choices. There are lots of us. I know that from the time I've already spent in the lock-up. My name will become irrelevant, just as it was before the trial, before the killing, and I will vanish, just like you.

Mohammad Ashadul. Who knows if that was his real name? Who knows if his identity card was genuine? It probably wasn't, because that was his line of work, faking ICs and passports. If you can print fifty counterfeit cards a day, you can print one for yourself, that's for sure. You

131

can say anything you want on the card. You can add the right digits to your IC number so that when the police stop you and check your details, you have a convincing explanation for your accent, your limited Malay vocabulary. I saw them all the time at the farm – 61, 62, 64, 68, 79. Especially 61 and 79. Indonesia and Bangladesh. You see those numbers, you know where the person was born. We're not talking about those flimsy temporary foreign worker cards that migrants are supposed to have – those are worthless. No one needs them. What I'm talking about is fake ICs that look exactly like the genuine ones you and I have. Pay the right guy enough money and you can get one. Or maybe you've married a local girl and got yourself an IC. Who knows. All I know was that guy was in the business of running cards, and in the days leading up to that evening, I never heard a single person refer to him by the name I heard in court. *Mr B*, *Bobby*, *the boss* – that was what people called him. Keong called him *sei hak gwai*. If you understand Cantonese you can translate that your-self. It was hard to know who Keong was talking about, because he often called dark-skinned people that name. That was what he was like. [*Shakes his head; laughs.*] Or maybe Mohammad Ashadul *was* his real name. All I'm saying is that you can't trust what you read on a piece of paper.

That was why we were going to see him – to sort out some paperwork. That's what Keong said. He laughed when he said it. 'It's like office work. I just need to sort out some problems.'

'What kind of problems?'

He laughed.

Even at that point, when I knew why Keong had come back to Klang, I didn't think things would turn out the way they did. He arrived in town about three months before that evening. He'd sent a few texts after he rang me at the farm – cheerful notes just to say *Hi, what're you doing today. Damn I can't wait to finish work and go home. Screw it the rain is just too bad today.* The type of message you send your best friend, someone you see every other day, who knows the pattern of your days and understands how you might feel early in the morning, or after a long day – not someone you haven't seen in years, someone with whom you've had no contact at all, with whom you share nothing apart from a couple of teenage years, when you were no longer boys but not yet men. When you didn't really know who you were, and were trying to figure out how to live. In the span of someone's entire life, that period amounts to little more than a few heartbeats – a time that means nothing. *Weather today reminds me of being back in our village.* Whenever I got a text like that from Keong, I thought, You kidding? Surely that time of your life doesn't mean anything to you now. He'd only spent a year and a half there. Now he was thirty-two years old, but still referring to things that happened half his lifetime before.

I didn't know how to reply to the messages. A guy like Keong turns up after nearly a decade's silence, what am I supposed to feel? I should have been happy, I guess, or at least relieved to know that he was safe and healthy. When someone disappears like that, as Keong had all those years before, it's only natural to be concerned. But instead I felt a numbness that spread through my thoughts and even the muscles in my body, as if I'd been bitten by a sea snake. Back in the village, people often got into trouble with snakes. They get tangled up in the nets, and when you try to free them, sometimes you get bitten. Unlike with land snakes or stone fish or urchins, a sea snake's bite doesn't swell up. No agonising pain, almost nothing at all to begin with. But later your head starts to ache, you feel your throat tightening, your breathing slowing down, your muscles refusing to obey your commands – a paralysis that overcomes you so slowly you barely realise it's happening. I saw this happening to people from the village, watched them succumb slowly to the venom as they were taken to the hospital – it looked as though their bodies were turning against themselves.

Once I got bitten myself – a flash of black and white stripes striking out from the mass of writhing silver fish; the dull ache spreading from my leg to the rest of me; the world turning into a place I couldn't control. And then – after a few minutes, half an hour, who knows? I really can't remember – it was over. It turned out that the snake hadn't released any venom. I'd been lucky. Who knows why that particular snake chose not to poison me that day. But my body had prepared itself for the shock, and started to sink into that unfeeling, unthinking state in order to protect itself. The body learns from what it observes. It remembers. It anticipates.

When I answered the phone that first day when Keong rang the farm, I just stood there saying nothing, just listening to his voice, as energetic and cigarette-rough as it had always been. I was remembering what it was like to be with him, and maybe I was already defending myself. My body knew how to produce sounds: *Yes, en, really, ya see you soon*. I thought he'd understand that I wasn't keen on seeing him again, that my lack of joy would mean something to him – but he didn't. I'd never been one to say much, and he probably thought I hadn't changed at all.

As that strange dull fatigue took hold of me, I thought of Jenny. I thought of her sitting at the computer in our new house, sending emails to customers, making calls to people across the country, all the way to Sabah, even

Singapore. Behind her, the sofa still covered in plastic to protect it from the last of the dust left behind from the construction work. The pure white walls, slightly chalky to the touch. The faint smell of paint and glue that we both found intoxicating. The sheen of the terrazzo floors. The certainty of things. We'd sometimes plug in our mobile phones to charge them even when we didn't really need to, and we'd joke that we missed trying to guess whether the socket would work, as we had done in our previous house, or whether the fusebox would trip when we turned the switch on. I'd turn on the lights in the kitchen and still be amazed that the bulbs underneath the cupboards on the wall glowed gently, just like the small glass dome on the ceiling. Jenny would laugh and say that I preferred the harsh light of the fluorescent strips that we had in the old house, that I couldn't see things clearly without that kind of low-class lighting. In the evenings, just before going upstairs to bed, I'd see her in front of the TV with a cup of *leung cha*, or spooning some *gui ling gou* out of a jar she'd bought at her favourite place in Jusco Mall. She seemed so settled in that spot that I never thought of asking her to join me in bed so we might fall asleep together, or make love, or talk – none of those things was more important to her than her place on that sofa. To disturb her space would be to destroy everything, for her and for us. Our house was new, it would last many years, maybe a lifetime, and in it we had found – quickly, so quickly – a way to live that would not be troubled by anything.

During that first phone call, Keong asked for my mobile number, and I gave it to him, not thinking that he'd ever use it. And if he did, I could simply not respond. That was what happened for two, maybe three weeks – every time I received one of his chatty meaningless texts I'd just delete it. But still, I'd feel the numbness start to creep into my body whenever I saw his number pop up on the screen of my phone. When the texts started to arrive more or less daily, I'd feel a kind of ache in my stomach every time I reached for my phone, wondering if I'd find a message from him. I knew I'd soon have to decide what to do. Ask him politely to go away. Tell him to fuck off. Meet him and have a Kopi-O and a stilted conversation so both of us could see once and for all that we had nothing in common – that I'd changed, that I was a different person. Tell him that my wife didn't like me getting texts from people she didn't know. Change my number. Take some of the boys from work to meet him and beat him up. Kick him until he was black and blue and half-conscious, just as I'd seen him doing to others when we were young. The options ran through my mind constantly, until I couldn't concentrate on anything else. '*Wai*, people are talking to you, dickhead!' Mr Lai shouted one day at work. 'Anyone at home there?' I'd been looking at him, nodding, but in fact I was thinking of my phone, clipped to my belt. It had just beeped twice, indicating a new text message.

What do you think I did? Of all the solutions available to me – some good, some bad, some complicated, others simple – I chose the worst. But when you have to make a decision like that, sometimes the most rotten choice, the one that everyone else knows will lead to disaster – that path seems the most sensible to you. Or maybe it only seems that way because you don't actually have a choice. Perhaps there's only one true way forward. All the others are false paths, illusions that exist only to give you the impression of freedom of choice. No one can alter the course of things. Your karma is set, it determines everything. I'd never believed in anything like that before – all the temples and prayers and amulets in my childhood, they proved nothing to me. But when I was in prison a few months later, I began to realise that it was all true. The joss-sticks and the offerings to the gods were a recognition of life's inevitability. Those attempts to appease the gods were our way of acknowledging our helplessness. We were trying to soften the rougher edges of our fate, but really we knew that nothing would truly change. If your boat was going to capsize, it was going to capsize. Your death in the storm was predetermined. God wanted it to be so. You could have stayed home that day, but you decided to go to sea, because it was the only thing you could do. Likewise, when I rang Keong, the choice had already been made for me.

Of course, that wasn't what went through my head the day I decided to meet him. My thinking was simple. I'd meet him out of respect for an old friendship. Village ties. The spirit of clans. It wasn't so much that I had to give him face, it was because I had to respect customs. Someone from your old village resurfaces in your life, you treat them to dinner. I guess I'm very traditional in that respect. I don't know what it's like to turn my back on someone from my past, who knew my mother, whose mother fed me when I was hungry. No matter how difficult the experience of meeting Keong might be, I would do what was expected of me by suggesting that we meet, and he would recognise that I was merely fulfilling an obligation. We'd chat about life, quickly run out of things to say, and finally try to end our meeting as soon as possible.

More importantly, he would realise that I had changed, was no longer the person he knew, and maybe when he heard about my achievements since we last met on the streets of Puchong, he'd feel chastened, embarrassed by his own lack of success. He'd think, Why am I still scratching around in the dirt like a skinny chicken looking for worms, when I could be a cow eating grass like Ah Hock? Our

137

meeting would be an awkward experience for him, even more than it was for me, and he would be the one to say, It's getting late, I have to go now. And he'd never contact me again. He'd see that the brief bond we'd shared in our teenage years and early adulthood amounted to nothing, that we were different people now, worlds apart.

That was the choice I made.

We met at Ah Chan's on Jalan Meru, a place I often used to stop at for dinner on my own before heading home, especially when I knew Jenny was having people over for one of her work gatherings, when they'd try out the latest products that had arrived from America, and discuss the various strategies they'd employ to sell them. They'd started to drink wine with the snacks they ate while they were chatting, and sometimes when I arrived home the house would be filled with voices as bright and clear as the clinking of their glasses. They'd smile at me as I walked in, and Jenny would wave from across the room, but their conversation would barely pause. I felt as if my presence was an intrusion, and it was safer to keep out of their world.

Ah Chan's place was set back from the main road into town, and although it was covered with a zinc roof it had no walls, so the rush of traffic was always present – a constant dull river of sound that I found comforting after a day at the farm, with its unsettling noises. The bark of men's voices, shouting, always shouting. The grinding of machinery. Even water, when it crashed down onto the planks of wood, had a jagged quality to it.

Ah Chan herself – in her sixties, with long, neat pure-silver hair – never spoke loudly. She talked to everyone – whether to me or the other customers or Hayati, the Indonesian helper who'd been with her for twenty years – in little more than a murmur. She and Hayati had got to know me over time, and I liked chatting to them. Hayati even spoke some Hokkien from working with Ah Chan. Can you believe that? We'd make jokes in our dialect that you wouldn't be able to understand. Sometimes, if it was raining hard and there were no other customers, they'd sit with me, drinking tea while I ate my *bak kut teh*. They asked about Jenny as if they knew her – how was her business, was she was eating well – but in fact Jenny had never been there, not even once. They'd tell me about their lives – back then Ah Chan was worried about her son in KL, who'd just lost his job because his factory was closing down and moving operations to Suzhou in China. She was hoping he'd move back to be close to her in Klang, but suspected that he'd leave the country altogether and look for work in China or Australia. He wanted to be successful, he told her, he didn't want to work in a factory any more. And Hayati, who'd just got divorced but was happier than she'd ever been. Dumped her cheating asshole husband in Bandung when she'd last gone home and found out that he was having an affair with another woman. Living in a house that they'd built with Hayati's money – all the cash she earned working a thousand miles from home. What do you expect, he'd said. You're away for so long, what am I supposed to do? I expect you to get out of my life and never come back, she replied. Now she had her entire month's salary to herself, didn't have to send anything back to that bastard. She could spend it how she wanted. Men, she said. No point relying on them – in this life, you gotta do everything yourself.

'You sure you don't want to find another one?' I sometimes asked. 'Now that you're single again.'

'Find me a man who's not a liar and a cheat and I'll marry him straight away!'

A few times, when it was clear that no one else would be turning up because of the bad weather, they'd close early. They'd leave me a couple of portions of leftover soup to take back to Jenny, and turn off all the lights before making their way home. But I'd sit there in the half-dark for a while longer, listening to the drumming of the rain on the roof that drowned out the noise of the traffic. The headlamps of the cars sparkling in gloom and mist, the water coursing along the open drains nearby. I'd feel like staying there all night.

Recently, just a few months ago, I went back to Ah Chan's after many years, and only Hayati recognised me. Ah Chan did not. 'Auntie! It's me, Auntie,' I said, but she just smiled briefly before looking away. At first I thought she might be going senile. She didn't look any older, but it had been such a long time since my last visit, it wouldn't have been surprising for her to have started losing her memory. Then I thought, maybe she'd heard about what I'd done, and didn't want to talk to me. That must have been it – there was no other explanation. Hayati said, 'It's been a long time,' but she too was subdued, distracted by the bubbling pots and the other customers who were calling for her. She didn't try to exchange any words with me, didn't smile when she walked past. I thought of asking how she was, whether she'd been back to Indonesia recently, whether she'd remarried – but I didn't. Couldn't. I finished my meal and left as quickly as I could. Didn't even wait for my change. I've never gone back.

Ah Chan didn't warm to Keong when we met there that first time. He looked much the same as he had nearly a decade earlier, only even skinnier, with dark rings under his eyes, his complexion slightly grey and powdery. Cheeks sunken. The long wispy ends of his hair, both front and back, were dyed coppery orange, just as they had been all those years before. But his clothes were smarter – a proper short-sleeved shirt, open at the neck to show off a gold chain, trousers with creases pressed down the front, and black leather shoes that made a clicking sound on the concrete as he approached. I thought, Those must have cost a lot.

He was talking before he even sat down, as though he was just picking up a conversation we'd recently had somewhere else. 'Klang traffic is crazy these days, I'm so stressed. They finish the new flyover then close it again after two weeks. Fuck. Why aren't you drinking beer? Hey Auntie, give us two beers, please. Carlsberg. What the hell, this place doesn't even serve beer, meh? Fuck. Life these days – everything costs so much. Alcohol licence, health and safety licence, even soy sauce. People can't run a decent restaurant any more. Look at this place. Poor bastards. How's anyone supposed to make a living when the price of petrol goes up all the time? That's what it's all about, you know. Oil. The moment there's a war in the Middle East, the garlic gets more expensive in Sekinchan.'

Hayati brought me my usual order. 'Same for your friend?'

Keong waved her away. 'No, I don't want to eat here. I'll get something later. I just need a beer. Can't eat without beer in my stomach.' He laughed, and started playing with the piles of small plastic sauce dishes on the table, arranging them into separate stacks. 'How was your day, anyway? All OK at work?' Just the sort of question he'd have asked when we were hanging round the streets of Puchong ten years back, drifting in and out of work. A lifetime ago.

Work? I thought. You don't know what I do for work, you don't know anything about me. 'Yes, all OK.'

'That's all we can ask for in life. That things are OK.'

He talked all the time I was eating – he had an opinion on everything. Whether the government was going to rig the elections. Buddhist monks on the streets in Myanmar.

Plainclothes police at Suria KLCC Mall. The price of wheat in Australia. Whether Andy Lau was better than Louis Koo in *Protégé*. The shooting in Virginia, USA. Things I didn't know about, and wasn't interested in. I finished my meal as quickly as I could, and when I signalled to Hayati that I wanted to pay, Keong reached into his pocket and eased out a thick bunch of hundred-ringgit notes, tightly folded and held together with a rubber band. He peeled one away from the others and let it fall to the table without interrupting his constant stream of talk. I looked at the wad of cash in his hand. He wore three rings on each hand.

'Got anything smaller?' Hayati asked.

He shook his head. 'Don't worry, if you don't have change you can just pay me back later. Take a small loan.'

I stood up and gave Hayati the right amount of money. As I made to leave, Ah Chan called out to me. She was holding a bag containing some soup and a small portion of rice, neatly tied up with pink raffia string. She had her own special way of tying up those takeaway servings, a double loop that came undone with a small tug, unlike the messy knots other people did. 'For your wife,' she said. 'With extra ribs as usual.' She turned away quickly without waiting for thanks.

'Where're we going now?' Keong said.

'I'm going home,' I replied.

'Come on, brother! I only just got here, we need to catch up on old times! I know a couple of places in town, people know me, we'll get free drinks. It'll be fun. Just a couple of hours. It's not even eight o'clock yet.'

I looked at my watch. Jenny's gathering at home would most likely still be going on. I could maybe have a beer, just one, with Keong, and then he'd go away and leave me alone. I rang Jenny and heard laughter – hers and others' – Jenny saying to someone, *We already knew that, sweetheart,* followed by more laughter before she finally came on the phone. 'Hello? Umm, yes, no problem. We'll be here a bit longer, take your time.'

The line went dead before I could say, Don't worry, I won't be late.

Sometimes I wonder how the last nine or ten years would have played out if Jenny had said simply, 'You joking? Come home right now, you good-for-nothing man. Call yourself a husband!' Perhaps I would have bought the farm from Mr Lai a few years later, and although it would have been tough at first, I'd just be starting to turn a profit now, with all the investment in new machinery finally paying off – big money coming in right at this point in time. You and me sitting here, my business growing even as we spoke. You'd be interviewing me not as a forgotten criminal with a little forgotten life, but as a successful figure in society. Jenny and I would have had children, we'd have plans for them. I'd be asking your advice about how best to have them educated – in one of those fancy international schools in Kuala Lumpur that I read about, or maybe boarding school abroad. I'd ask you tons of questions about New York, whether you enjoy being there – questions about your studies, what you eat, the weather. Things that would be of interest to rich people. Just think of it – that might have been what we'd be talking about. But these matters are of no relevance to me now, and we're talking about different things – about regret. And I'm sure you're thinking: There's no point dwelling on what might have been, because this is my life, my fate.

That first night with Keong, I never thought about how things might turn out – how could I? All the days that followed, it never occurred to me that things would end so badly. Not even on the night we met Mohammad

Ashadul. Driving up to the spot near the riverbank, I still thought I was just helping out a friend who had some problems, and the sooner they were sorted out, the sooner he'd disappear from my life and things would continue as before. Even when Keong and Ashadul started to raise their voices, I never felt that my life was going to change. When Keong started jabbing his finger in Ashadul's face, I thought, It's a small fight, it's nothing. The whole scene seemed so distant from my life, or at least the one I'd built for myself in my head. The two of them standing in the near-darkness, shouting at each other. Keong moving closer to the Bangladeshi guy until he's shouting in his face. Ashadul rooted to the ground, not backing off. Feet planted, solid as a tree trunk. Taking a drag on his cigarette. When he shouts back at Keong small wisps of smoke appear in the dark like threads of silver. He looks away and spits on the ground. Keong lunges at him. Doesn't punch him, slaps him. With one hand the other guy strikes out and knocks Keong to the ground – the other hand still holds his cigarette, so delicately that he looks like an actor in a movie. Keong lies there, suddenly silent. He's been taken by surprise by the swiftness of the man's retaliation. Keong has a knife. I've seen it. A switchblade he bought in Hatyai recently, 'in case of an emergency'. But he's lying on the ground, he's fallen in an awkward position, the knife is lost in the undergrowth. The other man turns to face me. He's short, powerfully built, with a moustache that even in the dark appears neatly trimmed. He takes half a step towards me – no, actually he's steadying himself on the muddy grass. I'm on the ground too. How did this happen – why am I surrounded by a tangle of branches and leaves? He reaches into his pocket and takes out a switchblade that looks very much like Keong's. The noise the blade makes as it flicks sharply into the night is smooth, almost

144

comforting, not at all alarming. He turns to face Keong squarely. And it's in that brief pause that I notice I have a piece of wood in my hand. As I stand up I think, It feels very light.

II

NOVEMBER

My father left for Singapore when I was four years old. Of course I can't remember anything about his departure, though over the years I've convinced myself that I was witness to certain things that happened on the day he left. For example: that he left his bus ticket in the kitchen and had to rush back to get it, but when he got home my mother had already gone to work, and he had to break into the house to retrieve it. It was late at night, my mother had just started a job as a cleaner at a fish wholesaler down the road, and I'd been asleep for a few hours. When my father broke the latch on the window it disturbed the dog in the yard next door, which began to bark. It was a thin mongrel the colour of sand, old and half-blind, and maybe because it was slow and couldn't see anything it got spooked easily and barked at the slightest movement. I remember that dog well, eyes like glass marbles that seemed as though they could pop out of their sockets at any moment. I woke up and started to cry in the dark. My father came into the bedroom to comfort me, but he knew that if he picked me up and held me until I was calm again he'd miss the bus, and all his chances of decent work and money would disappear, and he'd have to go back to gutting fish at the factory on the other side of Kuala Selangor.

It was raining heavily. The sound of the rain drumming on the tin roof, normally so soothing, agitated me that night, and I sat up in bed, blinking and sobbing in the dark. Outside: the barking dog, the yard turning to mud. My father stood in the doorway, staring at me. He'd been caught in the rain; his clothes were dripping and left patches of water on the linoleum that my mother would find when she came home some hours later. He'd been in a hurry, he hadn't had time to take his shoes off, and had ended up leaving muddy tracks all over the floor. He stood watching me for a while, then left. The sound of my crying followed him out of the house, all the way into the rainstorm as he boarded the night bus headed south.

I wish I could say that I remember him standing in the doorway, or that I could hear his breathing, heavy and rushed because he'd been running. But the likelihood is that I started to cry because I had a bad dream, and only woke up for a few seconds before falling asleep again. It must have been one of those nightmares that only children have, where sleep and awakeness and dreaminess and reality get entangled before evaporating into a cloud that hangs over them for hours, so that even when they're awake, they're really still asleep, still dreaming. You and I – we don't have this muddle. Everything is distinct. Work time. Play time. Eat time. Sleep time. I don't know how this change takes place in someone's life, but it does, overnight, and they don't even know it. I'm not sure how it happened with me – I just woke up one morning and thought, *Hurry up, it's time for work now.* I was fifteen years old. And that beautiful cloudiness on waking from slumber that I remembered from my childhood, sometimes sad, sometimes comforting – it had just vanished.

The story of my father coming home in the rainstorm to retrieve his bus ticket was told and retold to me by my mother numerous times over the years, until the image of him that evening became so sharp and true that I believed I'd seen him myself. She repeated the story so often that I thought: She wants me to believe that he cared for me. I cried, he wavered. Back then we still believed that he would be coming home to us, and when he did we would have more money and life would be easier. My parents were still in contact, on a more or less regular basis. A letter would arrive from Singapore from time to time, a single sheet of thin paper with a rough edge where it had been torn from a notebook. He could at least have bought decent paper to write on. My mother would read the few lines so intently you'd think it was the *I-Ching* or some special advice sent to her by Confucius himself. Sometimes she'd read just one line aloud, slowly and seriously, like a newsreader announcing a headline. *Singapore is Very Clean.* Or, *Here, Spitting is Not Allowed.* Or, *No One Has to Pay Bribes Here.* I have no idea what else he wrote to her in those letters – everything was just condensed into those single lines, like a public-service announcement.

A few times we walked to Ah Heng's sundry store half a mile away to wait for a phone call from my father, which I guess he must have promised in a previous letter. Only the call never came. Who knows why – maybe he had to line up for too long to use the phone at the warehouse where he worked, or maybe he had to work overtime, or maybe he just forgot. How did people live without mobiles? It feels like only yesterday, but life was so different. It seems strange now to think about how much time we wasted at Ah Heng's place. Hours and hours hanging around for that call that never came.

To hide the embarrassment and pain of that fruitless waiting, my mother pretended that we'd needed to come to the shop to buy things. I'd sit on the sacks of rice, filling the time by memorising the way the various things were arranged on the shelves, then closing my eyes and reciting them until I got the order right. *Mumm 21. Shelltox. Maggi*

151

Mee Perencah Kari. There was never very much stock, and what there was never changed position – biscuits, nappies, flour. Everything stayed where it was, covered in a thin film of dust. If I close my eyes now I can see every single object on those metal shelves, and I bet if you went there tomorrow, they'd still all be there, arranged in exactly the order I've told you.

My mother would chat to Ah Heng about all sorts of things, giving him news about my father, which wasn't actually news because it was the same set of things repeated every time: he had a new job, he was sending money home, he would come back soon and we would either build ourselves a new house somewhere in the Sekinchan area or move to Klang. Either way, we would stop living in that house – half-wood, half-cement – because the wood was rotting and my mother was tired of patching up the gaps between the planks with pieces of biscuit tins that she flattened out with a hammer. She spent a lot of time doing this, but new holes were always appearing – spots of white light, brilliant as stars. She couldn't keep up with them; nature was stronger than she was. We had to move. I would need my own room, I couldn't go on sharing with my parents. With my *father-mother*. She spoke as if we were a family, a normal, proper family, because that's what we were in her head and in mine, and probably in Ah Heng's and everyone else's too. When she talked about the life we were going to have, it all made sense. It seemed connected to where I was, sitting on the sacks of rice; it was part of the same story, a story of waiting, of waiting for things to get better, because they would. We all thought we knew how the story would turn out, because why would it turn out any other way? My father was in Singapore, he was earning a decent wage in a warehouse in a country that had rules about employment, where he got paid in full on the same day each month – a detail that seems small and irrelevant as I talk about it now, but back then seemed so important to us that we boasted about it. *Every month, without fail – no arguing, nothing – he gets his salary.* I can remember my mother saying that to Ah Heng one day.

Of course it was all fake. Our lives weren't getting any better. If they were, we would have been buying more than just a packet of cornflour or a single coconut which Ah Heng would split in two and scrape out in his old machine with its big metal bowl and spinning metal head. We would have been buying tins of Danish Butter Cookies, going out for meals in seafood restaurants, I would have had a new school uniform that fitted me, that wasn't four sizes too big because it had been bought to last me through the rest of primary school. Maybe a holiday – not anything fancy like a week all-included in Bali or a coach tour of Thailand that people do nowadays, but just some time away, on the other side of the country, visiting relatives in Penang or staying with my aunt in Kampar and spending a few days eating chicken biscuits. All the things that a normal family would do. How much could a bus ticket have cost back then? Even now it only costs twenty ringgit, max. We could have done all that if my father had actually been sending money to us.

That was when I realised that my mother's stories were intended not to comfort me, but to reassure herself. The more she repeated them to me and Ah Heng and whoever else cared to listen, the clearer it was to me that she needed to cling to the belief that they were all true – that my father was still part of our lives, that our future was bright, and soon we'd be living on the outskirts of Klang, in one of those new housing estates that were being built – just like the one we're sitting in now.

These days, I often take a walk through the neighbourhood after dinner. Sometimes I have trouble digesting my food, I don't know why – I went to see the doctor, she took x-rays but couldn't find anything wrong. Suggested it was stress. I said, Stress, what stress? I don't have stress, what the hell do I have to worry about these days? She said, In that case no one can help you.

It's true. It's not like it's going to kill me, it just ties up my stomach sometimes, as if all the blood's been squeezed out of my insides and replaced by a lump of concrete, and sometimes I have to get down on all fours like a dog to ease the pain. I close my eyes and wait for it to pass. Sometimes it takes an hour, maybe more, and suddenly I realise I'm crying because it hurts so much, this block of rough stone inside me, and I wish my body could explode and spill everything out. I stare at the cement floor, and it soothes me. I see that there are patterns in it. From a distance it looks totally uniform, but when my face is right up close to it I notice it has uneven swirls in it. One time I saw blood on the smooth grey surface – I must have bitten my lip while trying to endure the pain in my stomach, and hadn't even realised it.

Personally, I think it's those three years of bland prison meals that are to blame. I got used to tasteless stuff, so now I can't eat greasy food any more, nothing too spicy or rich. But I just can't help it – I love fried spare ribs and *laksa* too much. Sometimes the pain starts to ease after a few minutes, but then I'm worried it'll come back again, and that's when I go for a stroll.

The houses all look shabby nowadays. No one wants to live in these single-storey places any more, that's why. The people who live here wish they were living somewhere else. Secretly they all want to live in KL or Petaling Jaya. The drains outside the houses are blocked up by rubbish and dead leaves, the grass on the edge of the roads is overgrown and messy – the council doesn't bother to clean the streets around here. There used to be small gardens in front of the houses, now there are only cars, only Proton Sagas crammed into the concrete yards. A few doors down from me there's an old couple who use their Perodua as a kind of outdoor cupboard. At first you think it's just another small lousy old car, then you realise it's full of clothes and boxes and unwanted stuff like that. The neighbours – we see each other around and sometimes we say hi, sometimes we don't. I like it that way. No one asks me any questions.

But it wasn't supposed to be this way. When this neighbourhood was first built, I remember looking at the tiled roofs and thinking, *Whoa, they look so solid*. In some estates the houses have blue roofs, while others have green. My mother cut out an advertisement from the *Sin Chew Jit Poh* with a drawing of a house just like this one. Far from the sea, where we wouldn't have to smell the salty stinky mud when the tide went out, full of rotting fish that had slipped from the nets of the fishing boats. A house far inland, that couldn't be swept away by freak tides or floods or storms. A place close to the city – so near that you could feel part of it, be absorbed and protected by it. She pinned the piece of newspaper to the wall in the bedroom – a patch of colour against the bare board. These places, they felt so new. It's hard to imagine that now. You drive around this kind of estate and the streets look identical, house after house after house – they're all the same, it crushes you. I know that's what people from KL think. You come from the big city and you think, *These places destroy your soul*. Even I feel like that sometimes, and I've lived here for nearly ten years. I don't know how things could have changed so much in thirty years. The houses we dreamed

155

of then are exactly the ones we live in today, but they belong to a different world.

I used to wonder how my parents felt about each other during that long period of separation – those long years of hope. Sometimes we used to watch *Shanghai Tang* on TV, that Hong Kong series that had just come out then, which everyone was watching. We loved the costumes, the glamour – and that song! It made my mother cry every time. Once she dabbed her eyes and said, 'It must be beautiful to experience such things. To be in love like that.' And then, as if she heard the question that was forming in my head, she said, 'It's different for people like us. Your father and me, we don't have time *for all that.'*

I didn't think about it when she said it, but now I do. *Didn't have time for love.* Is that what she meant? They were apart from each other, romance was impossible, I understand that. But love – that's something else, isn't it? My father was in another country earning a living far from his family, but that was another form of love. Distance is love. Separation is love. Loneliness is love.

One day – I can't remember when, but a few years after my father left for Singapore – we received a letter from him. My mother read out a couple of sentences as soon as she opened the envelope. *I have been going to church for the past few months. The pastor says that my life will improve because Jesus loves me.* She stood reading for a minute or so, then took the letter into the bedroom and shut the door. I can't remember exactly how the rest of the information filtered through to me in the weeks that followed – my mother never said anything as clear as

Your father is not coming back.

He is living with someone else.

He has another family over there.

It was simply something I came to understand, in the

way children do – that things were no longer the same. One phase of your life is over, and suddenly you're a different person, even though you don't want to be, and hadn't been planning to change. The world rearranges itself around you, and all at once you too are no longer the same. For a few bucks, my mother sold the baby clothes she'd been storing in a small box in the bedroom. She took the necklace my father had given her on their wedding day to the pawnbroker in town. She didn't take her wedding ring – that would follow a few months later. You might say, So what? We needed money, we had to sell stuff – what was new? Still, it was different. There was a finality to those small acts that maybe the logic of adults – of clever, reasoned people like you – will interpret differently, will twist and reshape to form a kinder explanation. But a child always knows the truth, and in the end I was right. He never came back.

[*Pauses. Sips tea. Rubs belly.*]

Sorry. I have to stand up and take a quick walk now. Like I said, it's those three years of bland prison food that are to blame for my stomach problem.

Bang bang bang. Bang bang bang. Someone is hitting the metal grille on the front door, and I know it's her.

My body aches so badly I don't think I can make it out of bed. Every time I move there's a pain in my lower back – always in the same place, ever since prison. Like a knife deep in my flesh, twisting. I try to prop myself up, but the effort makes me cry out in pain. It's as if my body is attacking itself.

Hey, are you there? You OK? Open up. Her voice is strong but calm.

Give me a few minutes.

What did you say?

I said give me a few minutes. I realise my voice is barely more than a whisper, and I'm breathing heavily.

After a while the pain finally subsides enough for me to get to the door. I let her in, and slump into a chair. You can't read your emails or what? I say. I told you I was ill. I cancelled the session.

That was last week's session. You said you had 'flu. You haven't answered any of your emails or texts the last few days. I even called round a couple of times.

You called round? I didn't hear.

You look terrible. You've lost a lot of weight.

I shrug. I don't want to tell her that I haven't been out of the house for over ten days. I've barely got out of bed during that time.

Just sit down and wait, I have something for you. She

lifts up what looks like a large plastic container, and disappears into the kitchen. She comes back carrying a big bowl filled almost to the brim with soup. When she sets it down some of it spills over onto the table.

Ei, sorry. I'm so clumsy.

That's when I realise how hungry I am. But it's been days since I had anything to eat apart from some dry biscuits and an orange, and I don't know if I can eat so much food. Part of me feels like devouring it all in one gulp, another part of me feels like throwing up.

Come, eat. She pushes the bowl gently towards me. It's my mother's special double-boiled six-flavour chicken soup. I told her to add some extra ginseng. When you have 'flu you have to eat well, otherwise your body won't be able to fight the infection. Come on, just try a bit. It's very nourishing. It'll be good for you.

I stare at the bowl. Little swirls of oil make funny shapes on the surface of the soup. I take the bowl in my hands and lift it to my mouth. After one long gulp I set it back down on the table, and suddenly I find that I'm crying.

Later, when I'm back in bed, I drift in and out of sleep. Sometimes I can hear her typing on her laptop. When I open my eyes it's dark, and she's standing in the doorway to the bedroom. I'm going to go now, she whispers. I can't be sure what else she says, or what time it is. The following day she arrives with more soup, some rice and some medicine. She comes for the next three days, until I'm healthy again.

When my mother announced our move, she buried it in a jumble of other information in the hope that I wouldn't worry about it until much later, when, like all children, I'd have silently processed the changes in store for us and appreciated how they would affect our lives, without her having to explain it all to me. *You're growing up fast, we'll have to buy you a new school uniform. Next year you must study harder at school. History is a useful subject, but you should concentrate on maths. It'll be easier for you at Uncle Kiat's house. He has electricity from the mains. It's quieter there. He might even give you your own room.* There was a silence at the heart of all she told me, a missing piece of the jigsaw that was both essential and superfluous – her omission made the picture baffling, but it also explained everything. What she left out was, 'We're moving out of our house, because it's falling apart. Because we can't afford to live even in a shack on the verge of collapse. Because it's killing me to raise a child and work at the same time.'

I remember standing in the kitchen as she packed our possessions into raffia bags, waiting for her to elaborate on what she was saying – to give me an explanation, and maybe a hug, too, which might comfort me and give me the reassurance I needed to face this sudden shift in our circumstances. But she merely continued to talk about things that seemed unconnected to that moment – the price of fish going down that season because of an oversupply, the washing she'd have to do when she got back from work that evening, the list of chores she'd left me to do. *Collect more water from the well, ask Auntie Lian for some charcoal, make sure all your clothes are folded and ready to be packed in a bag.* I waited for reasons as to how and why the decision had been reached to move out of our home and into the house of a man we barely knew, but there were none. She talked, but the awful gaping silence remained amid her chatter. Nowadays when I remember that moment, I think: that is what shame sounds like.

I had known that our lives would be changing some months before, when my mother revealed that she had divorced my father. We'd got used to him being away, and I knew, with all the certainty that only a child can have, that he was never coming back. I no longer dreamed of his return, no longer imagined lying in bed one morning and being roused from sleep by the sound of a man's voice in the kitchen and knowing that it belonged to my father, even though I'd forgotten what he sounded like, or even how he looked. That he actually lived in another country just a few hundred miles away made his absence real. He wasn't living in some Greenland, or New Zealand or Somalia, or any other fairytale land that was so distant and magical to me that it kept alive the possibility of a miraculous return. For a few months, when I was smaller, I'd imagined my father living in an igloo. What exactly he was doing in the igloo I wasn't sure, but it was connected to making sure my mother and I were all right. It had been such a difficult journey to get there that he was still trudging through thousands of miles of snow to get home. The idea of distance made him seem close to me. But by the time I was ten or eleven, I knew that there were no igloos in Singapore, and that my father lived in a place that we could get to by sitting in a bus for half a day. He wasn't coming back because he didn't want to. His proximity solidified the gulf between us.

Still, when my mother sat me down and explained what a divorce meant – *it means Papa and I are still your parents but we are no longer husband and wife, do you understand?* – I knew that it signalled a shift. I just didn't know how that shift would play out. My mother could have disguised the divorce as something gentler, or hidden it in other half-truths or incomplete stories, as she had done before and would do many times later on; but for a reason I couldn't determine, she wanted to emphasise the split with my father after all those years of waiting. 'Mama is still your Mama, but she is her own woman now,' she'd said. 'She is free.' She referred to herself as if she was talking about someone else – as if she hadn't yet got used to the idea of being the woman she described.

For a few months after the divorce announcement our lives continued without fuss or noticeable change. School for me, the fish-processing factory for my mother. After school, the dead hours at home, playing in the yard on my own, or roaming the country lanes that I'd already come to know so well. Waiting for my mother to come home. I noticed she was staying out for longer than usual, and at first I thought nothing of this development. It had always happened from time to time, when she had to do longer shifts at work, often at short notice, and as dusk fell I'd know to make myself dinner from the leftovers in the refrigerator, and not to wait for her to come home before I went to bed. But in those months her absences felt more deliberate and consistent, and sometimes, half-roused from sleep by her late return, I'd notice that the noises she made as she moved around the house were somehow different – more purposeful, even energetic, unlike the slow, heavy sounds of a normal evening when she'd worked overtime and would barely have the strength to fix herself dinner before falling into the raffia armchair and turning on the TV.

The new night-time noises confused me. The quick padding of her footsteps, criss-crossing the little house as she darted from kitchen to sitting room, back and forth. Sometimes she'd come into the bedroom, pausing to make sure she hadn't woken me before taking something from the chest of drawers. I'd pretend to be sleeping, but in fact I was kept awake by the strange energy that filled the house – an energy that should have enthused me, but that filled me with a dull dread. A fear of something that remained hazy and unnamed.

It was soon after that I learned of our move to Uncle Kiat's house on the other side of the village, and as the move drew closer I began to understand that my mother's new optimism was linked to the end of everything I found reassuring in my life. Our little house. Our evenings and Sundays together, occasionally riding on the scooter into Kuala Selangor to buy candy from the store. The feeling that we didn't need anyone else in the world to survive. My mother sighing as she dozed off in the afternoons, saying, 'I could sleep until the end of our days.' The comfort in knowing that I could sit on the bed next to her for all that time, and that when she woke up our world would still be the same. The beautiful boredom of it all, when we were together.

'You'll see, Uncle Kiat's place will be much more comfortable for us,' she said as she packed the last of our things into the raffia bags. 'He's being so generous in taking us in.'

I didn't figure out until later that Uncle Kiat was a distant cousin of my father's, who'd grown up with him until the age of twenty or so, when he'd left to work in Penang for a couple of years before returning home. I didn't remember him from earlier in my childhood, and his sudden entry

163

into our lives was baffling to me – not because he was new, but because my mother talked to and about him as if he'd always been with us. 'Go fetch Uncle Kiat some tea,' she would say when he came through the door. 'You know he likes to drink tea. Hot weather, hot tea – only Uncle Kiat does that!' At first I thought I might be going mad, and that I'd forgotten the presence of this man throughout my growing-up years. I became anxious, worried that the problem was mine – why couldn't I remember him at all? But then I realised it wasn't me. The familiarity my mother showed was real – she knew this man well. Had done for a long time. She'd just never shared that familiarity with me, until now.

The journey wouldn't have taken more than twenty or thirty minutes by foot, and we didn't have many possessions to transport – three large raffia bags that between us would have been unwieldy but manageable – but Uncle Kiat came to pick us up in his green Datsun. The back doors were stuck and couldn't open, so I had to climb in over the front seat. The upholstery was torn and stuck together with black tape that chafed against the backs of my thighs as we made the short drive. My mother had been chatty all morning, but in the car she fell silent, and I wondered if she thought she'd made a mistake and was now regretting her decision. I knew, though, that she wouldn't be changing her mind – she had no choice but to follow through.

Uncle Kiat was silent in the car, and even that first day, without knowing the man at all, I sensed that he was by nature uncommunicative and slightly withdrawn. I wished that I didn't compare him to my father – or the version of my father who lived on in my imagination – but I couldn't help it. My cheeky, silly father, who rarely stopped talking. I closed my eyes and tried to scrub out those images. *In order to survive and be happy, I had to forget that I'd ever had a father.* I didn't know why that thought came to me just then, sitting in that hot, airless Datsun, but it did.

'Uncle Kiat likes you so much, he just doesn't know how to express it.' My mother spoke softly as we unpacked our things. The sentence had the neatness and tenderness of something that had been planned in advance. 'Did you hear me?'

I sat on the bed and looked around. 'Yes,' I said. The room was small but bright, and recently painted white. The floor and walls were constructed from brick and concrete and felt solid, unlike the timber boards of our old home. The mattress on the bed was soft, and I suddenly felt sleepy, even though it was only midway through the afternoon, or maybe towards the end of the day – I can't remember exactly. It was still light, in any case. I lay my head on the pillow and fell asleep at once – the deepest sleep I'd had in a long while. I heard my mother talking to me as I drifted off, but couldn't make out the words. I felt her hand sweep the hair off my forehead, the smooth warmth of her palm on my skin. Later, I heard her and Uncle Kiat talking in the next room, their voices muffled by the thick walls, reduced to low murmuring that at first surprised me – what was that sound? In our old house, noise passed through the wooden partitions as if they didn't exist – but then lulled me back to sleep. I opened my eyes briefly and blinked at the clean bare walls, but when I shut them I saw my old bedroom and believed that I was in it once again.

I felt as though I was slipping into another world, where everyone looked different, wore odd clothes and spoke in a foreign accent that I found difficult to understand at first, but soon made sense of. I recognised some of them – my mother, Uncle Kiat, the people of the village – but they too were wearing strange outfits and speaking in that alien manner, in voices that were dull and mumbling. My father was there too. I didn't recognise him, but he was familiar. I knew he was my dad. All this was taking place in a city made of stone and steel, indestructible, immune to floods and winds and mudslides. The rules in this new world were altered. I slept in the day, went to school at night. Sometimes I didn't go to school at all. As I roamed through the streets of this new city I had the ability to become invisible to its citizens. Others had this gift too, but not everyone. My mother drove a car, she didn't ride her scooter any more. The car was blue, and it travelled without the need for wheels. Everything was different here.

A whole lifetime later, when I was in prison, I'd remember these childhood dreams that spilled over into the following day and made my waking hours seem shorter and easier to bear. I'd try to recreate that haze-like state in my cell, try to hang on to those wisps of sleep, but it never worked. The noise of the other men shouting, washing, eating – it ruined everything.

For several months after we moved, my mother continued to work at the factory. 'Not for long,' she told me, 'Uncle Kiat is going to find me better work down in Klang. He's got friends in town, people who run businesses. I could even work in an office!' It was clear from the start that whatever Uncle Kiat did for a living was unconnected to the life of the village, just as the house itself felt different from the others around it. Even though it wasn't a new house, its efficiency made it feel fresh – doors and windows that worked, framed by metal that wasn't rusting. Inside, white-painted walls, a ceiling fan that spun without wobbling or stuttering. The cleanliness of it all made it seem almost suburban, as if it didn't belong in the village.

Uncle Kiat would still be in the house when I left for

school, wearing only his red Liverpool FC shorts that he never changed. Sometimes he'd still be in bed when I left, other times he'd have just woken up – he seemed in no rush to get to work. When he did finally leave he'd drive to Klang, where he was a supervisor in a factory near the port that made rubber gloves. 'From Telok Gong to the rest of the world,' he once boasted. 'Germany, USA, Korea. Go to a hospital anywhere in the world, you'll find our gloves. Even China can't compete with us.' There were boxes of them throughout the house, half a finger of a glove sticking out and inviting you to pull it out like a sheet of tissue paper. Uncle Kiat wore them all the time to clean the house. He was always cleaning, wiping the edges of the window sills or climbing onto a chair to brush the dust off the blades of the fan. I'd never seen anyone else in the village tidy their house with such determination and precision. No one else had as much time or energy to devote to domestic chores as he did. If you come home after a night at sea or doing the late shift at the factory, the last thing you want to do is tidy the house.

What I couldn't figure out was his work routine – why the world's mightiest manufacturer of rubber gloves didn't demand his presence on a regular basis. I'd grown up with people who worked in factories. I knew the rhythms of their days and nights, the way their shifts changed according to the seasons and public holidays. But Uncle Kiat's days were regular only in their irregularity – the only thing I knew for sure each day was that I could never tell what time he'd be leaving for work, or if he'd be leaving at all.

Deciphering his routine was important, because I needed to reduce my time with him to a minimum, if not eliminate it altogether. Sometimes I'd arrive back from school and he'd be sitting in front of the TV, shirtless and still in the same shorts he'd been wearing that morning and in fact

the night before. He'd look up briefly without acknowledging me and turn the volume up even louder on the TV,
so that the gunshots and explosions of the cops-and-gang-
sters shows he liked would vibrate through the walls. Even
when I shut the door I'd hear the screeching of brakes, the
crunch of metal on metal as if there were real-life car chases
going on just outside, threatening to smash their way into
my room at any moment. I'd put my head under the pillow,
but would still hear the noise. *Leave me alone!* I screamed
one day. *Leave me the fuck alone!* I wanted to flee, but I was
trapped in the room by the noise, which formed a barrier
that made it impossible for me to leave.

I was staying out later and later, heading home only
when it got dark and I could be reasonably sure that my
mother would be there too. At first she'd be worried that
I'd stayed out so late, and would give me extra portions
at dinner. 'Where have you been? What have you been
doing?' she'd ask. 'Nothing,' I'd reply. 'Just roaming
around.' Which was entirely true. That was what I did,
sometimes with other kids but often on my own. But
soon, when she realised I was fine, that I wasn't getting
in trouble, she was relieved to have a bit of time without
me. I'd come home to find her and Uncle Kiat already in
front of the TV, dinner cleared away and the table wiped
clean with the disinfectant Uncle Kiat favoured. The smell
of it was always in the air, the special perfume of the
house. Other homes had the odour of joss-sticks, or of
food. In that house it was bleach. My food would be on
a plate under a net cover in the kitchen, and I'd eat it
alone, standing at the sink and looking out of the window
at the back of the boatsheds. 'Don't forget to tidy up when
you've finished,' my mother would shout over the noise
of the TV.

In those first months my mother would sleep in the

same bed with me as she'd always done. 'See? Nothing's changed,' she'd whisper as I fell asleep. In the night, when I stirred, I'd look across and see her sleeping on her side, facing me, her mouth pursed slightly as she exhaled – a sight I'd known since the beginning of time. But despite her assurances I knew that things were different – how could they not be? – and so one night when, thinking I was asleep, she got up and left the room I wasn't surprised. It was confirmation of how our life was beginning to reshape itself – the mattress giving way slightly as she rose from the bed, the door clicking shut as she closed it behind her, the warmth of her presence when she returned later in the night. Was she gone for one hour, or two, or eight? I never knew for certain, but at some point, when it was still dark, she would return, and by the time I woke up properly in the morning she was always there, just as she had been when I'd fallen asleep the night before.

After about three months, my mother quit her job at the factory – or maybe she was fired, I'm not sure. 'Can't stand that place any more,' she told me. 'When you're big, you're not going to work in a place like that.' She got a job in an office down in the port area, much further away from the village than she'd ever worked, but the distance from home seemed to free her. Each day she'd set off on her scooter as if she were travelling abroad for the very first time – briskly, but a little hesitant too, as if unsure of what lay in wait for her. But that sense of discovery soon gave way to the same fatigue she'd known – we'd both known – in her years working at the fish factory, replaced by the boredom of routine. It was some time before I found out that she was a janitor, not a book-keeper or sales manager or any of the other things she could have been, and thought she might have been. I saw her name badge once, attached to the end of a ribbon that she would have hung around her neck. Her photo made her look older than she was – all the promise squeezed out of her life, an idea that started to gather on the edges of my own brain, like the shards of frost in the freezer that grew thicker every month until they formed a dense crust. The idea that my mother's life had run out of possibilities. Her life frozen. When she was not even forty years old. Under her name were the words *Hygiene and Sanitary*.

Now, when I think about it, what strikes me isn't the idea of my mother emptying waste bins in an office block under the white glow of fluorescent lights. I think of the impossibility of that happening now, when every janitor in the country is a foreigner. People like my mother – what would they do for work? Maybe by a process of natural promotion she would have become the book-keeper she'd always dreamed of being. One layer forms underneath you and pushes you up towards the surface, just like the geographical formations I was learning about at school. But maybe not, maybe she would have just ended up exactly as she did.

It was around that time that I began to notice that my mother had virtually stopped spending time with other people in the village, and that, by extension, I rarely went to other people's houses. I don't mean that it was a particu-larly social kind of village – not the way you would understand it, at least. You didn't invite people round for fancy meals, but you'd often drop in on neighbours when you needed something – a length of string, a screwdriver, some salt, whatever. You'd meet them in the street and they'd say, 'I've just boiled some barley-tofu drink, come and have some,' and you'd spend the next half-hour catching up on news. My mother had been especially social in that respect. When I was very small, riding on the scooter with her, I'd become aware of how ready she was with her greetings, how open she was to other people, even those she barely knew, like a new bus driver or a neighbour's relative visiting from another part of the country. She was always slowing down to wave to someone, and if anyone called out to her she'd stop altogether. My first memories of the village are of observing it from the scooter, sitting in front of my mother, cradled in her lap and reaching out for the handlebars as if I was steering it myself. The number of times I heard people say, 'He's growing up so quickly,' or 'Watch out – soon he'll be stealing that bike and riding down to KL with it!' I noticed the warmth in their voices, even when they were breathless and defeated by a night at sea, or a day at the factory, or working with the nets under the sun.

At that age – four, five, six – you don't understand every word, and you don't remember what you hear, but you sense the impression of the voices. Brightness. Jealousy. Affection. Danger. And when people spoke to my mother it was almost always with a sort of tenderness mixed with surprise, as if they were intimately tied to her, and their meeting on the street was a special occasion, even though they saw each other all the time. Looking back on it now, maybe what I heard as warmth was in fact pity. Or relief. *Young woman like her, bringing up a small child all on her own, husband probably gone for good. Poor miserable thing. Thank God we're not in that position.* Whatever the reason, I knew one thing: people liked my mother.

Now that I was older – pushing eleven, I guess – I rode on the scooter with her less often, so it took me a while to sense the loosening of her contact with our village, or the changing nature of her relationship with people she'd always been close to. I put it down to her job, more time-consuming those days even than before. She had little time to spend with me, let alone others. She was tired. She was getting old. But most of all, she was spending whatever free time she had with Uncle Kiat. Often they would just sit in front of the TV the whole evening, but sometimes they'd go out – I never knew where. At first there was a display of concern. 'Tonight, Mama and Uncle Kiat have to go out, OK? You promise you won't be frightened? You won't be scared to stay at home alone?'

'It's OK,' Uncle Kiat would say in an exaggeratedly manly voice. 'He's a big boy, he'll be fine. Won't you?' He'd pat me on the back, a bit too roughly, more like a blow than a gesture of affection, and I'd say, 'Sure. Don't worry.'

Soon I recognised this as an elaborate performance, more for themselves than for me. They knew I'd be all right. Back then kids were different. At ten, eleven, twelve, we knew how to look after ourselves. But very swiftly, even this pretence stopped, and when I came home late in the afternoon, when the sun was just beginning to lose its vigour, the house would be empty, and I knew it was one of those days when my mother had finished work early and planned an outing with Uncle Kiat. Their absence felt deliberate. Like a statement of something they couldn't bring themselves to pronounce in words. Or maybe they couldn't even articulate what it was. But I knew: they preferred it when I was out of the picture. It was easier for them when they didn't see me, or have to explain the changing ways of adult life to me. I wasn't so much a burden – how could I have been? I was hardly around those days, my life was breaking off from theirs, even from my mother's – as a reminder of their guilt. I didn't know what they'd done to feel guilty. All I could feel was that they *were* guilty. Of something. And every time they looked at me, they felt it too.

The first Chinese New Year after we moved in with Uncle Kiat, my mother went with him to visit some of his relatives who lived on the east coast, not far from Kuantan. They were fishermen too, my mother told me, people just like us. Nice people. How do you know? I thought. You've never met them. They were away for three days, and during that time they left me to stay with neighbours. They were good to me, they gave me tangerines from Taiwan and an *ang bao* of five ringgit. On the second day, a visitor – someone from the village who I'd known forever – asked about my mother.

'How is she? We never see her these days. She's spending New Year with Kiat?'

I nodded. 'In Kuantan.'

'She OK?'

'Mmm.'

'Happy in the new house?'

'Yes.'

She picked up a newspaper and started to flick through it. The other kids were unfurling some firecrackers out in the yard. Someone shouted, *Go out in the street! Get away from the house!* 'Huh,' the neighbour said as she looked at the newspaper. 'I always knew.'

I left the room and ran to join the other kids out on the street. One of them had tied the string of firecrackers to a tree trunk and was dragging it across the dirt. It looked like a sinewy red animal tethered to the tree, limp and about to die. I pushed my way through the crowd gathered around the fuse and seized the cigarette lighter from the boy who was holding it. In one swift motion I flicked it alight and held it to the fuse. The other kids dispersed like smoke carried on the wind, screaming with joy and terror. *He's nuts, that guy!* I held the lighter steady and waited for the fuse to catch. Even when it started to fizz and sizzle I

remained crouched by it, making sure the purple flame of
the lighter didn't blow out. *Get out of there you're crazy you're
gonna die!* the other kids were shouting. I watched the tiny
sparks run the length of the fuse. Don't run, hold steady,
I thought to myself. I imagined the firecrackers exploding
in my face, the hot smoke singeing my skin, ripping it.
Don't run. At the very last moment I leaped away. The
brilliant eruption of colours, so close, too close, blinded
me for a few moments, but I didn't shut my eyes. The
other kids were laughing, cheering, screaming wildly. 'Ah
Hock is mad!'

We stood watching the remains of the firecrackers strewn
across the street – charred bits of paper, black and blood-red,
like pieces of skin. The smell of gunpowder hung in the
air for a long time.

I always knew.

I couldn't get the neighbour's words out of my head.

When she and Uncle Kiat came back from Kuantan my
mother rushed up to me and gathered me in her arms.
She held me tightly and didn't let me go for a long time.
I wanted to surrender to the familiarity of her, the deep
comfort of her embrace, I wanted to cry with relief and
happiness; but instead I found that my body was rigid and
unresponsive as she hugged me. I wanted her to go away
again, leave for some place far from me.

'Leave him be,' Uncle Kiat said as he unloaded the car,
carrying a basket of fruit into the house. 'He's happier on
his own.'

In the weeks that followed, my mother made a special
effort to spend time with me, with and without Uncle Kiat.
We rode all the way to Tanjung Harapan on her scooter,
just the two of us, and sat on the low stone ramparts eating
a small picnic of slices of fried Spam and bread. We watched
the tankers and container ships cruise slowly towards North

Port, the colourful containers stacked on top of each other like pieces of Lego. Beyond the green-grey water, the line of low mangrove trees on Pulau Klang looked as soft as a thick green rug. It was late afternoon, the sun was just beginning to sink, and young couples began to appear, holding hands and strolling along the path that traced the water's edge. Groups of young men horsed around on the huge rocks that protected the shoreline from tides and wayward ships; they leaped from one boulder to another, pausing sometimes to pick up empty whisky bottles which they'd fling out to sea. A group of Indonesian workers on their day off had made a little fire in a metal drum nearby, and were cooking pieces of food over it – I couldn't tell what it was because the smoke was too thick, a column rising straight into the sky. There was no breeze at all that day, but it wasn't hot.

My mother stared out at the sea for a long time without saying much. I reached out and touched her hand, and though she clasped mine tightly, she didn't look at me. For a few moments I felt as though she was about to tell me something, but she remained silent. The sun had sunk almost to the crests of the mangrove trees when we gathered our things to leave. I sensed a sort of finality – the end of yet another period of my life, but not yet the beginning of the next.

Once, we went with Uncle Kiat to the movies in Klang. It was my first proper outing in the city, or at least the first I can remember. He bought us a box of Famous Amos cookies that my mother rationed carefully, passing me one at a time and waiting for me to express my gratitude sufficiently before handing me the next. 'Say "thank you" to Uncle Kiat,' she'd prod if I didn't do so, and I dutifully obliged. I must have thanked him fifty times that day. The film was *Honey, I Shrunk the Kids*, and Uncle Kiat laughed loudly throughout, throwing his head back to release a full-throated roar. 'Shh,' my mother said, giggling and pretending to smack him on the shoulder. I couldn't understand why he found the movie so funny. The story of ordinary kids who suddenly found themselves reduced to the size of insects terrified me, and I spent most of the film with my hands in front of my eyes, screening out the worst of the horror. One moment you have a normal family life, next moment you're being chased by a giant scorpion and taking refuge in a worm hole. No one notices you. You're so tiny your own dad sweeps you up like a piece of dust and dumps you in the trash like the piece of garbage that you've become. 'Look at them!' Uncle Kiat pointed at the screen as the kids tumbled into the huge metal container. I didn't find any of the film funny, and I hated Uncle Kiat for laughing so much. The man in the seat in front of me was asleep, his snoring clearly audible. '*Wei*, old man, wake up!' Uncle Kiat barked at him, and laughed. '*Aiya*, leave him alone,' my mother said, but she was giggling too. She held Uncle Kiat's hand, and they leaned in towards each other as if they were about to kiss, but didn't.

To avoid looking at the screen, or at my mother and Uncle Kiat, I watched the man, fast asleep with his head tilted to one side and his mouth hanging open. He wasn't so old, about the same age as Uncle Kiat. He looked peaceful, completely docile, and I wished that he was the one sitting next to my mother instead of Uncle Kiat.

On the drive home, my mother turned to look at me in the back seat. 'Wasn't that the best day of your life?' she asked.

I nodded.

She turned towards Uncle Kiat. 'He's really so happy,' she said.

I began to understand the widening gulf between her

176

and the people of the village, and knew that it was to do with her decision to move in with Uncle Kiat. I felt a separation between us and our neighbours, as if the earth was opening up and dividing the landscape in two. On one side was my mother and Uncle Kiat, on the other, everyone else. I was her child, I should have been happy standing on her side, but all I wanted was to leap across the chasm and be with everyone else.

In the end I started to drift away from the rest of the village too. I was fearful of hearing things about my mother that would hurt me. I stopped hanging out with the other kids, especially the older ones, who would have more knowledge of the ways of adults, and less fear of expressing what they knew. I roamed the paths and tracks that cut through the countryside, going further and further afield. I'd always done that, but in that period of my growing-up years I can't remember anything else. The further I walked, the more the landscape seemed to close in on me, suffocating me. I wondered how old I'd have to be before I could leave home and work in another city, or preferably another continent. Seventeen, eighteen? An eternity away.

I didn't realise it then, but there was to be no return to the fold, not even when the original cause of our separation from the other people in the village had been scrubbed from our record. About a year after this, when we'd been living at Uncle Kiat's for about two years, I came home and found my mother sitting on the edge of the bed. This was a surprise. I'd grown used to arriving home at dusk to find an empty house. Grown used to the comforting bitterness of knowing that my mother was out with Uncle Kiat. I'd become accustomed, above all, to having the room to myself, as my mother had given up all pretences and was spending her nights in Uncle Kiat's room. 'It'll be nicer for you,' she'd said, 'now that you're growing up.' She was reading a newspaper when I entered the room that day. When she saw me she put it down and folded it neatly. I stared at her, expecting a scolding. *You're late. You're lazy. You haven't cleaned the house.* Such admonishments were common, and I never knew when they'd be thrown my way. Instead she said in a flat tone of voice, 'We're moving out. Very soon.'

The clarity of the statement was confusing to me. This time it wasn't obscured by a mass of other information – there was nothing for me to decipher, no codes or signals for me to piece together. Maybe it was because I was older that my mother trusted me with this directness, but from that moment I knew that she had changed yet again, and that this new certainty and decisiveness would stay with her forever. 'It'll be much better for us,' she said as I stood blinking, unable fully to digest what she was saying. 'You wait and see.' That night she slept in the bedroom with me, and though I wish I could say it was a relief, and that I was happy, the truth is that I found it impossible to sleep. Her sudden presence after many months unsettled me. Her breathing, turning to a soft rumbling noise now and then. The way she sighed deeply in her sleep – as if a word had become stuck in her throat and emerged only as a twisted groan.

The day we left, Uncle Kiat hung around the house, pretending to wipe the floors with a bleach-soaked rag, but I could see that he was watching us pack our things. Every time he walked past the open door of our room he'd look in, and sometimes he'd cough, as if to make sure we knew he was there. But my mother ignored him, didn't once acknowledge his presence. She was checking the empty drawers one last time when Uncle Kiat appeared at the door. 'You don't have to go today, you know,' he said quietly. 'You can wait until your new place is ready to move into.'

178

'Don't worry,' my mother replied without looking at him. 'The sooner we leave, the happier your family will be.'

Uncle Kiat looked at the floor. He unfolded the rag he was clutching and rubbed his fingers on it. He continued to stare at a spot on the floor as if he wanted to scrub it away.

My mother zipped up the last of our bags and started to carry them towards the door. As I helped her I noticed that we had less than we'd arrived with.

'You sure you don't want me to drive you there?' Uncle Kiat said. 'It's a long way.'

'Don't trouble yourself,' my mother replied. 'Save your petrol to go visit your parents in Kuantan. Anyway, my son will help me. I'm an *unmarried woman who already has a child* – remember?'

I never saw Uncle Kiat after that day. I had no reason to go near his house, and not long afterwards I heard that he'd moved to the east coast to join his cousins there. Once he was gone, people in the village would occasionally refer to him as *that good-for-nothing man*. When I was a bit older I learned that he'd had an injury of some kind and been laid off work from the glove factory. He'd managed to arrange a compensation payment, which made him think he was rich, and better than everyone else. All those days when I thought he was at work, it turns out he was just driving into Klang and hanging around in coffee shops, watching the world go by.

My mother never mentioned him, or the time we spent living with him. There was no need to – we both understood what had happened, and neither of us wanted to discuss that time of our lives. Besides, we had new challenges on our hands now, which kept us occupied day and night.

Let's go out, she says. Buy some food. I don't think you're eating properly, that's why you get sick.

Food? What food? I'm the healthiest person in the world.

You need to eat more healthily. Fresh fruit and vegetables. Nuts, grains. Decent protein.

Curry laksa doesn't have protein, meh?

Actually, no. Not much. It has plenty of fat, though. Let's go to the mall, get some groceries, and then I'll drive you back. We won't get anything expensive, just decent basics. When you were ill a couple of weeks back I looked through your cupboards and there was nothing.

We've finished early today. Our talk didn't last as long as it sometimes does. Maybe I had nothing special to say. Sure, I say. Why not.

In the mall we head to Giant supermarket, and she pulls a trolley from the row of them at the entrance.

Why do we need such a huge trolley? I say. Just a small basket is enough. I don't need much food.

Let's just see how it goes.

We go straight to the fresh produce section and she begins to put things into the trolley, so quickly it seems she hasn't even looked properly at what she's taken. She chooses things I would never think of buying – freshly-sliced fruit, neatly wrapped in plastic boxes. Fuji apples from Taiwan. Big bunches of leafy vegetables. Shiitake mushrooms.

Wai, this stuff is too expensive.

180

It's good for your skin, she says, holding up a big purple dragon fruit.

I can't afford it, I don't have money.

Don't worry about that. She turns away from me and continues putting things in the trolley. I try to keep up with her but she moves quickly. She's mapped everything out in her head. It's like the way she questions me during our talks. She has mental lists and she works through them without being distracted. Packets of dried herbs for soup. A whole fresh fish. A chicken. Pork ribs.

Why so much? It'll all go rotten.

We'll freeze the meat so you can use it whenever you want. How about some New Zealand beef? You like beef?

I don't eat beef.

I don't either. In fact I'm vegetarian. But I think you should eat meat. You need it right now. Shame there isn't good organic meat. All this is just pretty . . . industrial. Anyway. You need to eat.

By the time we reach the checkout, the trolley is so full that it keeps banging against the shelves and other people's legs. It takes us a long time to load everything onto the conveyor.

You pack, I'll pay, she says.

After a long while, when the bags are nearly full and she is getting ready to pay, I hear her scream. Oh my God. She is staring at a shelf not far from us, at a row of tinned food. *Oh my God.*

The Burmese guy at the checkout turns to look. The other people in the queue behind us do so too. One young man looks concerned. We can't see what she's staring at.

What's the matter? I ask.

There. Oh my God. Fuck.

A rat darts out from under the shelves, across the aisle to the shelves opposite. After a few seconds it scurries back again. Oh my God, that's disgusting. Someone call management!

The checkout guy starts to laugh. The people in the queue chuckle too. Everyone relaxes. They continue to pack their groceries or check their phones.

What the hell are you people laughing at? Can't you see there's vermin over there? We need to do something about it!

It's just a rat, I say, packing the last of the bags. It's no big deal.

What do you mean, just a rat? You're going to just let it run around like that? Call your manager, she says to the checkout guy, lodge a report right now.

Miss. Hey, miss, someone calls from the queue. It's an older man. Could you please hurry? My legs are aching.

Yeah, someone else says. We have to go back to work.

You're all just going to stand there and do nothing? she says. Where's the manager? I'm going to report it! Otherwise the whole place is soon going to be infested and diseased!

I gather the bags into the trolley and begin pushing it to the car park. Forget it, I say. It's just a small thing.

What the hell are you smiling at? she says. It's not funny.

Nothing, I say. She keeps talking about the rat all the way home, and even after we've put all the shopping away, she's still grumbling about how no one did anything. That's the problem with this country, we let stuff happen that shouldn't happen, we turn a blind eye to little things, then the rot sets in. No one cares about anything any more.

I look at the fridge. I've never seen it so full. I want to thank her for all the things she's bought for me, but she's in a bad mood until she leaves, and I can't find the right time to tell her that I'm really grateful.

We bought the piece of land with the last of my mother's savings, a small amount of money I didn't even know she had. Doing the kind of jobs she'd done, you wouldn't have expected her to have put any money aside, but she had. Just enough to buy an acre and a half of scrubland, with a small house already on it, run-down and full of roosting bats, but with a roof that didn't have too many holes, and surprisingly solid walls built from cinder blocks on a concrete floor. I could remember the man who used to live in it, Pak Awang, who collapsed one day from a heart attack, and when he came home had to hobble around the place with the aid of a walking stick. *Poor old man*, people said. *All on his own in a place like that.* When he finally got too weak to walk, his children moved him up to Shah Alam, close to where they lived. In only five years, his land – a small vegetable plot and two fish ponds – had turned wild, reclaimed by nature so you couldn't tell it had recently been home to a human being. Long grass obscured the shape of the land, the prickly shrubs he'd planted as boundaries had meshed together, and small trees had taken root, blending into the forest beyond. The ponds were shrouded by weeds and looked like puddles of marshy water. We couldn't even get near them that first day.

I remembered what the people in the village had said about Pak Awang – why would anyone want to live so far from everyone else? Now I knew. For my mother and me, isolation was our saviour.

'The land is messy because that guy was old,' my mother said as we set about cleaning the house. 'Besides, he was alone.' She was attacking the rough, bare concrete walls with a wire brush while I mopped the floor. She stopped for a moment and looked at me. 'There are two of us. It'll be easy.'

She was determined to turn that patch of land into a small fertile farm, with vegetables and maybe some tilapia that we could sell at the market. It would all be ours, we wouldn't need to depend on anyone else. No one could sack her, no one could evict us. We were secure now. We were the masters – of our own piece of earth, of our futures. And so we set about clearing the land even before the house was patched up; the rich red earth was going to provide us with our income. We had two spades, a small axe and a rusty *parang*, whose curved blade bore traces of red paint, as dark as blood. That was the tool my mother used more than any other, hacking away at the undergrowth with long, powerful strokes. From twenty or thirty yards away I'd look up and see a sapling shaking as though caught in a gust of wind, and I'd know that my mother was chopping at its base, and soon it would topple and fall. She worked with a concentration so intense that it blocked out the rest of the world, and sometimes when I called out to her she wouldn't hear me, wouldn't stop until she had managed to slash all the branches from a bush. Often I'd stand and watch for a few moments. The rhythmic arc of her arm. The strength of her back as it curved to bring the blade down onto the foliage, time and time again. She moved methodically, as if she knew the effect of every cut of the *parang* – as if she was trying to match her strength to that of nature, and she knew

184

she could win. I don't know what my father did for work, or even what he looked like, but I know that I inherited my capacity for physical labour from my mother. I was not yet thirteen, and my body was ready to imitate my mother's. I copied her movements, learned to use the axe with speed and certainty, until after just a couple of days I no longer had to think about what I was doing. The tools became part of me.

At the end of the third day we stood on a mound of branches that we'd chopped down, balancing carefully on the springy pile. The land looked barely different from how it had when we started. The sea was just a few hundred yards away, shimmering in the late-afternoon sun, flat and waveless that day. The impossibility of our task lay before us. We'd worked without pause for nearly three days, and we hadn't made any difference to the landscape. My mother went back to the house without saying a word, leaving me to contemplate the days ahead. We had no choice but to continue.

It took us three or four weeks to clear the land. I became so used to working with blades of all sorts that when I closed my eyes all I could see was the slashing and ripping of foliage, the splintering of wood. In that short time I had learned to wield those tools as skilfully as a martial-arts disciple trained in the Eighteen Forms of Combat. It wasn't just my arms that had grown accustomed to this new awareness – I could use either hand to chop at a stump of wood, even though I wrote with my right hand – but my back, arcing and twisting to support my shoulders, and my legs, planted firmly on the ground. I could feel my body filling out, growing stronger and surer. I moved with the assurance of someone older, swifter. Sometimes, cutting away at the base of a tree with the same repetitive action, I'd imagine that I was a hero from the *wuxia* stories I'd started to read, wandering the countryside redressing the wrongs of an oppressed people. Old villagers bullied by unscrupulous landlords, isolated farming communities preyed upon by bandits – I would save them all, my elegant weapons cutting through the air with noble authority. Sword, staff, spear and broadsword: I had achieved total mastery of all of them from years of practice, and I could even slay the demons that roamed the country, terrorising all those who tried to confront them.

In one of my favourite reveries, I pictured our own village being menaced for years by a monster that rose from the sea in the form of a white half-dragon-half-cat. No one understood its history or origins, or where it lived and why it chose to ravage our village. We only knew that it had always been there, from the earliest days of our existence, and even before. Some said it represented our sins from former lives, others that it was part of our karma – either way, there was nothing we could do about it. We didn't know how to predict its appearances, though some thought they were linked to the cycles of the moon. It would snake its way silently out of the sea and devour the livestock – the goats tethered in the yards and the chickens in the coops would disappear at night, and sometimes small children too. Old folk and people with illnesses would be found dead in their beds in the morning – from fright, from the curse of the beast. The Night of the Monster. We'd realise it only when it was too late. The strong, healthy men and women knew it was futile trying to combat the beast – it was an understanding passed down from generation to generation. Lock your doors, mind your own business, and maybe you'll remain unscathed, your family frightened but alive.

People had tried to fight the monster in the past, and each time they had been crushed, their bodies mutilated and left behind as proof of the creature's power. This continued until I was born. I, humble little Ah Hock, who no one noticed, was devoting my childhood to training my mind and body, every day under the blinding sun. Not even the monster itself would know I existed. But I did. And that was its mistake, underestimating someone like me. Because I was there, improving myself with every cut of the blade, and one night there I was, standing at the end of the lane that led down to the inlet from which the awful creature rose. *Die, evil demon! I am the vision of your hell!* The thick tangle of vines and branches warped into the flesh of the monster for me. I hacked and beat at it with all my might, feeling my razor-sharp blades sink into the denseness of it. I didn't stop until I had vanquished the beast. Mortally wounded but not quite dead, it slithered back into the sea, fearful now of the people it had terrorised for so many years.

The following morning the people of the village would see the trail of monster blood in the fields, and know they were at last free. They would not know the identity of their *wuxia* hero, but some would whisper as they gathered at home to celebrate, *It was Ah Hock who saved us all.*

Those elaborate fantasies kept me occupied during the long hours working on the land. I slipped into such daydreams as easily as my mother tumbled into a deep sleep at night. I'd stay awake for a while after she fell asleep. I wanted to be sure she was resting before I surrendered to sleep myself. It didn't matter much to me if I slept or not. Tomorrow, I thought, in the full light of day, I'll have the chance to dream again.

Speaking of dreaming: during the trial, when my thoughts began to drift away in the heat and endless talking in the courtroom, I'd think back to those long days on the farm, my whole body training itself to cut and slash at everything that stood in my way. Maybe it wasn't surprising that my arms and legs reacted the way they did all those years later, on the riverbank facing that as-yet nameless man. When my defence lawyer insisted that I had no control over my actions, and that they had been *totally without precedent*, I suddenly remembered the sharpness of the blades of my childhood – their lightness in my hands.

As I began to see the boundaries of our piece of land – began to see bare earth and water now that the thorny scrub had been cut back – I started to feel a sense of permanence that I'd never experienced before. A feeling that I was connected to an unchanging place that belonged to me. A place that owned *me*. The sea was always restless, constantly twisting and warping, flowing away from us or overwhelming us. We were never certain of anything with the sea, but the soil – our soil – was solid. It would not leave, not even after we had left it.

When we were digging the first of the vegetable beds, my mother would often stop and stare at our plot of land. She'd shield her eyes from the glare of the sun and stand motionless.

'What's the matter?' I'd ask.

'Just looking,' she'd reply. 'Checking.'

'What do you think is going to happen – the land is going to disappear like smoke?' I joked. 'Even if you set fire to it, the land will still be the same.' It was true. When we burnt one part of the land to clear space to plant vegetables, the flames had danced over the surface of the earth, but after the fire had died out the soil remained exactly as it had been before. Rich red-brown in colour.

She laughed as she resumed tilling the soil. We were working the earth with *cangkuls* at that point – the one I was using was the same size as the ones adults use, and each time I lifted it and brought it crashing down into the thick red mud I knew that I was now able to do as much work as my mother. I hadn't fully realised up to that point how much of a burden I'd been to her. Perhaps I'd sensed it in the way that children do, but once that awareness had fully entered my thinking, I had to prove to her that I could make her life easier, not harder.

We planted the first of the vegetables just at the end of the rainy season, when the heaviest downfalls were over and the earth was heavy with moisture. We chose leafy vegetables we knew would grow quickly, as well as sweet potato, which in just a few months began to grow like a weed. Towards the end of the season we harvested some things for ourselves – for the first time in our lives we enjoyed a feeling of abundance, of having a supply of food that wasn't dependent on someone else. Nature, from which we'd always protected ourselves, was now providing us with a means to survive and be independent.

The rains were just right that first year – constant but never too heavy, and all our crops grew well. My mother was able to take a stall in the market in Kuala Selangor and sell whatever we grew. We dug a second vegetable plot, and a third, and soon my mother had a bigger stall, and regular customers who especially liked our string beans and *choy sum*. The first time I helped out at the stall, on a Saturday morning, I heard people greeting my mother by name. *Boss Lee* they called her, as they exchanged their news. 'That's your son that you've been talking about!' they said when they saw me. 'What a strong healthy boy – you're lucky!'

'Must be joking,' my mother laughed, and ruffled my hair. 'Look at this good-for-nothing lazy worm.'

Her customers dressed differently from the people of the village – not exactly like big-city dwellers, but not country folk either, with proper shirts and trousers, that didn't look as if they came from a night market. They spoke to my mother politely, even when they haggled over the price. They seemed to know about me – the fact that school was becoming a problem because I wasn't very good at maths or science – and sometimes my mother talked to them about me as if I wasn't there at all. *What can I do, he's lost interest in school. His teacher says he doesn't pay attention, he's tired all the time. Boys must be good at maths, otherwise die wor.* I hated being invisible, but I was comforted to see the customers' familiarity with my mother. She had a life outside the farm, a life that included other people than me, who knew about the problems she faced, and even if only for a few minutes a day, she could feel as though they took an interest in her.

It was about that time that her hearing began to fail. I'd always known that she had a slight problem, because she spoke louder than she needed to. I don't mean that she shouted, it was just that her voice was pitched as though she was constantly making an announcement. It was the result of an infection in her inner ear that she'd suffered as a child, she'd always explained. 'Too much playing in the rain.' I never believed she'd ever had a proper medical assessment of her condition. How could she have? Families like hers wouldn't have had the means to send her to a doctor for something as minor as that. During that period, when the small farm was expanding and we often found ourselves working the soil fifty or sixty yards apart from each other, I'd call out to her and she wouldn't look up, but continued carefully pressing the earth around the base of the seedlings she was planting row by row. I thought it might have been the intense concentration on her task that distracted her; I thought she was in her own bubble, savouring the knowledge that those little sprigs of green – barely even recognisable as leaves – would soon be sold

190

for money. *Ma!* It was only when I emptied my lungs in a full-throated cry that she'd look up in surprise and wave at me. Otherwise she'd continue working the soil, squatting so she could get close to the ground. Her back had started to ache from all the work we were doing, so it was easier that way. 'Look, my hips are still flexible,' she'd say. 'I'm still a young woman!'

I knew for certain that the problem was getting worse the week we released the fish into the ponds. We'd cleared the edges of the two murky pools of water to reveal a pair of neat squares. Old Pak Awang must have used a bulldozer to dig them all those years ago – there was no way nature was capable of such perfection. Once the edges of the ponds were defined, I slid into the water to clear away the weeds that had entirely covered their surfaces with a thin carpet. I trod water carefully – growing up in a fishing village teaches you never to trust what lies under the surface – and I was afraid of cutting my feet on sharp pieces of wood, or sheets of metal or other junk that had been thrown into the ponds' surprising depths. Unlike the sea, their water was stagnant and slightly cold, and I wondered what lay at the bottom, whether if I dived down to the muddy bed I'd find old bones – the skeletons of fish or monkeys, or even humans. I scooped the weed out of the ponds and dumped it on the grassy banks, where it collected in small piles.

I'd been in the water for some time on the second day when I felt my leg twitch – a sudden sharp contraction. A monster, I thought. A real goddamn monster. I writhed in panic as I felt my leg tighten from the toes all the way to the calf. I didn't know what was happening, and I began to thrash about, but I was in the middle of the pond, and the safety of the banks seemed far away. I tried to swim towards the edge, but the more I moved, the more my leg seized up, weighing me down like a block of concrete. I looked around for my mother, and saw her walking along the edge of the other pond. *Ma*, I cried weakly, but my voice was strangled by the pain and the fear that gripped me. Later – much later – I would know that I'd just had cramp, and that if I remained calm it would pass. But that first time I had no idea what was happening to my body, and the terror of the unfamiliar sensation was worse than the pain itself. I began to sink, my mouth and nose dipping below the water. Where were my superhero powers now? The monster was dragging me to the depths of the pond, and I was fighting, but losing.

My mother must have walked farther away – I could no longer see her. I called out for her again, loudly now. Again and again. I found strength in my legs and kicked towards the grassy bank closest to me, but I was still sinking. *Maaa!* I didn't know if I would make it. The monster was ferocious, it had caught hold of my leg and wasn't letting go. I pulled and kicked. I would make it. I would escape the beast, and one day I would return to kill it. My head dipped under the surface, but by then I was no longer afraid, I was close enough to the side of the pond to know that I had won. The creature would not claim me. We would duel another day.

I lay on the grass and looked around for my mother. She was not so far away, on the other side of the second pond, crouching on all fours as she reached into the water to salvage something from under the surface. 'Ma!' I shouted. I wanted to tell her about my ordeal, but she didn't look up, peering instead into the water as she fished around for something I couldn't see. My leg began to relax, and I felt as if I wanted to cry – out of embarrassment more than anything. I stretched out my leg and stood up. My body felt perfectly normal, as if nothing had happened to it. Why had I reacted so badly? I felt ashamed at having been so afraid, and even wondered if I'd imagined the whole pain. *Call yourself a wuxia hero.* It had been nothing. But my mother hadn't looked up – she hadn't heard anything.

We bought twenty tilapia and released them into the ponds. 'They're like us,' my mother said. 'They can survive anywhere.' They sank slowly into the water, as if they were too surprised to swim, and I never saw them apart from when I came to feed them. My mother and I spent even more time outdoors – now that the vegetables were under control we had to devise ways to chase away the egrets that came to fish in our suddenly fertile ponds. At the start, welded by the invisible ties that bond a mother to a child, I worked in close proximity to her, and she'd give me instructions on how to carry out my tasks, but now we often worked on opposite ends of what we referred to as 'the farm'. That meant calling out to each other, and I soon got used to the fact that she could no longer hear me unless I was standing close by.

'Buy her a hearing aid,' Keong said. I'd become friends with him by then, and – being older and from the city – what he said carried weight. In fact I had been thinking of a hearing aid for some time, but I knew we couldn't afford it. When I'd suggested it to my mother she'd said, 'But I can hear just fine.' Which I knew meant: We can't afford to buy anything.

'Leave it to me,' Keong said. 'You're my little brother. I'll fix it for you.'

The next day, late in the afternoon, I was harvesting some water spinach when I heard an unfamiliar beeping noise – a scooter coming down the lane that led to our farm, its rider honking insistently. No one ever came our way at that time of the day. The moment I saw the little red scooter I knew it was Keong. He stopped, and beckoned me over.

'I don't want to get mud on the wheels!' he shouted.

I jogged over to him and admired the scooter, a Honda with red and white stripes on its fuel tank. 'You're kidding me! Where'd you get that?'

'Outside the Nasi Kandar shop in Kuala Selangor.'

I knew what he meant, but I still asked, 'You bought it from someone?'

'Dumb fool!' He threw his head back and laughed. 'Of course I didn't buy it. This old guy went in for lunch, wasn't paying attention. I knew he was the type of idiot who wouldn't keep an eye on his bike. I broke the lock and rode off. Easy as anything.' He produced a screwdriver from his pocket and held it in front of my face as proof of his cunning.

'Better not let anyone see you riding it.'

'Relax, brother. I'm taking it down to Klang to sell it right now. New bike like this will attract maaaaaany customers.'

'How much will you get for it?'

'Enough!' he shouted as he rode away. I wanted to call out and tell him he should wear a helmet, but he was already too far away.

The next day, when my mother and I were packing up the stall in the market, I saw Keong sitting under a tree across the road, smoking a cigarette. He waved at me and I went over to see him.

'Don't let your mother see you hanging out with a scoundrel like me.'

'Think you're such hot shit? She's got better things to worry about than you.'

He reached into his pocket and drew out a fistful of cash. 'Well, she can stop worrying about her hearing.' He handed me the money, and I put it in my pocket without counting it. I felt the thick bundle pressing against my thigh, and suddenly I felt scared of losing it. What if it fell out of my pocket? What if someone stole it? What if the police knew I had something I shouldn't have had? Later, I'd feel guilty that I didn't feel more shame. That I didn't think, This money isn't mine. This money was stolen. This money belongs to someone else. But at that moment I didn't consider any of those things. The only fear I had was of losing the cash.

'Thanks, Keong,'

'No need to thank your big brother.' He stubbed out his cigarette. 'Now I'm going to take you to the shop in Klang to buy the damn thing. I don't trust a kid like you to do it yourself.'

We sat on the bus in silence, and later we cycled back to the farm together. He had nothing to do, he said, so he might as well come with me. Get some fresh air. 'Otherwise I'll be bored and get into trouble again.' He took charge of the hearing aid, strapping it tightly to his handlebars with some raffia string he'd brought along specially. 'You're such a bad cyclist,' he said. 'If you fall, you'll fuck everything up. Better that I take it.' He wouldn't let me touch the hearing aid until we were at the front door, and he didn't leave until I'd gone inside the house.

I waited until the next morning to give the new gadget to my mother. She eyed it suspiciously and said, 'But I don't need it, I can hear just fine.' I waited for her to ask me where I'd got it, whereupon I'd tell her the story Keong and I had prepared: that he had an aunt who worked in a shop in town, and who occasionally got to buy unsold stock at bargain prices. But she didn't ask, she just kept turning the small lump of flesh-coloured plastic over in her fingers. 'My friend Keong got it,' I said.

'I don't need it. My hearing is good.'

'Please, Ma. Just try it. If you don't need it I'll sell it.'

'OK. Make sure you get a good price! I'll just use it once, so it'll be like new.'

Of course she never took it off again after that, except to wipe it clean and put it in its box every night before she went to bed. 'I'll keep it in good condition in case you need to resell it,' she'd say from time to time, even a couple of years later when it had begun to malfunction, and would make all sorts of high-pitched screeching noises in the middle of conversations, or in the middle of a working day when we were digging the soil in the vegetable beds. I'd hear that strangled wail drifting in the air, and I'd chuckle at the thought of selling it on to someone else.

The farm gave us three years of stability, and although we never had enough money to live the way we wanted – the way people did on TV or in magazines – we had the sensation of control. We had mastered the small patch of land we owned, were extracting from it everything it was capable of giving us. We sold vegetables and a modest but steady catch of tilapia at the market each week, but we knew that we could never afford to expand the farm. We felt the limits of our potential – but the presence of those boundaries also felt comforting, in a way. For once we had a sense of our place in the world.

Curiously, the only other time I felt properly rooted to somewhere was when I was in jail. The routine, the frustration that was common to all the inmates, the meaninglessness of time, the absence of options – I was locked in a space that was mine, and nothing could change that, not even all the books I read to pretend I was somewhere else. I could read stories about life in Brazil or snowy Sweden, but when I finished I'd still be in my cell, just as I was before, the days stretching ahead of me.

That third year at the farm, people in the village began to talk about the spring tides, but we weren't concerned.

When you grow up by the sea in an area like that, the tides are as constant and present as the air around you. You think you know everything about them. You understand how destructive and regenerative they can be. How they carry the boats out to sea and bring them back again. How they swell with the seasons, bringing greater harvests at some times of the year, growing lean at others. When you know something so intimately, you don't fear it. We'd seen the spring tides before, always towards the end of the year, which doesn't make sense because that's not springtime. You'd get a sense that the tides would be higher than usual, because of the way the moon shone – with an unusual glow, not really brighter than a normal full moon, but with a strange intensity. You wouldn't notice this unless you spent a lot of time studying it – unless your livelihood depended on it. The winds would gather from the southwest, and you'd know that cyclones were building further north in Asia.

During these times, the village would prepare to defend itself against the onslaught of the sea. We'd rebuild the flood defences and move the boats further up the creek. Sometimes the families closest to the sea would move themselves and their belongings into the homes of relatives further inland, and resign themselves to rebuilding their houses once the floods had subsided. They'd done it before, and they'd do it again. It wasn't the end of the world.

People said, *Looks like it's going to be bad this year.* They said that every year – we didn't care too much. Just to be safe, though, my mother and I borrowed sandbags from someone in the village, planning to stack them around the seaward boundary of the farm, three bags high. That would stop the worst of any floods, we thought. They were so heavy it took both of us to lift them. *Wuxia warrior, you have to help this poor villager*, I told myself as I strained to

197

lift each bag. *Without you the sea monster will claim your mother and all her land.* We hadn't finished building the barrier when my mother pulled a muscle in her back. I could see her struggling, but she was barely able to hold her end of the sandbag. When she bent down to lift the next one with me she let out a sharp cry. *Aie!* Followed swiftly by a sharp intake of breath. Sucking in the air between her teeth.

'Take a rest, Ma.'

'It's OK, I'm fine.'

But when she tried again to lift the bag she could hardly move. She bent over, her hands resting on her knees, breathing heavily. I could smell her hot sour breath from where I was standing.

'Ma, please, go and drink some water. I'll finish this.'

'It's OK. Give me a minute.' She tried to stand up straight, but instead sank to the ground. I rushed over, and helped her up to a sitting position, leaning against the low pile of sandbags.

'That's better,' she breathed heavily. 'I'll be OK.'

I looked up at the sky. Rain clouds had gathered out at sea – thick and slow-rolling, the colour of coal, blotting out the sun and casting a twilight glow across the land, even though it was the middle of the afternoon. We'd already had the first of the rains that year, heavy drizzles that would turn to steady downpours. I continued to drag the sandbags myself, feeling the muscles in my legs and back thicken and strain with each one I lifted into position. My mother remained propped up against the sandbags, watching me. She waved, but made no attempt to get up. We both knew that I would have to finish the barrier on my own. 'Keep going!' she yelled, and pumped her fist. My knees felt as though they would buckle at any moment, but I forced my body to do what it needed to do. I was a *wuxia* hero. I was invincible. I had to defend us against the monster from the sea. I heard my mother's hearing aid squeal and whine, like the noise of an alien spaceship. I wanted to say, *Don't worry, I'll make sure everything's OK*, but I knew she wouldn't hear me.

Her back was bad for some days, and that Saturday I had to take the vegetables to sell at the market myself. When I got home I started to dig a trench that ran the length of the sandbags, so that if any water penetrated the barrier we'd have a second line of defence. The hard work was worth it, we said – an investment for the future. It wasn't just for this year, but for all the years ahead. Who knew when the next big tides were going to be? From time to time my mother's back would feel a bit better, and she'd start to work again, but it would give way within minutes, and in the end she had to stay indoors.

'I have no energy,' she complained. 'I'm getting so old.' She must have pulled a major muscle, because the pain was now in her stomach as well as her back. It was true that she hadn't been eating well. The harvests hadn't been good because of the rain – a lot of vegetables had rotted in the wet soil, and we hadn't been able to sell as much as usual. She'd lost her appetite, and I thought it was because of the stress – we both did.

When the first swells appeared we had no idea the tides would be as strong and high as they turned out to be. I heard the waves gathering in the night, and when I walked out of the house I found my mother already standing on the bank of sandbags, watching the sea rise. The rocky beach a few hundred yards away had been smothered by a foamy wash, and we knew that by morning it would have reached us.

'Better get some sleep,' my mother said. We went back inside and she told me to push some sandbags against the door, 'Just in case,' but we both knew that it was a certainty, not a possibility.

It was still dark when I heard the noise. The rushing of the wind, I thought. Then a low groaning – as if a monster had actually emerged from the sea. Then a silence. I didn't think I'd fallen asleep, but I obviously had, because the sounds came to me as hazily as in a dream, and I couldn't be sure of what I was hearing. What woke me was the touch of water. I turned over in bed and let my arm fall over the side. My fingers felt cold and wet. I jolted awake and sat up in bed, looking at the silvery black slick just a few inches below me. It wasn't a dream, I knew that at once. Things were floating in the water – my canvas shoes, my slippers, some clothes. In the dark they looked like dead fish.

This is the sea, I thought. *The sea is in my bedroom.*

I stepped off my bed into the cold salty water, slowly, not knowing what to expect underfoot, but it was just the floor of the house, reassuring and solid. I walked to the door, forced open by the water, and into the main room. My mother was already standing there, trying to prise open the door, which was wedged shut by the sandbags. I dipped my arms into the water, lifting my chin to keep my head above the surface, and pulled the sandbags as far as I could. We squeezed through the door and slipped outside. All around us we saw only what we had seen inside the house. The sea.

There was no distinction in the landscape – everything had turned to water. We waded waist-deep, trying to figure out the strangeness of our new world. Underfoot, everything felt uncertain. Where was the concrete platform outside the house, or the line of heavy earthenware pots in which we grew herbs? The sea had consumed everything. All we could see was the swirling surface of the water, as slick as petrol. We looked out into the dark and could not discern the vegetable plots or the ponds or the sandbags, or even the bushes and trees around the farm. Neither of us spoke. We walked until the ground beneath our feet became too soft and uncertain for us to continue, and then headed back to the house, which at least offered us a sense of boundaries, with its walls and roof, even though it was no longer the house we had known just a few hours previously.

'What are we going to do, Ma?' I asked.

She didn't answer. At first I thought it was because she was in shock. That she was too scared to answer. Then I realised she wasn't wearing her hearing aid, and couldn't hear what I was saying. She hadn't had time to put it in before the tide arrived, and now it was lost in the floodwater.

We found the ladder and climbed up onto the roof with as many things as we could gather from the cupboards – anything that hadn't yet been claimed by the water. Two candles. Some clothes, bundled up in a raffia bag. Biscuits. The tin of money that represented all our savings. We'd seen it floating in the water, knocking against the wall of my mother's bedroom as if to remind us it was there. The tiles of the roof were slippery, but at the top there was a flat concrete ledge that we could straddle comfortably.

From our vantage point we began to reconfigure what we understood of the land in which we lived. The place that was once our home. The sea had erased everything we had thought unmoveable. Scrubbed it all out and absorbed it. Our ponds, full of fish. Our farm. All of that was now part of the sea. As we waited for daybreak my mother pulled me close to her. The wind was gusting, blowing patterns on the surface of the water, sometimes ruffling it into waves. Occasionally there would be a surge in the sea, and the entire watery landscape would tremble and swell. At last the skies began to lighten, turning a faint blue-grey.

I can only recall that first spring tide in any detail. There was another one the year after, less powerful; and another the following year, stronger even than the first. The others felt inevitable, as if they were predestined. That first year, the waters subsided a few days later, and we tried to rebuild what we had lost. The second year, we didn't even try. *Global warming*, people said – strong tide surges would be normal from now on. Apply for a subsidy or loan to buy a new place, someone in the village suggested half-heartedly. But even at that age I knew, like everyone else, that it was hopeless. We were the wrong race, the wrong religion – who was going to give us any help? Not the government, that's for sure. We knew that for no-money Chinese people like us, there was no point in even trying.

It didn't matter. By that time my mother's stomach and back pains had got so bad that one day she collapsed on the street in Kuala Selangor and had to be taken to hospital. She'd been stressed, she hadn't been eating properly, she told the nurse when she woke up in the ward. But what she had thought was due to her bad diet turned out to be a tumour in her colon the size of a small apple. The doctor was angry. 'Why didn't you get it checked earlier?' she yelled at me. 'It's been growing for at least ten years,' she said, pointing at the fuzzy circle on the x-rays that she held in front of my face as if it was my fault. I just shrugged. She explained that there were treatments in KL or Singapore that might possibly shrink the tumour, but she wasn't all that hopeful. My mother said she didn't want to see any more doctors, that she needed to face her destiny. She tried to make her reasoning sound Buddhist, but the truth was that we had no means of paying for the hospitals. She struggled on for another year before her body gave up. I'd already made the decision to leave for KL to find work. Her death

202

made it easy for me to leave what was left of the land and the house we owned.

When I think back to that period of our lives, what comes to mind isn't the floods or the way the farm looked after the water had subsided, flattened by a blanket of grey mud and sea-sand. It isn't the storms, or the house with its cracked walls. It isn't the early promise of wealth either, when my mother's market stall was doing well and she came home every day with bags of sweets and cakes as a treat. What I remember is our days working on the farm – my silly, happy fantasies of being a martial-arts hero wandering the countryside slaying beasts and helping the oppressed. In these images that come back to me, clear as sunlight, I am slashing away at the dense foliage, or digging the thick mud. I feel like a hero. I am a hero. I look up and see my mother by the ponds. Squatting so she's close to the ground, repairing the small nets she'll soon throw over the water to snare the week's catch. Her hearing aid is playing up, crackling with static and squealing its high-pitched whine. I don't know why I'm smiling.

III

DECEMBER

December 4th

The encampment lay in a scrubby bit of forest, scattered among the trees and bushes, clearly visible from the road. A row of tarpaulins was stretched between tree trunks just a few yards from the edge of the road – grey-brown canvas and bright-blue plastic sheets that you couldn't fail to notice if you were driving along the long, straight route that linked the plantation towns to the highway, and further on to the coast. It was a road like any other in the area, cutting through palm-oil estates and scrubland and patches of forest. Occasionally you'd see a small abandoned wooden shelter that might once have been a bus stop, or a food stall. You could be driving down the road, make a turn at a crossroads, and suddenly find yourself on another, identical stretch of cracked tarmac, and soon you'd be lost. You wouldn't be sure if the makeshift camp you glimpsed between the trees was the same one you saw twenty minutes before. In any case, there are so many of these kinds of temporary dwelling places in this part of the country. So many temporary workers. If you want to hide a large group of men, this is the best way to do it: in full view of anyone who chooses to notice them.

Even though Keong knew where the camp was, we sped right past, and had to reverse a few hundred yards to get back to it. I was driving, and Keong was smoking, making his way steadily through his pack of Salems. We were always taking small detours to track down shops that sold them.

He was fussy, wouldn't smoke anything else. The window was down, but the hot air that swirled around the car didn't seem to chase away the smoke. It had taken us only two brief meetings to fall into an established pattern – I drove, while Keong smoked and talked constantly. First time, it was because he had a problem with his car. The next time it was because he said he wanted to appreciate the landscape. 'It's been so long. I realise now that I really miss this place.'

He'd point out things he remembered from the past, from way back in the nineties – a stretch of jungle that flooded one year, when the rains didn't stop for three days and nights, and the rivers and monsoon drains overflowed. For a few days afterwards, under heavy grey skies, the trunks of the trees were submerged, with only their leaves protruding from the muddy water like giant origami decorations floating on the surface of a pond. A dirt track where a wild boar charged at us while we were cycling early one evening. *It had its babies with it, it was aggressive, it really scared us!* The stretch of the main road where he had his first crash on his scooter – lorries carrying their loads of palm-oil seeds would squeeze him too close to the concrete kerb, and more than a few times he'd been forced off the road. Once he ended up in a ditch. There – the noodle place he'd taken that girl to on his first date, my God, what was her name?

I let him talk. I nodded. Sometimes I laughed, just to give him the impression that I was confirming the clarity of his memories. I never had the heart to tell him that he'd got it wrong – that the stretch of jungle he remembered had been cut down years ago, the trees felled in the space of a week to make way for a new plantation that was now so mature, the palm-oil trees so tall, that it seemed to have belonged to that landscape since the beginning of time. The noodle stall he talked about was actually on the other side of Sekinchan, and it too had disappeared years

208

ago. How do you expect a ramshackle place like that to survive more than a few years? As for other details – maybe he was right. I don't remember exactly where we were when we crossed paths with the mother wild boar and her babies, or where we saw a monitor lizard eating the carcass of a goat. I just nodded in agreement when Keong dredged up those memories. They'd ceased to matter to me.

He wouldn't stop talking about the past, and soon I found myself driving faster than I should have, just to reach our destination and put an end to our one-sided conversation. That was why I went past the camp without realising it was where we were meant to stop. He was still talking as we got out of the car – recounting one of the endless antics of Auntie Ah Hua, who had developed a taste for whisky after her marriage broke up, and used up all her savings on Johnnie Walker Red Label and Mekhong, and often appeared drunk at the temple, which everyone thought was funny – while I strode on ahead. I could barely remember those events.

'What is this place?' I asked.

'It's where the workers stay before they move into their permanent jobs.'

'So what kind of work are they doing right now?'

Keong lit another cigarette, and shook the box to see how many he had left. Almost none. 'You dumb or what? They've got no work yet. Why do you think I'm so stressed? Twenty men sitting around doing nothing for three weeks. Think of the money I'm losing.'

The camp looked deserted. The air was cloudy with the last remnants of an open fire slowly dying in the sticky air – I got the feeling that someone had thrown damp leaves on the embers to hide its glow. The smoke that rose from the pile of foliage and ash was thin and blue, and made the shapes that lay in the shade of the tarpaulins indistinct. But as we got close to the first of the shelters I noticed movement through the haze. One of those dead mounds – of earth? Of vegetation? – began to move, and a man emerged from the gloom.

'Haven't heard from you in two days.' He addressed Keong in bad Malay, mixed up with some words from a foreign language I didn't understand. In fact he said something like, *Two days something something never something call phone*. But I could make out what he meant all the same.

'Been busy.'

'We're out of food. The men haven't eaten since yesterday morning. Had to walk to the stream to get water. Some of them are sick.'

Keong kept striking his lighter, but the air was so humid that the flame wouldn't catch. 'Let me see them.'

As we walked through the camp the motionless shapes under the tarpaulins began to stir and unfurl into human form, men – all men – stretching into life, sitting up, coughing, running their hands across their faces. A few of them looked at us, and though I returned their glances I looked away quickly. Our eyes barely met, but in those two, three seconds, I knew that we shared something. A sense of shame. A desire to flee – to escape that camp, that forest, that country, the whole universe that made that life possible. Did they avert their gaze before I did? One of us blinked first and lowered our head to avoid seeing the other, but I couldn't tell who it was. Probably me. I didn't need to examine them any closer to figure out what they were, or what they were doing there – I didn't need Keong or anyone else to explain. Once they realised that they were in no immediate danger, they lay back down and continued to rest. What else could they do, I thought. Rest.

'They're not the ones we're looking for,' Keong said as we drove away.

'They're Bangladeshi?' I asked.

'That's where most of the labour comes from these days. Many from Myanmar and Nepal too, but in this area I handle mainly Bangladesh and Indons. Better for plantation work.'

I didn't ask any questions. At that point I was still hoping that Keong would go away and leave me in peace, and I didn't want to show any interest in his business.

On the drive back to Klang he explained that he worked as a 'labour contractor', that his employers were a company – a real, proper company with an office – that brought in people from all sorts of companies to work in all sorts of jobs. Construction sites, plantations – but these days also hotels, restaurants, toilet cleaners, you name it. The kind of work that locals don't have the taste for these days – and even if we did, what employer would give us the work? They can get two Bangladeshis for the price of one local. 'It's like at the supermarket,' said Keong. 'Who can resist the buy-one-get-one-free offer? That's why they're everywhere. Walk into any shop or eating place and a foreigner will be serving you.'

'Really? I don't see so many Bangladeshis around here,' I said.

'You must be blind. Anyway, up in KL they're everywhere. The other day I was waiting for my wife at the hair salon and I heard an old woman say, "I don't want a foreigner touching me, I don't want that dark-skinned person touching my hair." And I couldn't help myself, I said, "*Wei*, Auntie, better get used to it, because dark-skinned foreigners are here to stay. No one else going to be shampooing your hair any time soon." '

Whenever his company got calls from a construction site or a plantation, Keong told me, he would contact the labour brokers and say, 'How many Bangladeshis or Burmese can you get me by next month?' Or, 'I need eight men and six women for a new hotel in Johor by next Wednesday. Can?' *A middleman*. I thought it sounded like a suitable job for him. He didn't come in with any ideas at either end of the deal, he just got things sorted out in between. The messy stuff that no one else wanted to do – that was always his strength.

The brokers were the ones who got the men into the country, and Keong's company was responsible for the paper-work. Keong himself didn't do any administration. 'You know how bad I was at school – reading papers and contracts, that's not for me.' But any old fool could do that work. What Keong did was far more important, according to him at least. He had to go out into the field, drive around the country for days, making sure the foreigners were in half-decent shape when they turned up for their first day's work. Give them enough food in the three or four days before they start their jobs. Patch them up if they've got any wounds or bruises. Can't show anything ugly, no raw flesh, obvious fractures, that sort of thing – no employer likes to see men riddled with disease or carrying too many injuries. Women even more so – they have to look washed and clean. Thank goodness there weren't that many women in the plantations. God knows what women have been through by the time they got to this country. 'I wouldn't like to be the one in charge of getting them in shape,' Keong said. 'But someone out there has to. Sit down in your seafood restaurant in KL and the Myanmar girl who's serving you – well, chances are she didn't look like that when she stepped off the boat.'

Give them enough food. Patch them up. I thought of the people in the camp and wondered if any of them had open wounds. I drove fast down the narrow straight road. I was impatient to reach the wide lanes and streaming traffic of the highway. The sooner I got there, the sooner I'd leave Keong and his mess behind. I lowered all the windows to

212

get rid of the smoke from his cigarettes. 'You're the same as before, always judging,' Keong said. 'What I do is a proper business – just like yours. You think it's dirty work, don't you?'

I hesitated. 'I don't care what you do. It just seems a bit complicated to me. We never have these kinds of problems hiring workers at the farm.'

'Problems? What do you mean? Motherfucker. How do you find guys to work, then?'

'Mostly they're friends or relatives of people who already work for us. They know we pay on time – not a lot, but always on time. They get days off, holidays. Sometimes they just turn up out of nowhere. They walk into the farm and ask for work, we ask to see their foreign worker's card, that's it. We don't need to go through middlemen and brokers and all that nonsense.'

'*Sor hai*,' Keong laughed. 'You run a shitty little fish farm and you think you understand everything. Little guy, let me tell you, we supply workers to all the plantations. The biggest ones. They need dozens, hundreds of men at a time. The palm oil gets exported to China, the US, Europe – everywhere. Those imported American cookies you see in the supermarket, the ones you can't afford to buy – all made with our palm oil. You see, I'm working in an *international business*. And you think you can look down on me? Makes me laugh.'

'I like my job. I don't need to work for an international company to be happy.'

He didn't answer.

We kept the windows down even on the highway. The noise of the traffic filled the car, swirling around us just like the smoke from Keong's cigarettes, but its presence was comforting. I thought, Now he'll leave me in peace. Now he realises at last that we've become different people.

*

In truth I should have known, even on the first day of our so-called reunion, that he was going to be hanging around for a while. When we left Ah Chan's that evening, we drove into town separately, me following him as he led the way. I didn't know where he was taking me; it was just like the old days, only now we were in cars, not on scooters. He wanted to have a few drinks, sing a few songs at a KTV place, and we ended up at K-Fire Karaoke. I heard it closed down some years ago, and I'm not surprised. Got raided too many times. It looked just like any other karaoke joint, but back then even I knew what kind of reputation it had. At the farm, visiting contractors used to refer to it with a smile. They talked about going there after dinner 'for some dessert'. You had to ask discreetly, you had to look like the kind of man who'd spend a lot of money, not someone like me. There'd be women, young and not so young, who'd serve you drinks. What happened after that was up to you and your hostess. 'It's a free market,' I'd hear people say. 'You can do whatever deal you want.'

But that night Keong didn't want to do any deals. He didn't ask for any girls, didn't even look at passing women the way he used to when he was younger, didn't stare and make comments. He ordered a bottle of Johnnie Walker, which we didn't finish. All he wanted to do was sing. Danny Chan Pak-keung. The entire repertoire. Sometimes he stood up, holding the mike as if he was on stage, performing in a huge auditorium, his arms spreading swanlike as if he wanted to embrace the entire audience. *So why do I still keep on secretly loving you* he sang, facing the screen and closing his eyes as if addressing the words to himself. His voice was rough, gritty, even more so than before, and I remembered him singing the same songs more than a decade previously,

214

when we were hanging around the streets of the capital every night, that big-city life that seemed so full of promise. Sometimes, in the half-dark of that padded KTV room, in the middle of a song, Keong would turn away from his imaginary audience and look at me while singing a line or two, and I'd notice how much he'd aged since we last met.

And then I was singing too, with a mike in my hand, joining in the chorus to a few of the songs. I don't know how that happened, I'd only had two drinks, and I hadn't even finished the second one. Somebody opened the door and stumbled into the room – a middle-aged man with his shirt half-unbuttoned, mumbling, 'Darling, where are you?' before falling into an armchair. We helped him up and pushed him out into the corridor again. We were laughing. The music was playing loudly; we hadn't bothered to stop the disc. Keong sat down, breathing heavily, and eased his wallet from his trouser pocket. He paused for a while before opening it and showing me a photo, tucked neatly behind a plastic cover.

'My wife and baby,' he said. I couldn't see clearly in the gloom – the photo was hazy in the flickering light of the TV screen. Three people. A man, a woman with a young child in her arms, shot against a blue background in a studio. The man didn't even look like Keong – he was neatly dressed in a long-sleeved shirt, buttoned all the way to the collar. I thought of showing him a photo of Jenny, but the moment seemed wrong.

I said, 'That's nice.'

He leaned back in the chair and sipped his drink. 'I want to make some cash and start my own business. Make life good for my wife and kid. Emigrate to California. Australia. Wherever. Somewhere I don't have to do this shit.'

'Thought you loved your big-time job. You must be making decent money.'

He stared at the screen, which was playing the kind of

karaoke video that doesn't make any sense at all, just home-made shots of people walking in parks. He looked almost sad as he turned to me and said, 'I have a problem.'

As he talked his voice lowered slightly, as if softened by doubt. By reality. And that made him seem more certain, more truthful, than I could remember. He'd been wanting to leave his job for some time now, but he couldn't afford to. The work was tiring, he was on the road many days at a time, sometimes a week, ten days. He didn't see his family enough. He'd go away to visit a plantation in Kedah or Johor, and when he came back his daughter would have learned another few words. Once he came home after a long trip up north and she spoke in a full sentence. He had the feeling he was missing out on things. On the small things that made up this thing we call life. One day he got into a fight with some Burmese guys who hadn't been paid in a while. They were demanding their money, but Keong hadn't even known about the situation, so he stood his ground. *You know what I'm like*. They roughed him up before disappearing into the jungle. No one could find them – not the police, not the other workers, but in truth no one tried very hard. Guess who got the blame? Five lost men – that's a lot of money. His employers were furious. Worse still, try explaining to your small child why you've got a bloody bruise on your face. *Papa fell down. Stupid Papa!* She just stared at him, blinking. Then her face crumpled and she started to cry. Wouldn't stop crying. That was when he thought, I must get out.

Now there was another matter. Eighteen missing workers. Keong's company had already paid for these men, but they never turned up. That was why he was back down here, to try to find the men and sort things out with the broker, the guy who shipped them in from abroad. If he could clear things up, his boss had promised him a bonus. When he got that money, dear God, he would resign the very next day and start his own business. He'd already thought of a plan: his uncle had connections with factories in China that made clothing for Western luxury brands. He'd heard they threw tons of clothes away – one bad stitch and a perfectly good item would be rejected. Keong would buy all those rejects and sell them here at knockdown prices.

Still staring at the screen, he said, 'Will you help me?'

'How the hell can I help?'

'You know people down here. You know all the plantations. You hear things. I'm an outsider now. If I go around asking questions, no one will help me. You're a local.'

I laughed. 'In your dreams. I have a quiet life now. I don't know anyone.' I stood up to leave. It wasn't late, but my head was hurting and I had an early start at the farm the next day.

'I'm all on my own here,' Keong said. His voice had dropped so low that I could barely hear him over the music. Outside, muffled, off-key voices came from the other rooms. On the screen, a carefree young couple were running through the Lake Gardens, or some other pleasant park with a boating lake in the background. They looked impossibly happy, and slightly out of focus, as people always are in those sorts of videos. I left without saying goodbye, honestly thinking that was the last time I would see Keong.

I'm writing a book, she says.

Book? What book.

About you.

I pause. What for? I thought you were doing research for your PhD.

Well, I am. But, umm, I'm sort of thinking of turning it into a book? She says this as if it's a question. Only it isn't a question.

What kind of book? I say.

It's a bit hard to describe, she replies. Something between biography and journalism. Narrative non-fiction, I guess. That's what I'd call it. Or maybe true crime, only, well, different. Better. I don't know. Publishers have so many strange ways of marketing books these days.

Publishers? I repeat the word as if I've never heard it before. I know I'm coming across as stupid – that I'm turning the conversation into a sort of merry-go-round, where every so often we have to pass a point where I say, *What book?* Or *Publishers? Narrative what?*

You're kidding, right? I say. A book about me? My little life? No one's going to be interested in that.

You'd be surprised. I think a lot of people would be interested.

You're nuts.

The point is this. I need your permission before I can publish anything.

Why? You can do anything you like. I don't care.

Well, I do care. I wouldn't do anything unauthorised. I'd feel very uncomfortable acting without your blessing. It's your story, not mine. You should have the final say about whether it gets released into the world or not.

I pause and look at her. She smiles. That same smile that transforms not just her face but the entire room, scrubbing out any possibility of sadness.

A book, huh? What a crazy idea.

Did you read in the newspapers a few months ago about a man who went berserk and killed his entire family? Up in Penang. They ran a small chicken factory – the kind of place where live chickens are delivered to be slaughtered, cleaned and packed for sale in the supermarkets. The family lived in two shipping containers inside the factory, one stacked on top of the other. Their entire home consisted of these two metal bedrooms. I couldn't make out from the photos whether they had any windows or not – I don't think the photographer was interested in capturing anything other than the blood on the mattresses. The man – a young guy around thirty, I think – turns up at the factory and gets into an argument with his mother and her boyfriend. It's 2 a.m., and the workers in the factory are getting ready for a long shift slaughtering and plucking chickens. Imagine that, plucking chickens while it's still dark outside every day of your life. Machines are whirring all around them, the chickens squawking their heads off. The workers don't think anything about it – the guy's got a temper, he's always shouting at his mother. His brother hears the commotion and comes down from the top container. He's carrying his two-year-old son, who's sleeping in his arms. We don't know what the argument is about. Suddenly the guy pulls out a handgun, a 9mm pistol, and shoots them all. Point blank. From that range, you can't miss. Then he drives off in a Toyota Hilux and the police can't find him. Maybe he just drove over the bridge and up into Kedah and Thailand – who knows. And all that time, the Nepalese workers are plucking those squawking birds while the family are lying dead in their cramped shipping containers.

Police ask everyone who knew the family, but no one knows for sure why he did it. Killing a stranger is one thing, but your own mother? Your brother? His baby kid? Some people say it must have been drugs. Others that it was over money. Others that it was because he hated his mother's boyfriend. Others that it was shame. Mother gives him thousands of bucks to fund his chicken stall at the market, but then one day some guy from City Hall turns up and takes everything away because there's a problem with his licence. He's lost all his money – his mother's money – and doesn't know what went wrong. Maybe he didn't bribe the right person, maybe he forgot to fill in part of some form, but whatever the case, his business is finished, and he's so ashamed he can't face the family. Can't look at them without feeling a terrible pain somewhere in his skull. Every time they stare at him it's as if they're accusing him – of what he doesn't quite know, but they're accusing him. Of everything.

But the truth is that there is no *because*. And because there is no *because*, there is also no *why*. He did what he did. Sometimes things happen that way. Or maybe the *because* was buried so far in his past that it's impossible to figure out what it is, so it ceases to be real. For many months, while waiting for my trial, and afterwards in prison, I tried to find the reasons behind what I did. I tried to excavate the layers of my thoughts, my memories, digging patiently the way I used to in the mud on our farm when I was a child, and later at the fish farm. Sometimes you hit a layer of rock, other times the mud was compacted so solidly that your *cangkul* couldn't dig through it, no matter how high you raised it over your head, how hard you brought it crashing down into the earth. That was how I felt. I wasn't going to give up. I would sit on my bed with my eyes closed, sinking deeper into the mess of people and sounds in my head, of events lasting five seconds or five years, trying to recall anything in my past that might have given me a clue to why I'd done what I did. A reason for those five, ten seconds. When you have so much time on your hands there's little else to do. But those hours, those long nights alone, searching – they yielded nothing. That's why I don't question myself in the same way these days. Prayers are all I need. There's no point in questioning God's will.

The month Keong reappeared in Klang, I was busier at work than I'd ever been. The farm had just taken a huge order from a supermarket chain in Singapore, but Mr Lai's mood was as bad as ever. Said he was stressed. 'Stressed from success,' Jezmine said without looking up from her computer screen one day. 'You men are useless. Business is bad, you get grumpy. Business is good, you get grumpy. Can't handle anything. Look at him – doesn't even have time to dress himself properly or comb his hair in the morning. I can't even look at him these days, all that dandruff on his shoulders.' She laughed as she scribbled a note on a piece of paper – she wrote so quickly, typed even faster. 'Lucky your wife takes care of you,' she said to me. 'At least you look presentable.'

Outside, we could see Mr Lai gesticulating at some of the Indonesian workers. They weren't working hard enough, he'd complained to me, and it was true, a few of them seemed slower than usual. We were building more ponds and installing an irrigation system to fulfil the order from Singapore – a long-term contract with payment guaranteed every quarter. I'd devised the new pumps, imagined how the water would flow across the land, filling the hollows in the earth. I thought of my mother, bent over with a shovel in her hands, scooping out mounds of wet mud from our fields. I remembered our little farm, which wasn't even a farm but a stretch of soil and thorns, and thought how it might have looked if we'd had the technology I was now building, and the absurdity of it made me smile. That miserable unyielding land would never have given us anything, no matter what we did to it. Earth and water – that was my livelihood once again, but now I had money and machines on my side.

Even Mr Lai was happy with my plan, and promised to give all the men a two-hundred-ringgit bonus when the construction works were completed. 'I'm such a softie,' he said, 'always paying you guys too much.' He never promised to give me a bonus, though, and I wasn't expecting one. It was enough for me to see that the men were working well, darting across the yard, joking as they worked. Two hundred bucks isn't a lot of money to you, and not even to them – let's face it, even a packet of fried noodles in a shitty roadside stall costs five ringgit a throw, so how long can that kind of cash last? But in these kinds of jobs, small gestures like that mean something. They signify kindness, even though the person making the gesture doesn't do it out of kindness but as a sort of automated response. I remembered my time in KL, working as a waiter. Sometimes people would give me one, two ringgit as a tip, and for some minutes afterwards I'd be walking with more energy and being just a bit more polite to customers than usual. They'd hand me the notes without even looking at me, but still, I'd feel that I was important. That I existed.

The first days of the new works started in this way, but then there was a change – as swift as a thunderstorm on a hot afternoon. One day the workers were fine, the next they had slowed down to a near stop. Tasks that usually took a couple of hours, like digging a small trench or repairing the floating cages, lasted nearly a whole day. I tried to reassign them to different jobs, change the workload, but often I'd find them sitting on the bare earth, in a patch of shade under a tree, heads bowed. The patient rise and fall of their shoulders as they breathed. Even the air seemed to weigh down on them.

'What the fuck?' Mr Lai said every time he saw them. 'I paid for men, not livestock. Look at them, just sitting under the trees like goats!'

'What's up with you guys?' I asked several times, but nobody would answer. They just shrugged and looked away. 'Sack them, hire new ones,' Mr Lai said. He was spending all day on his mobile phone, and it seemed like wherever we were on the farm we could hear his voice, clattering away like a machine gun, always on the verge of shouting. I wouldn't fire the men, I'd replied, I'd clear things up. Besides, these men knew the farm, they knew me. I'd never had a problem with any of them.

'They're sick, they probably caught colds when they had to work in the rain last week,' I said. The winds that week had been very heavy – the tail end of the typhoon that blew down from the Philippines. 'Just give them a few days, they'll get better quickly.'

One by one, in the space of two, three days, they all succumbed to a lethargy that I'd never seen in them before. Their mouths were hanging open. Eyes bloodshot and sinking into their sockets. Lips cracked as if they'd been shipwrecked on a desert island. They were always drinking water, but it was never enough, and sometimes they'd hold the hosepipe above their heads and gulp down as much as they could. Still, they didn't get better. By the end of the week half of them weren't showing up for work, and the ones who did could barely walk from one end of the farm to the other without sitting down to rest. In the meantime the works we had started lay virtually abandoned, the earth scarred with half-dug pits filled with rainwater and beginning to collapse in on themselves. Piles of nets and wire, rolls of black tarpaulin. Men sitting half-asleep in the shade. Around us, the black stumps of trees we'd cut down and poisoned so the roots would die.

When I asked Hendro what was wrong with him, he shrugged and said, 'Stomach ache.' His cheeks were sunken; he seemed to have lost ten pounds in two days.

'You can't stop work just because of a stomach ache.'

He shook his head. *Muntah, muntah*. He made an action with his hand in front of his mouth to indicate vomiting. Lots of vomiting. Everyone was vomiting. In the village where they lived, someone had started vomiting and having violent diarrhoea one night. By the end of the next day, three other people were sick with the same symptoms, the day after it was ten, then twenty, and now everyone who lived there was ill, nearly fifty people in total. I'd seen where they lived, I'd driven past it, on the outskirts of the port area, and it wasn't surprising that they were all ill. One tap for all the inhabitants, the drains clogged with black water. Cats picking through small heaps of rubbish. Children playing with sticks and pieces of string, lines of washing hanging outside the houses, sagging under the weight of clothes that looked grey even after they'd been cleaned. You know the type of place I mean – you drive past them in two seconds and you don't even notice them. Funny how people use that word – *kampung* – when what they mean isn't a village in the countryside, surrounded by trees and flowers, but a semi-slum, a shanty without amenities except for one or two cheap generators that everyone chips in to feed with diesel now and then.

225

'You have cholera,' I said. I'd seen the symptoms before; there had been an outbreak in the village when I was small, and nearly all the children had fallen sick. Suddenly I felt sweaty, a slight shiver ran down my neck. I thought of all the things we'd touched that day – the oil drums, the packs of fish feed, the shovels – and wondered if I had cholera germs on my hands too. I wondered if I was going to be sick. I wondered if they were going to die. In the washroom I cleaned my hands with soap as thoroughly as I could, twice, three times. I found some bleach and poured a few drops into the basin and filled it with water before soaking my hands in it, submerging half my forearms. The sharp smell of chlorine on my skin afterwards felt reassuring; it followed me around for the rest of the day.

Later, I got all the men together in the yard and told them to go home. 'Go see a doctor!' I shouted as they trudged off, knowing that they wouldn't because they couldn't afford to. It wouldn't even cross their minds. I remembered how it felt. If you were sick like that, you just waited to get better, and if you didn't, well, there was nothing you could do about it. I looked at the pools of stagnant water collecting on the ground. Collapsing trenches of grey sludge. No doubt the men had relieved themselves in them, and now there was cholera in the water, seeping into the red soil everywhere around us, into the fish enclosures, into the rivers and the sea beyond.

Mr Lai rang from Kuantan – he was on the east coast looking for more business ('Hunting for more stress,' Jezmine said) – and asked how it was going, whether I'd hired more men.

How the hell could I hire ten men just like that? I felt like shouting down the phone. You think they're just going to appear out of thin air? That's not the way things work. You have to ask the guys if they have any friends, a cousin from their village back home, someone reliable. We needed ten men to finish the job in time, maybe fifteen. Now we had maybe two healthy ones. There was no hope for us.

'Everything's OK,' I lied. 'By the time you get back next week, you'll see the difference.'

'*Die lor!*' Jezmine screamed with laughter as I hung up. 'You're in big trouble. Don't count on me to help you with your lies.'

At home that evening I couldn't concentrate on anything, couldn't even keep up with the story of *Winter Sonata*, which we were watching again. Jenny had bought the DVDs from some counterfeit place, with Japanese subtitles, so we couldn't understand any of the Korean words. It didn't matter – we'd seen the entire series years before, when we were dating, and had found those tragic love stories romantic. I guess that's why Jenny had bought the DVDs, to remember how it was to be moved by the beauty of love affairs that don't work out. By the failure of love. I wasn't keen on the idea at first – why watch something you've already seen? – but from the very first episode, I was the one who was hooked, more so than I remember having been the first time round. Those frosty northern landscapes, people wrapped up in scarves. The idea of someone not remembering his past, becoming someone entirely new because he no longer had his memory. Oh, the poor unloved young man. And yet, love remained in his heart!

Jenny kept making noises – snorting, laughing quietly at the most tender moments, sighing impatiently when the characters looked at each other for a long time without saying anything. Sometimes she'd make the odd comment. *Ridiculous. Just hurry up. Hei, little girl, just move on, forget about the past.* She'd pick up a magazine and read it. But still, I knew she was sneaking a glance at the screen now and then. Why else would she have sat watching it with me almost every night?

'What's the matter?' she asked that evening.

'Nothing,' I said. 'Nothing's wrong.'

She leaned against me and put her head on my shoulder, as if she needed comforting, when in fact we both knew that I was the one who was troubled.

'This episode is really boring,' she said. 'I don't believe anyone can just turn up in America and become a famous architect.'

'You're so cynical,' I laughed, putting my arm around her.

'I mean, one minute you're just some Korean kid, next minute you're a hotshot architect in the States . . . just because you had a car crash?'

'*Ya lor*, that's what happens in TV dramas.'

She sighed – a long, slow breath that seemed to fill the room. She closed her eyes and mumbled as if she was getting ready for sleep. 'I don't know what's happened to me. These days I only find real life interesting, not all this made-up nonsense.'

Later, as I lay in bed, I thought of the workers at the farm, the cholera drying them to their bones, their eyes dark and bulging. Staring at me. I tried to ignore the germs in the water, spreading everywhere. I thought of pouring concrete into all the holes, covering the entire surface of the farm with cement – was that even possible? Driving the cholera deep underground until it suffocated and died. I didn't know if cholera breathed. Or maybe I'd burn it. Set the whole place on fire and rebuild it all within a week. I imagined the flames sweeping across the flat land, cleansing everything in their path before moving on in search of something else to consume and transform. They would leave only me in their wake, but that would be enough. One solitary human being who would resurrect the whole damn place. Mr Lai would come back and find new, healthy men, a farm transformed beyond recognition. He'd stand there and say, *You are a genuine wuxia superhero*.

In the dark, Jenny turned over and her hand brushed my arm. I wished I could sleep, I didn't want to wake her. I lay perfectly still with my eyes closed. The men. Water. Earth. I listened to Jenny's breathing, and knew that she wasn't asleep either.

I decided to call Keong the next day, when all twelve men were so sick that none of them could come to work. Jezmine came out from the office and stood with me as I surveyed the farm – the uncompleted jobs dotting the land with piles of bare earth and sand. Two concrete mixers, a stack of timber beams. In the distance the automatic systems continued to pump water through the ponds, but the fish wouldn't last more than a couple of days without being fed. In the shed, the fingerlings needed tending to. Someone had to check the filtration systems, make sure the water didn't become too hard, or too salty, or too hot or cold – any of which could kill the tiny fish and lose us thousands. I looked at the enclosures, neatly divided into squares by the wooden walkways, and I'm sure Jezmine knew what I was thinking: could I do it all by myself for a whole week? I'm sure she also knew the answer.

'Two of us won't be able to cope, right?' she said.

I shook my head. In truth it might have been possible in the past, when I was a younger, different person. I knew that if I'd arrived early and got into my work clothes I could have started the rounds before Jezmine arrived, pushing a wheelbarrow filled with feed around the enclosures. If I'd started at seven, before it was properly light, and finished twelve hours later, when it was beginning to get dark, I could have done it. And the next day, and the next. But even as my thoughts began to fall into place and devise a plan of action, I knew that my body was no longer capable of performing such tasks. I thought of some of the workers I'd met in the past, older than me, who'd still been working on farms and construction sites, outdoors the whole day. I remembered their hands, bony and strong. Their milky eyes. Then one day they'd just disappear. Gone back to Palembang or Sylhet or wherever they came from. Or died from a heart attack at the age of forty. One day you're working on a building site for a new mall, you look up and the sky is white, no haze, just pure sunlight, and suddenly your chest tightens and you drop dead. It happens all the time.

I knew that wouldn't happen to me. My body had slipped away from that kind of life, escaped into a safer place. The elements could no longer kill me now. The sun, the tides, the wind, the end-of-year floods – I was safe from them, but I was also incapable of facing them. I thought of my mother, squatting on the bare earth of our smallholding for hours as she tried to dig out a tree by its roots. Was she older then than I was now? She must have been.

'Anyway,' Jezmine pointed out, 'even if we manage to finish all the smaller jobs, who's going to do the construction work?'

I didn't answer, I just stood looking at the scarred land.

'You're really, truly, going to get sacked,' Jezmine added as she walked back into the office.

When I joined her there she was scrolling through some numbers on her computer screen, murmuring the names of people I didn't recognise. 'What are you doing?'

'Trying to find the name of an agency,' she said without looking away from the screen. 'Someone who can supply us with some workers – fast.'

'Tomorrow?'

'Like, today.'

'If we get new workers, what happens when our guys come back?'

She shrugged. 'That's your problem.'

'It won't be fair on them.'

'You want me to do this or not?' She turned away from her screen to face me. 'Listen, I can get another job in town by next week if I want to. But you can't. What are you going to do if Mr Lai comes back and finds this mess?'

I nodded and went to make some tea, making sure to wipe the kettle and the work surfaces with a cloth that Jezmine had soaked in bleach. We took care never to touch anything outside without putting on rubber gloves, but we didn't want to take any risks. I heard Jezmine ring one number and speak to someone, and I was surprised, as I always was, by the way her voice changed when she talked to people about work matters, even though I heard it every day. Her pitch dropped, the words slowing down so the other person could hear every syllable clearly, the way a parent talks to an uncooperative child. The sound of the words slowly pinning down the squirming kid. After a few minutes she hung up and rang another number, then another. Every time, there was a problem. No, this week was too soon. No, we don't supply temporary workers. No, we only deal with three-year contracts. No, you have to provide accommodation. No, you must be joking.

'What kind of idiots are you talking to anyway?' I said.

Jezmine was spinning a pencil with her fingers, twirling it back and forth around her thumb. She only did this when she was annoyed – the only sign she ever showed of being flustered. 'Legal ones. Like, they're actually licensed?'

'Licensed my ass. If you go and meet the guy you just spoke to, give him a thousand bucks, he'll sort something out for you.'

'Well I'm not going to break the law.' She sat back in her chair, crossed her arms and looked at me without blinking for a long time. 'What other ideas do you have in your brilliant mind?'

I won't sit here and tell you that I hadn't thought of Keong before that point. Of course I had. I considered ringing him the moment we lost the first man to cholera. I heard his voice in my head, boasting about the deals he'd cut, the tricky situations he'd been able to negotiate. *Anything you want, I can get it for you.* Half of what he said was lies – I knew that for a fact – but what about the other half? If he had achieved only 50 per cent of what he claimed, there was a chance he could solve my problems in a heartbeat. Even 30 or 20 per cent would have been fine. But on the other hand, I would have to speak to Keong, eat with him, go to karaoke bars and sing old songs with him. He'd have a reason to call me whenever he liked. He would expect gratitude; I'd have to pretend to be grateful. A 20 per cent chance of truth – of a solution to that one problem – measured against the return of someone you wanted to forget; of a life you thought you'd left behind.

That was the calculation that ran through my head over and over again as I sat looking at Jezmine. Her gaze was like a challenge. Eventually I said, 'I know someone. An old friend.'

She turned away and began to scroll through the numbers on her screen again. 'I didn't think you even had any friends.'

I looked through my phone for Keong's last text, which I knew lay buried somewhere in my messages from a few weeks before. I hadn't saved his number as a contact in my phone, but I hadn't deleted all his texts either. I don't know why I kept a few of them – I can't say it was because

I had a premonition of some sort, an anticipation of his usefulness. It was nothing like that, nothing logical. I'd simply laughed at the silliness of a couple of them, and thought I might want to look at them again. The coarse tone, the cheerfulness. The swear words he used, which no one else I knew would use in a text. When you hear them on the street their vulgarity seems funny, but written down, they acquire a different weight. They shocked me, but they made me laugh too. If Jenny ever saw them, she would have been disgusted – not just by the words, but by the mere knowledge that I knew anyone who would write them down. And she'd be right: decent people don't use words like that.

I found the message, and walked out of the office before dialling the number. When I was a safe distance away I turned back and saw that Jezmine was watching me, waiting to see if my conversation was animated or subdued – to see if I could actually achieve something. I didn't want her to overhear anything I said or to make fun of the way I spoke. I knew my voice and my manner changed when I talked to Keong and others like him, who had no time for pleasantries and didn't respect other people unless they acted the same way. If you wanted something from them you had to be like them. 'You're not very convincing as a hard man,' Jezmine had once teased me after I finished a call to a cement supplier in Kuala Kubu Baru. I didn't want that kind of comment this time; I didn't want to be distracted while talking to Keong. I turned and walked slowly until I was down by the ponds and out of sight of the office. But Keong didn't answer the phone, and my call went through to the automated voicemail. I hung up without leaving a message. Maybe he'd changed phones, maybe that number didn't even belong to him any more – I couldn't be sure of anything. I redialled quickly; again, no answer.

I stood for a few moments looking at the ponds, the surface of the water ruffled evenly by the jets of water coursing through the pumps. Beyond them, the mouth of the river fringed by small trees that would soon be half-submerged by the tide. And further on, the mouse-grey sea, flat and calm as it often was.

What would I do when Mr Lai sacked me the following week? I could slip away before he arrived and saw the extent of the damage, vanish overnight just like migrant workers do. Or I could hang on, try to salvage my position. (But how? Impossible.) I could ask Jezmine to take me along when she went hunting for a new job. That was it, that was the solution. She'd take pity on me, find some way of finding me decent work wherever she found some. She wasn't exaggerating when she said she'd ease swiftly into something new, and probably better. She didn't fear rejection – not because she was young, but because she knew she could survive in the world. In fact more than survive; she could control what happened in her life. She was good with people – so good that it surprised me some-times, hearing her speak on the phone or watching her at meetings. Her ease, her confidence. My astonishment was so sharp that on occasion I experienced it as a sort of wonder that turned into a brief pain.

We never talked about her family or her childhood, just as we'd always avoided mine, despite the numerous mentions of my being a local boy. But I knew she wasn't so different from me. We understood each other. When she looked at me perhaps she remembered a brother or cousin she had, someone not as quick-witted as she was. It wasn't unusual in families like ours. The older boy wants to pull rank, but never can, because his younger sister or cousin is smarter and braver, and in the end it's the young girl who has to help the boy with his home-

235

work and translate his furious adolescent shouting into something their parents can understand and accept. And because she does that she starts to pity him; but her pity also attaches her to him. He is hapless, she is clever; so she has to look after him. I saw that all the time in our village, the bright girls who should have moved away to the city and never come back, but instead chose to stay behind to run the household while their kind, slow brothers fished the empty seas and brought no money home. Pity. That was why Jezmine would help me get work. She felt sorry for me.

I had already worked this out in my mind as I started to walk back to the office, more calmly now. Once you accept the end of a particular time in your life, the past starts to slip away rapidly, even if nothing new appears in its place. Just as I had decided one day that I was going to leave KL, I knew then that my years of working at the farm were over. No drama. I'd ask Jezmine to find me a job, and if she didn't I'd find something on my own, just as I always had. I'd find a way of telling Jenny, but only after I found something new. I wouldn't tell her I'd screwed up and got sacked, I'd say I wanted a change. I'd figured everything out by the time I reached the office – that was how clear my thinking was, now that I had made my decision. After I left the farm that evening I would never come back to it. I'd leave it to rot.

I'd just walked into the office when my phone rang. I'd replaced it in its pouch, clipped to my belt; its vibrations felt stronger than usual, or maybe it was the heat of the day, rising with the midday sun, or the sudden quiet of the office after the noise of the water pumps outdoors. I'd been so resolute in my decision to move on that it took me a few moments to register that it was Keong ringing. The number flashed on the little square screen, but I didn't instantly recognise it, even though I'd dialled it just a few minutes before.

'Please answer that before it drives me insane,' Jezmine said, looking at a piece of paper as she typed on her keyboard.

'*Hey, little brother!*' Keong's voice was even louder than usual. In the background I heard metal clanging and people shouting in a foreign language I couldn't quite make out. Some laughter. Then a sharp grinding noise that briefly drowned out Keong's voice. 'You called me? I'm in a processing plant. The bastards are –'

'What? Where are you?'

'I told you,' he said, shouting now. 'In –'

'Keong,' I said, trying to imitate Jezmine's professional phone voice, 'I rang because I wanted to ask if you could help. I mean – not me, the farm. My employer has a slight problem. I mean, not a problem, just a . . . situation.'

Jezmine was typing a document, glancing between her papers and the computer screen, but I knew she was listening intently.

'Situation? What the fuck does that mean?' Keong laughed.

'I mean, it's a situation that requires a professional solution.'

'Wait, I can't hear you, hang on.' He walked away from the noise, holding the phone to his ear all the time, so I could hear his breathing, heavy and troubled in the heat. 'Yeah, what's the problem?'

I looked at Jezmine. 'We have a manpower issue.'

'*Manpower issue*. What the fuck you talking about? Manpower issue my ass.'

'We have a labour shortage,' I said. 'The situation is quite, umm, urgent.'

'Your hotshot boss with all his business in Singapore, he doesn't have any friends meh?'

I went outside. 'Keong,' I said, holding the phone tight to my ear and lowering my voice. 'I need you to help me.'

There was a pause, and when he spoke again his voice had changed, no longer cut with his rough laughter. I heard some rustling, the metal clink of his lighter.

'I need some workers. Fast. Men capable of heavy labour. Construction guys who know what they're doing. A big job. I can pay them a decent wage but I need them quickly. Can you help or not?'

He exhaled slowly, and I could imagine his face, the way his eyes narrowed as he blew out the cigarette smoke. As if life was hazy and somewhat beautiful. 'Don't worry about salaries, it won't cost you much.'

'So you can help?'

Another pause, long enough to make me think that I'd misunderstood, or that he was going to change his mind.

'You can always count on me. You have a problem, you can just call Ah Keong. You know that.'

'Sorry to trouble you with this,' I said. I was standing in the middle of the yard, and the sun was so bright I had to shield my eyes, even though I wasn't looking at anything in particular. 'It's just that I'm in a really tricky situation.'

'If you can't rely on your old childhood friends, who can you rely on? We're more or less brothers. We have to help each other out, don't we?'

Back at the office, Jezmine was texting someone. She spoke to me the moment I walked in, but didn't look up. '*Wah*, your friend always talks so loudly? You're just on the other end of the phone, he doesn't need to project his voice all the way from the other side of the country for you to hear.'

'Just finish your text. I'll talk to you when you're done.'

'I can do two things at once.'

I tried to deliver the news as casually as possible, as if

the outcome had been as predictable as daybreak. 'I'm getting the workers. It's done.'

She lowered her phone and stared at me. 'You're kidding.'

I smiled and pretended to look through some papers, as if searching for an important piece of information. 'If you don't believe me, that's your problem.'

My phone pinged, twice, signalling new messages, which I knew even before I looked at them would be from Keong.

Meet me tomorrow Problem solved
Brothers help each other

Every time we meet I watch her looking through her papers. Some of them are loose, kept neatly in a folder. She also has a ring file where she keeps them in separate sections marked by coloured dividers. Most of the papers are typed sheets, mainly in English and Malay, but there are news clippings too, a lot of them from the Chinese press. She also has many sheets in her own handwriting, and sometimes as I'm talking she'll scribble something down, very quickly in perfectly neat lines, the tip of the pen running lightly over the paper. I could never write like that.

I know that all these papers and notes are about me.

I pretend that I'm not watching her. That I'm not interested in what she's writing. But most of the time, when her head is inclined and she's concentrating on reading or writing, I'm trying to read what is on the papers. I can never make anything out clearly. She's just a bit too far away from me. Whenever we pause for one of us to go the bathroom or the kitchen, she closes her notebooks and files, even if we're only taking a two-minute break. She doesn't want me to see what's inside.

Wah, you've got so many papers. You typed them all yourself? I said one day.

Not so many. It's kinda normal when you do a research project.

What's written down in all those notebooks?

Oh, just bits and pieces. Wouldn't make sense to anyone but me. It wouldn't be interesting to you.

240

This morning she was writing something and drawing diagrams on a large sheet of paper while I talked. I wanted to see what she was doing, but every time I looked my voice faltered and I lost concentration on what I was saying. She'd look up, and I'd have to pretend I wasn't observing her. A research project. I wondered how I would appear in her project, whether I would be a nicer version of myself. Or a worse one.

Just before midday, she looks at her phone. So sorry, she says. I really hate to do this, but I really have to call my mother. She's got a hospital appointment later today and I have to make some arrangements. I won't be long.

She goes to the kitchen and disappears from view, but I can hear her conversation. I wait for a few moments before reaching across for the notebook closest to me. I open it without hesitating and begin to read.

Keong was waiting for me just off the Meru highway, at exactly the spot he'd described – a layby in front of a small row of shops. He was sitting in his car with the door open, smoking a cigarette and eating, dipping his hand into a large packet of prawn snacks that he'd set on the dashboard. I saw him from the other side of the road, while I was at the junction waiting to make a U-turn – one foot hanging out of the car, tapping on the grassy kerb, lifting his chin to blow out smoke the way people did in all those Hong Kong gangster movies we used to watch back in the nineties. There was a slowness to his movements, an impression of leisure, as if he could have hung around on that dusty stretch of road for hours, the way teenagers do. He got out of the car when he saw me pulling into the space in front of him, flicked his cigarette into the dirt, emptied the remains of the packet of prawn crackers into his hand and shoved them into his mouth.

'You shouldn't eat that rubbish,' I said.

'I don't care, my body's already fucked.' He wiped his hands on his jeans and opened the passenger door of my car. 'We're going to take your car. My air-con doesn't work.'

We drove northwards, then cut inland into the heart of the plantations, where the roads were long and narrow and straight, and mostly empty, except for the lorries that carried the loads of palm-oil seeds to the factories for

242

processing. On either side of the road the view was the same, the palm trees deepening into a shade so dense and resolute that it seemed to last infinitely, as if on the other side lay not just the east–west highway or Pahang, but Russia or Alaska, or the seventh ring of Saturn. Once a contractor who came to the farm showed us maps of the area, and some photos taken from a helicopter. Away from the sea and the narrow, irregular strip of human habitation along the coast there was nothing but a flawless, flat green carpet of plantations stretching as far as you could see, with not even the smallest patch of forest to break up the uniformity of the land. Plantation after plantation, each one the size of Singapore, or Luxembourg. 'Actually, Luxembourg is much bigger than Singapore,' Jezmine had said. 'I think you mean Liechtenstein. Or Andorra. Someplace like that.' I never figured out how she knew such things.

'This whole damn area all looks the same to me,' Keong said. 'Gives me the creeps. If you wanted to kill someone all you'd need to do is send him for a walk in there, tell him there's a shack that sells stolen brandy or something. Poor fucker would walk around in circles for days before dying. Fuck. That's why I always hated living here. Messes my head up.'

He was right, in a way, and that was why he needed me with him. If you wanted to find your way around without driving in a huge loop you had to know how to read the differences in the landscape – the way the palm trees were of a slightly different age and height, how some estates were older or newer, the way the roads faced the sun in varying ways, the villages that were each different, or maybe the small *surau* or Hindu temple that lay obscured by the trees – a tiny landmark that you could easily drive past unless you knew it was there. All these things told you how far you'd gone, whether you'd taken a wrong turn somewhere, how much time you had left to your destination. This was before GPS, remember – or maybe it already existed, but only very rich people could afford to have it in their cars. Nowadays even my neighbours round here look at their phones just to drive into the city or other places they've been to a hundred times. *It's because the roads change so fast*, they say, but that's not the reason. It's because *we* change so fast. No one wants to risk getting lost any more. No one has any time to lose. But I'm sure that out there, not so many miles away, when you're on those small roads, your phone won't be able to tell you the way. Don't think Google cares about Sabak Bernam or Kuala Selangor.

'You really have to be a local to know your way round these parts,' Keong said. 'Thank goodness you're here. I'd have driven halfway to Taiping by now.'

We were looking for an estate whose name meant something to me. I had a feeling I'd driven past it a couple of times a number of years ago, when Mr Lai and I had to take a few trips up that way to buy some cheap weedkiller and netting, in the days when we were just getting started and no one would deliver goods to us because we didn't order enough. He would cut the deals himself with an old man to whom he spoke Hakka to get a good price – he couldn't really speak the dialect, but he'd learned enough from his mother to be able to make decent connections when he needed to. He couldn't even afford to hire a foreign worker back then, so I would go along to load the small lorry we owned, carrying the sacks to the edge of the open platform at the back before climbing up onto it and hauling everything into place. I'm talking fifteen years ago at least, more maybe, and I was stronger then. *Wah, you're really made for this!* Mr Lai would say as he watched me pack the goods tightly onto the back of the lorry, and he wasn't wrong: my body took easily to that kind of work, whether due to the genes I inherited from my parents or to the years I spent working on the farm. But nothing ever remains the same, not even a labourer's genes. Only a few years later I would lose the ability to work like that. I got married, got promoted, my body forgot what it was like to toil in the sun and rain. But on those long slow drives back to the farm, cutting through the plantations and stretches of forest, the small bridges that wriggled their way across the flat land, I didn't question my body, and my body didn't question what I asked of it. I used to hang an arm out of the window, holding the steering wheel with one hand, never wondering what would happen to me in later years – never believing that I would ever be anything other than twenty-three years old.

At that point in my life everything seemed new and slightly wondrous to me. My years of stop-start work in dead-end jobs in KL had come to an end, I'd had steady employment for over a year, and more lay ahead of me. I remembered every detail of those days – Mr Lai falling asleep in the passenger seat with his mouth open, a trail of saliva tracing its way down the side of his cheek. The clutch that stuck and screeched loudly every time I changed from second to third. The way the leaves of the palm trees turned silver-grey rather than green in the lowering sun late in the afternoon. The broken-down *attap* huts set back from the road, whose dried-foliage roofs had blown away in the previous year's storms – things that had always been in my life, so constant that they became invisible by their permanence. They came into focus then, just for those few months – or years, I can't remember exactly – before they faded away again.

That was how I knew the name 'Golden Land', the general location of the plantation, the quickest way to get there. 'You sure you know?' Keong said as we drove along slowly, stuck behind a lorry that held up the traffic. 'When was the last time you went there?'

I shrugged. 'Before you were born, so just shut up.'

He laughed and leaned his head back, as if he was going to sleep, but he kept talking, continuously and without need for any response from me. He had a really rough time when he lived down in these parts, he said. When he lived in the village. Everyone hated him. Even his mother disliked him – she disliked him for being disliked. Why can't you get along with people? she used to say. Why can't you be friendlier to people? We're outsiders, we come to this place, we have to behave properly or no one will accept us. Be gentle in your manner. Be polite. If the other boys insult you, just walk away. If they beat you, just run away. What the fuck. Single mother with a teenage son, you think she was ever going to be accepted? All that time spent cooking and sewing for other people in the village, cleaning their houses, often not even getting paid – it made no difference, they still looked down on her. Imagine, people in a shithole like that, looking down on her. Sometimes he used to fantasise about going around the village at night dousing all the houses with petrol when everyone was asleep, then setting the whole damn place on fire. Of course he never did. Petrol was too expensive! Anyway, too late to regret that now. He didn't fit in, and that was the end of it. Thank God I was there. I, Lee Hock Lye – *Jayden* Lee Hock Lye, *wahlau*! – was the one who kept him sane. And yet his mother had told him, more than once, not to hang out with me. She liked me, but didn't want him spending time with me.

'Why?'

'Because your family was too much like ours. A broken home.'

'But she made dumplings for me. Steamed buns. Biscuits.'

'Don't ask me,' he replied, easing a cigarette out from its pack. He paused for a moment before lowering the window. The air that rushed around the car muffled his voice and I struggled to hear him. 'I guess if you want to be respected, you have to hang out with people who are respectable. Rich ones. *Normal* ones. You don't want to be associated with –'

A lorry went past, travelling in the opposite direction, drowning out what Keong was saying. I wasn't interested in what he and his mother thought of us. *We were normal*, I thought. In that village, at least, we never stood out. I chose not to argue with him, I just let him carry on. It didn't matter anyway, it was such a long time in the past; it had no bearing on the life I had now, no bearing on my future.

We were passing a convoy of lorries, strung out over a few miles – it must have been a time for harvesting the palm-oil seeds, because the trucks were heavy with the orange-brown fruit. The rumble of their engines as we passed them made it difficult for me to hear Keong clearly, and I was glad for this. I picked up the word *sorry* once, and perhaps a second time, and when we broke clear of the lorries I understood that he was apologising for having left KL so abruptly when we lived there as young men. Remember the friend of his that he used to mention, the one who was going to work in a hotel in Hong Kong? (*No, in fact I didn't remember*.) He'd been asking Keong to go and join him over there. The salary was great, they'd rent a room together in Mongkok or somewhere further up in the New Territories, and they'd save up enough money to go back home in a few years' time and set up their own business, a restaurant or something like that. In hindsight it was a stupid move, but when you're young and in his position, even vague promises sound like concrete career plans.

He'd been having a lot of problems at the time. (*Yes, I remembered that.*) His head was muddled, he couldn't think straight. He'd started taking some of the pills he'd been selling, and they screwed with his brains, exhausted him. (*I suspected, oh I suspected, but I never knew for sure.*) One week he would imagine living in a penthouse on the Peak in Hong Kong, the next week he saw himself lying down on the tarmac and dying in the middle of Chow Kit market. He'd stay awake for two, three nights in a row, then sleep for two or three days afterwards. He had no money, he was always in danger of getting into trouble – with the police, with the gangsters who hung around the same places he did. That's why he woke up one day and thought, I have to leave. Now.

He used all his money to buy a cheap ticket to Hong Kong, but we all know how that story ends – right there, where it began. He landed in Hong Kong with his friend, but after two unsuccessful weeks of looking for a job, he had to come home. No one would take someone like him – no papers and no qualifications. Not even low-grade shops like those selling herbal remedies or school uniforms would accept him. He could have got a job washing dishes in a cheap restaurant, like his friend did, but if he wanted that sort of work, might as well do it at home. He still remembered the feeling he'd had, sitting in the departure lounge at the airport in Hong Kong and hearing that his flight home had been delayed. He'd thought that if he didn't get on that plane within the next ten minutes, he was going to explode, he was going to smash the whole goddamn place to pieces, he was going beat the hell out of whoever was making those announcements telling him he had to wait, longer and longer and longer, before he could go home. For the first time since he'd been a small child, he thought he was going to cry. The thought of returning to where he belonged made him tearful and weak, and he didn't know if it was out of shame or relief. Then he did cry.

When he got back he thought of calling me, but didn't, because he was embarrassed. What would he tell me? That he had gone away and failed? After just two weeks? He couldn't do that. He knew I'd be upset with him for just disappearing on me (*I hadn't been angry, I'd thought: I'm glad*); he couldn't think of a way to explain why he'd been such an unreliable friend.

The experience sobered him up. On coming home, he started that course in computing that he'd always said he'd take, and it enabled him to get a job at a construction firm. That was when he started noticing the number of foreign workers in the country. Everywhere. One day he'd seen a team of men of all sorts of foreign nationalities fixing the wiring in the ceiling of an office block that was about to be completed. From a distance the men looked as if they were holding up the concrete above their heads, and Keong had thought: Without them, the whole damn building would collapse. In fact, take these workers away and the entire country would crumble. That was when he realised how much money there was to be made in bringing in workers from abroad. It didn't take him long to find a job with a small company that did just that.

But he had felt bad. All those years, he'd wished he'd said a proper goodbye to me.

'Forget it,' I said. 'I didn't really care.'

He kept talking, and with the noise of the wind swirling through the open windows it took me a few moments to realise that he had moved on to another subject, changing his focus without warning, the way he always had. He was telling me about Bangladeshis. Did I know that the average Malaysian earned ten, fifteen times what the average Bangladeshi earned? That's why there were so many of them here. If a Bangladeshi worker went to Singapore, he'd earn fifty times what he'd earn back home. Fifty times! Anyone would get in a boat and take some beatings if they thought they were going to earn that much money. But mostly they end up here, because in Singapore there are rules, permits, all that nonsense you can't change. Try and bribe someone, you go straight to jail. No permit, no talk. But here it's different. They can get in all sorts of different ways. There are people out there who help them enter the country, and once they're here they can go to the mosque, eat *halal* food – it's easier for them, so they settle for less pay.

We were on our way to find a group of them, Keong explained, some Bangladeshis who had recently arrived in the country. Eighteen of them, mostly men, though he wasn't sure. With Bangladeshis it was rare to find any women in the group – unlike the shipments from Myanmar, where you'd often find women.

The shipments. He used the word in the way Mr Lai did when he talked about lorryloads of frozen fish travelling to the city, or the ground soy and corn that we used as feed. But when I glanced across at Keong I saw that he hadn't noticed how strange the word sounded. He hadn't meant anything unusual by it – a shipment was a shipment to him. It was just work.

These workers hadn't yet been placed in a job, he explained, and were waiting to be assigned to their first contract, which Keong had lined up somewhere close by. That job wouldn't be starting for another month, so he could lend them to me for two, three weeks – long enough to finish the construction work at the farm and save me from getting sacked. Then, if I thought the men worked well, he could fix it so that they stayed on the farm for the rest of their time in the country. Three years at least, and easily double that if I wanted.

'I don't need them for that long. Just enough for my men to take a break and recover from their illness.'

'What do you pay your Indonesians?'

I told him.

'You'd save 25, 30 per cent every month if you take my guys. Bangladeshis are so much cheaper. Think about it – your boss will build a whole fucking temple at your grandparents' grave when he learns how much money you're going to save him.'

'I can't.'

'Huh? Why not?'

'What would I do with my guys when they recover from their illness?'

'Sack them, *lor*.' He laughed, and started whistling a tune – the chorus to an old Anita Mui number that was so off-key I couldn't recognise it at first. Then, as if remembering something, he said, 'In fact, they've already sacked themselves. Put it this way. In any of those lousy jobs we worked at when we were younger, what would have happened if you fell sick and didn't turn up to work for a week?'

'I never fell sick.'

'But if you had, by the time you went back to work, your boss would have found someone new. What else would you expect them to do? You get sick, you get the sack.'

We were entering the area of the plantation, the trees on either side of the road lined up in perfect straight rows – taller now, obscuring the rise and fall of the land in the distance. Where was the low hill I remembered, with a telephone mast or electric pylon on it, a metal pillar of some sort? I started to wonder if my memory was as reliable as I'd thought, but then we saw a sign that announced the plantation. Keong said, 'OK, now we have to find the north-eastern boundary. That's where your men will be.' He leaned forward and looked up at the sky, as if he could figure out our position relative to that of the sun – a feat that both of us knew he was incapable of. 'Turn left at the next junction, probably.'

'No, we turn right.' I drove faster. I wanted to get there quickly, sort this mess out as soon as I could. I knew roughly how big the plantation was, and I worked out how long it would take us to get to our destination – only another ten minutes at most if I hurried. I'd worked out, too, what I'd do with Keong's men. I'd keep them for a couple of weeks, max, maybe just one week or ten days, then I'd send them back to him, make an excuse that both of us would recognise as a weak pretext; but out of respect for an old friendship we'd pretend it was fine, and Keong would place them somewhere else, and I would never see them, or him, again. In the days they were with me, they'd accomplish little, but it would be enough for Mr Lai to see them at work – proof of my reliability and ingenuity. There would be no time for either party to form any attachments, for them or for me. The farm would be just another place of work to them, as familiar and alien as any other they'd worked at before. I knew that feeling from my younger days – remembered how it was to work somewhere just to survive. They would make sure they didn't rely on the farm to provide them with anything more than a few days' wages; they'd know it could end at any time. And so, when Hendro and the others came back, I'd simply call Keong and have the Bangladeshis sent away. There would be no drama in the whole affair.

I slowed as we approached the end of the estate, where the trees thinned out, allowing the sun to spread across the land and reflect on the surface of the marshy fields nearby. Keong checked a message on his phone. 'This is the right place,' he said. We cut our speed until we were going so slowly that we could see even the ripples in the pools of rainwater that had collected in the open ground, shrinking now in the midday sun. The plantation was behind us now, the landscape becoming ragged and untamed, with long grass and scrubby bushes before it ran into the next plantation, about half a mile ahead. When we reached it we doubled back, searching for signs of human dwellings, but there was no one around. We stopped the car and got out – still nothing. I began to wonder if Keong had made up the whole story, as I knew he'd fabricated things in the past. Bad shit that people had done to him. Fictitious enemies. Beautiful coincidences that he'd experienced. Places he'd visited. Nothing was beyond his imagination.

He checked his phone again, and made a call. 'Fuck. No signal. Damn this place!'

'What the hell are you playing at?' I shouted. The words sounded sharper than I'd expected, or maybe it was just the sudden noise in the midst of all that silence. In the full heat of the day there was no sound – not even the rushing of the wind that accompanied the changing of the tides, or the noisy jungle insects antici-pating nightfall. 'I should've known better than to trust a loser like you with something important.'

'Fuck you,' Keong said as we got back in the car and I started to retrace our route. He kept pressing buttons on his phone, but the signal was too weak. 'That guy who gave me the information, I'm going to beat him to death, I'm going to chop him to pieces.' He repeated this a few times, but I wasn't listening to anything he said. *Hallo, hallo!* He shouted into his phone, but the line wouldn't connect.

'Wait,' I said. The sudden braking of the car startled Keong, and he fell silent abruptly. 'Look there.' I pointed to a spot in the distance, where the neat line of the plantation palms gave way to a messy tangle of shrubs and young trees. Keong lifted his sunglasses and squinted. '*There*,' I said, but he still couldn't see. A sheet of grey canvas, hanging from a tree trunk. Nearby, what appeared to be empty raffia sacks on the ground, dirty white mostly, though I thought I could make out a tiny patch of red.

'What the fuck you looking at?'

I got out of the car and began to pick my way through the long scratchy grass, heading towards those old bits of cloth that hung unmoving in the shade of the trees. It wasn't easy to make out exactly what they were, and at times, with the sun in my eyes, I thought they looked like carcasses, pieces of dead animals. When I was a child, I woke up one day to find the villagers agitated. Someone had lost a dog, one of those small thin mongrels that spent all day on the streets, and at night wandered around in packs that drifted into the forests to play or to hunt small animals or God knows what. The owner of this particular dog eventually found it dead, halfway up a tree, half eaten by a black panther. The other kids and I ran over to see its remains, but all we could see was a grey-white piece of skin dangling overhead. Any blood or flesh had turned black, and we couldn't make out its face, or anything that identified it as the creature we once knew. We were frightened not by the death, or the savagery of the killing – we grew up by the sea, don't forget, we'd seen worse – but by how easily a life could be scrubbed out without trace. Without any mourning, or sadness, or even realisation that it was now over. *It looks like a dirty dress*, one of the kids said as we walked away. We laughed, but we couldn't stop thinking about the dog, and how it was now just a scrap of cloth.

It was that same feeling of dread that I experienced as I walked towards those pieces of canvas snagged in the branches ahead of me. *A dirty dress*. I tried to avoid the patches of ground that were soggy, but it wasn't easy. Sometimes I'd step firmly onto what looked like a mound of grass only for it to give way to a pool of brown rain-water. Behind me, Keong was cursing loudly. Where was I going, what the hell did I want to see, why did he even agree to help me. He started running, splashing through puddles and cursing even more violently, and by the time I reached the thicket he had almost caught up with me.

We stood for a while and stared at the canvas tarpaulin. Close-up, we could see pieces of string hanging from its edges, clearly showing where it had been attached to other tree trunks, stretching it to make a shelter that seemed too low for an adult to stand up under, though maybe that was the point of it. String up a length of canvas at ceiling height and it's obvious that it's meant to shelter human beings. String it up two or three feet lower, below the line of the bushes, and no one notices it. The undergrowth had been cleared away, and the space was littered with plastic bags and wrappers, flattened by the rain into the ground and the foliage, but not yet bleached of their colour – they couldn't have been there for more than a few days. Further away was a large mound of burnt sticks. When I nudged it with my foot, a layer of powdery white ash came loose at its base.

'This is where they were,' I said. 'They've only moved recently.'

Keong walked around the small clearing, kicking at bits of rubbish on the ground. *Bastard bastard bastard*, he repeated. *Cheating lying bastard.*

'Guess you were right,' I said.

'I'm going to mess that guy up so much.' Keong was already making his way back to the car. 'He's going to regret ever double-crossing me.'

'Who?'

'The guy I mentioned,' he said. *'That black devil.'*

Back at the car we took off our shoes and wet socks. I tried to wring them dry but the swampy water had got into them and made them smell bad, so I tossed them into the grass. Keong laid his on the roof of the car, hoping they'd dry in the fierce sun, but it was useless, and eventually he threw them away too. I drove barefoot, the pedals hard and gritty on my toes. Keong was silent, and I drove fast, surprising myself by how easily I slipped from one road into the next, always finding the smoothest route. As we got closer to town I said, 'I guess we can forget about getting any workers for the farm.' The moment I said it I regretted it, and expected Keong's silence to erupt into another tantrum. But he remained quiet, and just stared straight ahead into the afternoon light that slanted directly into our eyes.

'I'll get them for you,' he said. 'But you have to help me. We need to find the guy who's taken them.'

What strikes me are the lists. There are lists of everything.
Often the most boring everyday details. Like:

*

   Home décor: (use details in introduction??)
      Calendar (Mei Fung Confectionery) from 2014.
         (November: pic of Guilin cliffs)
      Chinese New Year scrolls, faded. (*Sui sui ping an,*
         wan shi ru yi.)
      Danish butter cookie tin (empty?), rusting in places.
      Crochet table mat, blue/red/yellow, torn top corner.
      Lucky cat, arm not moving.
      Rattan armchairs x2, string armchair

*

Or:

*

      Fridge (Tuesday 3 December):
      Preserved bean curd (for Hokkien congee)
      Eggs x3
      Gardenia bread loaf (half)
      Tin of sardines, open, half-eaten
      (Notes on DIET →→ rough skin, bad teeth)

*

I can't figure out why she's interested in this sort of detail,
or how this is related to her research project.

At times it felt as though a sickness had settled over the entire state, carried downstream by the two rivers that drew all the maladies from the populated hinterland before meeting at the port and spewing them out to sea, where even the salt water was not enough to kill the infection, which then spread up and down the coast, spawning mysteriously and releasing itself back into the air. I know that's not the way it works, I know that science wouldn't back up that view, but that's how it felt. There was a disease upon us, and it wasn't going to lift.

I met Keong at the same layby as the last time, and as I drew up I thought about how swiftly habits formed. See you at the usual place, he'd texted the night before, and it was true – on just the second occasion this spot felt as if it occupied a particular position in our lives, a fixed point that linked us. I saw the tip of his cigarette glow in the early-morning gloom – it was not long after 6 a.m., and the grass was still damp with dew. 'Motherfucker,' he said, yawning. 'Why am I up so early? I must be mad.'

'Just a usual working day for me,' I replied. 'You want some coffee?'

'I don't need coffee, I need drugs.' He stretched and let out a sharp, barking groan, as if the movement had caused him pain. 'Just kidding. Come on, we're taking your car.'

We drove to a new housing development in the middle

of a huge stretch of scrubland not far from the highway, before the roads narrowed and led into the heart of the plantations. The houses were almost finished, rows and rows of simple two-storeys with green-tiled roofs and neat front yards – nothing special, you know the kind, you see them everywhere – but workers were still installing the windows and doors. 'Who the hell would want to live here?' I said. 'We're miles from town.' The road hadn't yet been surfaced, and the dust we raised was like a gauze that made the workers look like phantoms – figures emerging from a dream.

'There's no more space in town,' Keong said. 'These houses are cheap as dirt. Come back in a couple of years and I bet you'll find a huge mall here, with cinema and bowling alley.'

He held up his hand, signalling for me to slow down as we reached a crossroads. Up ahead, a group of workers were lowering a length of pipe into a trench. Keong got out of the car and walked towards them, barking an indistinct word that made them look up. One of them straightened up and wiped his hands on his trousers, as if cleaning them in preparation for a handshake, but in the end he just wiped the sweat from his face. Keong stood with his hands on his hips, watching the men as they started shovelling mounds of earth into the trench. That was when I noticed their movements – laboured and heavy even when performing the simplest action, like sticking a shovel into a pile of earth – the red clay that seemed to become as unyielding as stone before them. Every gesture was slow, a split second's hesitation between the start of the movement and its completion, as if they were considering whether they had the strength to complete what they had started. One man bent his knees and looked down into the hole. A pause. Then he *tumbled* in – an accidental fall rather than a deliberate motion. It took the help of two of the others to get him out of the pit.

I felt a twinge in my knee joints, and then in my shoulders. The memory of work. My body was recalling its years of hard physical labour, as it did from time to time when I watched workers toiling over a job. Even now, I can be having noodles at a street stall, and if I see someone lifting sacks of concrete, or taking a pickaxe to some cement, my arms and legs want to perform the same actions, even though I know they would be incapable of carrying them out. Still. I read somewhere recently about a former soccer player who kept waking up on the floor because his body was taking free kicks or something like that in the middle of the night, and the action was so violent and real that it lifted him clean off the bed. Fifty years old, covered with bruises. He never even dreamed about soccer, no longer had any interest in it. Our bodies – every fibre of every muscle, every tiny nerve – they remember what our minds forget.

When you work in the sun at jobs like that, your only thought is to complete them as soon as possible so you can have some rest in the shade, even if it's only five minutes. Even if it's to move on to the next job. And the next. You don't think about how well you're doing; you don't have to. Someone is giving you orders, so you just obey. Your body obeys what you tell it. Your movements are swift, instinctive. Harsh, even. They are harsh because what you are engaged in is a battle – a battle to finish the job before it finishes you, a battle to gain those five, maybe ten minutes in the shade. A battle for time. There was none of that in that group of men, nor in any of the others we saw later that day. They didn't have the strength to fight.

'Are they sick?' I asked Keong as he got back into the car.

'No,' he replied. 'Nothing's wrong with them. Apart from being lazy bastards.' He pulled down the sun visor so he could see the mirror, then brushed the dust from his hair and smoothed it down.

They were his men, he explained, meaning that they were working under contracts provided by him. That was how it worked, usually. A property firm or a plantation or a hotel – whatever it is – needs manpower, usually in a hurry. They can't go out and find thirty Bangladeshi or Nepalese or Myanmar workers themselves, so they call Keong's company, who have a bunch of people on standby. The employer pays the salaries, Keong takes a cut. The men we saw had been due to complete their work on that site nearly a month earlier, but one thing after another had got in the way, and they were still on that stupid housing estate, with no end in sight. Keong had hoped that their job would have been almost done by now, and that he could steal a few of them away to work for me, but that was impossible.

'The clients are a big-time developer, a listed company,' Keong said. 'I can't mess with them.'

'Are you sure there's nothing wrong with those guys? They really look sick.'

'They're all like that,' he replied.

We visited a sheet-metal factory, then a processing plant in the middle of a palm-oil plantation, then another construction site – a row of small commercial units marooned on the edge of ricefields. Then another plantation, where thirty or forty workers, Bangladeshi and Indonesian, were returning to their quarters – a low concrete block with a rusty tin roof; I couldn't see what was inside. It was nearing the end of the day, and the light was beginning to lose its brilliance, turning rich and orange above the trees. I saw the same lethargy I'd witnessed in each group of foreign workers we'd visited that day, a heaviness beyond the normal boundaries of fatigue, to the point that even breathing seemed an effort to them. Some of them stood outside, splashing themselves with water that they gathered in their cupped hands from a tap. It seemed such a feeble action, incapable of relieving the heat or cleansing their bodies of sweat. The meagre handfuls of water trickled down their torsos and stained their trousers with dark flecks, and they looked no fresher afterwards.

By this point I knew it wasn't my imagination. All day, I'd watched closely, stood close enough to the workers to see their red glassy eyes and hear their rough breathing, as if their throats were coated with a film of fine sand. At the processing plant there had been a few women – Burmese, I think, though I couldn't be certain – working the machinery and organising the loading of the lorries, and at first I thought, I hoped, that they were somehow immune to the weakness of the men I'd seen, that they were more resistant. But they weren't. It was as if they had all given up and succumbed to this malady. There was a sickness in the air. In the land, the water. Everywhere.

'You're crazy,' Keong said when I told him my theory. 'You're desperate and panicking. Your brain is *deep fried*.'

We stood in the yard of the workers' quarters and watched them queue to fill plastic bottles from the tap. They sat down on the cement, sipping from the bottles without talking much. Out here, the water must come from a well, I thought. I wondered how much of the chemicals and the germs in the earth and the rivers around us had worked their way into it. I thought of our farm, our workers – I'd had no news of them for nearly two days.

Keong was talking to the foreman, who was himself from Bangladesh. From the way Keong stood, with his hands on his hips, head slightly bowed, I knew what the man was telling him. It had been the same story all day long. There were no spare workers – man, woman or child. They were all taken. And as for the ones who had disappeared, there was no clue either. 'Guess I should be happy that the global economy is booming,' Keong had said earlier. His lips curled into a smile, but he didn't laugh. Now, talking to the foreman, he seemed resigned to the silent, dead-end situation.

'This group of people are from the same province in Bangladesh as the ones who disappeared,' Keong said. 'I thought they might have heard something, been in touch with them.'

I started walking back to the car. 'What made you think they might know anything?'

'They'll have friends among them, maybe someone from their home village, maybe even a relative – someone will know something. They might even have been in touch. These people arrive, first thing they do is lay their hands on a phone.'

'I have to go home now,' I said.

'There's one more person we need to talk to,' Keong said. 'Please.'

'Time's up, big brother.' I started the car and eased it out of the yard. The sky was darkening slowly now, dotted with quick-flying bats.

'Ah Hock,' Keong said, 'I can sort this out. Those missing workers are out there. Some bastard is hiding them, and we have to find them.'

'My wife will be home. I have to go.'

'Just one drink,' he said. 'It's important.'

In the bar of the Tokyo Hotel, which was also the lobby – since it wasn't, and still isn't, a big or elegant place –

there was the usual mix of travelling salesmen, a couple of Korean businessmen and a small group of tourists from mainland China, their heavy northern accents audible from the other side of the room, cutting through all the noise in the lobby, which on that night felt like a sealed box to me. Maybe it was the hard, polished floor, that kind of shiny fake-marble that you see in fancy places, or at least places that wish they were fancy, or maybe it was the long day out in the countryside, with little noise apart from the monotone of Keong's voice and the wind rushing in through the lowered windows whenever he smoked a cigarette. Whatever the reason, the noise seemed amplified beyond what humankind could naturally produce. The little *ping* of the lift doors as they opened startled me with its brightness, the ringing of the phone at the reception desk was as shrill as a fire alarm. I needed to open all the windows, I thought – that would make the sounds feel normal and real once more. Or maybe I was falling ill, my body being claimed by the same sickness I'd witnessed earlier, out there in the countryside.

'Who the hell would want to travel across Asia and do business in a shithole like this?' Keong said, pointing at the Korean businessmen. He'd been silent for the final stretch of the drive, except to give me directions on how to reach the hotel, and now, slumped into an armchair, he seemed as drained of energy as I was. *A shithole like this.* I didn't know if he meant the hotel, or the town, or the whole goddamn country, but I didn't ask. I reached for my beer, which was turning warm, and after just one sip I put it down – it tasted bitter and unappealing, and I watched the beads of condensation collect on the glass and slowly drip down to the table, where they formed a little puddle.

A Filipina singer – announced on a poster in the lobby

as *The One and Only Sarita* – was setting up her act for the evening with her accompanist, a young man wearing a tuxedo about three sizes too big for him, testing the sound system by playing short little melodies on the keyboard. A long screech from the speakers as he adjusted them, followed by a low growl that seemed to be made by a primeval beast, like the roar in a horror movie when the unknown monster makes its appearance. I covered my ears. *Testing, one, two*, the singer said into the microphone when the speakers had settled. *Hello everyone, now is this working?* More whining, this time from the mike. *Sorryyy*.

'Where the hell is he?' Keong said, looking around. He dialled a number on his phone and held it to his ear. He took a long gulp of his beer, tilting his head backwards. I watched his Adam's apple move in his throat – a small lump that seemed unnaturally hard and jagged, rolling back and forth as if it was a living thing. Its liveliness disgusted me.

My throat was dry from thirst and dust after our long day. I wanted some water, but lacked the energy to put my hand up and catch the attention of a waiter. In any case, there was no one around – the man running the bar, who had brought our drinks earlier, was now doubling up as a receptionist on the front desk. For a few minutes my vision began to tremble, to feel unreliable, as if I couldn't judge how far away people were, or how quickly they moved across the room, or what each human action was intended to do. That man over there, leaning forward in his chair to get closer to his female companion – was he about to strike her, or speak to her? The hotel manager, hurrying towards the exit – running to pursue someone, or to escape something? I was dehydrated, I told myself. I wasn't falling sick, I was just dehydrated. I should have drunk some more of my beer, but the thought of it revolted me.

The singer and the keyboard player returned to the stage to begin their act. The One and Only Sarita was saying something, but the mike was too close to her mouth and I couldn't make out the words, only the sense of energy that she communicated, which made me feel even more tired. She started singing – 'Hero', by Mariah Carey. My head was spinning. I couldn't figure anything out. She clutched her hand and raised it slightly, letting it float upwards, away from her body – what did that mean? I looked over at Keong. He was mumbling the words, or at least what he thought were the words, but which came out in a low, off-key string of sound that didn't match the singer's timing.

A man emerged from a door in the far corner of the room, behind the bar, dressed in black trousers and a white shirt with a bow tie. A waiter. I put up my hand, but he didn't see me. I should have, could have, simply stood up, but my legs felt as uncertain and unreliable as the rest of me, so I remained in my seat, waving at him. Keong looked up. 'There he is, the bastard.' He put his hand on my arm to stop me from waving. Without knowing why, I let my hand fall. I'm thirsty, I wanted to say. I need some water. I need to go home.

The waiter walked slowly towards us, and just as with the other people, I was unable to figure out his intentions. He looked around – nervously, it seemed to me, but why?

'Water,' I said when he arrived at our table. 'I need to drink something.' He wore a badge that displayed his name – Uzzal.

'You didn't answer your phone,' Keong said, glancing at him briefly, and speaking as if addressing someone else. 'I need help.'

Uzzal spoke softly, in Malay that was heavy with a foreign accent – Bangladeshi, I guessed – but fluent, or at least fluent enough to make it clear that he'd been in the country for a long time. He was at work, he said. How could he answer his phone while he was at work? He would meet us in a couple of hours, when the last of the customers had gone and he could close the bar. He looked at Keong and said, 'You shouldn't come here next time.'

'We were thirsty,' Keong replied. 'We wanted a drink.'

'I'll bring you something,' Uzzal said. 'But you'll have to pay, otherwise my boss will be suspicious.'

Keong shrugged.

Sarita was singing 'I Will Always Love You', and Keong seemed less tired now. The beer had made his cheeks go slightly red, and his eyes moist, which gave him the look of someone who'd just emerged from a hot shower, quietly revived. Uzzal came back a few minutes later with another Carlsberg for Keong and a bottle of water for me. Although I'm now sure I couldn't have done so, in my memory I drank it in one long gulp. I can't remember ever having been as thirsty as I was in the Tokyo Hotel that night – not before or after.

Uzzal was Keong's fixer in Klang. A fixer's fixer. Someone with his ear to the ground. A foreign worker who'd made good. Keong didn't know how long exactly he'd been in the country, but it must have been at least eight or ten years, possibly more. Keong had met him while Uzzal was working at a cement factory in the area – just another foreign worker, one of a team of fifteen, twenty. But this one guy stood out because of his clothes, which always looked laundered and pressed, and gave the impression that he was different from the others, when in fact he was just the same. He was the only one of the lot who smiled, enough to make people think he was happy doing his job, so of course he got promoted, and every time Keong came back to the factory to check up on the workforce, he noticed Uzzal wearing sharp clothes, organising the people under him as if he'd been doing it all his life. It was strange, Keong had thought: he behaved as both their commander and their comrade. Which is to say, he was one of them, but also not one of them.

'Put it this way,' Keong said. 'Are you friends with the Indonesians who work for you at the fish farm?'

'We get along.'

'But are you friends? Do you take your lunch with them, exchange stories about your wives and kids – that sort of shit?'

'No.'

'See? They don't really like you. Whenever you have a boss, you have an enemy. But not with this guy.'

Watching Uzzal at work, Keong had realised that he was good with his fellow workers, he could get them to do things that the bosses couldn't – he never threatened them, but coaxed them. He joked with them. Delivered stern warnings quietly, out of earshot of the others. *This guy is smart, I can use him some day*, Keong thought. He knew that Uzzal would soon find a way to get himself the right papers and a regular job. Sometimes you'd get that feeling with a migrant. You don't know exactly why or how they're going to break free and make a life for themselves in this country, you just get a sense it's going to happen – maybe because they're a bit more desperate than the others, maybe they've got a few more IQ points than their friends. Who knows. He also thought, *This guy knows how to hustle*. Sure enough, when Keong called at the factory the following year to deliver another team of workers, Uzzal was no longer there. Found himself a wife, his colleagues said. A local. He'd quit his job and was working in a restaurant somewhere in town. It was easy finding him – he'd answered his phone within a few seconds of Keong calling.

Keong's hunch was right. Uzzal knew all the Bangladeshis in the area – knew which ones were good workers, the ones with a bad attitude, the ones hiding an injury or a sickness that was soon going to finish them off. He knew the ones who were planning to run away from their jobs, knew where they hid – the invisible slums in town, on stretches of the riverbank, or out in the countryside, in the middle of the forest. He knew all the different routes migrants used to get into the country, by sea and especially by land, across the border from Thailand. He was familiar with all the techniques the smugglers used, from hiding human cargo in containers to plain old bribery. That was the most common. Customs officers see a big lorry loaded with sacks of rice or cages of live chickens, of course they know what's underneath all that. They could spend an hour unloading the lorry and finding the migrants hidden underneath, but pay them enough and they won't bother. Maybe they don't want to find the real stash; maybe they're afraid of discovering dead bodies, children suffocated in that tiny hollowed-out space under a mound of squawking chickens. Just because you work at a job like that, it doesn't mean you don't have feelings. But a tiny bit of cash makes it easy to turn your head and look the other way – someone actually pays you not to see dirty, upsetting shit. Anyone would do the same.

Uzzal knew all these tricks. He stashed them away in his head the way other people might do with money stuffed into a mattress. All that information – how to get in, how to get out, how to survive. He kept it secret, never revealing any of it to anyone except people who'd pay. Foreigners and employers alike. That was how he made his money.

'Like I said,' Keong smiled, finishing his Carlsberg, 'I know a player when I see one.'

'You go and see him yourself,' I said. 'It's none of my business.'

'Hey, do you want your workers or not? You're going to get your ass fired.' He stood up and checked his watch. 'We'll find out from Uzzal where the workers are, then you can go home and tell your wife and boss that you've got things covered. Tomorrow I'll deliver the men to your farm, and you'll look back at this evening and think, "Why the hell was I so grumpy? A favour for a friend. It was the easiest thing I ever did." '

The singer and her accompanist stopped for a break, sitting on a couple of plastic folding chairs next to the bar. Suddenly the lobby felt empty and silent – the cluster of people at the reception area had disappeared, and there was no one in the bar apart from us. Keong was staring at his empty glass, turning it slightly as if examining the traces of foam that left a snakeskin pattern. 'We're brothers, you have to back me up,' he said, his voice sounding flat and deflated once more. 'All I'm doing is trying to help you out here.'

You're thinking, Why didn't I just get up and leave? That moment of escape, of flight, presented itself, as it had done before and would do again. I recognised it for exactly what it was – an opportunity to say, 'You know what? This is too messy for me' – but spotting a chance and taking it are two separate and unconnected things. When faced with a door that's wide open, how many of us actually walk through it? We never take the chance to flee. We stay. We recognise the danger, but something in our brains tells us it isn't going to be so bad. We believe in life's power to iron out the kinks in our existence and make things turn out OK. We don't think anything fundamentally evil will occur to us. Everything will turn out just fine.

I said, 'I'm tired. My head hurts.'

Keong looked around the empty lobby, then reached into a pocket and took out a small plastic bag with three or four pills in it. 'Panadol,' he smiled. 'For your headache.'

I knew what they were – definitely not painkillers. I shook my head. 'Call the waiter. Let's just get this deal done.'

The meeting point was a car park in the Old Town, an empty space in a row of shophouses where an old building had collapsed over time, or been torn down. The far end of the unsurfaced yard was shaded by a large tree from which vines hung thickly towards the ground, as impenetrable as curtains. It was here that we waited for Uzzal, listening to the traffic on the highway drifting across the night. It began to drizzle very lightly, and the sound of the rain on the leaves overhead seemed muffled, as if it was occurring some distance away, hundreds of feet in the air, and I had the impression of being separated from the noise around me, as if I was insulated by a giant bubble of invisible foam.

Keong had taken a pill and was standing perfectly still, concentrating his gaze on the street. The pills gave him concentration, he said, made everything as clear and bright and optimistic as a magnificent sunrise. I remembered how he'd been a decade earlier, how he wouldn't sleep all night because the pills he'd taken gave him too much energy. 'Even if I climb Mount Everest I won't be able to sleep,' he used to say. Now he no longer displayed the nervous energy of before – he stood with his hands in his pockets, occasionally kicking at the gravel underfoot, but otherwise he moved very little. Every time a car approached he would stiffen and shrink back slightly into the shadows before relaxing once the glare of the headlights had faded. We stood well back from the soft orange glow of the street lamps. At that time of night there were few cars in this part of town, but I'd seen enough of Keong's work to know that caution was part of the job. It was part of *him*, I thought. He didn't know any other way to live than in the shadows.

When we heard the scooter approach we both knew it was Uzzal. The stutter of its motor as it slowed down. The way it glided into the unlit parts of the street, like a creature that instinctively seeks the margins. The deliberate dimming of its headlight before it was switched off altogether as it neared the parking lot. He killed the engine as he drew close, hopped off and pushed the scooter towards us. He seemed younger now than he had at the hotel, where he'd been dressed up in his waiter's uniform. His movements were quick and easy, and he covered the ground swiftly. I found it hard to believe he'd been in the country for ten years – he must have been a teenager when he arrived, I thought. A boy.

Keong didn't move; he waited until Uzzal was close to us before speaking. 'I keep telling you,' he said, 'you should quit that lousy job of yours. The uniform makes you look like a penguin.'

The way Uzzal laughed gave me the impression that he and Keong knew each other better than I'd assumed. 'What am I supposed to do?' he said. 'Just wait for you to turn up and pay me a few hundred ringgit now and then? I got a wife and a kid to feed.' He parked the scooter, propping it up gently to make sure it didn't fall over on the uneven ground.

'I forgot you're a dad now.'

'*Ya*. Like being a waiter.'

Keong laughed. 'You're a real joker.'

Uzzal was still smiling, but he was eyeing me, while also looking around as though there might have been others lurking in the darkness.

'Don't worry, he's an old friend of mine,' Keong said. 'From childhood. A local boy. He's helping me sort out this mess.'

Uzzal kept his gaze on me for a while, taking in every bit of me, as if he might find something that would test the truth of Keong's statement about me. I wanted him to notice a detail – the way I dressed, the way I deliberately refrained from smiling, the heavy shoes I wore, suitable for light agricultural work, whatever minuscule note he'd think was suspicious, and that would indicate to him that I wasn't any of the things Keong had made me out to be. I was willing him on, silently urging him to say, That guy, he's no friend of yours, he's not like you. He's not one of us. Get him out of here, I don't trust him. I even shook my head, wanting to communicate to him that I was there by accident, that I had a home, a job, a wife – a whole separate life away from this shabby parking lot surrounded by derelict buildings.

He continued to stare at me for a few moments, and that was when I experienced, for the first time, that curious sensation I would encounter later that week, and again during my time in prison – of time slowing down, folding in on itself, almost as if it had taken a physical form and was collapsing, just like the buildings around us. I remembered the feeling I had when I was a child, of joyously sliding down an imaginary rabbit hole and emerging on another continent, or even another planet altogether, with landscapes and people that were so familiar to me I'd sometimes have trouble believing I was in a new place – only I was, because in these new surroundings I would understand how to make decisions, choices that would turn out all right for me and my family, and everyone else who populated this world would behave with similar clarity and ease. But now I wasn't a child. I knew such things couldn't happen.

I don't know why that thought came to me at that moment. It was so ridiculous that I smiled to myself.

Uzzal turned to Keong and said, 'I know what you want, but I can't help you.'

Keong laughed. 'You're kidding me, right?'

'My friend, I can't help you.'

Keong took a step towards Uzzal. Just a small, quick step, but it was enough to make Uzzal react – a tiny shuffle of his feet, a hardening of his stance to mask the instinctive reaction to back away.

'I pay you but you don't help me,' said Keong. I wasn't sure if it was a question or a statement.

'It's the boss. The one who got them into the country. He has the people you're looking for.'

'My company paid that bastard to get them in, now he's hiding them. I'm going to get that damned Bangla, make him pay.'

Uzzal remained silent for a while, and in the half-dark I saw him look up towards the canopy of leaves overhead. It was still drizzling – so lightly that it felt like a fine mist on my face. He laughed, making a noise like a soft snort. 'He's doing you a favour.'

'He'll do me a favour when he delivers the people he owes me, and gets the fuck out of here.'

'You were supposed to get permits for them but you didn't, so what's he supposed to do? He can't just let them loose.'

Keong took another step towards Uzzal. This time he did back away. 'That guy – he smuggles people into our country. And now he's telling *me* to get permits?'

'I'm just telling you what he told me,' Uzzal said firmly. 'If those people don't have permits, they can't work.'

Keong laughed. A loud, full-throated roar that cut through

the gentle hush of the rain and echoed against the walls of the parking lot. I looked around us, checking to see if there were any stray pedestrians passing by who might have heard the noise, but there was no one about. I was becoming like Keong and Uzzal, I thought – cautious, afraid.

'Look at you, mister lawyer,' Keong said. 'Who the fuck cares about permits? Today we saw two hundred workers. Two hundred people without papers, working away happily. So don't give me that bullshit.'

'I'm just telling you what he said.' Uzzal turned and walked to his scooter.

'How much do you want?' said Keong. 'Find out where they are, I give you a thousand.'

Uzzal laughed but didn't turn around.

'Hey, how much?' Keong shouted.

Uzzal climbed onto the scooter, but didn't turn on the engine. 'There are women in that group,' he said. 'And two children. They need papers.'

'Which Bangla need papers? Once I have them, I'll sort things out.'

'They're not from Bangladesh. They're Rohingya. They need refugee papers.'

'Rohingya, Bangladesh – whatever. You're all the same.'

Uzzal started the engine and eased the scooter towards the road.

'My friend will call round tomorrow,' Keong said. I knew he meant me. 'You give him the news. I'm going to sort out your Bangla boss.'

'Even I don't know where he is,' Uzzal called out as he rode away slowly. Once he reached the road he flicked the headlight on, but it wasn't until he was some distance away that he began to accelerate.

Keong cursed. Called Uzzal that name again, the one he

used all the time for dark-skinned people. We walked towards my car, and the only thought in my mind was whether anyone had noticed it, parked where it shouldn't have been at that time of night, and been suspicious enough to write down the registration number. But of course no one had. I wouldn't have. It was ridiculous even to think that someone might have done, but that was what a couple of days with Keong did to my way of thinking.

'Refugee papers. Do they know how long it takes to process those? None of the Rohingyas have them.' Keong lit a cigarette as he climbed into the car. 'I don't understand the difference between Rohingya and Bangladeshi. They all look the same to me. Can you tell which is which?'

I shook my head. 'Listen, it's too complicated,' I said. 'Let's just forget the whole thing.' I was expecting him to argue with me, give me all the reasons I should continue to help him, make excuses for not telling me earlier all the things I'd suspected, which were now out in the open: that he was dealing not just with illegal migrants, which was bad enough, but half-dead refugees. I expected him to say that it wasn't such a big deal, because let's face it, how many foreigners are legal in the country these days, so why would he bother to tell me? He'd try to convince me that I needed to help him in order to help myself. He'd refer to the bonds of a friendship that had never really existed, but it would sound convincing because they meant something to me.

Instead, he kept silent and lowered the window to let out the cigarette smoke. The wind shuddered through the car, reminding me of the long day we'd spent together, reminding me of my fatigue. 'Maybe you're right,' he said after a while. 'Maybe we should just forget this whole business. Pack up, go live on a desert island in the middle of the Atlantic Ocean.' He held his face close to the window and felt the rushing of the air, as if tasting it.

I wanted to say, You fool, there are no desert islands in the Atlantic. But I was too tired to speak any more that night.

A noise. Nothing unusual, just a car. But I sit here all day, so I know the tiny variations in the sounds outside. Without even looking, I know that the car is a taxi, and that she is in it. For the first time since we started our talks, she is late.

She checks her watch as she comes through the gate.

Sorry I'm late.

What happened to your car?

I have a problem with it. But it's cool. I took the KTM Komuter to Klang, then a cab. It's no big deal.

Your car broke down?

She steps into the house and sits down in her usual seat. Breathes out, slumps back in the chair as if she's just run ten miles and doesn't have enough strength to sit up straight.

No, it got taken away.

Ha? Stolen?

No, towed away. DBKL guys did it right in front of my eyes. I was parked perfectly legally, my ticket had run out like one fucking minute before, and they were standing by ready to tow it away. Said if I paid them the fine they'd let me go, so I said, Fine, what fine? You mean BRIBE, and they just laughed in my face. *Ei Ah Moy, janganlah macam tu.* Jesus. I could have slapped them. Why the fuck do I put up with such misogyny? How dare they call me *Ah Moy*? Racist misogynists. I'd forgotten all about that sort of thing. Fuck.

Your language. You're sounding like me.

I don't care. Can you believe it? One minute. One stupid minute. They were laughing at me while I argued with them. Laughing and smoking. I couldn't do a damn thing. Right up until the truck came and took the car away.

Why didn't you just pay?

She stops and looks at me as if she can't understand what I said.

It's only fifty, a hundred bucks, I say. You should have just paid.

She narrows her eyes, and I get the feeling that I'm the one who's done something wrong, not the DBKL men who took her car away.

That's not the point! Why should I pay? I did nothing wrong. They were just out to make some extra cash, and I was *not going to pay*. Hello? That's called *corruption*. That's what's wrong with this country – everyone's just looking out for themselves, looking to make a quick buck at someone else's expense. Those idiots, they can just go *fuck themselves*.

Calm down, stop shouting.

I'm like, Do you even recognise this as corruption? Please.

She pulls some papers out of her folder and puts her phone on the table, ready to record as usual.

Anyway, no use in complaining. I'll deal with the process in due course. Now we have to get to work.

No. We're going to get your car back.

I go into my bedroom to get the cash I keep in a biscuit tin in the wardrobe – the money I've managed to save over the last six or seven months. I don't know how much there is, so I take it all. Better to be safe. I come out and head straight to the door.

Waiting for what? I say to her. Better deal with the problem now.

At the car pound she insists I stand to one side, tells me not to say anything.

You think just because I'm a woman I can't deal with this sort of thing? she says.

Aiya, don't say like that. I'm just coming to support you. What can a guy like me do to help anyway?

I pretend to read the announcements on the noticeboard, but actually I'm listening to the argument she's having with the guy at the desk. I say argument, but in fact she's the only one talking, trying to persuade him to cancel the fine.

The parking warden should have exercised discretion, she says, I was only one minute late. We should reform the system to make it fair and flexible.

The guy isn't even looking at her. He's staring at the screen of his phone, his thumb gently swiping at it every few seconds.

She raises her voice. Hey, listen to me! You're so rude. She's almost shouting.

Sorry miss, rules are rules. He smiles and starts to flick through a newspaper.

You people are hopeless. How do you expect this country to progress if you behave like this?

Her voice is so loud that people at the other end of the room turn and stare at her. I'm afraid of what might happen next, even if she is not. One of the other men – they are all men in that office – stands up and says, What's that stupid girl shouting about?

Stupid girl? she shouts. Who are you calling a stupid girl? You want to come out and say that to my face?

Hey hey hey OK OK. I come and stand next to her at the counter. No problem here, I say. We just want the car back.

You know something? the man who has just stood up says. Your fine is now one thousand ringgit. *Ya*, it's gone up, because yours is a special case.

280

What? You can't do that, she shouts.

Hey, *Ah Moy*. Rules are rules.

You know what? she says. Keep the damn car.

She turns and walks quickly out of the office. There's air-con in the room, but it still feels very hot. The men are looking at their phones or flicking through magazines. It's as if we'd never entered the office, never even existed.

I find her outside, sitting in the shade of a tree on a low concrete wall. Behind her are the remains of some small plants that are slowly dying in the heat. The bare earth is dry.

I really need a cigarette, she says.

I hold out my hand and open my palm.

What the hell? she says, staring at the car keys. How did you get it back?

I shrug.

You paid a bribe?

How else?

How much did you pay? Oh God, you shouldn't have done that. You're just perpetuating the system. You're encouraging those guys.

From the time I give her the keys until we find the car and get into it, she doesn't stop lecturing me.

It's because of people like you that they dare to ask for bribes. Corruption is a two-way thing. The victim doesn't even know they're a victim. In fact, you could say that the victim becomes not only the enabler of corruption, but the perpetrator.

Aiya, enough already. I'm sorry, OK? I just wanted to get the car back.

We drive out of the parking lot and into the traffic. Neither of us says anything. Finally, when we reach the Meru road, she says, How much did you pay?

Six hundred.

Ha, they gave you a discount.

It was all I had with me.

She doesn't answer, and I think maybe she doesn't want to talk about it any more. But after a while she says, That's a lot of money. I'm sorry.

It's fine, forget it.

We drive on in silence, and it isn't until we're almost back at my house that she speaks again. Thank you, she says. I appreciate it. I'm sorry I yelled.

That night I open the biscuit tin. It's been a long time since I've seen it completely empty, so I take one of the four ten-ringgit notes that are still in my wallet and put it in the tin. I know it's a meaningless thing to do, but it makes me feel I still have some money to spare. I make a quick mental note of how much food I have, how many days I can live before I get some money. As I fall asleep I tell myself, It'll be fine.

'Have you taken up smoking again?' Jenny asked. We'd only just got into the car and she was doing up her seat-belt. 'Stinks in here.'

'No,' I replied. It was the truth. But the smell of Keong's cigarettes was everywhere, hanging in the air even when I flicked the air-con to max and lowered the windows.

'It's really horrible.' She put her forearm to her nose and sniffed it. 'It's even getting into my clothes.'

Still, after a few minutes she was forced to raise the window on her side of the car. The wind was blowing dust into her eyes, and her hair was starting to look dishevelled. She'd spent a long time getting ready for the conference that morning, and we hadn't spoken much from the moment we woke up. Sometimes, when she had something important going on with her work, I'd feel that anything I said would break the spell of her concentration – the sound of my voice felt rough and inappropriate, especially when I was not long out of bed and my throat was still a bit dry from sleep. That morning she was preparing for a gathering of all the people who sold Skin-Glo, which was being held at a convention centre on Leboh Gopeng. She'd got out of bed a little before me, and as I prepared break-fast I could hear her typing quickly on her laptop. She'd been one of the few people selected to give a speech at the conference. This involved her putting together a pres-entation filled with colourful interlocking circles and wavy

283

graphs, which she'd spliced together with photographs of happy people who used Skin-Glo. I brought her tea and eggs – she liked them boiled for two minutes and broken into a shallow saucer, the way you get in old Hainanese *kopitiam* – and set the tray down quietly next to her. I looked at the screen – she was flicking through the pages of her presentation, her lips moving as she silently rehearsed her speech – and saw that she'd added a few photographs I hadn't seen in a long time, and hadn't noticed in the jumble of material she'd accumulated on her desk. I'd been so distracted by events at work that I hadn't asked her how her work was going.

There were five or six photos, of Jenny or the two of us. The first was of her standing in front of the Merlion in Singapore, on a trip we'd taken not long after we got married. We were going to save up for a proper honeymoon – a week or two abroad, somewhere nice like Taiwan, where we'd put on smart clothes and pose for portraits in Alishan or Sun Moon Lake: pictures we could then frame and use as decorations in our living room the way other people did. We'd talked about Phuket, too – we had visions of ourselves dressed in flowing white outfits that blended into the perfect sand on the beach, snaps of ourselves doing star jumps against the backdrop of a sea so brilliantly blue and green that no one would believe it was real. *Like the colours of a peacock*, Jenny had said.

But all that lay in the future, when we had a bit more time and money, so in the meantime we thought we'd spend a long weekend in Singapore. Four days, nothing fancy, just looking at the shop windows on Orchard Road and seeing the orchids in the botanical gardens. We stayed with relatives of Jenny's in their apartment in Toa Payoh, with a view looking over the rest of the estate, rows and rows of identical apartment blocks – white and rectangular, with strips of darkened windows on each floor, lined up like soldiers on parade. Between them, neat squares of concrete or patches of grass. The sound of people singing to a karaoke set in the distance. Our room was so small that there was barely space to walk around the bed, and as we sat on the mattress listening to the conversations of the people going past on the walkway just outside – what they were planning to eat at the food court, what bus they were going to take to get into town – we joked that it was *just like being in a luxury hotel*. Outside, in the living room, the TV was on, the volume turned up loud because Jenny's aunt was getting older and starting to lose her hearing. A Korean drama, dubbed into Mandarin. *Big brother! Big brother!* a woman's voice screamed over and over again. Jenny and I laughed. 'We need to get the fuck out of here,' I said.

We spent the whole of the next two days out, only returning to the apartment late in the evening, when Jenny's relatives had gone to bed and the TV was finally off. We walked in the sun, got sweaty, went into air-conditioned malls to cool down. We strolled around the marina, posing for photos in front of the Merlion and the carpeted steps of the Fullerton Hotel, as if we were staying there. Other guests – real ones – came up the stairs and nodded at us as if in acknowledgement, and we nodded back. Later, we couldn't stop laughing at the idea that they'd thought we were just like them. 'We should go to Raffles tomorrow,' Jenny said. 'Pretend we're staying there too.' We went to the cinema and saw *Harry Potter and the Prisoner of Azkaban*. It was nearly the end of the movie's run, and the cinema was half-empty. We sat near the front because we wanted the screen to feel as huge and all-engulfing as possible; the sound drummed in our ribcages and we felt its vibrations even after we'd left and were having *mee pok* and barbecued wings at a late-night hawker centre in Balestier.

On the second day I caught a chill from the air-con in the bus on the way home, and came down with a cold. On the third day Jenny fell sick too, and we spent the afternoon in bed. It was so hot and sticky that we had to keep the windows open. We lay there for hours, listening to Jenny's relatives preparing dinner, talking loudly over the noise of the TV. We wanted to hold each other but we both had a mild fever, we were too hot and sweaty, so we lay side by side, her hand on mine. *Why are you doing this to me?* a man screamed on TV – one of those stilted dubbed voices. We began to giggle.

'Promise me our real honeymoon won't be like this,' I said.

'What are you talking about?' Jenny replied. 'This is all the honeymoon you're going to get!'

She was joking, of course, and so was I. But as the months dragged on and it became clear that we weren't going to go away on a honeymoon anytime soon – because of work, because we didn't have enough money just yet – the talking about possible honeymoon destinations became just that: talk. We'd see adverts for cruises to Benoa, or tours to see the cherry blossom in Kyoto, and we'd discuss how much we'd have to save up for the trip, how we'd tell our respective bosses that we'd like to take ten whole days off work. 'Mr Lai will kill you before he lets you take ten days off to look at cherry blossom!' Jenny joked. She mimicked his voice: '*You turned into a woman, meh? Take holiday go see flower?*'

At some point we stopped using the word 'honeymoon' when we discussed these fantasy trips abroad. I guess we'd stopped thinking of our marriage as something that needed to be celebrated, or cemented, by something as sentimental as a honeymoon. We'd missed the chance to do something only available to newlyweds. I'm sure Jenny felt the same way I did. We were both old enough then to know that in life, these lost opportunities never come round again.

And yet. Looking over Jenny's shoulder that morning, and seeing those photos that she'd included in her presentation, I wondered if our trip to Singapore all those years ago had been more than just a long weekend. I looked at the photo of Jenny in a hawker centre, holding an *ang ku kuih* to her lips as if it was an oversized clown's mouth, bright red and fleshy. Another of me in bed the day I came down with the cold, my hair roughed up and even spikier than usual. In the photo I am pulling a sad face which somehow manages to look comical and happy – so ridiculous that it made me smile all those years later. I remembered handing the camera to an old man who was walking by in the botanical gardens, and asking him to take a photo of Jenny and me. He had difficulty framing us, and backed away. Jenny started to get nervous – she was worried that he was going to run off with our camera – but I said, 'Don't worry, this is Singapore. No one steals anything.' In the photo we are striking a pose around a tree fern, in the style of Bollywood actors – hands clasped, arms forming a neat circle. Our smiles are exaggerated, but they were real.

Above the photos, Jenny had written the words 'My Life', followed by 'Happiness' and 'Skin-Glo'. She continued looking at the computer screen, but her lips had stopped moving. I went back to the kitchen and made myself a cup of Nescafé. I was still thinking of those four days in Singapore, which I'd almost forgotten. And I experienced a sense of loss, though I couldn't discern what it was that I'd lost. Maybe nothing. Maybe everything. Sometimes, we don't realise something's happening until it's over, and then it's too late to celebrate it – you can only regret its passing.

'I hope your presentation goes well,' I said as we drove slowly through traffic. Jenny was leaning forward, sniffing the air-con vents for traces of cigarette smoke. 'I'm sure you'll be great.'

'If people like my presentation, I might get a lot more customers.'

'I'm sure you'll get loads. You deserve it.'

'I've heard that someone's going to make a video of the presentations and send it to head office in America. People in Colorado are going to be watching me!'

'That's amazing.'

'I had a dream a few nights ago that when I finished my presentation, the whole auditorium gave me a standing ovation. People were chanting my name. By the time I got back to my seat, the head of operations in Hong Kong had already offered me a job in KL. She wanted me to move there immediately. Then all the salespeople from other parts of the country came up to congratulate me. Actually, I wasn't asleep when I dreamed that, so it wasn't a true dream. More like a vision of what could happen. Why shouldn't it? One special moment is all it takes to change your life. Imagine. This time next month, maybe even next week, we could be looking at houses in Damansara Heights or Kenny Hills. Choosing furniture.'

'I don't really know KL that well. Anyway, our house is nice, isn't it?'

She fell silent, and when I glanced at her I saw her lips moving silently, rehearsing her speech again. Her eyes were trained straight ahead, and I knew that she was looking not at the smoky exhaust pipe of the van in front of us, but at an auditorium full of attentive salespeople.

'How's your work, by the way?' she asked after a while. 'Did you sort out that manpower problem?'

'Yes. Yes, I did. Well, almost. Everything will be finalised soon. Things will be even better than before. You know, sometimes you have to face serious problems at work before you can move to the next level. That's something I've heard you say in the past, and it's true. I'm only learning that now.'

She turned to me and smiled. 'I feel very optimistic about the future.'

'Me too.' We were nearing the convention centre, and the traffic was flowing more freely than before.

'Mr Lai will finally give you the huge bonus you deserve for saving his farm, and we'll use that as the down-payment for our new house in KL.'

'Maybe.'

'You have to stay positive,' she said brightly. 'Be like me. Have faith in yourself!'

'You're going to be late.'

'You'll see,' she said, reaching for her briefcase. 'Everything will turn out great.'

Looking at her then, I truly believed her.

'Wish me luck,' she said as she stepped out of the car.

You've been smoking.

Huh? She looks up at me briefly, but quickly returns to her notes, as though she hasn't really heard me. She coughs. A rich, wet cough.

I said, you've been smoking. Haven't you?

So what? You smoked for years.

It's bad for your health.

Look who's talking. You were smoking at fifteen.

But I stopped, didn't I? You look very tired.

I'm OK.

She starts to cough again and tries to stifle it, but she can't. The cough is stronger than she is – the more she tries to suppress it, the worse it gets. She bends over, covering her face with her hands. Her back is heaving, as though the cough has taken over her whole body. Finally she stands up and goes to the bathroom, and I can hear more coughing. When she comes back I give her a cup of hot water and some cough sweets.

I don't need sweets, I need a cigarette.

You joking? You're an amateur. You don't even know how to smoke. Drink some water, it'll make you feel better.

She takes a sip of water and slumps in her chair.

I don't feel so good, she says. Her voice is hoarse.

You don't look well. Do you have a fever?

She touches her brow. No, I don't think so. I'm not ill. Maybe I am. But it's not a physical sickness.

I see. A love problem, huh. With your partner? You've never told me her name.

My ex-partner.

Sorry?

We broke up at the weekend. I mean, I broke up with her.

You're joking, right? It was going so well, you were so happy.

She shrugs. I just realised I couldn't actually live with her. We're too different. Of course we knew that before we got together, but we thought we could overcome our differences. We thought love could conquer all, blah blah. But you know what? It can't. So I thought, better to end it quickly than endure a long, angry decline.

You sure? I mean, you've only just moved in together. Maybe it's because you're not used to each other yet. When Jenny and I got married and started living together we fought over everything. I didn't wash up my cup, *fight*. She didn't close the door properly, *fight*. We didn't know how to share a house. Then, after a while, it all disappeared, and I even got anxious when she wasn't at home. What I'm saying is, maybe you should give it more time. Learn to live with her.

It's not that. The apartment is huge, we have tons of space. We don't get in each other's way. Our differences are . . . let's say, too deep to be bridged.

Why? You love her, don't you?

I just can't stand her principles. Her politics. She's so . . . so fucking *conservative*. Such a reactionary. Thinks everything is fine, and that the only thing wrong is that poor people don't work hard enough. You know what she said the other day? Our friend Shafik got mugged. Some guy on a scooter went by and grabbed his phone. My partner said, *It's all these migrant workers we let in. They're the ones who commit all the crimes.* Obviously I went ballistic.

I told her that statistically, foreign workers commit only 10 per cent of all crimes in the country. You know what she said? *Huh, why don't you tell that to the old woman who's just been beaten and robbed, or the seventeen-year-old girl who got raped in Setapak last week. We should just deport them.* She's an educated person, she's rich, she should know better than to peddle such nonsense! I tried to convince her otherwise, but she just shrugged. *Whatever*, she said. *The facts speak for themselves.*

Maybe she's right.

She's wrong!

So you don't agree on crime. Is that a reason to split up?

It's not just that. It's everything. Her whole politics. She's a corporate lawyer, right, so I know she's a capitalist, but I didn't expect her to turn out to be so damned conservative. All she thinks about is making money. She had a small Honda when I met her, now she has a huge Audi 4x4. What next, a Bentley? I joked. She said, *Mmm, maybe in a couple of years' time.*

What's wrong with making money? Your family are well-off too, aren't they?

We're not rich, but yeah, we're OK. That's precisely why I'm trying to do more interesting things with my life. Useful things. Her parents are so *stinking* rich. Why does she need more? What makes me sad is that she wasn't always like that. I remember the first time I saw her. She was sitting alone reading a trashy novel in the Hungarian Pastry Shop. In New York. We were both studying there. She was smiling to herself as she read, and shaking her head, as if she was reading the funniest thing in the world, and I thought, Now *that* is someone I could live with my whole life. She was fun, she loved to laugh. It wasn't that long ago. Now we sit on the sofa and discuss mortgage rates all evening.

She's just trying to provide you with security for the future. If you don't have a nice house, how can you feel safe?

You know the worst thing of all? She supports the government. Doesn't see why I went on the anti-corruption march, said it was a waste of time. Actually laughed at me and my friends, as if we were kids. *Yeah, just go and pretend to be revolutionaries, if it makes you feel better. You're crazy if you think you'll change anything.* I felt like leaving the apartment and slamming the door and never seeing her again.

She stares at her cup of water, but doesn't drink. She keeps her head lowered, and I think, Maybe she's crying.

Do you love her?

How can I live with someone who votes for this corrupt government?

That's not what I asked. I said, do you love her?

She keeps looking at her cup, but still doesn't take a sip. When she finally lifts her head to look at me she sighs heavily.

She's called Alex. Actually her real name is Intan Alexandra Sulaiman, but all her friends call her Alex.

December 30th

Last night I woke up with a jolt. One moment I was in a deep sleep, the next I was fully awake. My head was still on the pillow, my entire body as it had been in the minutes and hours before that rupture, but suddenly I was as alert and clear-eyed as I am right now, sitting here talking to you. It was a crack of thunder that woke me up. A single streak of lightning that came out of nowhere and split the night neatly in two. I don't know what the weather's been like in your part of town – sometimes when it's raining heavily here, it's as dry as the Sahara where you are. Thirty miles away, but everything can be different where you live. Out here, the skies have been heavy for days now, full of the sort of thick low cloud that usually announces downpours that last for days, even weeks – only we haven't had any rain at all. Every morning I keep thinking, Better not go out today, the rain will be too heavy and there won't be any buses. Every evening I smell the moisture in the air and expect to hear the drumming of rain on the roof in the night, but in the end nothing happens. Just a lightless blue-grey sky full of swollen, twisted clouds, like strange ripe fruit about to burst.

Then, last night, that single, sharp crack of thunder, like an oil drum splitting in two. My eyes flicked open. I waited for the next burst of lightning. That's it, I thought, here comes the rain at last. But still nothing. I lay awake for a while, not even blinking, just listening, waiting, even when

294

enough time had passed for me to know that there would be no deluge after all. Thunder in a dry sky – that was all it had been. As I drifted back to sleep I wondered whether I'd simply dreamed it; that maybe the sharpness of the lightning strike, the loud booming of the thunder – all that had occurred in my mind, and nowhere else. I get caught in this state sometimes, trapped between two worlds, not knowing if I'm fully awake and present in one, or if I've actually passed into another. Sleeping, running, raining, burning. Sometimes it's all the same to me, I can't discern the difference, can't shake myself into a state of clarity and divide my days into distinct portions with lists of things to do. It's worse since I came out of prison, but to tell the truth I've always been a bit like that, even when I was small. Look at the sky. It's the same as yesterday and all the days before. This morning the alarm clock told me it was seven-thirty, but it was so dark I didn't feel as if night had properly ended.

[*Rubs eyes; pauses; stares into space.*]

I almost didn't recognise Uzzal when he walked out of the Tokyo Hotel. I'd been waiting for him for more than an hour, watching the back entrance that led into the side street where there was hardly any traffic. I'd parked my car just across the street, where I was sure to spot him – yet I still almost missed him. He'd changed out of his hotel uniform and was wearing long camouflage shorts and a Liverpool football shirt, the kind of clothes you might expect a local to wear, not a foreign worker.

It was very hot that day, and even with the car windows fully wound down there was very little air, and I was sweating heavily. The drains that lined the side street were clogged with rubbish – the usual tangle of biscuit tins and plastic bags and broken branches. It wasn't surprising that people got sick, I thought. Once the rain started it would only take a week of heavy downpours for all the trash to accumulate in a great heap that would block the deep monsoon drains, and then the town would be flooded. I could see it so clearly: the street in front of me disappearing slowly under a rising tide of floodwater, bits of driftwood and plastic floating in the muddy filth, bacteria spreading everywhere. The awnings of the makeshift food stalls huddled against the sides of the buildings would be sagging limply into the water. I'd sit there watching it, trapped in my car, and after a while, even with the doors and windows closed, I'd notice water seeping in through tiny cracks, maybe even through the undercarriage of the car itself. Was that even possible? In any case, eventually I'd feel the car begin to shift, feel the weightlessness of it as the water carried me away in its stream, along with the other bits of rubbish.

It was then that I noticed someone walking swiftly from the back entrance of the hotel to a row of scooters parked nearby, and it was only once he'd started to put on his helmet that I realised it was Uzzal. I started to get out of my car, but the lights of his scooter were already on, and a puff of exhaust billowed out from the engine as he drew away. I got back in the car and began to follow him, not caring whether he saw me or not. It was the opposite of all those cop films you see on Astro, where Aaron Kwok or Andy Lau is always trying not to be noticed as they trail someone in an SUV, but their target always sees them anyway, and they end up in a high-speed chase. I wanted Uzzal to spot me, but he didn't, he just rode through the traffic at a steady pace, not slow but not fast either, sometimes speeding up and disappearing between lorries, at other times waiting patiently at traffic lights.

I got closer to him as the traffic thinned out beyond

Taman Kelana, and just as we were approaching the Sementa area he turned off into an industrial area separated from the main road by a monsoon drain and a row of small trees so covered in road dust that they were more grey than green. It was a place I'd driven past often but never paid any attention to. A lot of the small factories and go-downs there had ceased to operate over the years, and it was hard to tell which were still in business and which were abandoned. The port business isn't what it used to be, and now that so much work is done by computers, there isn't any need for a lot of things we used to take for granted. One of the factories facing the highway had a sign that showed paper, pencils, wastepaper bins, but the place had long since closed down, shrouded by trees whose branches and vines hung so thickly they would soon hide the building from view entirely.

Uzzal drew to a halt outside a long, high fence of red-painted corrugated iron topped with two strands of rusty barbed wire. It looked as if it was protecting a small industrial unit – behind it I could see a flat-topped concrete roof, but I could also make out lines of washing. I pulled up alongside him just as he was pushing his scooter through the gate of the compound. When he looked at me, his eyes were clear and slightly wet, irritated from having ridden through the dust on the road. He didn't recognise me at first, but then he said, 'I already told you, I can't help.'

'Please,' I said. 'I've got nothing to do with Keong. I don't even know the man.' *I don't know him.* As I was saying these words, they didn't seem like a lie, they seemed to form a truth so perfect and deep that I myself was convinced I'd never set eyes on Keong. Maybe it was my dreamlife speaking, my desire never to have known him. In that other life – the one that was safe and decent and true – Keong had never been a friend. 'I have a family. A job. I'm in trouble.'

'I can't do anything for you,' he said, propping his scooter against a wall. There were other people in the yard, men and women washing clothes in plastic buckets. Two children stood on the steps of the building, framed by the doorway, ready to disappear inside at the slightest sign of trouble. The older one – seven or eight, with enough life behind her to recognise danger – stared at me with the closed look of someone who did not welcome strangers; the kind of expression she had no doubt encountered all her life on the faces of the people who looked at her as she walked in the street, to the extent that she had absorbed it herself, and it was now fixed on her own features. *Don't come any closer. Go away*. That was what her young face said. She had one arm around the shoulders of her sister, who must have been a couple of years younger at least, not yet closed off to the world, though that would come soon.

I had once been those children, standing on the threshold of our house, watching people approach and judging the danger they posed to us. Debt collectors, people from the village, distant relatives from out of town. At first I was caught between fascination and fear, but later I became suspicious of everything. I suppose there must have been a time when I feared nothing and was enthralled by the newness of all people and all things, but I can't remember that time.

I explained my situation to Uzzal without needing to add or exaggerate. I told him I would be sacked and my wife would leave me, and I would be alone again. I would have to start from scratch like a young man of twenty, only the body I lived in now was not a twenty-year-old's, and it might not be capable of creating a new life for me.

That was why I was scared. Already, my body would often not obey my commands; my thoughts and my actions were diverging. Even if I wanted to work at a job digging trenches and ponds at a fish farm somewhere else in the country, my body would refuse to do it. If I had to go back to sharing a room with two other guys in a low-cost flat two hours from where I worked, my body would rebel, it wouldn't be able to take any rest on the thin mattress on the floor after a day in the sun.

'Now that you work as a waiter in a hotel, can you imagine doing an eighteen-hour shift in a factory again?' I asked.

Uzzal looked at his children, and went up the steps to greet them. He took the smaller one in his arms and picked her up. The older one leaned lightly against him. She still hadn't shifted her hard-eyed gaze from me. Uzzal turned to go into the house, and beckoned me to join him inside. Beyond the initial gloom the concrete space was lit by a brilliant square of light that fell from a hole cut in the roof. Around us, in a large room that must once have housed light machinery, there were plastic chairs and makeshift beds spread out on the floor. In one corner, a sort of kitchen built from plywood boxes arranged against the wall, a small stove and a row of three gas canisters.

'If those explode,' I said, 'you'll be in heaven before you know what's happened.'

He lit the stove and began to heat the kettle. 'How do you know it won't be hell?'

The children went out into the yard to play. They'd arranged some sticks on the broken concrete, and were hopping over them in a pattern that I couldn't figure out. They spoke in a language I didn't understand, but once in a while, amid the warm swirl of their chatter I heard a few Malay words, as striking as trees poking out from the water at high tide. *Satu, dua, tigaaaaaa*. I looked around the concrete box that Uzzal and his family had made their home, and I thought, It's dry and safe, and that's something.

More than just the three of them lived there, that much was clear. There were bags of clothes and pairs of rubber sandals everywhere. But where were they? He must have had a wife, and maybe cousins from his village in Bangladesh, or friends he'd grown up with. I didn't ask, and he didn't volunteer any information. With migrant workers, you learn not to ask questions about their families – you steer clear of the topic, because you don't want to hear the explanations. How did you end up in this country? What happened to your parents? Where is your wife? How did your husband die? You know that the stories are always going to be the same – you've heard them before, read about them in the newspapers – and if you don't have the stomach to hear them again, you learn not to ask questions.

He gave me some tea in a steel mug. It was hot and slightly bitter.

'You should stop your search,' he said. 'The people you're looking for – they can't work.'

'We can arrange permits,' I said. 'We can bribe the police, it'll be OK.'

'It's not a question of law, it's a question of reality. They're sick, they're too weak to work. It's useless.'

I was thirsty, but the tea was too strong for me to drink. 'Are you sure?'

He nodded. Their journey had been harsh, he explained, harsher than usual; most of them hadn't arrived in good shape. They'd taken a boat from southern Myanmar, from a place called Sittwe, not far from where he himself had grown up. From there they'd taken the usual sea route to southern Thailand, cutting in from the Andaman Islands and heading to the point where Thailand narrowed into Malaysia. It wasn't such a long trip, and conditions were good at that time of the year, between monsoons, the waves gentle. He'd done almost the same trip some time before, from further up the coast towards Chittagong, in fact, so he knew how long it would take.

But something went wrong, the boat got lost, they ran out of water days before they reached shore, and people died – he wasn't sure how many. All it takes is for one or two people on board to die and it changes the way you feel on the boat, changes the way you feel about the days, months and years ahead of you. Even if your body holds up, your spirit wishes you were dead. Drifting on the sea, you feel you've died too. The friends you lose take something away from you as their bodies are thrown overboard, and that something – what is it? No one knows – that something never comes back.

Once they'd reached land, they were held in jungle camps in southern Thailand, recovering enough strength for the journey across the border. One or two bodies – of people who'd died after they landed – were buried in the jungle. This happened often. When Uzzal was in one of those camps he had to dig a grave for a seventeen-year-old boy he'd met on the boat who'd dreamed of becoming a carpenter. Why a carpenter? Uzzal never found out. The boy had got sick with dysentery, and died of dehydration. As Uzzal was digging his grave, he kept thinking, This could be me. If I die, someone else will be digging my grave, and I'll be buried here, in the soil of a country I don't know, before I even have a chance of getting to know it. My body will nourish the earth of this new land, I will give myself to it after all, just not in the way I expected. (The Chinese have a saying, I wanted to tell him right at that moment, but I didn't. *Falling leaves return to nourish the tree's roots.* Do you know it? All things go back to their source. Wander far and wide, but you'll always return home. That is the natural way of things, that is how we expect life to turn out, and maybe it does for some. But not for most.)

They were smuggled in lorries across the border, all the way down into southern Perak, and now they were in the area, moving from one makeshift camp to another. Uzzal's so-called boss, the one Keong was looking for, was trying to find them medication, but it's hard to get help for people who aren't supposed to be in the country. That's what Uzzal had heard – that many of this group of workers were sick and dying. It didn't sound good. Not so long ago he might have stepped in, tried to do something to help them, maybe house them with families that were already established in the country, people who could nurse them, give them the shelter and comfort that was more healing than any medication. But these weren't the sort of people he knew. They were Rohingya. Do you know what that means? They were refugees, they lived in a war zone, they were being driven from their homes, they would have been weak and injured even before they set off on their journey. When you come from a place like that, it's not just your body that suffers, your brain is fried too, and Uzzal didn't know how to help people like that. The smugglers don't care who they bring in, they just count the numbers. As long as they fill the boats, they're happy. A man or a woman – they're just a body. That's what Uzzal's boss said one day, but Uzzal already knew it, he'd known it since the day he left Bangladesh. He knew because he'd once been that body himself.

That was when he decided he wouldn't be part of this business any more, and that was why he couldn't help me. He had a job now, a proper one. He'd got his papers, and in a few years he hoped to get a passport. He couldn't get involved in this kind of work, he had to leave it all behind.

'What am I supposed to do?' I said. My voice sounded suddenly too loud; it reverberated in the concrete room. I wanted to shake him by the shoulders, scream at him. What did he think – that he could leave it all behind just like that, and forget all about it?

'It's not my problem,' he said, finishing his tea. We were still standing in the middle of the room, and he looked at me for a few seconds before taking my mug from me. 'I have to make dinner for my kids now.'

I can't explain to you how it happened – how my hands reached out suddenly, violently, to push him sharply in the chest. It was both a surprise and not a surprise to me. In my head, I was registering the fact that I'd reached a dead end with Uzzal, and that he wasn't going to help me in any way. I'd even begun to imagine how angry Mr Lai would be when he came back to discover his farm without any workers – without me. I'd begun to imagine Keong sulking for a few days before disappearing back to KL with his ego hurt.

That should have been the end of it. I should have been walking away by then. So I don't know why I struck him like that. It was just a push, not even very hard, but it caught us both by surprise, and he stumbled backwards, just a couple of steps, not enough to fall over, but enough to unbalance him. The tea from my mug splashed onto the concrete floor, and we both stared at the stain, as if that was the most important thing in the world at that moment. Outside, the children were still playing, counting out numbers in a sing-song manner. *Tu-juh-be-las-la-pan-be-las* . . .

303

I turned to leave, but as I reached the doorway Uzzal called out.

'I can give you his number,' he said. 'The man you're looking for. I don't know where he is, and I don't want to know. Take his number, but don't say who gave it to you.'

I forwarded the number to Keong, but didn't get a reply. Later, lying on the sofa at home, I heard my phone buzz and vibrate on the dining table. I didn't bother to get up and look at it; I just continued to flick through the channels on TV, not watching anything in particular. When I finally listened to my messages, Keong's voice sounded unusually flat and calm. *You're my brother. You're the best.*

But it's illegal, she says.

So? Just because something's illegal doesn't mean it doesn't happen.

We have laws against that sort of thing. I mean, the kind of abuse you're talking about. We have rules against exploitation and brutality. Child labour. We do have regulations.

I laugh. Do you know which country you're living in? You think you're in Switzerland or Singapore? Miss, this is the real world. Even in New York or wherever you did your studies, you think illegal stuff doesn't happen?

I know, I'm not naïve. But even so.

You don't believe me?

No, it's not that. It's just that some of what you describe is . . . pretty difficult to take in.

I look at her and shrug. Sometimes I can't help it. When I talk about things that are unpleasant, I know that I should choose my words more carefully, try to make the story more pleasant and acceptable to her. I look at the phone that is recording my voice, and her pen scribbling in her notebook. I want her to think, *I like this story*. I know I should be more measured and tell a nice story, but I end up doing the opposite. I tell her every terrible detail, I can't stop myself. *Hold back, hold back*, I think, but it all tumbles out despite myself. She doesn't say anything, doesn't interrupt, and that makes me talk even more. Today when I told her about the stories I'd heard from foreign workers who'd travelled from Bangladesh, I'd had a simple line prepared in my head. *It was a very difficult journey, people died.* But instead I told her exactly what I'd heard from the foreign worker I met. The smugglers slashing the stomach of his dead wife so her body wouldn't balloon and she'd sink quickly when thrown overboard. Migrants who were so weak they were dying, and still they had to dig graves. Their own graves. So when they died the smugglers could just push them in. No strength to fight, just enough strength to die. People seeing the gangrene set into their wounds, feeling that their legs were being gnawed at by an animal.

She would look up, her face pale as the moon, her eyes wide and confused like a child's when they hear bad news. At first I wanted to protect her from these stories, but as I was talking I realised that I wanted her to be a part of that pain, to make sure that it seeped into her world, her clean, happy world. I wanted it to be a cloud that hung over her everywhere she went, just as it does over me, all the time, and that's why I didn't stop talking. But each time I finish, the inevitable happens. I feel ashamed for having introduced this bitterness into her life, and then I feel like scrubbing it all away, except I can't, I can't repent in any way. I can't even say sorry. (What for, anyway?) I feel completely powerless. So I just sit there.

Hmm, she says after a pause. That's very hard to digest.

IV

JANUARY

The day before I was supposed to meet Keong and the man I'd later know to be Mohammad Ashadul, I called in at the farm for the first time in a while. In truth it hadn't been so long, maybe only four or five days, but it felt like a month. As I drove down the track towards it, it seemed as though I was revisiting a scene from a past life, a place I'd once known but had left behind. The vines hung lower from the trees than I remembered, the *lalang* had grown so thick and tall that it was spilling from the verges and narrowing the lane to half its former width. We'd planted it just six months before, to hold the banks of earth in place and stop land-slides in the rainy season, but it had grown thick and lush in that time. We were meaning to cut it the previous week, before the men fell sick; now it no longer resembled long grass but the folds of waves on a bright-green sea.

There must have been strong winds in the night, because the parking area was strewn with broken branches and fresh leaves ripped from the trees. Jezmine's car was in the yard, but I could tell at once that things weren't right – the hum of the engines that ran the pumps was lower and rougher than usual. In the distance, the neat squares of the ponds looked calm and silvery, but that too was a bad sign. The stillness of the water bothered me; everything else in the world seemed to be shifting.

Jezmine came out of the office to meet me. Mr Lai had called several times, and on each occasion she'd said that

309

everything was under control. What did he expect would happen? A tsunami in the Straits of Melaka or something? Stop being so paranoid. Everything's fine.

I could just imagine their conversation. I'd heard her speak on the phone hundreds of times. She could put anyone in their place, make men like Mr Lai feel like primary school boys with her directness and flat tone of voice, as if she was slightly bored and waiting for them to keep up with her. Her lies had bought us an extra day or two – Mr Lai had decided he wouldn't rush home from Penang, that he'd stay another couple of days, take it easy, go out for a few meals with his wife. Good idea, Jezmine had said.

'Do you smell that?' I said. We were standing in the yard, neither of us daring to ask the next question: What do we do now?

'Smell what?'

We started walking towards the ponds, and had just reached the first of the enclosures when I figured out the source of the sharp, sour odour hanging in the air, growing stronger all the time. Ammonium and decaying flesh.

'Ugh.' Jezmine had her hand over her nose.

At the halfway point on the wooden walkway, I began to notice that the pumps at the far end of the farm weren't working. Fish had gathered close to the surface, sometimes breaking the water with a flash of their tails. As we walked along, it occurred to me that most people wouldn't have sensed the panic around us. If you were an outsider, someone unconnected to our farm, you wouldn't have seen anything but still, green-grey water, the darting of fish. You wouldn't have sensed the disturbance below the surface, the agitation of the fish, the way some were swimming frantically in tight circles, others drifting so slowly they seemed suspended in the water, as lifeless as a

310

painting. Without the soft jets of water from the pumps, you would have remarked upon the flatness of the water, so natural and peaceful. We, Jezmine and I, saw only the stagnation that preceded death. Where you saw calm, we saw chaos. You saw the beautiful order of things, we saw decay.

I knew that many of the fish would have been suffocating, that they weren't getting enough fresh moving water, that their feeding had been interrupted. Maybe something had got into the water, some chemicals from up the coast. We didn't need to walk all the way to the furthest ponds to see the damage, but we did anyway, staring at the silvery carpet of fish, the sun glinting on the scales of their upturned bellies. The wind had died, and if no one had told you that you were looking at dead fish, you could easily have thought it was a trick of the light caused by the sea and the small shifts in the cloud that change the way the world appears. But the stench made the truth clear; the acidic chemical smell burned the insides of our nostrils and made us choke.

Jezmine was still covering her mouth and nose with her hand. She muttered something, almost a whisper. *Cham lor*. She might have said the same thing when she couldn't find a parking space in town on a busy Saturday afternoon, or if she was late in paying her mobile phone bill, or realised she'd forgotten her purse – the minor incidents of modern daily life. But in this instance it seemed particularly apt. Just one hushed little observation. We were screwed.

By the time we reached the office it was clear that even Jezmine couldn't think of a solution. 'What are you going to tell Mr Lai?' she asked. 'Maybe you can just blame it on the men. Say they all disappeared without warning, tell him the truth.'

I shook my head. I was still trying to figure out how

much money we would lose with two ponds full of dead fish, trying to equate each carcass to a sum of money. If we could get some new workers, cheaper ones, how quickly could we make the money back? It wasn't as though we paid the Indonesians a lot anyway, but from what Keong and Uzzal had told me about the others, I was sure we could pay them even less, to start with anyway. When someone is desperate for work, they're not going to ask for permits and insurance. They wouldn't even know about that sort of thing. I couldn't work out exactly how much we'd save, but surely quite a lot over the long run. If I could have them in place in the next couple of days, working hard by the time Mr Lai returned, it would soften the blow of losing so much money. I knew what he was like. He wouldn't care about losing the workers, he'd only care about what that would mean for his profits. It didn't make any difference who worked for him. As long as they kept his business running smoothly, he didn't mind. All those years, he barely knew the workers' names. Maybe he wouldn't even notice that I'd taken on completely new people.

'I have some men lined up,' I said. 'Almost ready to work. Tomorrow or the day after.' In my head, I was convinced this was true. All the rules and routines I'd known up to that moment had changed, the world I inhab-ited no longer seemed to belong to me, and in this new land, whole groups of men and women could disappear from their homes and appear in an entirely foreign country without knowing where they were, or how exactly they got there. They could be alive one minute, dead the next, just from the same water they'd been drinking for months.

The normal order of life no longer applied. When you leave your old home you're a child; when you reach your new one, you're an adult. You don't even know how it happened. You get a job. You get sick. You get married. You get high. You get sacked. You get a break. You get screwed. You get nothing. You get everything. There was no longer any logic in this world; things happened in random order. I couldn't figure out how one event led to another, so why was it so ridiculous to think that by the next day I would have found twelve new workers? I'd lost the old ones without any warning, I'd get new ones just as quickly.

'You kidding?'

I shook my head. 'I have a meeting with someone tonight. Tomorrow, we'll have the workers.'

Even in the messy sequence of my thinking, I knew that failure was a far greater possibility than success. But in spite of this – or perhaps precisely because of it – I felt free to imagine what would happen if I did succeed in finding new workers that evening. They'd arrive the following day, tired and maybe a bit sick. I'd feed them, buy them new clothes, make them shower and get clean. I'd give them a bit of cash from my own pocket to show them we were serious employers, maybe give them half a day's rest. By the next day they'd be fully at work, and by the time Mr Lai got back it would seem as though nothing had changed.

When I met Keong at the layby that night the darkness meant that I couldn't make out the expression on his face – couldn't tell if he was nervous or scared or angry.

'You eaten yet?' he asked. Even though it was a standard greeting, I found it odd that he'd say it at that particular moment. It was way past dinner time, nearly ten o'clock, so of course I'd eaten. I was waiting for him to tell me about how he'd got in touch with Ashadul – what they'd discussed on the phone, what they'd agreed – but instead he started describing what he'd had for dinner. He'd been very hungry, he said, he hadn't had lunch, or very little, too early in the day, so at about six o'clock he'd gone to a seafood place and ordered enough food for a whole family. He had steamed prawns, a kilo of crab, some Marmite ribs, a big bowl of soup. He didn't know why he was so hungry, but he couldn't stop eating – it felt like he hadn't eaten in days, and had never tasted food so good. Everything seemed so new and delicious, and of course all that food had made him thirsty. Maybe they used *ajinomoto* in the cooking to make it tastier, and those sorts of chemicals always made his throat dry, so he'd washed it down with three big bottles of beer. He was thinking, This might be a long night, better eat well.

'Why a long night? We're just going to talk to the guy, right? Confirm what time he'll deliver the workers. We don't need all night for that.'

Keong shrugged. 'You never know with these people. He said he'd call me when he's ready, but the bastard hasn't called.' He checked his phone, its green glow making his face look shapeless and flat, but I still couldn't make out his expression. When the light went out and his face blended into the darkness again, he said, 'Want a drink?' He went around to the passenger seat and reached into the glovebox. He handed me a plastic cup and unscrewed a bottle. When he poured from it into my cup I could smell the strong, sweet odour of XO cognac. 'I don't have any Coca-Cola to mix it with,' he said. 'It's OK just as it is.'

We leaned against the bonnet, staring at the headlamps of the cars going past in the distance. At this time of night there was hardly any traffic, and I started to count the seconds between each car. Five, nine, twelve.

'What did you say when you called him earlier?' I asked. 'Does he have the men?'

'*Aiya*,' he laughed. 'You're always worried. Relax. It'll

be fine. He's got the men, we just need to agree the price.'

We had another drink while Keong checked his phone. He dialled a number, and I could hear the ringtone clearly, even though I was standing a good few feet from him. I can remember how still it was that night – I remember the total absence of wind, because I could hear each long beep of the ringtone as clearly as if someone was shaking a bell in my ear.

'I'm feeling sleepy,' Keong said. He reached into his pocket and produced a small plastic bag, the kind with a Ziploc top. He held it up against the night sky, but I couldn't see its contents. He emptied it into the palm of his hand, and manoeuvred his phone to shine a light on the small pills that lay there. I noticed how worn and creased his hands were – rough hands that seemed to belong to a much older man. 'Take one,' he said. 'It'll make sure you're wide awake.'

'I'm not tired,' I lied. It felt as though the previous fifteen years had disappeared, collapsed into another realm, and that we were acting out one of our Friday nights in KL, when we were barely out of our teens and trying to get started in life. The cheap pills of dubious quality, the long nights – the rituals of our youth. I took one, without knowing what it was, and without believing it would really help me stay awake and alert, and in the minutes and hours that followed, I can't honestly say that my mental state was affected, in a good way or a bad way. That was something else I remember from the trial: my lawyer trying to argue that I'd acted under the influence of drugs, even though I'd told her the pill had made no difference to my behaviour. Four, maybe five cups of XO, one amphetamine tablet, or something similar – it would have changed nothing. In the end, her defence failed, the jury didn't consider the alcohol and the drugs to be *relevant factors.* And neither do I. Looking back at that evening, as I've done many times in the years since, I agree with them.

Keong's phone rang, and I could hear a man's voice on the other end. Keong grunted a single syllable in agreement, and put his phone away. He threw his cup into the long grass and said, 'We'll take my car.' When we were inside he reached under his seat and pulled out a long, thin object wrapped in a cloth. He handed it to me and said, 'Hang on to this. Just in case.'

'You're fucking kidding me,' I said. I didn't have to undo his little parcel to know that it was a knife. 'We're just going to have a talk. Why would we need that?'

'Like I said, you never know with these guys.'

'You take it,' I said. 'I'm not touching it.'

'Suit yourself.'

It didn't take us long to drive back into town. At that time the traffic is always light, but that night it seemed quieter than usual. Who knows – maybe the port business was slow, and fewer container ships were docking, so all the lorries ferrying goods up to KL had called it quits. Sometimes work at the port slowed down and you'd see migrants drifting into town looking for a few days' casual work here and there, from whoever would employ them. During these periods the town appeared to function normally, which is to say that a visitor like you wouldn't notice anything unusual. You'd see the buses and the markets, shopkeepers sweeping the pavements outside their doors, people sitting down at roadside food stalls – but you'd miss the feeling of anxiety, the knowledge that the entire town depended on trade from faraway places, goods being bought and sold by people we would never know. Some politician in America decides that they can't buy Malaysian rubber gloves; suddenly ten factories in the area have to shut down. The Europeans want to save the fucking planet so they ban the use of palm oil in food; within a month the entire port is on its knees. Life continues, but you feel it slipping quietly away, and you worry that it'll never return. And because of that fear, you feel caught in a suspended state. On the outside, life seems normal, but inside it's drawn to a standstill.

That night, driving into town, I felt the same sense of being lost, as if events were being controlled by things and people I didn't know, far away from me. We drew in to a parking spot near some abandoned houses, not far from the riverbank. Keong led the way, picking a path through trees until we were walking along a rough track that led closer to the river's edge. There wasn't enough light in the night sky to see clearly, and I had to hold up my phone and point its faint glow towards the ground so I didn't trip up. Keong was walking quickly, without any hesitation, and I got the impression he'd been there before, walking this exact route.

'Turn off your phone,' he said. I stumbled a few times in the dark, unable to keep up with him. Later, after the killing, when I retraced my steps, I'd find myself thinking how clear the path was, how light the landscape, even though it was the middle of the night. But in those first few minutes I couldn't even see my feet. All I could hear was the sound of Keong marching steadily through the long grass, the ground getting slightly swampy underfoot.

I started to fall behind, and after a while he was so far ahead of me that I couldn't make him out. When I caught up with him, under a large spreading tree, he was already talking loudly. I'd heard his voice from a long way off, agitated from the start. Now he was shouting. *What the hell, money doesn't mean anything to you any more? I'll chop your stupid head off.* The other man didn't answer. In the

317

dark, the tip of his cigarette glowed deep red, then faded again. Keong continued to talk in his machine-gun way, the words tumbling out in long jagged streams. He was waving his arms, occasionally pointing his finger at the man's face, and as I drew closer he glanced at me. Suddenly I could see his face, as if the clouds had cleared to reveal the moon, and in those moments every detail of the land seems sharper than at midday, every blade of grass and curve of a leaf becomes highlighted by the moonlight. Only there was no moon that night – I'd only realise that later on.

I don't know how I started to notice shapes and textures at that point in time, when only a few minutes previously everything had been obscured by darkness. Keong's face was twisted in rage, deep lines scarring the skin around his mouth and eyes. How he'd aged. I heard every sound, too – the way both of them breathed. Keong's short, heavy breaths, drawn sharply at the end of sentences, three, four quick breaths after he cursed. Ashadul's slow, rasping breaths, his lungs and throat coated in tar and phlegm. A smoker's cough rising from his chest. The flat tone of his voice contrasting to Keong's hysterics. The clarity of it all.

Who's this?

My cousin. Why you care?

The man turns to me. Then he laughs – laughter so rich that for a moment I feel this is all a joke, and we're friends.

Brother, he says, looking at me. *You come to threaten me is it?*

And then: Keong cursing in Cantonese. (What's the point, I remember thinking, the guy can't speak Cantonese.) *Lia ma, I chop you dead. You owe me money still don't pay.*

The man laughing. Standing firm, unmoving as Keong comes right up close to him. *Not scared ah I can kill you right*

318

here no one will care my brother will fuck up your family screw you for seven generations. Still in Cantonese.

Why?

Cigarette smoke, like a puff of bird feathers in the dark. Then a quick movement, a scuffle, and Keong has pulled out the knife. *Chop your head see if you still laugh.* But Ashadul stands as motionless as the trees around him, and I know he isn't going to budge. I know it's Keong who's going to lose this fight.

Give me my money and we let you go, Keong says.

(We. He says *we*.)

He makes a swift lunge towards Ashadul, and suddenly Ashadul is on the ground. They're both on the ground. I back away, I need to get out of there, but I stumble backwards, I trip over a pile of logs, a branch. Keong's knife has fallen to the ground, lost in the undergrowth. Ashadul is first to his feet. He faces me, and waits for a second or two before taking a knife out of his pocket. The blade makes a sharp, clean noise as it flicks open, as if claiming its place in the night. He walks over to Keong, and I don't know what he's going to do. I can't see Keong's face, but I can still hear his breaths, quick, desperate. As if he can't breathe. Ashadul stands over him, looking as if he's examining the knife, considering his options. I hear Keong's voice.

Ah Hock.

I struggle to stand up. I put my hand on the branch next to me, but as I lean on it to rise to my feet it breaks and I fall again, the piece of wood useless in my hand. Ashadul laughs and turns back towards Keong.

I don't know how I manage to stand up, but I do. I get to my feet, and in just three or four steps I've reached Ashadul. I know he can't see me as I raise my arm. I think: This is stupid, I'm not strong enough to hurt him, he's

319

going to kill me. I'll hit him, but not hard enough to knock him out, and then he'll kill me. The first blow catches him squarely on the back of the head, and he falls straight to the ground. As I watch his body collapse slowly, I think: He's a heavy man. He tries to get up, but I'm already raising my arm to strike him a second time. And a third. And it continues. I aim each blow at his head. At first he tries to move his head, to shield himself with his arms, but soon he's motionless. I continue to hit him. I don't know how many times.

Later, when my case was in court, I heard that the autopsy showed I'd hit him fourteen times. The number didn't hold any meaning for me. It was the same as if they'd told me it was a hundred, or a thousand times. I remember raising my arm time and time again until it felt like the only thing my arm was capable of doing, that it had been created for that purpose and nothing else.

After I'd stopped, I looked at Keong. Now I could see his expression – pale and wide-eyed. *We were just meant to scare him. We didn't mean to harm him. That's why I asked Ah Hock to come with me.* I remember the things Keong said during the trial, when he appeared as a witness for the defence. *I wanted the Bangladeshi to pay back the money he owed me, that's all. Two against one works better. He'd be frightened, he'd pay. It was simple. We didn't mean anything more than that.*

Keong lay on the ground for some time, staring at me as if I was someone he'd never seen in his life. He didn't blink, didn't speak, and for a moment I thought that maybe he'd been fatally wounded, that Ashadul had stabbed him without me seeing it. I even thought he might already be dead. The human body is capable of all sorts of incredible things beyond the control of its own muscles. We are after all creatures of nature. Chop off the head of a snake and it'll still bite you, still be capable of injecting poison into your flesh, only it's even worse than a live snake because the poison glands don't know when to stop. Sometimes people are dead but they sit up and look at you with open eyes as if they're still alive. I felt that Keong – the dying or already dead Keong – was asking me a question without speaking – the way people sometimes do when they can't understand why you've behaved in a way that seems so extreme to them, so bizarre and inexplicable, they can't even bring themselves to ask *Why?*

Jenny used to do that often, like the time she found I'd kept a whole drawer full of used toothbrushes. I kept them because I hated throwing them out, and thought I could re-use them in some other way, like cleaning shoes or bottles, but mostly because I hated the idea of throwing out something that hadn't broken, something I'd paid money for. She held them in a big bunch in her fist, and when she looked at me she didn't need to say anything. Why the hell have you done this? Why are you so strange? There was no need to ask, because there was no explanation for my behaviour. In any case, she'd already supplied her own answer, and anything I said would have been superfluous. That was how it was with Keong and me at that moment. It was pointless for either of us to say anything.

After a while, when I was almost fully convinced that he was dead, he got to his feet and scrambled up the bank, through the trees and undergrowth, in the direction of the road. From the crashing and tearing of the foliage I knew he was running blindly, as fast as he could. He didn't turn back to look at me. That was the last time I saw him before the trial.

When I could no longer hear Keong I knew I was alone on the riverbank, and that I was very thirsty. So thirsty I found it difficult to breathe. I swallowed a few times, but my throat felt as rough as sandpaper. My legs began to buckle, and I had to sit down. I realised that I was next to the dead man, so close that his outstretched hand was almost touching me. Mohammad Ashadul. Maybe if I'd known his name at that moment I might have felt more afraid – more anguished about what I'd done, more terrified by what was to come, the life that would follow. Instead, all I felt was an aching in my limbs so intense that I thought for a while I might pass out.

I lay down next to him. Two bodies, side by side in the darkness. In the way that human beings do, by pure instinct, I listened for his breathing, as if we had both lain down to sleep.

The drive is longer than I expected. It's a Saturday afternoon, so even the highways that snake around KL are
clogged. I've never driven out of this side of town, heading
into the hills towards Genting. We reach the final toll plaza,
and the cars are backed up for three or four hundred yards
waiting to get through. The air-con is blowing in my face,
and I'm glad I'm not driving.

We'll be OK once we get through this bit, she says.

Sure enough, the traffic clears once we pass the toll
booth and the road begins to climb.

It'll be fine, she says. You'll love it.

I didn't reply to the invitation when it arrived by email.
It wasn't addressed to me alone, but to a whole bunch of
people, and it came from someone I didn't know – someone
from her publisher, I later found out, which was throwing
a party to mark the publication of the book. Yes, *your* story,
she said when she rang me to ask why I hadn't responded
to the email.

That's nonsense. It's your book, not mine.

But it's *your* story. You have to come! I'll collect you and
we'll drive up there together. I won't take no for an answer!

We pass a guardhouse manned by Nepalese men who
tick our names off a list and let us through. Although we're
driving slowly through jungle the roads are immaculate,
and now and then a mansion rises out of the trees. I see
people sitting on balconies overlooking the forested valley
beyond. Eventually we drive into a sort of farm – not the

kind I used to know as a child, but a place with neatly manicured squares of vegetables dotted with papaya trees. A sign at the entrance announces that it's an organic farm, and there are a few Indonesian workers still out in the fields, even though it's late in the afternoon. A passionfruit vine hangs over the space where we park the car.

We seem to be the last people to arrive, and a cheer goes up when we walk into the room, which is in a large wooden house on stilts overlooking a lotus pond. There are no walls, and a breeze rises up and blows a stack of paper napkins all over the floor. Most people are drinking wine or champagne. Someone offers me a glass. I decline.

Oh, you don't drink? That's cool, the young man says. He has long hair tied in a ponytail, and his skin is as clear as candle wax. I'll get you some juice. Pineapple OK?

Most people are speaking English; some of them sound American to me. But they're all locals, all her friends. After a few minutes someone makes a speech, describing the novel. I guess he's the editor. He's speaking too fast; I can't hear him properly, and suddenly I realise I can't really understand anything he's saying. At one point during the speech everyone turns to look at me, smiling, but I don't know why. There's applause, and Su-Min turns to look at me. She says something that makes everyone laugh, but by now I can't understand what anyone is saying. When she finishes, everyone applauds, and people drift away. Some of them wander over to the buffet table, others hang over the edge of the banisters, smoking and laughing. I wait a while, wondering if she'll come and speak to me, but I can see that she's deep in conversation with a group of people, including her editor. Very discreetly, I move away, walk down the path to the far end of the pond, and sit under a rambutan tree.

From where I'm sitting I have a view of the party, but no one can see me. The light is just starting to fade, and further up the hill some kerosene lamps appear, like fire-flies in the jungle. That must be where the workers live. Although lots of people are laughing, I can hear her laughter in particular, rising above the others'. I look up and see her talking to a woman about her age. They talk together, just the two of them, for a long time.

Circles ripple gently across the surface of the pond, and I know there are tilapia in it, even though I can't see them in this light. There's a small pump at one side of the pond, next to a clump of banana trees, and all of a sudden I think I'm hallucinating. In fact I know I'm hallucinating, but it feels real anyway. I see my mother, squatting by the edge of the pond, wiping her brow with the small towel that hangs around her neck as she hacks away at some weeds that are growing into the water. She's weaker now than before, and her arm rises and falls slowly. From time to time her hearing aid squeals, and I call out to her. Ma, enough, go back inside and relax, but of course she can't hear me.

Hey. What are you doing out here all on your own? You escaped the party.

A bit noisy in there. I needed some fresh air.

Yeah, lots of people came. Everyone's fascinated by your story.

I think they're more interested in your book.

Same thing, isn't it?

Is that her? The one you were talking to. Your partner. Alex, isn't it?

My ex-partner, yes.

You look good together. You seemed to be getting along well.

You think? She laughs. Well, a bit late for that now.

Nothing's too late. If you still love each other, why not give it another go?

Let's see. Anyway, what about you? Why don't I introduce you to some of the people here? You never know, you might meet someone.

Good idea. Convicted murderers are always so popular.

It wasn't *murder*. She laughs. The same laugh I've heard all evening, drifting across the farm, mingling with the sound of the water. I could marry you if you want. A militant queer girl and a depressed felon – a perfect match.

That's not even funny, I say, but I'm laughing. We both are. The moment lasts just a few seconds, but seems to stretch into the night.

I think I'm going to go now, I say.

No, please stay! There's lots more food, lots to drink.

I'm tired, I'll just go home.

That's crazy. Give me a few minutes to say hi and bye to some people and I'll drive you.

No, no, please. Just enjoy yourself. I checked the bus timetable, there's one every hour from the village nearby. She knows I'm lying, but she decides not to argue.

Are you sure?

Really, I'm sure. I'd feel bad if you left your party now. You worked hard for it, you should enjoy it. I'm tired. I need to move my legs, otherwise my back will seize up.

OK. But call me if you need help. I'll keep my phone on.

We stand facing each other. It's almost completely dark now. I think that maybe I should extend my hand, but that feels wrong, and she doesn't move either.

Goodbye, I say.

The walk down the hill takes nearly an hour, and by the time I get to the village all the shops are closed. I sit on the concrete steps of a coffee shop, listening to the noise of the traffic from the highway nearby. The rush of the cars and lorries sounds fuzzy and soothing, like the sea on a windy day.